VILEST THINGS

VILEST THINGS

Flesh & False Gods
Book Two

CHLOE GONG

SAGA PRESS
LONDON SYDNEY NEW YORK TORONTO NEW DELHI

1230 AVENUE OF THE AMERICAS, NEW YORK, NEW YORK 10020

This book is a work of fiction. Any references to historical events, real people, or real places are used fictitiously. Other names, characters, places, and events are products of the author's imagination, and any resemblance to actual events or places or persons, living or dead, is entirely coincidental.

First Saga Press hardcover edition September 2024

SAGA PRESS and colophon are trademarks of Simon & Schuster, LLC

Simon & Schuster: Celebrating 100 Years of Publishing in 2024

Interior design by Erika R. Genova

Manufactured in the United States of America

1 3 5 7 9 10 8 6 4 2

Library of Congress Cataloging-in-Publication Data
Names: Gong, Chloe, author.
Title: Vilest things / Chloe Gong.
Description: First Saga Press hardcover edition. | London ; New York : Saga Press, 2024. | Series: Flesh & false gods ; book two
Identifiers: LCCN 2024028127 (print) | LCCN 2024028128 (ebook) | ISBN 9781668000267 (hardcover) | ISBN 9781668000274 (paperback) | ISBN 9781668000281 (ebook)
Subjects: LCGFT: Fantasy fiction. | Romance fiction. | Novels.
Classification: LCC PS3607.O524 V55 2024 (print) | LCC PS3607.O524 (ebook) | DDC 813/.6—dc23/eng/20240621
LC record available at https://lccn.loc.gov/2024028127
LC ebook record available at https://lccn.loc.gov/2024028128

ISBN 978-1-6680-0026-7
ISBN 978-1-6680-0028-1 (ebook)

For the d.a.c.u.—

Christina Li, Racquel Marie, Tashie Bhuiyan, Zoe Hana Mikuta.

You know why.

Look you sad, friends?
The gods rebuke me, but it is tidings
To wash the eyes of kings.

—Shakespeare, *Antony and Cleopatra*

TALIN
BORDERLANDS
YOULIA
RINCUN
ACTIA
XIMILI
MEANNIN
LAHO
EDISO
LANKIL
JINZI RIVER
KELITU
JANTON
DAOL
LEYSA
PASHE
CIREA
GAIYU
YINGU
DACIA
EIGI
WALL
SAN
ER
N
W
E
S

CHAPTER 1

BEFORE

Power has a certain taste to it. A hot, golden tang slinking down the throat and trailing smoke in its wake, like seared meat or aged liquor. Something to settle the body, soothe the heart. It is the answer to every type of hunger, an addictive luxury that requires little else in accompaniment, some salve solely made to take up every bit of space it can find.

Power also has a certain taste coming back up. And Anton Makusa can't say he finds it very pleasant at all.

He takes a shaky breath, fighting to keep his stomach under control. The guards inside the throne room peer through the gold-thread curtains, calling in concern, but Anton wipes his mouth and waves them off. His vision flickers and doubles. His skin screams with raw misery, his qi at once too big for his body and too ill-fitting in its mold. The last minute of his existence tries to escape from understanding. He's struggling beyond belief to hold on to consciousness, to cling to life. Memories that are both his own and not flash before his eyes. He looks at his hands, and the image lurches. He's washing blood off. Writing with old ink.

Then, in a snap, the pain eases. Though the nausea remains, his body stands intact. His surroundings register again. One guard steps onto the balcony to ask if he would like assistance to come inside now, and Anton throws his gaze out over the ledge in disbelief.

He doesn't entirely know how he's done it, but he has. The guard prompts him again, her eyes flickering to the sludge on the balcony floor where Anton emptied his stomach, and Anton raises a hand to stop her, barely holding down another shudder. Maybe he's only squeamish over the gruesome image below. Princess Calla Tuoleimi—player Fifty-Seven—has just been declared the victor of the king's annual games, having slaughtered her final opponent. The loudspeaker continues bellowing the results: *A decisive battle . . . the Juedou draws to a close . . . the final challenger is dead . . .* and even if Anton shuts his eyes, he can't keep the images out. His last moments in the arena are trying to coalesce with August's most recent memories: Calla, luring him close; the council, meeting late at night in the war room; Calla, her forehead resting upon his shoulder; a dove, pressed into the wax seal of an envelope before the paper is torn open; Calla, Calla, *Calla*—

"I am perfectly fine," Anton says. The voice is foreign. The voice is entirely familiar. His eyes open, and the world stabilizes. His previous body is facedown on the arena ground. Bleeding, still, even though player Eighty-Six is dead. "Pardon me. This is rather repugnant."

Asking for any pardon is enough to make the guard uncomfortable, and she steps back into the throne room obediently. Anton doesn't leave the balcony—not yet. He overlooks the arena, takes in the thousands upon thousands pressed tight against the rope barriers. When his hands curl around the railing, his knuckles are as smooth as marble, silver rings carving dents into his long fingers.

An armory shield hangs from the stone walls of the balcony. His mere conscious existence here proves that he's succeeded in his escape, and without notice among endless witnesses. Though he knows what he has done, he's still stupefied when he leans in, when the metal of the shield reflects back a shock of blond hair, combed and ordered under a circlet. This is August Shenzhi's face. August Shenzhi's body. The only difference is his black eyes, catching light with the hint of purple instead of blue. Anton's eyes.

Delirium sets in. A bubble of laughter pushes out, and Anton hardly realizes he's the one laughing until his reflection moves too—*it's you making that sound. No one else stands on the throne room balcony. It's you wearing these silk clothes, wearing the prince himself.*

There's an incredible distance between where he stood in the arena and where August was watching. Yet he jumped, without having August in his sights first, without giving off that obvious flare of light. No evidence remains to show what he has done except for the pool of blood in the middle of the arena, noxious with the qi he drew from his previous body to fuel his move as he was dying. Amateur experimentation.

Anton clutches his hands behind his back. August's sleeves whisper with the movement, the light blue unstained and perfectly unmarred. No one below cares to watch him too closely in this moment, especially not while Calla is being led out by the guards, directed forward into the Palace of Union. He eyes her coldly, waits for a show of regret or some sign that *killing him* has affected her, but she disappears from view without looking back, her gait steady.

He dared to believe this would have ended differently, but that was his mistake. He may get caught in the next few minutes; he may get away with this forever. Neither one is more likely than the other when such an invasive phenomenon has been performed before, and as soon as Calla strikes, that throne will be his. This should have been impossible. And yet.

And yet.

"You're weak," Anton says out loud. He lifts his arm, waving goodbye to the arena audience, and half of them wave back instantly, summoned to attention by the gesture. He hadn't thought anyone would notice, but of course they do. A jolt runs down his spine, so strong that he has half a mind to check for a wound.

He's comprehending, slowly, the full implication of what he's achieved. Royal and noble bloodlines have been preserved over the centuries with the belief that their lineage holds favor with the old gods. August Shenzhi was born August Avia. As much as he's tried to escape it, he can't change that.

"Please, please, hold your applause," Anton whispers under his breath, turning on his heel. The words are reminiscent of a different life he lived long ago. This time around, there really is applause to accompany his exit: innumerable eyes upon his gestures and the knowledge that anything he proclaims upon the balcony will be heralded as law. He straightens his shoulders, smooths down his robes. The guards startle when he pushes back into the throne room, the curtains billowing to either side of the door. Though they hasten forward, Anton says nothing—not yet. He had little reason to enter the throne room back when this was the Palace of Earth and he resided in the other wing. The walls shimmer velvet red. Gold pillars prop up the high ceiling, their details carved with renderings of Talin's old gods. While he walks, slowly taking in his unfamiliar surroundings, his shoes sink into the deep green carpet threads, plush and soft. A smarter man would ask for the vault to be opened, gather whatever he can, and run before the opportunity slips by.

"The war room," he declares instead. "Let's go."

The royal guards must find the request strange. One steps forward—orange eyes, not a Weisanna—and says, "Highness, you're expected at the banquet. It will begin soon."

"I know." Something smells different about the palace, he decides. It's been years since he was last inside, but his memory of the rest of its layout hasn't faltered. Exile is lonely. Unforgiving. There was little to do during his quieter nights, and he turned to imagining these rooms in his mind, pretending he had clusters of priceless objects at his disposal rather than another sparse meal of a single fried egg when he woke in the morning.

"Your Highness?"

Anton is already on the move despite the guard, hurrying the few steps down and taking care not to trip when the flooring turns uneven. He passes the nobles at the door and pushes through the flurry of activity, paying no heed to the surprised greetings, the double takes. It's late. There must have been lurkers waiting to walk with him to the banquet, wishing to gain favor. Now they blink after him striding in the opposite direction, and the royal guards are quick to scatter the waiting palace nobles promising, *His Highness will be with you shortly if you could please make your way . . .*

Anton doesn't stop.

Outside the entrance to the war room, two guards step aside quickly upon sighting him. He asks them to stay there, alongside the royal guards who have followed him from the throne room, and he closes the door after himself before any of them can respond. There's cheering, somewhere in the distance. The crowds will be dispersing after the arena battle, drifting closer to the palace, hoping to catch sight of the banquet or receive scraps afterward.

Anton bites down hard on his teeth, marching straight for the filing cabinets pressed to the far wall. Talin's borders have been at peace for the past century, protecting the kingdom within from conflict, but the war room is well used, treated as the center of palace affairs. His fingers skate along the ornate table to the left, brushing across the rough surface and jostling the teacups that haven't yet been cleared. He opens the first filing drawer he sees, yanking all the way until its latch makes a metallic clang to signal it cannot be pulled any farther. A flurry of dust bursts upward when he fingers through the tabs, reading each one quickly. *Theft, Assault, Property Violation, Weapons Use, Protective Orders . . .*

He slams the first drawer closed. Only petty charges within San-Er. Not what he's looking for. He makes a wider glance around the room, considering where the information he needs would be stored. Instead of screens and machines, the war room is populated with shelves of thick books. The walls are covered in maps with curling edges, browning from age. Someone has drawn the window's heavy curtains partway closed, but there's enough of a gap left to allow in the electric light from outside and illuminate his way.

Anton tries the next cabinet. Here, the tabs are separating different provinces of Talin, ordered by proximity to the capital. *Eigi, Dacia, Cirea, Yingu, Pashe, Daol . . .*

He closes this one too. Tugs open the next. Employee positions in the palace. Next. Property purchases under the council.

"Where *is* it?" Anton mutters. He still tastes acid on his tongue.

When he crouches down to open a drawer situated between two overgrown potted plants and no taller than his knee, he finally finds tabs ordered by aristocratic last names. *Makusa* waits near the back, a file thicker than all the rest.

He stares. A lock of hair falls into his eyes—gold and fine, like sunshine twisted into spun silk. He pushes it out of the way, barely resisting the urge to tear the piece right out of his scalp.

"Your Highness?" A guard is knocking on the door. "Would you like any assistance?"

"No," Anton replies shortly. It's not as though August would have answered any more kindly, been any more considerate. The evidence of that is before him, within the file he takes into his hand.

"I'd help if I could," August had said, when this place was still the Palace of Earth, when Anton practically lived in the training halls, vowing revenge on the attackers who killed his parents. "If there was any resource in the palace I could use, I would. But the palace knows so little. These people are entirely outside of our control."

Anton flips through the pages in the file. He scans past the family tree, past the different reports that note when each of his relatives was born and when they died, past the graphs showing the other noble families who were connected to the Makusas by blood.

On the last sheet of the family logs, he finally finds what he's been looking for.

Anton Makusa—storage room 345, north wing.

After Otta fell sick and only Anton remained to suffer the consequences of their crime, the palace took his birth body as punishment. True exile, flung into the cities without any ties to his former life. He has always known that they stashed his body somewhere in the Palace of Union; he just never knew where. The location was purposefully kept secret to prevent Anton from trying to get it back, and the councilmember who delivered the fateful verdict of his penance promised that the palace would take care of his body, that they might return it one day if he served his exile without trouble. He's almost surprised that they've held to their word. The palace puts up a front of valuing nobility—by their own law, the bodies of aristocratic bloodlines should never be destroyed—yet he suspected they would discard his after a few years, merely because they could. Every other Makusa was gone. Anton was the last one left until the palace could sweep this entire file under the carpet, blow away the imprint of dust, and pretend none of them ever existed. How tidy, how neat.

"Can't you ask Kasa to send people in?" Anton asked. "Come on, August, he's the *king*. He has complete reign over Kelitu. He can order palace guards to investigate. Someone in that province must know who did this."

August was always the reasonable one, Anton the one whose voice got too loud with theatrics. Adults in the palace liked to listen to August.

"He's tried," August said levelly. In all the years they remained friends, Anton never could distinguish August's tells between lie and truth. What other choice was there than to believe him each time? "Trust me. They've found nothing."

Anton rises, brings the file to the desk in the middle of the war room, and lays it down so he can spread out the various sections. The Makusas come from a long history, but not any longer than the rest of the nobility, not enough to justify this much information kept under guard. He pushes away the atlas on his left and the paperweight shaped as an anvil on his right. Section after section, the desk becomes covered with loose paper, scattered with every document Anton reads as he grows more and more confused by the contents.

Copies of his parents' administrative letters in Kelitu. Snapshots of rural villages and tax reports with boxes circled in red. When Anton peels apart two inventory logs that have become stuck together over time, a small photograph falls out, and he sees himself as an infant in his birth body, staring straight at the camera so that they could put his face into the kingdom registry alongside his identity number.

He can't fathom why any of this would be collected. Not until he reaches the end and his eyes land on a missive. Digitally typed, then stamped with King Kasa's personal sign-off.

> I will keep this short. While your loyalty should belong with your councilmember, there has come undeniable evidence that Fen Makusa is a revolutionary insurgent. Where ambitions of usurping the throne usually call for arrest and a quick execution, his harm extends much further: he plots for the utter collapse of the kingdom. There is no scenario where this can be allowed to spread. For the sake of your province, and the sake of your people, see to it that the Makusas are eradicated in a manner that will not radicalize their followers. The palace cannot be associated with this punishment.

Though Anton continues reading onward, the rest of the missive stops registering past that line. He returns to the start, then again, and again. Finally, when it seems nothing more will change his understanding, his hands lash out of their own volition, flinging the file off the table and sending documents skittering across the floor.

He inhales shortly. Exhales, but can barely get the breath out of his lungs.

He's certain, in that first moment of panic, that August is trying to kick him out. When he's still heaving a few minutes later, he holds his breath in a snap decision, and his body responds accordingly. He's doing this to himself. The only harm to him right now comes from the fact that he can't keep himself under control. His panic shifts into red-hot rage. It finds its targets in front of him, within him.

His parents are dead because of King Kasa, not because they were the target of some random rural attack. After all these years wondering why his family had suffered something so awful, why his sisters needed to die as collateral, it turns out that the reason was because *the palace had ordered it.*

Another knock comes on the door. "Highness? What is that noise?"

"Come in," Anton says. "Just one of you."

A guard pokes her head through. Her silver eyes take in the papers littered on the floor, then flicker up. "Yes, Your Highness?"

"Who was the last person who put anything away in this room?" Anton gestures around him. "It's a mess."

The Weisanna shifts on her feet. She hesitates, and Anton knows she'll only confirm what he suspects. What he knows, given the guards posted outside the war room.

"Only you and His Majesty are allowed in here outside of council meetings. I garner it must have been the wind if a window was left open for air."

It's a tactful excuse that she has come up with on the spot. What she must be thinking is: *Your Highness, it could only have been you who made the mess.*

Anton glances at the name emblazoned on the front of his family file, which is lying askew by one of the potted plants now. He wants to tear the label off. Slap it elsewhere, as if that might change the fact that this heinous massacre happened to his family instead of someone else's. *A revolutionary insurgent.* That's preposterous. He never heard his parents say anything close to revolutionary. They were palace nobles . . . why would they have wanted to change that?

"No, it wasn't the wind," Anton says plainly. "Wasn't I the last person to go through these cabinets? *I'm* the one who keeps this information for King Kasa when he can't keep up with what happens in his own kingdom."

The guard flinches slightly, trying to gauge if this is some sort of test. It doesn't matter. Anton knows: there's no file in this place that has gone unread under August's watch. The crown prince takes it upon himself to stay informed using what he has access to. And there was plenty of time between August acquiring access to these rooms and Anton being exiled from the palace.

"Ah, never mind," Anton says, saving the increasingly anxious Weisanna from a response. He scoops up the file, then the papers, gathering them haphazardly before tucking them beneath his arm. "Make sure no one else comes in here."

"Yes, Highness—"

He strides past her, through the door. Farther down the hallway, Anton doesn't take the turn that'll lead him toward the banquet hall. He proceeds in the direction of August's bedroom, his polished shoes beating a war drum underfoot. Perhaps Calla has made her strike at the banquet already. King Kasa will die, and then Calla will be free to luxuriate in the only matter she truly cared about.

"Prince August." Someone hurries to catch up to him. Another guard. "Your presence is strongly requested at the banquet."

"No, that's okay," Anton replies.

Confusion dampens the air, a beat taken where the guard is perhaps wondering whether he was misheard. Anton is expecting rebuttal—of course there should be rebuttal. This is the Palace of Union. Affairs can't be derailed simply because he doesn't wish to tend to them.

But August Shenzhi is the heir to the throne, not some noble who has to capture favor. The guard nods in understanding, and Anton is free to continue onward without argument. He pivots left, then into August's anteroom.

"You can go."

The guards stationed outside August's quarters are exclusively composed of Weisannas. No Galipei, so he must be at the banquet, waiting for his charge's arrival.

"All of you," Anton prompts. He waves vigorously toward the door.

It takes a few seconds more, but the Weisannas nod and step out, entering the hall. Only then can Anton toss his file onto the desk. Only then does he immediately follow the movement by slamming his fist against the paper too, a zip of pain spiriting down his arm.

See to it that the Makusas are eradicated.

That was all it had taken. A single command, and life as Anton knew it had been decimated. Did King Kasa invent the excuse because his father upset him over some arbitrary matter in a council meeting? *Revolutionaries*. It is laughable, knowing their lineage. Yet the suspicion worms its way into his mind, wiggles free the faint impressions he has of his childhood. He remembers little of their trips out to the provinces, but they were frequent. There's a possibility that this was true, but still—

A drum beats throughout the palace, declaring the banquet coming to either a start or an end. Shouting echoes through the halls, either in ecstasy or horror. When Anton glares up, the mirror upon the wall catches his face, reflecting his expression. August dresses so regally, his hair combed neat and his posture straight as a needle. Anton's sneer turns his appearance off-kilter. He has the desire to pick up the decorative vase on the table and hurl it at the mirror, so he does. The glass shatters. A few jagged pieces fall off, littering the carpet.

"You knew what he took from me," Anton says to August. August's mouth moves with each of his words. A mockery, even now. "You let him get away with it."

August doesn't have the decency to look remorseful. The broken mirror cuts away parts of his cheek, carves into his forehead, distorts his mouth, yet Anton can find no scenario where his former friend might have apologized. The golden crown prince, only working to procure the throne he desired.

Fine. *Fine.* If King Kasa wanted to brand the Makusas as revolutionaries, then that is the inheritance Anton will accept. He'll finish what they say his parents started.

And then, Calla Tuoleimi is going to answer for what she did too.

CHAPTER 2

AFTER

At the farthest edge of Talin's border lies a province called Rincun, but that wasn't its original name. Ask the people living there how they used to refer to their home, and they aren't allowed to answer. A decade of the soldiers posted in the villages has instilled a healthy dose of fear, coating the villagers' teeth like a plaque they can taste any time their tongues press up to speak. They have seen the decapitated bodies staked by the yamen to make an example of those who kept using the old name. They would much rather survive than become the next example.

Calla Tuoleimi used to know Rincun's true name. She lost it at some point over the years, along with her own.

"Have you been out to the provinces at all, Councilmember?"

She's trying to ignore the conversation in the carriage. They entered Rincun this morning, picked up General Poinin where he lives, and are continuing onward to the yamen in West Capital. The general didn't have any luck starting a conversation with Calla, so he's moved on to lecturing Rincun's newest councilmember.

"First time," the councilmember answers. Her powder-blue eyes flicker over to Calla, silently requesting help. "My father never brought me when he visited."

Venus Hailira is the firstborn daughter of Buolin Hailira, who recently passed in his sleep. His council seat passed to her, and though the rest of the council questioned whether it was wise to continue with their delegation visit to Rincun while she was so green, their king was more impatient to get his newest palace advisor out of his sight after his coronation. There was no time for Calla to plead for forgiveness, to ask him how in the high heavens he was standing in front of her like this. The moment the coronation finished, Calla was ushered away, pushed out by the Weisannas with one wave of the king's hand. Hours later, while she paced the sitting room outside the royal quarters with each of her requests to speak to the king denied, she was told that she would be accompanying the delegation visit to Rincun.

"You'll be surprised at how backward everything is out here," General Poinin says, slapping his palms on his thighs. "The first time I met someone who still worshipped the old gods, I thought they were joking."

"I'm aware that the provinces still pray," Venus replies politely.

"They don't merely pray. You should pay attention to the number of bird figurines in the villages. I suggest ordering a province-wide sweep one of these days to get rid of them. It's unseemly."

Calla frowns, turning so that she's looking out the window. There are small clumps of snow still frozen where the paved road meets clay ground. Keeping bird figurines is about the most an ordinary villager can do in old worship anyway—it seems like overkill to be ridding them of that.

"I will add that to the agenda." Venus clears her throat. "We can ask the soldiers to make note of the numbers first."

That seems to mollify General Poinin. He settles into his seat, lacing his hands over his white jacket.

Calla senses the moment his gaze wanders back to her.

"Princess Calla, you appear to disagree."

She holds in a sigh. This trip is a formality, a survey staged for show. The palace doesn't learn anything new, and the provinces certainly don't gain much either when their councilmembers come by with a retinue of advisors taking note of their grain numbers and water levels. Rincun and Youlia are the only provinces in Talin where delegation visits are still placed in the palace calendar: they're far across the kingdom, and too new to have reliable, well-marked roads out. They're also too ramshackle for their councilmembers to keep holiday houses, which usually suffice as *visits* for other provinces when those councilmembers are off escaping the hot weeks in San-Er. If anyone from the palace is to make a visit to Rincun, a whole delegation is indeed necessary. The horizon of Rincun stretches for miles and miles without life, plenty of excess land roped in after the throne's conquest took their villages and swallowed the lake in the middle. Palace delegations must make use of the local generals, the ones who have been stationed out here long enough to know the way and direct their path. Though there's a seaboard and the raging ocean at the western edge of the province, one would never know that for how long it takes to travel over from the villages.

"Don't speak to me."

The carriage goes quiet. The two other advisors shift uncomfortably.

"I—you—*pardon?*" General Poinin demands.

She considers backpedaling to conceal her overt disdain. She could say that his suggestion is unnecessary by the palace's own decree. It is illegal for the provinces to speak anything other than Talinese, and so the villagers cannot truly pray when prayers to the old gods were made in their original tongue. Excessive worship in the provinces has already been cut down. The palace has no need to draw more ire from their farmers.

"Don't speak to me," Calla repeats instead. "Your voice is so fucking grating."

Prior to his ascension, August Shenzhi put the decree in place to make Calla his advisor, to pardon her from any past crimes and come into power alongside him. No one can overturn the command, unless August himself decides to renege on his word and yank Calla away from her new title.

But then people might start asking why.

Then the council might start sniffing closer and realize that King August is not King August at all, but Anton Makusa, refusing to leave the body he has invaded. Now, for as long as Anton allows Calla to keep this power, there is not a soul in this kingdom who can say otherwise, and Calla is going to make the most of it.

They continue the rest of their journey in silence.

◇◇◇◇◇

"We're just about ready, I gather," Calla announces, stretching her neck and hearing a click. The sun is setting. They should leave before then, get on the road as soon as possible instead of spending a third night sleeping on village cots.

She's impatient. It took a full week to travel here by carriage, so it will likely take another to get back to San-Er. Time will not linger to await Calla's return. While she's been flung to the farthest reaches of the kingdom, Anton is at liberty to do whatever he likes, and she wouldn't have the faintest clue about it. The thought itches at her, inciting an overwhelming physical restlessness across her limbs.

"I'd agree. Do you need a blanket, Highness?"

Calla glances down. Surveys her torso, her legs, her dirty boots. She figures there might be some reason why Venus Hailira asked the question, as though she's unwittingly started to shiver, but everything appears normal. She leans on the yamen wall, her arms folded. Though the wall is rubbing grime onto her jacket, Calla remains clad in leather, not the fine robes and silk of palace dwellers. She still dresses like she's lurking around San-Er, like she needs to blend into the perpetual night of the twin cities while playing the king's games. If anything, she's probably the warmest here at present. Even the palace guards accompanying the delegation seem a little chilled in their practical black cotton. As do the horses, already saddled and latched to the carriages.

"No?" Calla's answer comes out as a question. "Do I look like I need one?"

"Uh, no. I only wanted to check." Venus's gaze goes over her shoulder, to the building enclosed behind the wall. "Maybe the yamen would like some extra blankets."

"The yamen doesn't want blankets," Calla says dryly.

"They're low on supply. Some of the windows are cracked, and—"

"Let me revise my statement." The day's shadows shift, light ducking under the horizon. "The yamen doesn't want blankets from *us*. Leave them alone. You've seen the way they've behaved during our visit."

It has barely been three days, and the reception in Rincun could not be frostier. The villagers stay inside. Rural dwellers have no use for the palace unless the palace has use for them. While the other advisors make their rounds and receive reports from generals and soldiers, Calla has spent her time either in the yamen or dully trailing after Venus Hailira while her mind remains back in San-Er. She can count on one hand the number of people who have talked to her.

Venus frowns. "Don't be such an aristocrat."

"That is what I am, after all." Calla picks at her gloves. "They don't like us. Let them have it rather than trying to feign generosity."

"I'm not *feigning*—"

"You are." More guards emerge from the yamen, finished with their final bathroom breaks. "We are, as you say, aristocrats. If you were truly generous, you would open the Hailira vault for them instead of giving bits and pieces. Say you won't. You're allowed."

Venus's mouth opens. Before she can say anything else, Calla—still ever casual—gestures at the councilmember's pocket. "Phone's beeping."

"Oh." With a start, Venus takes the cellular phone out from her pocket, pulls the antenna long, and walks off to take the call. Once her generals return from their survey of West Capital, their delegation can leave. The palace guards seem impatient too: the ten or so–strong force stays close while they wait by the West Capital yamen, ready to set off at a moment's notice. Venus isn't very good at controlling the operation here. Unsurprising. Calla only knows of the Hailira family through peripheral knowledge, but she remembers hearing about the Palace of Earth turning up their nose at Venus for abandoning her birth body. It's not as though palace nobles don't often help their children quietly swap bodies when they insist they're not a little boy and need to be addressed differently—the problem is that Venus did it herself when she was a teenager, and the Hailiras couldn't just claim that nothing had happened, as other nobles did.

"That was peculiar," Venus reports, striding back. Her headpiece has shifted to the left, the blue jewels on the side tangling with a knot of black hair.

"Don't tell me there's a delay."

Venus frowns, raising her cellular phone to the sky. Signal is always weak in Rincun, and only phones specifically suited for the provinces work out here. "Lieutenant Forin is having trouble getting in touch with General Poinin. He'll call back once he checks with East Capital's yamen. Shouldn't be long."

"Why are we waiting on General Poinin? All he does is give you bad advice."

Venus pretends not to hear the remark. "He's supposed to be here by now with East Capital's final report." Venus lowers the phone. She catches the look on Calla's face. "We need to take *both* province reports back to the palace."

"Oh, do we?" Calla muses, though she knows. "My mistake."

She would bet the councilmembers in Eigi and Pashe never struggle to receive prompt answers from their generals. Their chain of command flows cleanly from throne to councilmember to general to soldier. Loyalties are clear; tasks are cut-and-dried. Rincun, meanwhile, has been split into two since its conquest. It is the only province in Talin that distinguishes between a west side and an east side, yet still one councilmember remains in charge of a dozen generals operating in both. Venus Hailira is not incapable in the slightest. But she is Calla's age, and she's naive as any aristocrat raised without tribulation is, which means the palace is going to mangle her into pieces. Let a month or two pass, and another noble family will make a play for Rincun, even if it's the least desirable province.

Calla would give Venus three months here, at most, before her own soldiers turn on her and the palace slams its fist down.

They wait another few minutes. Nothing more comes over Venus's phone.

"If this goes on past sundown," Calla suggests, "let's just forge the report and leave."

"The palace won't like that."

"The palace will not *know*, Councilmember Hailira."

"But—"

"Your phone's beeping again."

Venus starts. Looks down. "It is indeed. Excuse me."

The councilmember strides off. Meanwhile, one of the palace guards appears to be calling for someone a few steps away, and though Calla hears it, though she registers that the words he's repeating are "Your Highness. Your Highness?" she doesn't think to respond. Not until the guard, finally, prompts "Princess Calla!" and her attention snaps up.

"I am only an advisor," she says. "No need for a royal address."

"All right, Highness," the guard replies anyway. No matter her objection, there's still a smooth band of gold metal on her head, stark against her black hair. Royalty or advisor or mere palace aristocrat, all these titles mean the same thing: she is an intruder in Rincun. "We should remain for the night if this report takes any longer. It's getting cold."

Calla unfolds her arms and takes one glove off, letting the breeze blow against her bare skin. The horizon has taken on an orangish tint, bringing an imminent sunset that stretches its own long fingers into the clouds.

She doesn't remember this scene, though she must have witnessed it before. Her recollection of Rincun feels faint and faraway, like the logic of a dream upon waking. She can recount the series of events she experienced shortly before she left this province, the events that pushed her to invade Princess Calla Tuoleimi when she was eight years old. Yet she cannot look upon Rincun and acknowledge that this was once home.

Her fist closes, her palm turning numb. All her memories have a fragile nature to them. She needed it to be that way to fool herself and everyone else in the palace. Now her stomach churns each time she looks too long upon the flat plains, plagued by repulsion and pining alike. Somewhere in this province, rotting at the bottom of a deep puddle of water, there's the body of the girl she was born as. This place may feel foreign, but the tether between Calla and that girl has led her to this. It pushed her hand in the Palace of Heavens, bid her to spend the last five years a renegade princess instead of a comfortable one.

"Strange," Calla remarks. "It wasn't this cold last night."

Even as she speaks, the temperature drops again. A sourness rises in her throat. Her pulse hastens, nudging against her ribs.

"*What?*"

On hearing Venus's sharp cry, Calla swivels her gaze to the councilmember.

"What is it?" Calla asks.

Venus doesn't immediately answer, though she does turn her shoulder, caught in half motion. She's clutching her phone tightly.

Calla pushes off from the wall. "Councilmember Hailira." Her voice is hard enough that Venus stiffens, meeting Calla's eyes properly. "I'll ask again: What is it?"

"They've located General Poinin," Venus answers in a whisper, her hand coming up to cover the bottom of the phone. "He's . . . he's dead."

The freezing temperature suddenly seems like more than a weather anomaly.

"Where? East Capital?" Calla demands.

"No, he's here in West. Outside the barracks," Venus manages, and Calla is already running for a horse and unhooking it from the carriage. "They're getting in contact with his unit, but there's no answer at—"

"I'll be right back," Calla interrupts, hoisting herself into the saddle. The palace guards stir, puzzled by the sudden commotion.

"Wait!" Venus puts her phone away. "If you're off to see what happened, I'll come—"

"No! Stay here. Stay with the palace guards." She points at one of the guards, catching his attention with a threat in her eyes. "Watch her!"

Calla snaps the reins. Her horse surges forward. She isn't certain she knows the way to the barracks they inspected earlier, but Rincun shudders beneath her at menacing speed before she can doubt herself. The wind turns razor-sharp as it blows against her face. Calla, wheezing, grabs the collar of her shirt and pulls it up beneath her eyes for protection, then continues charging forward with only one hand on the reins, her horse stomping a cloud of dust along the main path through West Capital. She rushes past two meager, gaunt villages. Scans their greeting gates, keeping track of the names.

There. The barracks were close to those brown trees. She remembers that.

Calla skids to a stop and rolls off the horse. It's quiet. Startlingly so, given that West Capital's main strip of shops stands to her right. Her jacket isn't enough to stop her from shivering anymore, and Calla pauses for a moment to stare up at the darkening clouds. There must be some better explanation than what her instinct is telling her.

"Where is this coming from?" she whispers to herself.

Without time to waste, Calla runs forward, curving around the barracks and drawing a knife from her boot. They didn't let her bring her sword—*this is a peaceful delegation, Princess Calla; the royal guards are your best protection*—so she's making do with a smaller blade she swiped from the palace vault. The wind pulls her long hair in every direction, whipping it back and forth, over and around her eyes.

At the back of the barracks, she finds three men outfitted in the clothing of officials. Yamen workers already in the area, probably sent to poke around when East Capital couldn't locate General Poinin either.

"Your Highness!" one of them says stiffly, spotting Calla as she approaches. The delegation was introduced to him upon their arrival; she doesn't recall his name. He bows, but Calla's attention is already fixed on the dead general lying before him.

General Poinin has one arm tucked beneath him and the other splayed out. The left side of his face is pressed hard into the ground, his stare an eerie, unblinking burgundy. Hard to believe he was chattering nonstop earlier in the day. Maybe a villager finally had enough of his insistence on ridding them of their old gods.

"What happened?" Calla asks, putting her knife away.

"It's hard to tell," the official in the middle answers.

"An examiner will be here soon," the third says. "We called this in the moment we saw him. They'll find the cause."

"Let me save you the investigation. Make some space." Calla leans down and rolls the general over. There's a moment when the left side of his face is terribly red—then, seconds later, unnervingly pale. The officials must have noticed too, because one emits a disgusted noise, and Calla waves a hand at him to back up farther. She drops to a crouch. Peels back his jacket.

Two of the yamen officials start to gag.

"I *did* recommend that you make space."

A gaping hole glares out from his chest. Despite the gruesome sight, it is shockingly bloodless—a clean carving that goes through the sternum, past the ribs, and leaves empty space behind. Calla reaches her hand in, and the gagging noises behind her get louder. She runs her finger against white bone, gently. Smooth. Before a weapon made this cut, the body had already stopped bleeding.

"This doesn't make any sense," Calla mutters, standing up.

It's happening again. In San-Er, these qi experiments were the work of the Crescent Societies under Leida's guidance. But Leida Miliu is currently in a prison cell underneath the Palace of Union, and the Crescent Societies have no temples or reach outside of San-Er's limits, so what gives?

Calla loosens her shirt collar, lowering it from her face. The temperature appears to be returning to normal, the switch back just as abnormal as the sudden glacial plummet.

"What was he doing out here, anyway?" the first official asks. He's fanning himself to prevent further gagging.

"Probably wanted to see what other complimentary remarks he could include about the soldiers," the third answers, his hand still grasped around his nose. "Poinin has been petitioning for budget changes. Less for the farms, more for palace operations."

"Well"—the second official searches the grass around the general's dead body—"I don't see the report anywhere."

"Perhaps he handed it off already."

"What was he doing lurking around behind the barracks if he had already handed it off?"

"What are you sniping that question at me for? Let's just ask a lieutenant in the barracks—"

Calla doesn't have much to contribute to the conversation. She says nothing before turning on her heel and walking toward the entrance of the barracks. Though the three officials fall silent at her sudden exit, they don't follow her. She's alone when she rounds the bend again, steps over the raised entryway, and enters the walled facility.

"Heavens," Calla whispers.

When Yilas was kidnapped during the games, they found her in the Hollow Temple, surrounded by other unconscious bodies. Enough time has passed that Calla can rewind back to that scene on occasion without flinching, try to recall the details and wonder if there might have been an easier way out that night than brute force. An easier way than being stabbed in the heart, than having Anton Makusa yank her out of there to recover under his watch, his hand threading through her hair and her fleeting sense of peace molded into his bedsheets.

Inevitably, each time she forces herself out of *that* thought sequence, her mind wanders back to the Hollow Temple. She should have tried harder to get those others out. The nameless faces, the wrong-place-wrong-time kidnappings. She counted her job done the moment Yilas was safe. But there had been so many other bodies there. Some were still breathing, still alive. She never went back for them.

Calla exhales, scanning inside the barrack walls. She takes in the swathes of grass, the water troughs at the far end, the climbing ropes trailing from the watchtower rising higher above the perimeter.

And the bodies. Countless bodies clad in the uniform of palace soldiers, splayed dead.

Slowly, Calla makes her way over to the nearest corpse. He's slumped at the waist, his sword still sheathed. She hardly dares to breathe as she leans down, pushing his shoulder carefully so that his head lolls back to face the rapidly darkening sky.

But he has no wounds. Calla frowns and lifts his eyelids, finds his gaze dulled but with color remaining. She pats his chest. Rummages around his uniform. His skin is clean, his organs appear intact, and there's no blood on the ground around him.

The soldier has merely fallen dead, without any indication as to *how* he died.

Calla stands. There's more than a thirty-strong force at these barracks. How could all of them go down without any sign of a struggle?

"What *happened*?" she mutters. "Did a god come down for vengeance?"

A rustle echoes from the water troughs.

Calla stiffens, drawing her knife again in one motion. There's another sound—a suppressed human sniffle—and Calla flips the blade so that she can secure a better grip on the handle.

Just as she's about to throw her weapon at the first sight of motion, two children poke their heads out from behind the trough.

"Shit." Calla barely reins in the knife, snatching it out of the air and shoving it back into her boot. "Hey! You there!"

The children disappear back behind the trough.

Calla hurries forward. It's not like there's anywhere they can run, but she doesn't want to startle them. She's making her nicest face when she peers over the trough, slowing her movements.

"Hello," Calla says. "Are you all right?"

The children start to scream.

"Shhh, shhh!" she urges. She tried her best. Clearly, her nicest face isn't as nice as she thought. "You're okay. You're safe!" She throws her hands up, palms outward. "See? I'm good, I promise. I won't hurt you."

The boy on the left takes a ragged breath. He calms, wrapping his arms around himself. It takes a bit longer for the girl on the right to quiet, but she does so in stuttered bursts, each sound coming softer and softer until she stops.

"There we go. Nothing bad is going to happen to you." Calla crouches to their eye level, hovering on the other side of the trough. "Can you tell me what happened? Why are you here?"

No response. For a brief moment, Calla wonders if the children speak Talinese at all, but the thought is swiped aside as soon as it registers. There's no world where children would be raised without speaking Talinese. Someone would have reported the family otherwise, knocking on the yamen wanting to be rewarded, and then the punishment would come down swiftly from the mayor.

Still . . .

"You can tell me," she whispers. The past hums in her ears, lands a strange taste on her tongue. Before she fully registers where the word has come from, she's saying it out loud—*please*, she's just said the word for *please*, here she was thinking she forgot every bit of Rincun's dialect—and the two children perk up, a new glint in their eyes.

"You speak our secret," the boy says.

"I do." Calla looks over her shoulder. The yamen officials are going to make their way around shortly. She's made her point: she switches back into Talinese. "I'm just like you. I can help. Tell me what happened."

The children exchange a glance. An air of deliberation passes between them, making them feel older, far more sensible than should be expected of their age. Whatever they decide, Calla catches the girl nod before she shifts forward to lean on the trough, only her two gray eyes peeking out above the wood.

"They let us play in here and eat the rice if there's left over from the meals," she mumbles carefully. "We're not soldiers."

Calla holds back the flicker of a smile. "Yes, I figured. Did an attacker come in?"

"No one came in." The boy, bravely, decides to stand then. "The barracks turned really cold. Mother says that we should run when we feel the air turn cold. Cold means qi is being stolen. Great-Grandfather died that way."

Stolen? Calla glances to the side, to the dead bodies littered across the grounds. In her mind's eye, again she sees the Hollow Temple, the bodies that had been carved open. Stealing qi. Such a claim would normally be considered provincial superstition, just as some people here believe that being too nosy allows the gods to invade one's body and suck out their qi.

"Is that . . ." She doesn't know how to phrase this, not without sounding like a dubious city dweller who believes all the old gods are dead. "Is that *common* here?"

The two shake their heads. They remain silent.

"But you didn't run."

"It was my idea," the girl insists. She stands, too, now, as though her dignity is at risk. She's so small, barely taller than Calla's waist. Calla has the absurd thought that she could pick her up and shove her into her pocket if she wanted. "It felt safer to hide."

"And you were right to do so," Calla murmurs. No attacker came in. The world simply turned cold; the throne's soldiers fell dead. In the midst of it, two village children remained perfectly unharmed.

"There you are!"

Calla turns over her shoulder. A woman runs in through the entrance, her eyes the same gray as the two children's. They both scramble around the trough, hurrying to their mother. It's then that Calla catches sight of the scuff marks by the trough where the children were hiding. Three lines—simple enough that it may be mere coincidence.

Few matters tend to be coincidence when the unexplainable has occurred.

"What is this?" Calla asks. She points to the lines.

"A sigil," the girl chirps immediately, clinging to her mother's dress. "For protection—"

"Deera," her mother interrupts. There's a scold in there, sharp but subtle. "Remember what we said about making things up?" The woman looks to Calla and says, "I'm terribly sorry. May I take them home? They shouldn't be seeing this."

Odd that the woman hasn't asked what happened. Nor does she seem shocked at the presence of so many dead bodies.

"Of course," Calla says anyway.

"Your Highness!" A new racket comes from the entrance. The three yamen officials, finally catching up. "Your Highness, your palace guards are nearing!"

She registers the announcement dimly, still thinking about the situation at hand, trying to make sense of it. Hearing the officials, the little girl echoes "*Highness?*" with an edge of surprise, and Calla nods once in response. For the first time, she's starting to wonder if the provinces are better at hiding secrets from the palace than she thought.

"Better hurry out of here before the guards come to clean up," Calla says lightly. She looks to the mother. "If these two have anything more to say about this incident, please ask your mayor to reach me directly."

The woman lowers her head. "Yes, Highness."

I'm just like you, Calla said to the children earlier. Then the officials called out, and all they heard was: *I am nothing like you.*

She watches them go. The officials enter the barracks. They talk over each other, debating what happened and what could have possibly caused this. Though Calla doesn't look again for fear of bringing attention to it, she traces the shape of the three lines on the back of her hand. It reminds her of the two lines that the Crescents in the Hollow Temple wore.

"Shit," she whispers under her breath.

Just as the palace guards rush into the barracks, Calla finally gathers her thoughts and makes up her mind, storming out.

"Let the yamen deal with this," she commands. "We're *leaving.*"

CHAPTER 3

On Galipei Weisanna's fifteenth birthday, the palace assigned him to Prince August. It was a random draw, pulled from a list of every Weisanna who was near the prince's age and could follow him around like a personal shadow disguised as a child's companion. It could have easily been one of Galipei's cousins—another Weisanna, since they were all interchangeable as long as they had the silver eyes, the genetic inheritance that protected them against invaders jumping into their bodies.

But by whatever chance, the councilmember who'd made the list had put their finger on Galipei's name and sent the instruction down the chain of command. August had just been named Kasa's heir. He needed someone to keep him out of trouble, especially when the Palace of Earth recently had a scandal of colossal height: Otta Avia and Anton Makusa caught trying to raid the vaults. With Otta half-dead and eighteen-year-old Anton tossed into the streets of San in exile, the poor prince had such few friends left.

"Through here, please."

They took Galipei into one of the sitting rooms, a second-floor location in the east wing with very little sunlight. It must have been rarely in use, because he was greeted by a burst of dust, and coughed up a storm while the captain of the guard gave him a funny look. Though Mayun Miliu said nothing, Galipei clamped down on his itchy throat, too intimidated to draw more attention to himself. The royal guard usually gave him his daily tasks at a distance, addressing him in tandem with the other younger Weisannas. He had never received personal attention like this before. Nor had he been in direct contact with the captain of the guard herself, who had brought her daughter along for the proceedings. That was Galipei's first time meeting Leida too. In his memories, it's always overshadowed by August's arrival.

"Sit, sit," Mayun said. "Can I get you anything? Water?"

Galipei swallowed. His throat was dry, but he wasn't about to ask Mayun Miliu for water. "No, ma'am."

The seat creaked underneath him. A large rug took up most of the room, though it did nothing to muffle sound against the floorboards. Old portraits hung somberly on the walls, overlooking the wooden chairs placed in a circular arrangement. There was very little else to survey; Galipei doesn't find it strange that he can still recall each detail of the room to this day, from the silver drapery around the windows to the burgundy red of the wallpaper.

"Don't look so tense." Captain Mayun Miliu dropped into the seat opposite him. "Think of this as a small change in your daily routine. You'll still eat and sleep and go to school the same. The only difference is that it will be at the prince's side."

Her daughter came to stand behind her, staring at Galipei with unabashed curiosity. There was glitter smeared across her forehead, the exact shade of Miliu blue. He had never come close enough to Leida to notice. Up until that moment, Galipei Weisanna had been a forgettable face in the palace. Another boy trained in the morning hours, then sent off to the academy during the daytime so that he wouldn't be an illiterate guard. Another orphan with nothing to do during his evenings except continue training. Long before his parents were killed in work incidents, he had been gifted to the kingdom as an expendable component. It didn't make sense for him to cross paths with Milius or Shenzhis.

Then August walked through the doors, and Galipei's life slotted into place, rewritten for a new trajectory. He had been given no choice in the matter, but if he were asked to do it again, he wouldn't have changed a thing.

"Hello." August inclined his head in a gesture of greeting. "You must be mine."

Yes, Galipei decided. His sole purpose was August. What August needed, he would provide. What August wanted, he would seek out. In the years that followed, he was not only a companion; he was an extension of August, going where the prince couldn't and accounting for what the prince didn't think about. He didn't need appreciation. He needed to fulfill his purpose, and when it came to August Shenzhi, it was day after day of unending, invigorating purpose.

Maybe that's why Galipei has felt thrown off lately. For years, there has been only one path forward. One purpose, coloring so much of August and Galipei's time together. It was first whispered into Galipei's ear on a dark night, when August got out of his bed and came to crouch beside Galipei. The moment Galipei tried to sit up, asking what was wrong, August put a hand on his shoulder and pushed him back down. His other hand rose to his mouth, a finger pressed to his lips. There were Weisannas standing guard outside, watching August's quarters. When August spoke, his voice was almost inaudible. Only Galipei bore witness to his declaration.

"I'm going to depose King Kasa."

It had taken no convincing for Galipei to join him. It was not treason, not in his eyes. There was only one royal who had Galipei's loyalty.

"Okay," he replied. He raised his right hand, like he was already swearing allegiance to his new king. "How do we start?"

Now it has happened. The twin cities have August on the throne. Yet San-Er feels more or less the same, which is perhaps the first treasonous thought Galipei has ever had against August.

"Fuck."

In his memories, August takes his hand and presses their fingers together, a rare smile playing at his mouth. In the present, Galipei's hand strikes hard against the boxing bag—which he's been hitting for hours at this point—then slips, sending a flare of pain down his wrist. The bandages across his knuckles are starting to loosen. He has been spinning the same two thoughts on repeat. One: something is wrong with August. Two: it's damn *hot* in here.

The bag swings awkwardly. Galipei finally takes a rest, blowing a breath out and leaning over to prop his hands on his knees.

This boxing gym is located in the south of Er, but with the amount of movement through the doors every minute, one would think it was the epicenter of San. It's frequented most by the businessmen who live in the area, stripped down to only training gear, kicking at the bags and wooden-man apparatuses during their lunch breaks. Galipei likes coming here, despite the six flights of stairs it takes to enter the facility. Even though the bags are of questionable quality, filled with rags that often cause misshapen lumps and peculiar dips. The palace training facilities may import sand for their boxing bags, haul them in from the coastal provinces to create items of the highest quality, but they're also surrounded by the eyes of his relatives. He wakes up and there's a Weisanna outside his room. He takes breakfast and there's a Weisanna eating next to him. He can't even seem to get a word in edgewise to August, because it's not just Galipei acting as his guard anymore; it's the entire royal force, his aunts and uncles milling around and on high alert.

Here, he is unwatched, unmonitored. When Galipei throws his arms back, trying to stretch out his tight shoulders, he almost hits a man behind him. The man doesn't flinch. He barely notices, in fact, despite their proximity.

Galipei wipes the sweat from his forehead. He should get going before he actually collides with someone. Every public space in San-Er is built compact—the floors here are partitioned with rope to allow multiple occupants in one section; the owners have opted to install curtains in the corners for changing areas rather than create separate rooms. An electric fan spins hard overhead. Though it does little to make Galipei less sweaty when he heads toward the changing area, it does blow a corner of the curtain to swish left and right before he smacks the whole thing out of the way. He opens his locker. Inside, his pager is lit up, the screen flashing to signal incoming messages.

Where are you?

Return soon please

The wall's renovation is starting soon and I haven't been briefed??????

And is the gala still happening this year?

Surely not, right?

Galipei answer

Galipei pls

The messages are from Seiqi. She's Galipei's cousin, two or three or however many times removed, who has been assigned as captain of a new unit within the palace guard. Since Leida Miliu was arrested for treason, the guards in San-Er have been reshuffled into units based on city quadrant, reporting to different superiors. That way, there will never be another Leida, plotting with enough force to threaten the throne.

Seiqi is taking her new role far too seriously, pestering Galipei incessantly for consultation. They're not even that close.

"Annoying," Galipei grumbles under his breath, shoving his pager into his pocket. He pulls a black shirt on, then his jacket, and drags the zip up so fast he almost catches his chin.

He's in a foul mood. At Seiqi for thinking he has more sway than he really does. At the city for being too crowded, too hot. The afternoon air is better once he steps out from the building, but he still brushes against other pedestrians in the alleys, still has to skirt around the stalls when he gets to the main thoroughfare. The more perceptive civilians try their best to shuffle out of his way, sighting his silver eyes and recognizing him for a Weisanna, but most do not care.

A tremble from his pocket. Galipei fishes the pager out again.

Are you coming back soon?

"I thought I turned you *off*," he says, hitting the button again.

The palace guard is a mess, stretched too thin despite their vast numbers. August—no longer their prince but their sovereign—has put sweeping changes into place, far exceeding the promises he had whispered about before he rose to the throne. Talin's new reign has been sending out supplies and surveys in the form of mass legions, converting palace guards into province soldiers. They're drawing up comprehensive reports to identify each province's problem areas, then turning over mayors and firing administrative nobles haphazardly instead of addressing those problems. They're building infrastructure, then ordering that statues of the king be erected in every village, made of the most expensive materials paid from councilmember pockets. August Shenzhi was always quietly perceived as the heir who would one day improve conditions for the people in Talin. But his new measures—and new taxes—are so overtly a power grab that any observer would think he is trying to upset his own palace on purpose.

It could all be chalked up to acting too fast, too rashly trying to establish himself as king, if it weren't for the wall.

August has decided San-Er should be expanded. The wall is to be torn down and repositioned deeper into Eigi. None of it makes sense. August doesn't do anything without planning for weeks—even months—in advance. August would not act on a whim. August would not plot anything without consulting Galipei first.

Yet in the two weeks since his coronation, he has done exactly that. Galipei surrenders to an involuntary shiver, feeling a bead of water land on his neck from the crawling pipes overhead. San-Er watches him move through the streets, omnipresent surveillance blinking from one dense walkway to another. It's the same inside the palace. He hasn't found a moment alone with August from the second he became king. On the few occasions where Galipei has tried to speak to him, to ask if he's all right and offer counsel, August has been much more concerned about what his cousin Calla is doing—*no, listen, Galipei, there must be some way to take her off this advisor role before she gets back from Rincun . . . Yes, I am perfectly fine, there's no need for me to read over that report if they're following instructions . . . Someone get me a list of the other royal advisors . . .*

The palace comes into view, one of its turrets catching a flare of sunlight coming through the clouds. An unusual sight. The twin cities are normally as gray as sludge, the sky clogged and the streets dark without its nighttime lights.

Galipei frowns, circling around the rough bricks of the coliseum and blocking out the bustle of the marketplace within. He enters the palace through a side entrance. The mud under his boots trudges in with him.

"Galipei! I thought you'd never show up!"

He suppresses a sigh. He should have known he would be ambushed.

"Seiqi," Galipei greets plainly. His stride doesn't slow. He's got work to do, and anyway, a Weisanna can walk and talk at the same time. "If this is about the wall, I'm not your reporting superior. I don't know whether you'll be posted on it."

"I know *that*," Seiqi replies, sounding a little offended that he would assume otherwise. She breaks into a light jog to keep up with him, her long braid flying up behind her. "You're on the king's private detail. Even my superior's superior should answer to you."

Technically, Seiqi's superior's superior would be August. So that is untrue.

"What is it, then? Must be important to spend so much time locating me." There's commotion ongoing in the south wing, somewhere overhead. Briefly, Galipei turns his head while they pass the junction between palace wings, curious enough to eye the servants who are hurrying down the broad green staircase. One of them has a soiled bedsheet bundled in her arms.

"I wanted to ask about the gala. Kayen says it's still happening."

"Then it's still happening," Galipei replies. The grand gala is just another occasion to have a banquet so the council can do a self-congratulatory pat on the back. "It's an annual event and it's been on the calendar for a while. Why would it stop this year?"

Seiqi grimaces. "It's technically Kasa's gala. You should tell King August to cancel."

"Council isn't going to like that," Galipei counters. If there's *one* matter that August needs to be careful with, it's the council. The common people must fall in line no matter what he declares. He could proclaim that all civilians of Talin shall walk backward from now on, and they would do it. So long as there are soldiers ordering it, they will do it.

But if the council turns on him, he loses everything. The council controls the generals. The generals dictate orders to their soldiers. That is the only way Talin knows how to operate.

"The palace is practically in shambles, and we don't have the resources to support another banquet tomorrow."

"Yes, we do. It's a large royal vault."

"It's not about the *money*. Regardless of how many new palace employees Calla Tuoleimi lets the staff hire, we don't have enough *guards*. I mean, listen to that rumble upstairs. A whole unit of Weisannas is doing reconnaissance on the palace infirmary because of that blood-vomiting interloper. Waste of our talents, if you ask me."

Is that what the sound is? Galipei, finally, slows down. There's another staircase at this end of the corridor, with an accompanying flurry of activity too.

"Wait a moment." *Blood-vomiting interloper?* "Is someone sick?"

Seiqi flips her bangs out of her face. They're short, so she barely moves them, but the attitude behind the motion is there.

"Too good for palace gossip, are you? I don't know how you haven't heard. Northeast Hospital brought her to the palace an hour ago and said she's been screaming about being a noble. Someone must have validated the claim if we're letting her stay."

Galipei halts completely, right next to the smaller staircase. A pit opens up in his stomach, as potent as a pulsing wound. There's no chance. Absolutely none.

Do you have cinnabar? he asked his aunt.

For what? Are you trying to create an immortality elixir?

He bolts up the stairs, his head whirring in disbelief. The south wing grows tall before him, a silver fan running fast at the center of the painted ceiling. A selection of the pantheon—the most important cosmic gods—stretch their arms above the foyer space.

In their earliest years, before their war with Sica, before Talin conquered places like Rincun and Youlia, the kingdom would send delegations through the independent provinces in search of gods. The borderlands supposedly granted entrance to the heavenly plane. The old gods had disappeared into the mountains and left the land to mortals, allowing kings to rule in their stead, but the kings—as kings tended to—desired more. It wasn't enough to accept the old gods watching over the kingdom once in a while on a prayer. The kings sought outright favors instead, if only they could find them.

So they dug through the mountains.

Though they found no gods, they did find cinnabar. The first people to mine the substance started to shake and seize. Later, they would claim to have seen the heavens and been within reach of immortality. They brought the mineral into the kingdom, into the Palace of Heavens in the north, then the Palace of Earth in the south. Royal chemists were given the instruction to carve open the line between mortal and god—their palace would supply them with as much of the mineral as they needed.

Eventually, after a considerable number of deaths, the palaces changed their tune. Cinnabar was no element of the gods; it was just stupidly poisonous and caused hallucinations. Now they had an abundance of the mineral and no immortality to squeeze from it. They dumped their supply en masse, loaded them onto carts to be wheeled into the provinces and discarded. The factories took one look at the barrels and immediately brought the bloodred color in for use. Despite its toxicity, cinnabar has never disappeared from the kingdom because of its pigment, which San-Er's factories still extract in abundance. Easy to obtain, if you know the right people.

Galipei turns the corner. The infirmary's double doors loom ahead. If there was a racket earlier, it has quieted since. He pushes on both doors, thudding them open.

"Oh, heavens."

CHAPTER 4

At the edge of San-Er, unending piles of construction line the path into the provinces and along the periphery of the wall. This central section will come down tomorrow. They'll detach the gate and rebuild farther out into Eigi, allow these steel foundations to infect the yellowing grass and new buildings to take root inside.

A large force of guards has been brought out to surround the new perimeter of the capital and clear away the rural civilians who like to camp outside the wall. Many in the provinces have come to watch the perimeter line change, waiting for their moment to slip into San while the wall is down. They haven't acted yet. As far as the palace guards have witnessed, they're merely camping patiently.

"We have someone claiming to be a lawful entrant," one guard on scouting duty says, coming to a stop in front of a Weisanna.

The Weisanna barely looks up from his tablet screen, too annoyed that he's been placed out here. A smattering of rain falls from the murky sky, wetting the text. They need a few elite units in case there's real trouble and a Weisanna's capabilities are required, but did it have to be him? For most of his life, he has been on the royal guard. Now he's overseeing a *wall.*

"Identity number?"

"She says that she hasn't been issued one yet, but her entrance date is today. Gave her name as Bibi."

"Bibi what?"

"Only Bibi. Didn't say whether it was first or last."

This is stupid. The Weisanna smears the rain off his face, then stabs a finger against his clunky tablet to type the two characters in. "I don't see her on the list. She must have been issued an identity number if she's been accepted for entry. We need to match her in the civilian registry or else she doesn't come in."

"All right. Hold tight."

Bibi, meanwhile, waits by one of the camp tents with an umbrella. It's a hideous yellow color, the last one at the stall in Eigi where she bought it. She clutches its handle with one hand, twiddles a lock of curly hair with the other, tugging and tugging. She has spent most of her life out in Laho Province, though she wasn't born there. Sometimes, out in rural Talin, people find themselves stuck in certain places. One day at a job turns into one month, waiting for the savings to go somewhere, but then it never does, because food prices keep increasing. One month at a job easily blends into a year, which then grows into a decade. Farm owners are good at using bartering systems instead of San-Er's central currency. A year of work for decent comfort. Ten years of work for a shed to sleep in. Eventually, one forgets whether leaving is even an option when leaving means starting over.

Laho, though, is too landlocked, and Bibi couldn't shake the urge to run, try as she did. The province produces grain and grows wheat in its plains, the same as those beside it. Nothing about Laho captures particular attention, not like how Gaiyu is known for its red wind-chime flowers, or how Daol has a glimmering eastern seaboard. Laho isn't a difficult province either, not like the outermost territories of Talin that were more newly swallowed. Rincun and Youlia are associated with unrest. Small, frequent fusses that the palace soldiers have to beat away.

Laho is just nothingness. When Bibi started making her way southeast toward the twin cities, waiting each round of the immigration draws, she felt the difference in her bones, in the creak of her knees while she crossed from plains to forestry. The Jinzi River rushing beneath her feet made up her mind; Pashe's hot climate breathed a damp thrill in her lungs. After failing to obtain entrance during her first lottery, she decided Eigi wasn't so bad for what she needed. The villages were busy. The food had strong taste.

Then she heard about the palace burning down Eigi's capital to transform it into a security base, and she had to make a choice: either enter San-Er proper and hide among its people or return to the provinces and get out of sight. There was far too much risk hovering in proximity to the twin cities, where the guards were most wary.

They could find out who she was. They could kill her a second time.

"Ask the palace," Bibi whines when the guard returns and prompts her for her identity number again. "I told you already—they said someone would be at the main gate with welcome materials. How was I to know you're not using the main gate today?"

"Fine, fine." The guard has a good spirit, unbothered by the rural dwellers who sneer at him from a distance away. "Give me a few minutes. I'll go to administration."

Bibi folds her arms across her chest, her sleeves bunching at her wrists. She's wearing her only nice shirt. Rural Talin doesn't produce much variety in fashion. Plain cloths and wraparound cotton to keep cool during sweltering wet seasons. Slightly thicker wool for dry seasons when the ice blows in.

"You don't really have an identity number, do you?"

The voice comes from the tent to her left. A man pokes his head out, looking unkempt with shadows under his eyes. There was a child who ran out from the tent before. Perhaps this is a tired father trying to relocate his family. It is equally likely that this is the head of a trafficking ring treating the wall as a ripe plucking ground, scooping up children to use for labor in Eigi.

"Of course I do," Bibi answers evenly. "I just don't know it yet."

"I heard it comes with your approval letter."

Though construction hasn't officially started, they've already begun digging in some parts, unscrewing the pillars of the wall and the joints of the concave bends. It makes it easy to glimpse into the city. To eye the buildings made of metal and imagine walking right in.

"Funny. I suppose mine was lost."

"How do you lose something like that?"

Bibi reaches into her shallow bag of belongings and rummages around for nothing. As some of the guards at the wall start to move, changing shifts, she takes her cue to walk forward.

"How silly of me," she says in lieu of a reply. "It's been here all along."

◇◇◇◇◇

San-Er feels it the moment she comes back.

The twin cities may have lost most of their stories, but their temples still worship. And where there is worship, there must remain remnants of the past. Practices that only make sense within their context, methods of sacred care passed on from old to young. It is there that fragments of collective memory cling to life, lurking in obscurity. No one alive now was around for the war, but there are some who remember growing up in its shadows, in those years after the kingdom's masses took refuge behind the wall. They remember their parents refusing to speak about why they fled the provinces; they remember the fear at any mention of the enemy.

Talin's borders have been undisturbed for over a century. When the throne won the final battle, it breathed a sigh of relief. It cleaned its streets, wrapped its history away with a neat bow so no one could haul it back into the light.

It didn't realize it had never been granted victory, only momentary armistice.

The enemy has achieved her greatest play. She isn't going to accept defeat this time around.

CHAPTER 5

The delegation finally returns to the capital shortly after nightfall.

Calla was quick to clamber out of the carriage as soon as they stopped outside the wall, but she's been waiting around for what feels like eons now. There's metal and rubble littered everywhere, decorating the ground with ladders and half-prepared dig sites. Muted green lights beam down from the top of the wall at two-meter intervals, enough illumination to let the incoming carriages navigate their way but not to disturb the occupants living at the edge of San. At this hour, most of the apartments taller than the wall have their blinds pulled down anyhow, preparing for sleep.

Calla wraps her arms around her middle and drums her fingers along her elbows. Every time there's movement near the gate, she thinks it must be opening wider, but it's only province migrants trying their luck to get closer to the wall before being shooed back by the guards and their batons. Calla has been tracking a young boy who keeps skirting in and out of sight to avoid them. First he was poking his head around the left of the main path. A few minutes later, he was sidling nearer and nearer the right side before a guard barked at him and he skittered away. No one has called for him. No parent, no adult to chide him to be careful and usher him inside one of the tents.

Calla shakes her head, pulling her attention away. It's not her problem. There are too many orphans in Talin. If she were to start tending to every one of them, it would drive her mad.

"What's taking so long?" Calla calls to the nearest line of guards, finally losing patience. "It's like a snail is pulling the gate open."

"Manual operation, Your Highness," one of them replies. "The electric wiring has been shut off and taken out."

There's a pause. She's waiting for the guard to elaborate, but he only stands at attention, watchful in the dark.

"Shut off and taken out," Calla echoes, "for what?"

"Renovation starts tomorrow, Highness. We're moving the wall a mile out."

The gate groans a colossal complaint. It lurches once in a taunt of speeding up—pulling just wide enough for a carriage to squeeze through if it didn't mind getting its sides scraped off—before the gate stops entirely, stuck.

Calla waits a moment. Someone is shouting from the other side of the wall, but the voice is muffled, as though water fills the space between rather than brisk night air. They're calling instructions for this disaster of a manual operation, she's sure. She's also sure that the manual operators aren't even listening, because the sides of the gate suddenly inch closer together again.

The carriage door opens behind her. Venus Hailira steps out, shivering in the cold. She likely heard every word Calla was exchanging with the guard, so she doesn't ask what's going on. She watches the wall for a few seconds before asking, "I don't suppose we could ride through anyway?"

"San-Er only has a small number of carriages," Calla replies. "The council won't be very happy with you for destroying these."

Venus sighs. "This could take a while."

"It could," Calla agrees. She makes up her mind. "I'll see you inside, then?"

"You'll *what?*"

Calla starts forward, her chin lifted high, the glint of her circlet beaming back the wall's green lights. The guards nearest to her don't find the fortitude to say anything when she strides past them on the main path. Movement flashes in the corner of her eye. The boy again, still circling the crowds. Right as he pushes to the edge of the cluster, surfacing among the other migrants, she reaches out to snag him by the arm.

"Move fast," she hisses under her breath.

"Your Highness—" The guards at the wall half-heartedly raise their batons at the sight of her, but Calla merely ducks under one of their arms and keeps moving, tugging the child along. She makes use of their shock, and then she's in, through the gate and scuffing her boots against overgrown yellow grass.

"Go," Calla hisses, letting go of the boy. "Hurry!"

He doesn't hesitate. The boy is running immediately, headed for one of the alleys. Behind her, the guards scramble to follow, calling protests, but Calla has already located her own route, crossing the short field behind the wall and cramming into another small alleyway between two residential buildings. They'll go after the boy first, but he didn't seem like he would be easily caught. By the time they send people after her too, she'll already be out of sight, and then why would they bother pursuing it further?

The cities vibrate beneath her feet, as though they're voicing agreement. Calla climbs a few steps up and emerges from the alley, turning right to use a narrow pedestrian walkway. She's not a little girl from Rincun anymore. She's not one of the rural dwellers waiting outside the wall, hoping to be granted entrance into the cities on the palace's whim. She's Calla Tuoleimi. The man on the throne may be doing everything in his power to squeeze her out of sight, but Calla's been wearing a weapon in the shape of a face far longer than he has. Anton Makusa doesn't even know what he can do yet. He can't play this game like she can.

Calla pulls a cellular phone from her pocket and presses it to her ear. Along with her small knife, this was also swiped from the palace—the surveillance room, specifically. It only works within the twin cities, or else the wireless signal isn't strong enough.

As the phone rings, a pungent smell suddenly hits her nose. It's coming from a half-shuttered storefront, and Calla hastens her speed. There could well be a corpse rotting in there, and she's startled for a heartbeat by her own callous reaction. Finding dead bodies out in Rincun is a reason to send her hurrying toward the palace, but not in San-Er. Dead bodies out there are a problem, a symptom of something terrible soon to erupt; here, they are another day, another damp gray afternoon turning into a cloying night where cracked ground-floor windows look onto addicts lying diagonal on insect-infested mattresses.

"Magnolia Diner."

The cheery voice crackles, answering right as Calla ducks into a building and hits a patch of rough signal. Her surroundings remain at a low drone: murmurs from a higher floor, an electric bulb buzzing overhead, a shudder along the walls that might be an air conditioner coming to life. Though she can run fast, it'll take considerable time to get to the Palace of Union on foot. Less, however, if she goes by way of the rooftops and cuts a direct line through the dense city.

"Hey," Calla says. There's a blue arrow spray-painted beside the staircase at the end of the corridor. "Is that you, Chami?"

"Unless I've been jumped unbeknownst to everyone around me, yes."

Calla almost misses the first step up, her grip turning bone white on the handrail. Chami is joking; of course she's joking. It's common sarcasm that children fire back at their mothers, something so impossible it can only be in jest. Still, Calla shudders as she corrects her stride, ascending three stairs at a time.

"Is Yilas around?"

"When is she not? One second—*my love? My dearest, softest baby?*"

Calla snorts. Despite herself, she cradles the phone close. She continues climbing, passing seven flights of stairs, then eight, nine, ten . . .

"Hello, Your Royal Highness."

Calla pushes through the rooftop door just as Yilas's voice bursts through the static.

"Your brother," Calla says without greeting. "Is he on shift in the palace surveillance room right now?"

In the one night she had as royal advisor before being booted from the palace onto a delegation mission to Rincun, Calla did everything she could to plant an extra set of eyes in the Palace of Union. Both Yilas and Chami said they would rather defenestrate themselves than serve the crown again. But Matiyu Nuwa . . . he needed a new job after his departure from the Crescent Societies. It was easy enough to maneuver him into place, especially with Anton distracted. Calla presented the edict to let palace employees come and go rather than reside inside the walls—to let ordinary civilians working the surveillance room or cleaning the kitchens take shifts and clock in and out for the first time since Calla's parents were murdered in the other palace and Kasa ramped up security in his own.

Their esteemed new king signed off on it right away to get her out of his sight.

"Princess Calla, you were the one who hired him. Shouldn't you know?"

"I haven't exactly carried his schedule out with me to the great provinces."

"Fine, fine. Let me see..."

Yilas trails off to the sound of rapid clicking. Her pager, probably. Moments later, just as Calla is leaping between two rooftops, Yilas reports: "Yes, he's on shift for the next hour. Why—"

"Tell him to get me in. I'll wait by the south entrance. One of the cameras should pick me up. Thank you, bye!"

Calla hangs up. She's being rude, but Yilas won't mind. It's hard to hold a phone to her ear and listen to San-Er under her feet at the same time. If there's any burst of noise, it will be civilians emerging from their homes and flocking to the main thoroughfare. They will want to watch the returning delegation while it moves through San-Er to return to the palace, and Calla needs to keep an ear out so she can get back first and check on some business.

"Oh, *shit.*" When Calla leaps to the next rooftop, her boot skids. It must have rained earlier, shallow puddles forming where the surface is uneven. Calla narrowly recovers her balance to avoid falling off the building, but her knee goes down fast, striking cement and whatever discarded electronic pieces have been left up here.

Sharp pain moves through her leg. Calla grits her teeth hard, then picks herself up and continues forward. A brief slip. She'll be okay. Though she's been away for some time, the twin cities don't warp around her absence. San-Er waits, ever patient, perking to attention the moment she returns like her best-fitted shirt, more easily indulged than resisted.

The south entrance of the Palace of Union protrudes from a section of the coliseum. Calla descends before she's within distance and returns to the pavement. Illegal drug trade starts on the rooftops during these hours, keeping operations close to the coliseum for the sort of patrons wanting to make a pickup after their late-night grocery shopping. Plenty of Crescent Society presence on those rooftops too, and Calla doesn't have time to be recognized.

Brief glimpses of the coliseum peek through the narrow spaces between shop buildings, flashing gray stone and golden lights. Calla takes a wrong turn at first, but before she can circle back, she catches casual conversation in the next alley over—palace guards. With a brief, muttered curse, she acts fast, rushing over to a window and tapping the glass a few times.

She pauses to listen. No response. When she hears the guards turning the corner, she nudges open the window and enters the apartment, keeping her tread light over the messy floor. The room is surrounded by scattered burlap sacks and emptied cans of precooked meat. Whoever the occupant of this apartment is, it appears they're unpacking from a fresh move, which strikes Calla as strange. People don't move around much in San-Er; the circumstances don't change enough to warrant it, unless someone is drawn in the migration lottery and allowed entry from the provinces.

She steps out the front door and hurries down the hall, then through an exit into the next street. The palace's south entrance looms ahead, around the dark bend and past the dilapidated fragment of an awning that has fallen from a third-floor restaurant. Calla presses forward just enough for the cameras to catch her, then checks her phone so the guards at the entrance don't notice her arrival.

While she pretends to tap the buttons, a real message comes through.

What number were you calling from? Will my pager come through can you see this

Calla blows out air in the shape of a laugh, her bangs puffing up before landing back in place.

I am on cellular. Yes I see this.

Yilas texts back instantly.

Oh fab. Matiyu says turn back and follow coliseum on right. keep going until you see wires

Wires?

Despite her confusion, Calla quickly follows instructions. She's loitered for long enough, and the guards have noticed her. It wouldn't be the worst thing in the world if she *did* walk right in through the palace entrance, but she doesn't want them declaring her presence. She doesn't want news of her arrival to reach the king's ear, at least not until she makes a stop first. If Anton's been sitting here simmering in his anger, maybe he'll throw her in prison the moment she returns.

"Over here, Calla!"

Calla stops. She's paced too hastily past an alley and slowly reverses back two steps, peering into what she thought was a dead end blocked off by the coliseum's exterior. To her surprise, Matiyu is waving at her from the end of the alley, standing by a large tangle of electric wires. *Ah.*

"I didn't know there was another entrance," Calla remarks, entering the alley. On the left side, there are two back doors that lead into restaurants on the upper floors, surrounded by trash cans overspilling with food scraps. If she weren't looking, she wouldn't see the other door hiding behind the wires that feed out of the ground and into the top of the coliseum.

"It's an emergency passage," Matiyu says brightly, turning to pull the door. When it doesn't move, he sighs, patting around the wires until he clears a tangle to reveal an electric panel. Calla watches him input what must be his identity number. A puff of air emits from the wall as the door unseals. Quickly, Matiyu grabs a corner to haul it open and waves her in first.

"I'm impressed. You've been here less than two weeks, and you've already discovered an unused entrance."

Matiyu dabs his sleeve against his nose to try to stop it from running—either a result of the night chill or his rapid dash across the palace to meet her here. He and Yilas look startlingly alike, down to the exact same mannerisms when they want to be polite. "Don't think I don't know why you got me this job. I registered my identity number for access through every emergency entrance on my third day."

"Good work. Now take me to the surveillance room, would you?"

"I'd better get a good year-end bonus for this."

Calla rolls her eyes and starts to walk. Before she can make an arbitary right turn, Matiyu reaches to steer her shoulders left. She pivots. Even when she made diplomatic visits here with the king and queen of Er, she never spent more than a few days in the Palace of Union—then named the Palace of Earth. Heaven overshadows Earth: the Tuoleimis were the ones who played host more often. In keeping with its name, the Palace of Earth was supposed to be the grounded one, satisfied with its portion of Talin claimed below the Jinzi River. The Palace of Heavens, meanwhile, stretched the kingdom's ambition north, higher and higher until the kingdom was complete at twenty-eight provinces, having conquered Rincun and each bite of uncharted territory up to the borderlands.

"This way," Matiyu says, pointing at the stairs. The moment they start to ascend, a rumble of voices floats from the top, signaling their impending descent. Matiyu grimaces, waving Calla off the first step and down the next corridor instead.

Though this is a different palace from the one she grew up in, Calla can almost fool herself into thinking she knows the way. When San and Er merged, when King Kasa took over the latter and his council grew from twelve seats to twenty-eight, any illusion of difference between the two palaces snapped away. Somewhere nearby, the throne room glitters coldly, its half-circle entryway decorated with ostentatious carvings, words and symbols of immortality for Talin's rulers.

"Servants' passages," Matiyu explains when they descend three steps and the plush red carpet suddenly turns thin and gray. "Hope you don't mind."

"How dare you. Fetch me a palanquin right now."

Matiyu snorts. Though Calla hasn't seen Yilas's little brother since the Palace of Heavens—when Yilas was her attendant and Matiyu visited on weekends to steal palace food—she feels the same sort of ease with him as she feels with Yilas. They may not know her truly, but they don't fuss about wanting to know the princess either. That's more than she can really ask for.

Three staircases up, two staircases down, and five sharp hallway pivots later, they're finally approaching the surveillance room with Matiyu huffing for breath. Calla follows closely on his heels, ever casual as Matiyu drops into his cubicle. The two people on either side of him glance over curiously before snapping their attention back to their monitors, pretending they don't see Calla Tuoleimi hovering over his shoulder.

"Show me the palace prison," Calla says.

"Which one?"

Which . . . one? Calla thinks back to the cell she was kept in after the victor's banquet. The chipping walls, somehow both water-damaged and charred with electric burns. The thin, threadbare blanket on the creaky bed. She only spent one night in there, believing Anton dead, believing that she had done everything she needed to in this kingdom and that it was time for rest.

She almost wishes she had been right.

"How many are there?"

"Two." Matiyu clicks around on his screen. A camera feed appears on the left side, showing the row of prison cells she remembers. Surveillance for the rest of the cities is nowhere near as sharp as this. During the king's games, sometimes the reels were too pixelated to see a player's limb being severed off. The light in certain alleyways made fights appear as clumps of shadow on-screen. Inside the palace, meanwhile, the quality of the footage is almost better than what Calla sees with her own eyes.

Matiyu clicks again. Another display appears on the right side of the screen, showing only one cell and one prisoner, her head lolled against the wall.

"Stop. Zoom in on that one," Calla says.

Matiyu follows instructions. He inches closer and closer, until the live surveillance is focused entirely on the prisoner.

So Leida Miliu is still locked up. There is no trick here, no possibility that the reality is anything otherwise. Yet something happened out in Rincun, with the same echoes of the events that unfolded in San-Er during the games. Calla rushed back in a fit because she was sure she would find an escaped prisoner. A part of her hoped for an empty cell, because that would mean she knew who to hunt; it would mean Leida was the adversary to best.

If Leida Miliu remains in the palace cells, then trouble has sprung from somewhere else.

"The Crescent Societies," Calla says out loud.

"What?" Matiyu asks.

"We should check on the Cres—"

"*Announcing His Majesty.*"

A drumbeat booms through the palace wing suddenly, reverberating low and long. Calla, though she swallows a curse, isn't surprised. It was only a matter of time before word spread that she slipped into the city ahead of the delegation. She entered the palace and didn't report to the king first. What a poor royal advisor she makes.

When Anton strolls through, unaccompanied by the usual presence of the royal guards, Calla barely keeps her arms at her sides. The roots of his blond hair are coming in dark, curling around the crown on his head. He hasn't been maintaining August's dye routine. It's a shock to see the change, as though the two of them have started merging into one. She wants to claw August's face off him. Then she wants to caress his cheek and beg him to understand what she did in the arena. But she stays put, because it doesn't matter what she wants. Anton Makusa is furious with her.

"Your Majesty," Calla says.

"Your Highness," he echoes back. "What a surprise."

"You couldn't possibly believe I'd remain in exile for long."

The surveillance room presses past quiet, growing tense enough to register as unusual. Out of the corner of her eye, she sees Matiyu wince, and Calla attempts a course correction, flashing a smile. The machines at her side blink green and red. The walls loom closer, each tear in the iridescent blue wallpaper growing larger to listen too.

You should have left the games. You should have run. You should have run with me.

"No one here can take a joke between cousins, it seems." Calla laces her hands behind her back. She grips the edge of her jacket, hiding the tremor that threatens to show. "I was so efficient at surveying the provinces that I have returned early ahead of the delegation. Aren't you pleased, Your Majesty?"

Anton, like he's already exhausted, drops into an open chair beside the surveillance cubicles. Their eyes meet; his are pitch-black. When Calla takes a step closer, his gaze narrows, still dark as night but reflecting a hue of purple. Anyone who knows August Shenzhi well enough should know that his eyes flash blue-black instead. But that list is very small, and given that Galipei Weisanna is nowhere to be found at present, Anton is probably doing a fine job keeping those people away.

"Protocol says the delegation must travel together."

"Oh, psh." Calla shrugs one shoulder. "Since when have I followed protocol?"

His expression darkens in an instant, sweeps that violet away like a midnight flash flood. This visit to Rincun was, of course, an implicit threat. Anton Makusa is the only one who knows the truth about her identity, and she is the only one who knows the truth about his current deception—so she should keep her mouth shut if she wants him to do the same. Her once lover looks at her with the ire of a battle adversary: she chose herself over him, over *them*, in that arena, sacrificed him to fulfill her ultimate goal. If the tables had been turned, she would have lunged for Anton's throat the moment she saw him again after the battle.

Then again, if the tables had been turned, they never would have ended up in that arena to begin with, but Anton wouldn't *listen* to her and pull his wristband. He chose the allure of victory too. She is not alone in this blame, and if she's being honest, she's growing increasingly irritated at the fire he's tossing her way, given his own role in this mess.

"I expected you to report to me first, Princess Calla. It is only proper."

Anton is alive, at least. She didn't lose him to her vengeance. She murdered King Kasa, and Anton Makusa still walks the earth. That's something. Even if it feels like a bomb that could blow up in her face at any moment.

"I'm here now."

"After I sought you out myself. I had to leave an important meeting about the wall."

His behavior is a good imitation of August, she can admit. Every movement is the graceful sort of casual, his limbs relaxed even while his attention remains alert. But she knows what to look for, and his small faults slip out in a silent herald. The quicker tilt of his head. The longer swing of his arm. August would never prop his hands against furniture like that. It's too cavalier. August would have both his feet flat on the ground, not rested lightly on his toes. That's the behavior of someone used to running. Though August's body isn't ill-fitting on Anton, it's *off* in the manner of a mirror reflection having a half-second lag.

"May I speak to you now?" Calla asks. "In private."

"No."

Someone in the corner gasps. A small sound, nothing that draws further attention. It only makes audible what every witness here must be thinking. In King Kasa's toppling, Calla Tuoleimi and August Shenzhi were certainly allies. While the palace servants whispered *King-Killer*, if it hadn't been for August, the council would have instantly had Calla executed for her crimes.

"Matiyu, clear the room," Calla orders.

"What?" Matiyu blurts. He looks between Calla and his king. "Is that allowed?"

"You may be overstepping, Highness," Anton says blithely.

"Confidential palace business," Calla offers without missing a beat. It is not entirely out of line to ask for the first convenient place of debrief—especially not for Calla Tuoleimi, whom the palace knows to be a wild card. If Anton Makusa has any sense of self-preservation, he will agree without argument. As he should have back then, in the arena. Yet instead, he's playing his own stupid games, and Calla wishes she could take him by the shoulders and shake him into submission.

The room begins to clear. Each employee gets up hesitantly enough to afford them deniability if their king were to declare that anyone leaving ought to be imprisoned, their bodies still facing their cubicles until the final second. Matiyu is the last to shuffle through the entryway, and he grimaces awkwardly at Calla before sliding the door shut. It clicks.

"You need to get out."

Anton's gaze is knife sharp when it pivots to her. He performs a haughty sniff, but no amount of feigned disdain can disguise his fury.

"Why?" he asks. "So you can kill me without consequence a second time?"

They haven't been alone like this since the arena. Since Calla put a blade into his back and through his heart. Where she hasn't changed her wardrobe from her getup during the games, he is dressed in a pressed blue jacket and fitted trousers, looking like he could lead a royal battalion across Talin and lounge back on the throne after a long day. This isn't the manner of someone wreaking momentary havoc. He's staying in August's body.

"Anton, please," Calla says, her voice dropping to a whisper. "The arena . . . you *know* I didn't want to—"

"Whether you wanted to or not doesn't change anything, does it?" Anton interrupts, rising to his feet.

"It changes everything." Calla is trying her damned best not to sound angry. "I don't—I'm still—"

The truth is, she doesn't know what she's trying to say. Whether this is the time to be deciphering why she did what she did. There's no way for her to say *Sorry I killed you* without the part that goes *but if you think about it, you forced my hand.*

"Anton," Calla pleads, stepping forward. It could be her imagination, but she swears she sees him flinch, even from several paces away. "You are causing trouble where there needs none. Didn't the palace keep your birth body? You can take it back, jump—"

"I'm not leaving."

The rest of her words sour in her throat. She doesn't understand what his purpose is here. Power? Money? If it were only this title he wanted to keep, he should have gotten rid of Calla the moment she placed that crown on his head. He should never have revealed the truth to her. Put her neck under a sword before anyone could question the decision, gain some points with the councilmembers who reported to Kasa and now report to him. Then he could have playacted as August forever.

"Don't force my hand further," Calla says tightly. "Leave, Anton. Let the kingdom return to how it should be."

"And how should it be? Another century ruled by a useless king, I gather."

"August has plenty to do."

"August wants power for himself, first and foremost," Anton counters. "You are a fool to think otherwise."

Calla has to turn away from him, has to look somewhere else, her eyes falling on the monitors that show her the scenes outside the palace. The marketplace has almost cleared of shoppers, save for a handful of stragglers here and there. "Maybe I am a fool." There is the truth. There is her pulsating heart, pulled bloody from her chest and harvested for the threads of deceit she wove into it herself. "Once August was on the throne, my job was done. Then everything was supposed to have been worth it, no matter how high the price."

You, the room whispers. Filling in the blanks where she won't, whispering impatiently from the monitors whirring around them. *If putting August on the throne meant nothing, then losing* you *meant nothing.*

"Unfortunately . . ." It's Anton who steps closer now. The metal buttons on his jacket catch each colorful flicker on the screens, and when Calla turns back, she finds herself focusing on that detail to keep her expression in check. She wonders if August had those buttons matched to Galipei's eyes, silver enough to appear perpetually cold to the touch, bright enough to reflect everything in the vicinity. "I'm not going anywhere. I have unfinished business."

Calla remains still. He couldn't mean their battle in the arena. Finishing that business is as simple as picking up the nearest heavy object and bludgeoning her in one quick swing. He could do it while the room is empty, with no one able to punish him for the indiscretion afterward.

She might even let him.

Anton reaches for a lock of her hair. The gesture appears affectionate at first, when he winds it around his finger. Then he yanks hard, and Calla has to yield an inch to stop him from ripping her hair right out. Her hand whips up and grasps his wrist. She doesn't dare look straight at him. She only squeezes with equal pressure, her breath locked in her throat. It seems absurd to recall how different the circumstances were the last time they stood this close. Maybe Anton is thinking the same thing: her touch and the dark of night, the storm outside raging white light through the blinds. The cluttered floor. The twisted bedsheets.

"What is it?" Calla whispers, her words strained. "Your unfinished business."

When she runs through the possibilities, she emerges with very few options. Outside of her, if there is anything that would keep a flight risk like Anton in one place, it has to do with August, and what he has discovered while wearing his body.

Anton lets go of her. Terribly, Calla misses his touch despite the sting. She needs more, craves a longer moment of contact to know that he is real, that although she has torn him apart, he has cobbled himself back together as no one else could.

The door to the surveillance room shudders, cutting short anything Anton might have said in reply. Calla has a mere second to get ahold of herself and flatten her expression before Galipei Weisanna appears at the entryway, yanking the door back.

"August, I have been outside your quarters waiting for you all evening," he says sharply. "You are *needed* in the royal infirmary."

Anton doesn't glance at his bodyguard, but Calla is watching Galipei carefully. His collar sits crumpled. His silver eyes are wild: an abnormal sight for someone who has spent his entire life training to be August Shenzhi's obedient half.

"Not now," Anton replies.

"What's happening in the infirmary?" Calla asks.

Anton shoots her a glare. "What part of *not now* is unclear—"

"Otta Avia," Galipei interrupts.

In an instant, Anton swivels around, rearing with shock. "*What* did you just say?"

"I said, it's Otta," Galipei says. "She's here."

CHAPTER 6

Midnight strikes in the Palace of Union. Floor by floor, the electric lights flicker on when they sense movement cutting through the sleeping hallways, chasing away the hazy indigo for Anton to march through the north wing, his heart pounding in his ears.

It's Otta. She's here.

The moment he had access to the royal vault, Anton made sure that Otta's medical bills were paid, made sure there wasn't anything outstanding that could prompt the hospital to clear her bed when they couldn't reach him. He hasn't checked in on her otherwise—he's been a little preoccupied—but he couldn't have imagined that she would *wake up*. The yaisu sickness is incurable. The doctors have never changed their tune. Although she wouldn't get better, she wouldn't get worse. A lifelong coma was no consolation, but it was still enough for Anton to clutch to, day after day. At least he had her. At least she wasn't entirely gone.

"August, one moment."

Galipei is calling after him. Just now in the surveillance room, Anton was quick to react, pushing into the corridor to make his way to the infirmary and see for himself. Calla has either taken another route or decided not to check on this matter, because it's only the palace guard at his heels. And Galipei. Galipei, incessantly needing to speak to him, even while Anton was holed up in his quarters, unwilling to see visitors all evening. Honestly, Galipei should have just passed the message to a guard on duty instead of asserting self-importance, instead of waiting around the hallways for a personal conversation and delaying delivery because Anton exited his quarters in the other direction to avoid him. Look at how quickly news about Calla's arrival in the palace breached a straight line into his ear as soon as the guards on duty started muttering with the rumors.

"It can wait, surely," Anton says.

When Galipei finally catches up, his posture is stiff and his shoulders are slouched. Anton understands the restlessness, the confusion spilling off him. But Galipei Weisanna does not yet suspect that his charge has been invaded. Anton needs to keep it that way.

"It cannot," Galipei intones, lowering his voice so only Anton can hear him. "I'm sorry, August. But at least Kasa is gone. Even if she tells someone—"

Anton should know better than to react. Unfortunately, he isn't quick enough to stop himself from giving Galipei a bewildered look, and Galipei cuts himself off midsentence. In that gesture alone, Galipei must know something isn't right. Before he's noticed the precise color of Anton's eyes, before he's registered any of Anton's strangeness in August's body, he's picked up on this one discrepancy, and Galipei simply stops talking.

"Did you bring her here?" Anton asks, trying to smooth over his error. *Did you have something to do with this?* he wants to ask instead. *Did August?*

"Not my doing," Galipei says shortly.

Anton pulls his loose sleeves back. All this fabric, gathering at his elbows, restricting his every movement. He's practically choking in it, the silk and the gold, the layers and the cover-ups.

Two guards pull open the doors to the infirmary. Inside, the clinical space is twice as large as any of the palace bedrooms, and for a moment, Anton doesn't even know where to look. He steps in. The soft, warm-hued bulbs on the walls illuminate the room with small circles, mimicking candlelight. Piles of blackened towels sit in the corner. Blood. He smells it despite the stink of bleach emanating from the marble floors too.

She almost blends in with the sheets. In the farthest bed by the red-curtained window, there's the shape of Otta Avia, her black hair poking out from the white. It's a familiar sight: an unmoving Otta, connected to the tubes and lines that keep her affixed to her last gasp of life.

Except here, there's nothing attached to her.

Here, when he draws to a stop at her bedside, her eyes fly open.

"Otta," he says; he exalts. He doesn't realize he's dropped to his knees until he feels the faint echo of pain.

Otta sits up hesitantly. Their eyes lock, and in the flickering light, it appears that her irises are yellow instead. He thinks of Calla, off elsewhere in the palace. When Otta blinks, her eyes return to the same black shade they've always been. *Perhaps*, Anton considers dimly, *this is an imposter*. It would be more believable that someone has conducted dirty work and planted a fraud in the palace. That they manipulated qi to invade Otta's dying body. Far more believable than Otta Avia suddenly awake and well again.

Then Otta takes a stuttering breath, her tears welling over in an instant, and Anton doesn't need to bring the firelight close to erase his doubts. Seven years later, fresh out of an eternal sleep, and she can still summon tears on demand. His vision distorts and blurs, trying to reconcile the present before him with the memories he has replayed over and over: of the days when they got in trouble across the palace, caught in someone's quarters, found where they weren't supposed to be, and Otta always got them out scot-free with the howl of her crying.

"Hey, hey, you're all right," he urges. "You're safe, Otta."

He reaches to cup her face. He's afraid that if he presses too hard, she'll disintegrate like a drawing in sand, but Otta is firm beneath him. Her sobs ease, a flash of confusion deepening the line between her brows.

"I hear you woke in the morgue," Galipei says from behind Anton's shoulder. "That must have been frightening."

Otta sniffles. "It was so awful," she whispers. "All I could see was darkness. I felt the fire."

"The fire?" Anton echoes. "What do you mean?"

"I don't know." She twitches, then nudges Anton's hand away. "Don't ask me to explain. I don't know!"

The infirmary is cold. Anton doesn't know why he's only noticing it now. It prickles his skin, up and down his arms. He glances over his shoulder, silently warning Galipei not to say anything more. Galipei, unrepentant, folds his arms across his chest.

"We will have to investigate further," Galipei says anyway. "It's nothing short of a medical marvel to wake from the yaisu sickness. Northeast Hospital will want to run tests and see what happened."

"What?" Otta's eyes well up again. "You're going to send me back there?"

"We're not sending you back there," Anton says. Almost instinctively, he tries to take Otta's hand, and she tenses, pulling away. He's taken aback for a moment. Then Galipei says, "August. You've got company incoming," and Anton remembers. He's August Shenzhi, Talin's newly crowned king. This isn't his first love before him. It is his half sister, and he should act like it.

Movement enters his periphery. Silent as a ghost, Calla Tuoleimi walks into the infirmary, a bag dangling from her hands.

For fuck's sake.

"Well. This is a shock," she says wryly, swinging her arm.

The bag lands beside him on Otta's bed. He didn't hear her approaching, though Galipei clearly did. He's let his guard down once again. No wonder he lost in the arena.

"Clothes for you," Calla says. "Figured you'd like them better than that awful hospital gown."

Slowly Otta reaches for the bag. She tips it upside down, and out tumble two large pieces of green silk. A bodice with bell-shaped sleeves, then another swath of fabric composing the skirts.

"That's very kind of you." Otta's tone doesn't give her away, but her frown does. Her tears remain dew-frosted on her lower lashes, glimmering as she holds the silk closer. Anton recognizes that dress. It's hers, indeed, having sat in her rooms for years.

"Truly, Highness, you shouldn't have," Anton says. It's as much a message for himself as it is for Otta. Calla was delayed merely minutes after him into the infirmary. If, in that time, she had a servant track down Otta's former quarters and retrieve the dress, then Calla Tuoleimi is priority number one in these gilded halls, the princess who the palace drops everything for. He wonders whether she's heard the chatter about her. Whether she planted her spies here while she was in Rincun to report the palace's whispered curiosities, people wanting to know where their King-Killer had gone. Kasa can't punish them for that any-more. The Palace of Union can say aloud that they love his destroyer, even if the council wants her out.

Otta zeros in on Calla.

"I know you."

"I should hope so," Calla returns. "We've met several times." She comes to crouch beside Otta, hovering on Anton's left. Something about the scene before him feels like a violation of nature. It churns his gut, not unlike the way his jump back in the arena felt like it was turning his body inside out. Someone like Calla was never meant to meet a girl like Otta. They will eat each other alive.

"I'm only a royal advisor now, so don't worry about bowing."

"Calla, thank you for bringing her clothes," Anton cuts in, before Otta decides to combat the subtle threat. "But if you must busy yourself with palace affairs, I suggest getting some sleep. The council will want a debrief on Rincun in the morning."

"I keep telling you I need to speak with you, given that what happened in Rincun may be related to what lies in front of us," Calla fires back. "You should consider the possibility that Otta Avia's body has been invaded by a hostile force."

"She hasn't." It doesn't surprise him that Calla would immediately hold this suspicion as well; an invader presently getting away with their identity theft will, naturally, be inclined to think everyone else could be equally guilty. Only after his quick defense do the rest of Calla's words dawn on him, and he backtracks. "What do you mean, *what happened in Rincun*?"

Calla stands, her leathers rustling. "We found an entire legion dead. Palace-delegated soldiers in their barracks. No weapons, no wounds. It's as though their qi was merely plucked from their body."

The news arrives at an awry angle, like a bird thrown at their feet with legs growing out of its head. Calla's delegation visit was supposed to be a formality. The idea of an attack in Rincun while she was there is so absurd that Anton only blinks—as does Galipei, his restless movements stilling.

"Has Rincun been invaded?" Anton asks, knowing full well that cannot be the case if it has taken Calla until now to announce this. Nevertheless, if Sica is going to cross the borderlands into Talin, the first province they will reach is Rincun.

"Unclear. Rincun is still investigating the incident."

Anton isn't sure what this means. Neither is Calla, it seems, given that she's reported the news so vaguely.

"Trouble follows you wherever you go, doesn't it, Princess Calla?"

Her glare whips to him. It grates him to admit it, but a surge of satisfaction rushes down his throat to see her agitated like this. To provoke her like this. Yes, perhaps he ought to get rid of her entirely, find some excuse to call the palace guard down on her, yet . . . this is a better punishment. A thousand lashings in answer for her fatal cut. She should feel the pain too.

"You know, I owe you an apology, Otta," Calla says suddenly.

Anton's stomach drops. Well, there's the problem with punishing her long-term: Calla likes to retaliate.

"Whatever for?" Otta picks at a thread on her dress. She doesn't see the glint in Calla's yellow eyes while they stay locked on Anton, homing in before she looses her weapon.

"Aren't you wondering how your brother's on the throne? Last time you were awake, it was King Kasa ruling this palace. Surely you don't think the natural passage of time put that crown on August's head."

Stop, Anton signals to her with his eyes. *Right now.*

"Perhaps it did," Otta replies.

"Ah. Alas." Calla smiles. "I imagine when you awoke, you asked for Anton Makusa."

Now Otta sits up straighter, her shoulder-length hair gliding back. Where her posture was soft, meshed into the lines of the sheets, she prickles to attention at Calla's words.

"What does Anton have to do with anything?" A pause. "Where . . . *is* Anton?"

"A fantastic question. I'm sure he would have greeted you himself if he were here."

Anton can hear the insects fluttering in the corner. The electric pulse beating through the lights. Instinct tells him to jump, to surge into movement before he can be caught and chained down.

"Where is he?" Otta repeats, an edge entering her voice.

Calla takes her time answering. She looks away from Anton, directing her gaze out as though she's doing penance. She wants to rankle him into giving himself away, into calling her a liar. He will not. He, too, wants to know how

Otta will react anyway. The curiosity pushes up beneath the surface of his skin, where his need to be needed flows in his brittle blood. *You were supposed to be the one who loved me most,* he thinks. *How will you mourn me?*

"He's dead," Calla says. "He entered the king's games to pay your debts, and I killed him in the final battle."

He didn't expect her to say it so plainly. It takes every effort not to scoff and demand she explain the circumstances of his defeat. When Otta lifts her gaze, he braces, waiting for either a wailing shriek or a pithy remark that she never loved him anyway—one or the other, surely—but her expression is unchanging, her eyes narrowed to make two elongated chasms, nothing of the whites visible.

Seven years have passed, and the world has moved on without Otta Avia. Seven years asleep, and those black irises still scare Anton if he looks too long, as though nothing has changed.

"Why do you sound like that?" Otta asks.

Anton can't help but blink. Dimly, he senses that this exchange between Calla and Otta has moved on without him—which is absurd, when it's supposed to be *about* him. He rises, and Calla looks at him sharply. Her elbow flutters, drifting closer to her waist where there used to hang a sword.

"I beg your pardon?"

Though she's speaking to Otta, she is looking at him.

"Your tone. Who was Anton to *you*?"

"If I may," Galipei interrupts. He has been all but forgotten, lurking by the wall. "Any trouble in Rincun should be reported immediately to the council, who can warn their respective provinces. We waste time debating it here."

"Yes, fair point," Anton agrees at once. "Calla, won't you write up the report?"

Calla has been saved from answering Otta's question. She reaches for her long hair, untucks the stray strands from her collar, and flips them outward with a huff. "Venus Hailira can make the report to the council. I've reported to the king. My duty is done."

She pivots. Her boots clunk through the door, into the hallway, and out of earshot. Galipei catches Anton's attention and meaningfully tilts his head in that direction too, urging them to take their leave.

"August," Galipei prompts when Anton doesn't move, and Anton jolts again. He remembers where he is—who he is. "It's getting very late."

"It is." He turns back to Otta. "Get some rest. There will be time to talk later."

"Yes," Otta says quietly. "I appreciate that."

A lock of black hair falls into her face, curling at the end and flicking at the corner of her mouth. It might give the impression of smiling if it weren't for the fire in her eyes. Again, for a flash, he thinks, *Your eyes. They could almost be the same yellow as Calla's.* Then the light flickers, the shadows settle back in place, and Otta is Otta.

He fears he is filling the space Calla left behind. The thought is frightening enough that Anton has to resist the urge to reach out and touch Otta once more, to confirm that she is real and not an illusion he conjured to reckon with Calla's betrayal.

"Is there anything you need?" Anton asks. He bids himself to keep still. Galipei's scrutiny prickles at the side of his face.

Do you have nothing more to say? he entreats silently. *Ask about me. Ask anything.*

"No," Otta replies. "But I'd like to be discharged tomorrow. I want to return to my old rooms."

"We can arrange that." Anton takes a step away from the bed. Before he can draw far, it is Otta who reaches out to touch the side of his hand, and he startles.

Otta blinks up at him, almost childlike.

"I appreciate it," she repeats. "I know we haven't always gotten along, August. But I am thankful that you will take care of me nonetheless."

"Of course." Anton releases her hand. "Get some rest."

He's quiet while walking out. Galipei, wisely, says nothing too, trailing three steps after him on their way to the king's quarters. Though he doesn't speak, Galipei's footfall comes down hard, each audible *thump* keeping rhythm like a heartbeat. Anton tries to block it out, but it is as potent as another pulse inside him: August, trying to come back to life the moment Anton falters.

Not a chance, Anton thinks. They reach his quarters. Without a goodbye to Galipei, he enters the antechamber and slams the door closed.

CHAPTER 7

Calla can't stop thinking about Otta Avia.

It kept her sleepless through the night. She tossed and turned, unaccustomed to the cold palace sheets and grumbling under her breath every few minutes when her annoyance reached a peak. Otta was aggravating enough when she was comatose. She was the reason Anton wouldn't withdraw from the games. The reason Calla and Anton ended up battling each other in the arena, why Calla was forced to land the killing blow—why Calla and Anton are in this absurd predicament. If she was capable of all that while lying unmoving, Calla doesn't even want to consider what Otta Avia can do now that she's awake.

Conversation sneaks under her door in excited whispers. Infuriatingly, Calla's quarters in the Palace of Union are situated near the central hub of activity, because palace advisors are placed by the meeting rooms, and the meeting rooms are often adjoined to sitting rooms, which the nobles shuffle in and out of around the clock. They've been chattering among themselves all morning, in shock that the yaisu sickness can be cured.

It can't, Calla wants to spit, shoving her last pair of leather pants into a small backpack. No one merely wakes up one day when their insides have been burned beyond repair. Something beyond their understanding has happened here.

"Mao Mao," Calla calls. "Mao Mao, come on, buddy."

Her cat trots out of the bathroom. Before she left for Rincun, she stopped at her old apartment and clicked her tongue until Mao Mao sauntered out from the hole in the wall where he had been hiding. Almost everything else was broken, the kitchen plates in shards and the mattress torn in two with its innards strewn across the bedroom. Nothing was retrievable except her cat and one potted plant.

That's all Calla has to her name. The council didn't exactly welcome her back in the way they're welcoming Otta. With council encouragement, some of the other royal advisors have decided it would be nice to commission a portrait of the king's newly woken sister. The servants Calla walked by earlier were gossiping that it would hang in the north wing where the Avias used to live, depicting Otta Avia's tiny face and dainty chin as the centerpiece of the main foyer to celebrate her miracle recovery.

Calla leans down, holding out her arms. "Are you coming with me? You don't have to."

Mao Mao makes a noise of protest, nuzzling into the fabric of her sleeve. He's gotten fat in the short time Calla has been away, well fed at every corner as servants sneak him treats. Someone's tied a giant pink bow around his neck too, fitted with a bell in the middle so he jangles as he moves. He's a fancy cat now. A royal cat.

His fluffy head twitches twice. Calla gets the hint and removes his bow and the bell. "Okay, I won't leave you here. You'll have to get in a bag again, though."

"Meowr."

"I know. But a rice field with me is better than this pit of vipers by yourself."

If she moves fast, they may not notice her absence until she's well out of range of San-Er's surveillance. She pillaged the royal vault while the palace was still sleeping in the early hours, plucking objects that would each go for the price of a house in the provinces' black markets. Her backpack rattles with valuables, probably totaling twice as much as the victor of the king's games receives.

It's taken Calla the full morning to prepare for her departure, and she can't spare a second longer. She shouldn't have returned to the palace in the first place, but she had to know about Leida, had to see what she could fix. While she was outside the wall, she should have found an opportunity to skirt off somewhere along the Apian Routes, disappear into a province and never be seen again. If she had moved in the night, the palace soldiers wouldn't have known she was gone until the next day when they cleared out of their roadside stop. She could have been deep in Pashe or Leysa by then.

Calla spares a glance at the clock ticking on the deep-purple wall.

"*Meowr!*"

"Hold *on*, you're so impatient—"

She holds open a shoulder bag and lets Mao Mao squirm inside. They'll leave in an hour, when the decorators enter the Palace of Union to prepare for the gala tonight. She can have Matiyu shut off the cameras along her path to a back entrance. The corridors will fill with people, and she's banking on the chaos to slip away.

There is nothing more for Calla here. King Kasa is dead, and everyone who was responsible for her village burning is gone. Advising a false king afterward isn't what Calla signed up for. If the kingdom descends into anarchy, that's a problem for the man on the throne, and Anton Makusa is not her fucking business, especially now that his first love has returned. She hopes they live happily ever after for the brief time they have together until August wins back control of his body and kills them both.

"Your Highness?"

A knock comes on her door.

"Busy!" Calla calls back, her voice bouncing across her rooms. The window alcoves are too long, echoing the slightest sound tenfold.

"Your Highness," the voice says again at the door. "I was told not to take no for an answer."

Calla performs a scan of the floor, making sure she hasn't dropped anything. "That's too bad. Come back later, perhaps."

She keeps circling to the same conclusion, again and again: there is no chance Otta will be fooled for long. Otta Avia knows August well, and she knows Anton even better. It will take only a single glance in good daylight for her to figure out that it is Anton inside August's body, which means it is only a matter of time before she causes utter catastrophe. As soon as Anton is caught, San-Er will course correct. Anton will be removed, August will return, and if Calla sticks around, she will be blamed. It's too late to fix her mistakes and take back what she has sacrificed. She lost Anton Makusa in that arena. She gave her all to the kingdom when King Kasa fell under her sword. It's time to go while she still can.

"Highness." The knocking grows more persistent. "Councilmember Hailira requests your presence. The council is convening on the matter of Rincun, and they're bringing Leida Miliu up for questioning."

Calla bites down on the inside of her cheek. She lolls her head back, glaring daggers at the ceiling, tracing her eyes across the floral patterns.

Fuck. *Fuck.*

In three long strides, Calla crosses her rooms, shrugging off both her backpack and her bag with Mao Mao. Her cat gives an unseemly yelp of surprise, and Calla whispers a quick "*Sorry!*" before yanking open her door.

The woman waiting at the entrance looks familiar. Something about her white hair and her steady eyes, a muted purple made darker by the lack of natural light in the hallway. The color reminds her of Eno, of the kid's glassy stare after he was killed in the games under her watch, and Calla forces the thought out as soon as it nudges into her mind. Besides, as the old servant steps back, gesturing into the hallway and turning her head, she's sure there must be another reason why—

"Let's go, Highness."

The old woman begins walking. It clicks. The servant, the one who prepared Calla before the coronation, before Calla went forward to crown the lover she thought she'd killed. Though she was dazed and near-delirious that day, she remembers those two words whispered into her ear, at once an indictment and exaltation: *King-Killer.*

"Today would be nice, Princess Calla." The woman has stopped and turned back over her shoulder. The councilmember urged the need for haste.

If Calla is detoured here for too long, she will miss her window of opportunity to leave. Without the shield of the decorators coming in, surveillance will notice her exit, and the guards will most surely block her route.

"Go play," she whispers to Mao Mao. Her cat ignores her and settles in to sleep in the bag. With a huff, Calla closes her door, then follows the servant.

"What's your name?" she asks. "I didn't get to ask before the coronation."

"Joselie. Would you like adjustments made to your wardrobe, Highness?"

Calla has a brief buffering moment wondering exactly how long Joselie's name is. A beat later, she registers the question and glances down. She was going to change on the streets of San-Er. While she remained in the palace, she figured it was better to raid the drawers in her rooms: dresses with bell sleeves and loose collars, bundles of fabric with ties around the waists. She's taken it upon herself to alter some of the items.

"You don't like my alterations?" Calla asks, smoothing down the rumples at her torso.

"Respectfully, it appears that you took a cheese grater to it."

"I did." A knife, but sure.

Joselie's expression doesn't change. "Perhaps reconsider in the future. This way, please."

The decorators have already entered the palace. While Calla was away, the other royal advisors busied themselves planning the gala and spending their allocated budget. With the new security rules that Calla's proposed edict put into place, they could hire outside the palace, bring in far more decorators for half the price. She watches all the tradesmen—carrying stepladders and paint rollers and neatly folded tablecloths—streaming en masse through the south wing. Calla cranes her neck, trying to determine what those large red buckets being taken into one of the halls are, but Joselie clears her throat, plucking her attention back, and opens a small door beneath the side staircase. Another set of steps lead down into a passageway, dark enough that Calla can't see much beyond the few inches of brick flooring and vague shadows. When they descend, she walks with her hands outstretched, brushing the wall to keep her footing.

At the end of the passageway, Joselie climbs up three steps and pushes through a door into a new hallway. There, she stops abruptly. Calla braces herself to run.

"I'm running an interception, Highness," a voice says. "I hope you don't mind."

She rolls her eyes, her vigilance easing as she climbs the three steps and exits the passageway too. Galipei is waiting with his arms crossed over his chest, his shoulders so broad that he could probably block a wind tunnel if he tried.

"An interception for *me*?" Calla says. "I'm honored. We'll have to make sure August doesn't hear about this. You know how jealous he gets."

Galipei scoffs, but a line forms between his brows—a momentary flinch. It wasn't his king who sent him, then.

"Come with me. Thank you, Joselie."

Joselie nods. Calla waves in farewell before striding after Galipei, deliberately keeping slower than his pace. They proceed past a green arch and a statue of an enormous rabbit, moving between the atriums. She's careful to count how many turns they're making in the hallways. If Galipei is leading her somewhere intending to get rid of her, Calla is going to pull his ribs out.

"We're still en route to the council meeting," Galipei calls back, as though he can hear her thoughts, "so you can stop trying to predict an attack."

"*You?* Attack me? That's unheard of." Calla, begrudgingly accepting that there's no need for suspicion here, hurries forward a few steps so she's walking at Galipei's side. "Why are we going this way?"

"They've already brought Leida out from her cell. I want you at the rear door with me."

"Venus Hailira wants me there to contribute to the meeting."

"I'm sure if there's anything you have to contribute, you can project your voice. You don't need a table seat."

Galipei has little reason to detest her, but he certainly doesn't trust her either. Not enough to personally fetch her for some friendly company, even if he must feel lonely these days with Anton blocking him from speaking to August.

"What prompted this?" she asks. "Am I playing substitute Weisanna?"

Galipei stays quiet. She's guessed right.

"The wall is coming down tonight to be rebuilt farther into Eigi," he allows. A group of attendants pass by in the hallway, going the opposite direction. One of them, dressed in blue, waves at Calla, but she doesn't recognize her. She waves back anyway.

"Ah. So you need me for manpower."

"I have made it very clear to the council that we should not bring Leida out," Galipei says, his volume dropping. "We put her in the most secure cell under the palace for a reason. She is dangerous."

Leida's cell certainly looked well-built, from what Calla saw in the surveillance room.

"*I* wasn't put there," Calla says, a hint of chagrin creeping into her voice.

"You weren't considered enough of a risk to warrant it."

"Oh. Oh, wow."

Galipei casts her a sidelong glance. "Are you . . . offended by that?"

"I murdered the *king*, Galipei. What else did you want from me?"

He mutters something that sounds like *Have mercy* under his breath. Galipei looks over his shoulder, checking their surroundings before speaking again.

"The situation you mentioned last night. It's bigger than Rincun."

All traces of humor evaporate from Calla's manner. "There have been other attacks?"

"Yes. The news has taken a while to reach us, but it is the same as what you witnessed in Rincun. Barracks of palace soldiers simultaneously dropping dead."

And that's why they're bringing out Leida for interrogation. If Calla thought the attack in Rincun resembled the Crescent Society experiments in San-Er, it is no surprise that others would come to the same conclusion. Especially if new attacks have hit provinces closer to the capital, provinces that are more important in keeping San-Er operational.

Unfortunately, Calla doubts they'll get much from Leida. Even if the former captain of the guard knows something, she has been locked up since she was caught. She's not the one orchestrating new movement against the throne in the provinces.

Galipei leads Calla past a set of ornamented double doors guarded by Weisannas, then around the corner. Rear door, as he mentioned. It's a much more modest entrance, one that doesn't even have a door handle, only a hinge that swings both ways.

"Stay on alert, Calla."

They sidle through. Calla spots Leida in an instant. She's blindfolded and handcuffed to a lectern at the front, her posture bristling with an alertness incongruous with that of a prisoner. If it weren't for the Weisannas surrounding her, it might appear like she was preparing a speech, readying a battalion to charge at her command.

"Leida has proven before that she can jump without light, in any proximity," Calla states dryly.

A large meeting table occupies the center of the room. More than ten feet of distance has been made for Leida in every radius, her lectern placed in the corner to give her a wide berth from the double doors, but councilmembers are oftentimes stupid, and if one of them gets up from the round table and wanders a bit, they will have gotten too close.

"Trust me," Galipei says. A vein stands out on the side of his neck. "I've made it very clear how easily this could go sideways. Just keep your guard up where you can. We'll be performing identity checks on everyone before they leave this room."

Calla scans the meeting table. Venus Hailira is staring intently at her hands, seated on the far end. On the opposite side, Councilmember Aliha and Councilmember Rehanou are in quiet, intense discussion, their graying heads bent together.

"Fair enough," Calla mutters. "Still risky, but fair enough."

Galipei doesn't bother countering that. He only repeats "Guard up," and then goes off to inspect the main entrance. He's got weapons hanging from his belt. Calla was given nothing. They could have at least offered her a baton. Even if Leida can't break out of the room, she may still attack for the sake of it.

Calla brings her thumb to her mouth and bites down on her nail. Miliu blue. Weisanna silver. Tuoleimi yellow. There are people in this kingdom who have long been marked for attention. The thought should put her at ease, that there's no chance Leida could escape and go unseen. But Calla lasted in the cities for a long, long time before she took herself out of hiding. She wouldn't underestimate Leida's ability to disappear either.

A low drum rolls down the hallway. Anton steps in through the main entrance, walking a beat faster than Otta Avia, who meets Calla's eyes briefly the moment she enters too. It's alarming how similar she and Anton look at present. August and Otta are half siblings; it would be only fair for them to bear a resemblance to each other. Now that Calla knows it is Anton wearing August's body, though, it is hard for her to consider any alternative. Every reminder that he should be August is jarring to her senses, nauseatingly wrong and especially so when Otta gets onto the tips of her toes, whispering something into Anton's ear. She's wearing a red dress, the bodice made of a heavy brocade. Alongside each of Otta's movements, the skirts follow suit like a tailed phoenix curling around her feet.

To the councilmembers, her proximity is a natural gesture from a sister. Calla forces herself to look away, knowing better. She can barely breathe past the fire licking up her stomach.

"Let's make this quick," Anton declares.

He doesn't take a seat at the table. He walks right past the guards toward Leida, and Galipei grabs his elbow. Calla crosses her arms over her chest, waiting for the outcome, and unsurprisingly, Anton pays Galipei no mind, brushing him off as he would any irritating councilmember bringing an irrelevant agenda to the throne. The lights in the room are dim. It is hard to argue that there is anything odd about the way Anton doesn't look directly toward Galipei.

He stops before Leida. While he inspects her, Calla looks down and stares at her own ragged fingernails, sighing to herself. If there is any danger, Galipei will step in. He's always been somewhat of a kicked dog in August's presence, and it's ten times as bad with Anton playing imposter. Poor loyal Galipei. It must hurt when the one you love most disappears.

Calla doesn't realize she's been picking at her nail bed until a bead of blood wells by her thumb. She winces, smooths down the skin, and clasps her hands firmly behind her back. Though the meeting room doesn't cleanly face the marketplace the way the throne room does, she can hear the bustle outside the palace. In her mind's eye, the coliseum flashes vividly—the circular walls that boxed her in when she entered the final battle, the imposing masses on either side that wouldn't let her leave when they dragged Anton in.

August hadn't given them a chance to run. The moment Calla and Anton faced each other at the end, only death would preserve whatever love they'd thought they possessed. Really, it's August's own fault he's been invaded as a result.

Yet he will still blame her when he comes back.

"Leida," Anton says. "Do you know why we've brought you here?"

"I'm blindfolded, not earplugged," she says. "I can hear all this muttering."

"Good. It would be a waste of my time to stand here and explain it. Did you plant more of your people in the provinces?"

Leida doesn't answer immediately. Her brow furrows, half disappearing behind the fabric of her blindfold. The air conditioner in the corner of the room blows lukewarm air. Calla can't tell whether it's supposed to be cooling or heating.

"No."

"No?" Anton mimics August's head shake. It's subtle: the smallest left-right-left with his lips thinned. Calla has never seen Anton do that in any of his other bodies, so surely this is a maneuver adopted intentionally for faithful emulation. It shouldn't, but the realization takes her by surprise. She forgets sometimes that Anton and August were once very well acquainted. Far more than she was with August despite their familial connection, and certainly more than she was with Anton despite the frantic, heedless time she had with him.

"I've already confessed to conspiracy inside the twin cities. I have nothing to do with the provinces."

Calla feels an itch skate along the side of her face. Her eyes flicker to its source.

"Somehow, no one in this room believes you. What about your co-conspirators in the Crescent Societies? Any names come to mind with connections to the provinces?"

Otta, upon catching Calla's gaze again, smiles. Calla looks away, then wonders a second later if she shouldn't have hastened, in case the response made her appear intimidated.

"No one in the Crescent Societies was my *co*-conspirator. They're religious fanatics. I offered them an opportunity to commune with the old gods, and they took it."

Someone at the table clears their throat. Calla can't immediately place the woman who stands, though her eyes are a steely gray, familiar in a way where Calla suspects she might have once been a councilmember for the Palace of Heavens.

"An attack in Laho found three generals with their chests carved clean and their hearts taken," the woman says. "This is nearly identical to what the Hollow Temple did on your instructions."

Leida tilts her head. "Is that you, Councilmember Savin?"

The woman grimaces. She glances around the table like she's seeking backup, but none of the other councilmembers look too eager to jump in. Most of their faces blur together—Calla could name a handful and would start to stutter after that.

"It is."

"I thought I recognized your voice. Is that all? Is this why I have been disturbed from my eternal imprisonment?"

"It doesn't have to be eternal," Councilmember Rehanou interjects. "We're at liberty to have you executed at any point."

Anton holds up a hand. His sleeve falls to his elbow. "We don't need to be issuing threats."

He was once friends with Leida too, Calla reminds herself. August Avia, Leida Miliu, and Anton Makusa—even from the other palace, she knew their names in tandem, knew that the three came together as a unit. She forgets, because the trio fell apart when Anton was exiled, and before that, when he and Otta became a unit of their own.

Otta is still watching her.

"As I stated to His Majesty weeks ago, I never instructed the Hollow Temple to do that." Leida's voice remains steady. "I shared my knowledge about jumping. They took it too far."

"Tell us this, then," Councilmember Savin says. She has a tablet in front of her. A clunky thing, probably only with enough storage to hold one picture and three documents. "What do you know of the Dovetail?"

Calla, almost unconsciously, steps forward, chasing that first appearance of a thread. Though a few guards look at her askance, she's saved from rudely interrupting when Venus Hailira grimaces and says:

"Were we briefed on this?"

Aliha and Rehanou glare at Rincun's councilmember. Though Calla is equally confused, she has to resist the urge to drop her head into her hands for the way Venus just asked. Perhaps before her own soldiers boot her out of power, the council will get annoyed enough with Venus Hailira to put a hit on her from inside San-Er.

"The Dovetail," Leida starts to answer, before any of the councilmembers can. "The largest revolutionary group in the provinces, with operations based out of Laho." She tilts her head. Her hair is tangled by her neck. "It sounds like there are others in the room. Deepest apologies. Under King Kasa, the council was prohibited by the crown from acknowledging its existence. I wasn't sure if that had changed or not."

Calla stays quiet. The only *others* in the room who seem surprised are the guards at the doors. Anton isn't facing Calla. Otta doesn't even look like she's listening.

Venus pushes away from the table slightly. "No one told me about this either."

"You will be told sensitive information when you're deemed capable in your seat," Councilmember Mugo rumbles. He has his hands laced across his stomach, his legs stretched long under the table. Rich of him to speak of capability when he was kidnapped in his own province a few months back.

Savin turns her tablet off and places the screen facedown. At some point, she seems to have taken over the interrogation, and Anton isn't doing anything to resume command. Calla waits for him to interject, but his expression is unfocused. He's following some other track in his head.

"The Dovetail, as far as we have gleaned, believe the old gods remain supreme, and the kingdom has taken its people away from this natural order. They regularly attack any delegation that encroaches on their operation route, largely in the provinces above the Jinzi River. The palace guards usually think they're common province rebels."

"I'm still not hearing why I have been made the scapegoat," Leida says.

"The Crescent Societies didn't start carving out hearts until you told them they could sacrifice qi and commune with the gods for more power," Savin says. "Now six provinces have experienced similar attacks across a few days that target royal soldiers and palace generals. The death counts have already exceeded those of the attacks in San-Er."

Leida squares her shoulders and tips her nose high. It should look ridiculous while she's blindfolded, but her figure grows in the shadows, the line of her jaw stark enough to catch light. "If you already suspect that the Dovetail are responsible," she snaps, "then ask their revolutionary insurgents outside the wall. I have nothing to do with it."

"Don't you think we have surveillance out in the provinces? The Dovetail were paid off from within the palace. A large sum of bills was taken out from the vault the day before you were arrested, and their serials have reentered circulation at each yamen where the attacks are taking place."

Anton swivels suddenly. "No one told me this."

It is almost the exact line Venus said, but the effect cuts differently. The councilmembers flinch. Some look away, not wanting to be the one to explain why. Others stare forward, as though it wouldn't be their job to explain to their king anyhow.

They resent you, Calla wants to say. They have always resented August, and now Anton isn't doing him any favors by digging into his plans and speed-running them without any sensitivity to the politics of the council.

"The perpetrator is evident enough," Rehanou concludes, speaking for the table.

"It wasn't me," Leida insists.

"Leida," Anton prompts again, urging her attention back to him, and Calla hears the change in that word alone. She's not the only one in the room who has noticed: Otta's attention finally shifts away from Calla, her black eyes narrowing. "Did you know about the Makusas' involvement with the Dovetail?"

What?

The councilmembers don't seem to be taken too aback. Calla, however, can't believe her ears. Anton is asking about the Makusas while posing as August. He's dropping his act, and if anyone in this room has even the vaguest suspicion about his identity, this would surely be the battering ram. Besides, why would *his* family have been involved with a province group? They were killed in Kelitu by rural rebels . . . weren't they?

"What are you talking about?" Leida asks in return. "What do the Makusas have to do with this?"

Councilmember Savin clears her throat, trying to steer the questioning back on course.

"If you provide us with names of the members of the Dovetail you communicated with, we may spare you from execution."

A sudden, metallic clang booms from the lectern, and the room collectively jolts in surprise. Leida's tried to tug herself free, rather aggressively but unsuccessfully.

"Have you considered that maybe the similarities between the Crescent Societies and the Dovetail start and end with their hatred for the palace?" she spits. "You don't think anyone out in the provinces might have tried sacrificing to their gods for the fun of it and realized it worked? You don't think they would then try to use that power to fight back?"

Mugo scoffs. "The old gods aren't real."

Leida goes very still.

"You're right," she says. "They're not." Her cuffs clank again, but this time, she's not the one doing it. "But we are."

Every light bulb in the room explodes.

Calla breathes a curse, ducking as the shards splinter outward. The Weisannas hurry into action, raising their weapons and training them upon Leida for the first sign of attack. Leida Miliu, however, hasn't even tried to free herself, her hands still looped in the metal holding her to the lectern. Low gray light from the window illuminates enough of the room to show the councilmembers slowly straightening from around the table. Only a false alarm, perhaps.

One of the guards stationed beside Calla shifts. She sighs, then nudges the rear door and steps out. Calla only caught a flash while the guard was turning her face, but it's enough.

In an instant, she follows suit, pushing out after the guard. She waits a beat—the door swings closed. Just as the guard hears motion behind her, Calla's hand shoots forward and grasps the back of her neck, digging in hard.

Inside the meeting room, the first sound of alarm is called. Someone has finally noticed that Leida Miliu has jumped without light.

"How did you know—"

"Don't struggle," Calla interrupts evenly, pushing her forward in the hallway. It's empty. "I'll kill you if you so much as flinch. Come with me."

CHAPTER 8

The palace goes into lockdown.

Anton wandered off at some point after being deposited into his rooms, taking advantage of the distraction among his guards while they argued about who they needed to report to. Under their new quadrant system, there's no particular guard in charge of the palace, only multiple Weisannas who have opposing opinions about how the halls should be searched and little difference between them in rank. They're scrambling around the atriums and hallways, inefficient in their delineation of roles while combing through the Palace of Union to find Leida Miliu. All exits have been sealed and windows monitored, so it is not as though she can escape. Calla has disappeared too. On the lookout for Leida, probably. Maybe she's already found her and refuses to report to the Weisannas or Anton. Fine—the farther Calla stays from him, the better.

Anton gargles, then spits out the water that's crept into his mouth. His rinsing finally runs clear down the sink, and he closes the tap, marveling at how quickly the pipes in the palace respond. In his apartment on Big Well Street, sometimes turning on the tap meant listening to it creak for a full minute before a light trickle appeared. Sometimes turning off the water had no effect, either, and he had to practically unscrew the spout in order to close the valve.

He leaves the bathroom, scrubbing a towel through his hair. No one has used these in years. What was once soft fabric has turned harsh from time, the threads scraping at him as he returns to the rooms and comes to a stop in front of the mirror.

After a generous amount of black dye and a small brush to reach every strand, Anton has gotten the hair on his head back to its natural color.

August would be furious. All those hours committed to climbing palace ranks, trying to set himself apart from the other leg-huggers. All that time spent ensuring his face was the one that people summoned in their mind's eye when they thought of the kingdom's inheritor, someone to appeal to the rich and grant promises to the poor, perfectly suited for the palace to the council's eye and, to the city's, a faultless outsider who worked for his stature. August Shenzhi wanted to appear hand selected by the gods.

Now, he looks just like everyone else.

"Your Majesty." The main door opens before Anton can give an answer. Immediately, the staleness inside the rooms alleviates, cleared by the air-conditioning in the hallways. "You cannot slip away from us when you please. It is a matter of safety—"

The guard halts midstep. Her silver eyes move back and forth in rapid succession, from Anton before the mirror to . . . Anton Makusa, lying on the bed. His birth body, at least. An unoccupied vessel.

"Seiqi, was it?" Anton asks, unbothered. "How did you find me?"

Seiqi Weisanna is still staring, her jaw slightly agape. She must recognize the face, if not the photos of the Makusas around the four-poster bed. These were Anton's rooms after his parents were killed: a corner section in the east wing, barely connected to the rest of the palace and placed as far to the wayside as possible. They have been left untouched since Anton's exile, with the exception of occasional cleaning, it seems. Past the thin layer of dust, the deep-green curtains still fall to the floor the same; the three ceiling bulbs still emit a hum when the brightness lever is set to low, the electric current pulsing through the wiring in a way that Anton has always suspected is too strong.

Despite everything, these rooms still feel like his. He can't say that about anything else in San-Er.

"How I found you," Seiqi repeats, trying to prompt herself out of her stupor. She shakes her head, her long braid flying over her shoulder, and says, "Um, we realized you left, so I looked at surveillance footage of the hallways."

Anton remains silent for a moment. Then:

"I may have to reevaluate the order of the royal guard, given how long it took you to find me. I've been away for quite some time."

Enough time to fetch dye from the palace tailor. Enough time to have his birth body moved out of storage and brought here, freshly dressed and arranged on the white sheets, looking to be merely asleep.

"I'm not sure that an unannounced test is fair, Majesty. Especially given the situation." Seiqi, even in the dim light, has turned visibly pale. Her eyes flicker to the door. She regrets coming to find him without backup. "Galipei was very concerned. I can fetch him."

"No need. I'll make my way out now."

Seiqi casts another glance at the door.

"Otta Avia is here for you too."

That takes him by surprise. His instinct is to decline seeing her, bid her come back later, and let later never arrive. The less time he spends with her, the less likely he will be caught out. Then again, there's no reason why August would decline seeing her in this moment.

"Otta shouldn't be walking around while we're under lockdown. Leida could be in any of these rooms."

"Yes, well"—Seiqi clears her throat and steps out into the hallway, gesturing for, presumably, Otta waiting nearby—"as we have observed, the guards couldn't exactly stop you from walking around either. I'll take my leave."

The mirror flickers within his periphery. Under better circumstances, Anton would be wearing his birth body instead of fetching it from palace storage, brushing off the dust that had gathered on his shoulders because his body became a forgotten insurance policy jammed between the discarded vessel of a councilmember's son and a stack of books about the war. August would be standing beside him as flesh and blood, rather than the light reflecting from silver and glass. And when Otta prances in to say hello, her skirts too long and trailing after her on the floor, her feet bare, it would be as casual as anything.

"Oh, goodness."

Otta draws to a halt.

But because these are the circumstances he has been given, he turns to get August's face out of his view. The clock is only counting down until one of them remains.

"So, the gala is proceeding," Otta says. Though she pivots, her eyes are still on Anton's body upon the bed. "The council doesn't think it necessary to call it off. An internal palace event won't be affected by a lockdown, anyhow."

"The council would do anything to avoid the appearance of conflict." Anton pinches the bridge of his nose, trying to lessen the tension in his head. August barely has any space up on his thin, delicate nose. It's near-impossible just to pad two fingers down on both sides.

"Including keep all of Kasa's secrets."

"Indeed." *Did* you *know?* Anton wants to add. *When Kasa killed my parents, did the Avias hear about it over dinner one night? Did you keep the unthinkable from me, caring just as little about the matter as August did?*

Soundlessly, Otta slinks up to his side. Her hands run along his shoulders before she presses a cold touch to his neck. He doesn't trust Otta. He doesn't know anything about her intentions upon waking except that scheming is in her nature, that maneuvering her way into importance is as instinctive to her as breathing. All the same, he relaxes into her without thinking—he exhales fully for the first time in weeks. Anton feels young with her, responsible for nothing except the assignments he needs to hand in at the academy. He feels as though it doesn't matter that he has no family in this kingdom, because he has her, and she needs him.

"August," Otta says. Her voice is soft. "Why did you ask about the Makusas in the meeting room?"

Anton freezes. His instinct is to cover his tracks with anger, spout out some disparaging remark he would expect August to say. Then his eyes drift to himself on the bed, and there is little he can feign when this evidence lies before them. He wouldn't have asked if he didn't care to know.

"Don't you miss him?" he returns gently. It's a careful line to walk. He hasn't a clue how August and Otta left off with each other before Otta fell ill. "I do."

Otta touches his ear. "You've never shown it, to tell the truth."

"He was my best friend."

"You thought he was weak. You said if his parents hadn't died, he never would have learned to jump, because his only motivation was anger and loneliness."

It takes everything not to react. Anton's neck flushes slowly, reddening with every new word. *Weak*. August thought him weak because his parents were murdered, their bodies shredded to such a state that the funeral proceedings were forced to cremate them ahead of time, leaving nothing but a canister of ash to mourn.

"In fact . . . ," Otta goes on, pulling away and drifting across the room. She taps a finger to her chin. "It was you who always warned me not to be with him. You said he would discard me eventually, once the wind changed direction. People like him only know how to run."

Anton snaps. He doesn't know what he means to do as he marches forward. His arm outstretches, reaching for Otta, and she pivots so fast to face him that her skirts swirl in a frenzy of reds and golds.

"Don't say anything," she hisses, and her demeanor changes entirely.

Oh, Otta. How I have underestimated you.

"I wasn't going to," Anton replies. His arm returns to his side. He smooths down his jacket. It is a performance, but no longer for the girl in front of him.

Otta tilts her head toward the door.

"They've put new cameras here. Let's go elsewhere."

◇◇◇◇◇

In the surveillance room, Matiyu Nuwa taps through the palace feed, idly keeping an eye out for Leida Miliu. He doubts that the former captain of the guard would be so stupid as to get caught on camera, so he isn't taking the task seriously, even though the entirety of surveillance was put on the task. One of the Weisannas will find her soon, surely. It's not as though Leida can hide for long when the exits are sealed and the guards are sweeping through each wing.

His cubicle phone rings. He brings it to his ear, throwing the long handset cord over his shoulder. "Hello?"

"Matiyu. A favor, possibly?"

Matiyu frowns at the voice. He recognizes it instantly. "How did you get this number?"

"Anyone can call the palace and request to be put through. I said I was your sister. The Weisannas aren't going to screen me for a phone call."

They should. Taking people for their word seems like bad security practice.

"I won't lie, Woya: I thought you were dead."

"Nonsense," Woya says, offended. "I'm in charge of the Hollow Temple again, I'll have you know. Our time under Pampi Magnes was a temporary hiccup."

"A hiccup that caused half your numbers to be jailed?"

"Says you, deserter—" Woya coughs, cutting himself off. Clearly he's called because he needs something, so it isn't smart to go offending Matiyu. "I heard you work in palace surveillance now. I need you to check on something very, very small for me."

"I'd rather not," Matiyu replies. "I'm not trying to get into trouble."

"How many times did I watch your back in the temple, hmm? I only need a yes or no from you—yesterday, sometime in the morning, did San-Er receive an entrant through the wall?"

Matiyu frowns and tuts, even as he types in a search for the footage Woya is describing. "There are no entrants into San-Er while the wall is undergoing construction."

"Just check the footage."

When Matiyu pulls up the camera pointed on San's wall, he realizes it won't catch any entrant, because the gate is on manual operation. After a quick calculation, he finds another camera, farther away but at a higher angle, pointed at a side path. He rewinds. Fast-forwards.

"Doesn't look like it. I'm only seeing guards."

The line stays quiet. Matiyu pulls the receiver away from his ear, checking the sound quality. If Woya hung up on him . . .

"Oh." Woya's voice returns, breaking the silence. "Hmm."

Matiyu presses the receiver back to his ear. He taps his keyboard, cycling through the other cameras nearby for the sake of it. "You know the surveillance room has technology that issues alerts when there's irregular movement by the wall, right? If it were that easy to sneak into the capital, there would be chaos."

"People do sneak in," Woya says, sounding defensive.

"Sure." Matiyu rolls his eyes. He resets his feeds, letting it return to live time. "As I said, there's no—oh. Oh, wait."

The line rustles. On the other side, Woya either sat up really quickly or dropped something. "What? What is it?"

"What the fuck?" Matiyu says.

The shoe is what catches his attention. The live footage on Gold Stone Street captures only a small part of the trash heap in the corner—there are cameras installed on just about every alley and street in the city, but they're not all actively playing on the surveillance room's screens, or else the people working this room would be overwhelmed by far too much useless footage. Camera three tends to remain active in the surveillance circuit for a broad view into the street. But that shoe is sticking directly up, and it can't really reach that angle without a *foot* in it, so if Matiyu activates camera four for a lower angle on the trash pile . . .

"Oh, *fuck*."

Swallowed within the trash, a dead man lies on his side, wearing the uniform of a palace guard. He couldn't have been left there long, given the color that remains in his face, his expression frozen in surprise.

The most bizarre part, though, is the yellow umbrella stabbed through his middle, both his hands curled around its handle as if he was attempting to tug out the weapon shortly before death.

"I have to go."

Woya splutters. "Wait, what did you—"

Matiyu hangs up the phone.

"Guards!"

CHAPTER 9

Calla hauls Leida all the way to her rooms and slams the door closed before any of the panic in the hallways can catch up to them. Her cat greets her upon entrance, but when he sniffs Leida too, he flees into the bathroom.

"I don't know what you think you're achieving by yanking me around like this," Leida remarks. She tries to extricate herself the moment Calla grabs her arm, but Calla is stronger. Leida grunts, throwing her body weight into her. They're in close quarters—it isn't easy to put up a good defense. Instead of finding a way to hit back, Calla only grits her teeth, putting her whole focus into the grip she has on Leida's left arm. If she lets go, Leida will flee in an instant, and this will be for naught.

"Let *go*." Leida's shoulder clips her across the chin. The moment Calla flinches, Leida seems to realize that Calla's other hand has been working on freeing something behind her: the heavy curtain, and the cord in the middle that keeps the fabric bundled. Leida tugs her arm hard, but it is too late. The curtain bursts loose, its cord secured in Calla's hand. As a last resort, Leida kicks out to take Calla's knee from underneath her, but Calla has already braced low. In this body, Leida is shorter than she's used to, and she doesn't put as much swing behind the attack. Calla pushes the cord around a pipe running up the wall, a thin tube stemming from the anchored radiator. Before Leida can throw herself free, Calla has her left wrist tied with the cord, then her right.

"Heavens," Calla grumbles, finally lurching back to catch her breath.

When Leida tries to move now, her arms stay welded to the pipe. Her blue eyes are bright, almost feverish.

"Were the prisons not enough of an indignity?" Leida demands. "Did you have to trap me to a"—she looks back—"a *cold* radiator?"

"Oh, did you want me to turn it on?"

Leida scoffs. "You can't, anyway. Heat systems in the palace switched to electric a decade ago."

Most of San-Er outside the palace still uses radiators. There are always a few apartment fires each year from faulty pipes and overheating.

"You must have observed the palace systems closely in your time as captain of the guard," Calla muses. She crosses her arms over her chest, hiding the reddened scratches from their struggle. "After they made me a royal advisor, I happened upon a file in the surveillance room that detailed your mother's work too. Lots of changes. Also lots of suggestions that went ignored."

Leida yanks against the curtain cord again. It doesn't budge. Calla has tied the knot tight enough that she herself couldn't undo it.

"Is that a surprise?" Leida says shortly. "No one in this palace cares about what is good."

Calla claimed to want the greater good once. In Anton's kitchen, when he asked why she was playing in the king's games, it seemed as fitting an answer as any. She wanted to get rid of everyone who had caused her suffering; she wanted dead bodies made of the nobles who ruled this kingdom, who couldn't have cared less that she was fated to sleep starving by the roadside as an abandoned child. Of course she was doing good.

"And you do?" Calla asks. "You, who have caused multiple massacres as a byproduct of poorly executed plans."

The thing is, if King Kasa had been the most decent man in the kingdom who'd made one mistake by burning her village, Calla would have lifted her sword regardless. It's not a lie to say she's invested in good, but she supposes that can't be the whole, unblemished truth either. If revenge brought guaranteed destruction upon Talin, she might still have continued onward.

"As I've told the council," Leida says, "I have already confessed to everything I am guilty of."

Calla expected Leida to counter the accusation. To say that she hadn't intended for people to die. Leida gave an anarchist sect the knowledge to siphon power. Plotted a conspiracy to crumble the monarchy from the inside. It's not that Calla disapproves: she's almost sad that Leida ran laps around San-Er thinking she could remain virtuous while others wouldn't hesitate to cut a line right through to reap their own gains. Leida Miliu had the right idea, but she can only be as good as her most crooked byproduct.

Calla kicks a foot at the radiator. Gray paint flakes off, dusting her shoe.

"The council is convinced that you're responsible for the attacks in the provinces," Calla says plainly. "They will execute you and hope that will solve their headache, just as locking you up seemed to stop the Crescent Society killings in San-Er."

Leida's mouth opens, but before she can say anything, Calla cuts in:

"No need to argue. I know that you have nothing to do with these province deaths. The timing doesn't make any sense. The Dovetail would've acted when you started working with the Crescent Societies, not after you got caught."

Another scoff. Leida leans back, her shoulder blades hitting the pipe. "I'm so very grateful you believe me, Your Highness. Why am I here, then?"

In her memories, Calla returns to the arena. She breathes deep, her heart tears in two, and she slides the knife out of her sleeve. She exhales, the sky shatters, and Anton dies before her, his vessel turning gray in that pool of blood.

And then he resurrects, clutching her hand in the body of her cousin, his eyes furious.

"Where did you learn those techniques?"

Leida frowns. "Excuse me?"

"You weren't *born* with the knowledge," Calla continues, "and I doubt it was fancy guesswork. You learned it somewhere, then passed it on to the Crescent Society members. People in the provinces learned it somewhere, and someone among them is using it to perform attacks on royal soldiers. That seems correct to you, doesn't it?"

Now Leida goes quiet. She doesn't know exactly what Calla is seeking, but she's smart enough to be apprehensive. By the time Calla has thrown a clear trap before her, there must be a dozen littered in every other direction, blown like winged seeds on each word. It is how the palace engages in combat. It is what Calla learned between physical training with war generals and relentless target practice, because speaking well is half the push toward winning a battle, regardless of how many legions she possesses.

Leida stays silent.

"I keep thinking . . ." Calla drops to a crouch, her leather jacket rustling. She needs to push harder; if Leida won't step into a trap, Calla is more than happy to offer a shove. "Maybe it's family tradition. The provinces don't have many resources. No books, no files, no digital databases. Knowledge is going to pass through stories, from mother to child." She pauses and drags her finger along the carpet threads, drawing lines. Three, like the sigil that the children in Rincun etched when the barracks turned cold. "The palace has plenty of resources, but it's hard to go digging without someone noticing. It's only in the privacy of your own quarters that your mother taught you how to carve people's hearts out—"

Leida jerks forward. The cord yanks her back, her head knocking hard against the pipe in recoil.

"Don't you speak about my mother."

"I'm not insulting her." Calla stretches out her neck, and her hair trails off her shoulder, unraveling like a cape around her. "If she's the one who taught you, it was quite an accomplishment."

Leida tries to pull against the cord again. "She had nothing to do with this." Again. Her wrists are red. "She *died* for this kingdom. She gave up her life for Talin, and still no one realizes her sacrifice."

Calla believes it.

"Then who, Leida?" Calla asks. "Who taught you?"

She doesn't need to add her silent follow-up, but it is heard nonetheless. Her hunger soaks into the air between them. It was there when she realized how easily Leida had jumped into the body of a guard standing on the other side of the meeting table. It was there when she watched the chaos that erupted in a few short seconds when there was no burst of light, when everything their kingdom knew was upended as those present merely imagined what Leida might be capable of doing.

Who taught you, Leida? How do I learn it too?

"Forget it, Your Highness," Leida says. "Put me back in my cell."

"If you want to do good, let me help."

Leida chokes out a short laugh. Despite the sound, her expression is furious.

"*You*, help *me* to do good? Do you take me for a schoolchild? You are a Tuoleimi. You are one of the two bloodlines whose foot has been heavy on the neck of this kingdom for centuries."

"And hasn't that puzzled San-Er for years now?" Calla fires back. "I was next in line for Talin's second throne, and I destroyed it."

"You are no better than the others just because you didn't like your parents—"

"Jump into me, Leida," Calla interrupts. "I know you're thinking about it."

Leida stills, her arms easing lax. She must suspect a trick. The room is dark despite the hour, the curtains draped across most of the alcove window. It allows for no signal of day or night, allows in no wind or pitter-patter of rain. The in-out of their breaths is the only way to track the passing time. The faint creaking of the floorboards down the hall is the sole confirmation that the rest of the palace continues moving.

A brush of nausea crosses Calla's chest. It twists her throat. Sours her tongue. Then, it's gone. She watches Leida play through a myriad of expressions, unable to settle on what exactly has just happened. Eventually, she makes the undeniable conclusion. Eventually, after another attempt, Leida goes tense.

"You're . . ." She trails off.

"Exactly," Calla says. "I'm already *in*. I'm your best chance."

◇◇◇◇◇

In a past lifetime, Bibi had quite a lot of people doing her bidding.

She's learned how to keep herself alive in this one. Not by choice, truth be told. She would have preferred an easier option, a life that could be described as comfortable even if it doesn't quite reach opulent, but when the inns in Laho have doors that open as easily when locked as unlocked, she's gotten good at behaving like a roach. If an intruder isn't looking too closely, they will rarely notice the occupant under the bed while they scavenge the valuables left on the table.

Bibi picks at the skin on her bottom lip. The city whispers have been abuzz since she entered. With King Kasa gone, San-Er's denizens are not shy about running their mouths on the streets, chattering about how the palace had a traitor some few weeks ago—the captain of the guard drawing up a plot to kill civilians and blame it on the foreign Sicans past the borderlands. No one in San-Er, nor in most of the provinces, has met a Sican, but they all know to fear them. The war took its toll on the kingdom, funneled most of their people into a tight corner and cut the heads off their resource bases. Despite Talin's victory, those who remember their great-grandparents still recall the haunted eyes, the refusal to speak a word about the past they had endured.

Leida Miliu's plan could have gone far. Crumble the monarchy. Stir enough dissent among the masses to cause lasting protest too great to be immediately crushed by Weisannas.

Then the cities' attention turned to Calla Tuoleimi and Anton Makusa in the arena, and the people had more important bets to make.

Bibi trails along the outside of the coliseum, her grip tightening on her shopping bag. She'll need to pick up some utensils. The marketplace is crowded today because the palace is hosting a gala. Not that anyone outside the palace is invited to attend, so she can't fathom why people are craning their necks like that, but city folk will do strange things in proximity to wealth.

"*You there!*"

She turns over her shoulder. Palace guards. Two of them: one alert, the other bored.

"Yes?"

"Identity number?"

Bibi frowns. She peers into her shopping bag. All that's of value inside is her apartment key—she's rented one of those rare units that still use a lock rather than an identity number pad. Makes things a lot easier, given that she doesn't have an identity number.

"I'm only doing my shopping," Bibi says. "Surely this doesn't require being checked?"

"We're under instructions to log everyone around the palace. Please co-operate."

The guard speaking has dark-orange eyes, the shade of sunset after a storm in the provinces, when the clouds clear just in time for nightfall. His companion is a Weisanna, though his eyes are drooping enough in boredom that Bibi requires a subtle double take to confirm the presence of silver.

"All right, all right." She makes a show out of rummaging through her bag. "I'm new here. I was drawn through the lottery last year and just emigrated from Laho, so forgive me for not knowing the full number yet."

It helps that her accent is strong. Provincial, even if the people in San-Er can't tell the difference between rural dwellers north and south of the Jinzi River.

"Oh no," she says. "I don't think I have my card."

The guards exchange a look. "We're going to have to take you in until we can verify your identity."

Bibi sighs. She slides one palm along her bag handle, gauging its circumference. "Really? Is that necessary?"

"It's only protocol."

"Come on," Bibi pleads. "There aren't cameras on this alley, anyway."

"Yes, but—" The guard pauses. Frowns. "How do you know that?"

Bibi swings the handle of the bag around the neck of the Weisanna in a sudden lurch. She has her hands tight around the ends, squeezing hard, and ducks when his arms flail out, trying to loosen her hold. The other guard is taken aback for a second, then he's scrambling for his pager, a weapon, any idea of what the fuck they're usually supposed to do when a civilian is stupid enough to attack an elite guard of the palace.

It takes a decent amount of time to strangle someone, but it also takes a decent amount of strength to hold them down for it. Maybe the other guard knows he will lose this fight if he engages. Instead of pulling his baton, he simply turns on his heel and runs out of the alley.

Bibi finally feels the Weisanna fall slack. She grunts, letting him collapse to the ground before closing her eyes, tapping into her surroundings. Her lungs seize. Blots appear before her vision: moving qi there, and there, and *there*—

She jumps, stumbling the first few steps when she takes over the orange-eyed guard's body. His legs are still in motion, running at high speed, before her qi seizes control entirely and she grinds to a halt, her hand bracing against the brick wall. The coliseum rumbles behind her. She rests her hands upon her knees, letting her frantic heart still.

The guard's uniform is unfamiliar on her skin. Rough and bunched at the elbows. She goes to scratch her arms, and then she's sobbing in loud gulps, trying to expunge the hot pellet that sits in her lungs.

Bibi cries every time she kills someone. It's not that she feels bad. She would cry just the same after she ran a lap around a farm in Laho or raced the neighborhood kids to climb the tallest tree in the sparse grove. The tears feel like a release after such exertion, confirmation that her body is capable of strong, strenuous matters.

She wipes her tears off her face, the scruff of facial hair scratching her palms. She's got to go back for her birth body. It'll be safe in her new apartment while she wears this guard. Then she'll check in, report that this little roach they've plucked out of the provinces is good at her job.

Step one is causing fear. Paranoia. The sneaking suspicion that something will come skittering over the palace's bare feet the moment they stop for a rest.

The next step is infestation.

CHAPTER 10

Galipei doesn't follow lockdown protocol. He hears that August has been sighted in the east wing, speaking with Otta. In that moment, he makes up his mind to leave him be. He puts on a long jacket in his rooms. Leaves his pager behind so that Seiqi can't annoy him any more than he's already annoyed. When he passes the guards watching the west exit, he nods, and they let him through.

A light mist of rain falls from the skies. Dreary afternoon hours. It's the time of day when no one has much energy for anything, and across the twin cities, activity draws to a lull. Night will breathe a second wind onto the day, push everything into motion again once the moon rises over the horizon. Until then, most of San-Er is only buffering with lackluster effort.

Not Galipei, though. He pats down his trousers, checking that he has his weapons. No one will stop him from going off to do his own thing, but it *is* rather frowned upon to be away from his charge for so long. Probably no one is stopping him because Galipei is usually the one frowning if other guards don't put in enough hours.

Nothing has made sense lately. He knows as well as anyone that August is prone to disappearing periodically, jumping across the cities to complete a task himself. But Galipei was always in the loop—always the one covering for him so that the rest of the guard thought August was resting peacefully in his rooms.

Galipei has never been on the other side of that before.

You only want his attention, the most vicious part of him whispers. *You're bitter that the rest of the kingdom needs him too.*

No, he fights back. It's not only that. The dismissals. The distraction. The new *dye*. August has been shedding every part of himself, and Galipei is flummoxed trying to parse the logic behind it. It took seeing the jet-black hair to be certain that this isn't merely his imagination.

That night years ago, when August asked for help the first time he bleached his hair, he was more upset than Galipei had ever seen him.

"What's wrong?" Galipei demanded. "Did something happen?"

"Nothing more than an ordinary day in the wondrous Palace of Earth," August replied wryly. It had been a few months since Galipei had been assigned to him. On the other side of the capital, the Palace of Heavens hadn't fallen either, which meant King Kasa hadn't yet gone off the rails with security. He was happy to provide when August requested a study of his own, up in the palace's highest turret. Galipei thought it was because the prince wanted the view; August would tell him soon after that he wanted the isolation, away from visiting nobles or aristocrats begging a favor. That study was his reprieve from the world, and only those who really needed to seek him out would climb that high.

Galipei remembers taking the brush from August and crouching down to help. There was a mirror hanging on the wall—it's since come down after Leida nudged it too hard two years ago and put a chip in the corner—and Galipei watched August's expression slowly ease while he spread the dye.

"This lightener is good quality," Galipei remarked. "Barely leaves a smell."

"Only the best," August replied quietly. "Or else it wouldn't be permitted in the palace."

Already, Galipei knew he was putting together a picture of August Shenzhi.

The crown's heir hated the palace with a volatile energy, yet he couldn't separate himself from it. To stray too far would be to lose the power it gave him, and to get too close meant sacrificing the grand ideas he had in his head about change. The Prince August of back then had wanted to wield the throne in his way, and according to his beliefs. It would be vastly different from the way Kasa managed it.

"Are you going to tell me what happened?" Galipei asked when August finally emerged from the bathroom.

"The paperwork has started." August dragged a hand through his wet, rinsed hair. "For the legal adoption."

The color had set in perfectly, an even application down to his roots. Blond suited him. The rest of his face was so sharp that this softened the edges and added a new air of pleasantry.

"That's . . . that's good," Galipei said, startled. "Right?"

"Depends who you ask," August replied. "But it is a necessary step, so that's all that matters."

Then he offered a sardonic smile to end the conversation and Galipei shut up in an instant, the same way that mortal sacrifices stilled in the presence of their gods, a second prior to being consumed.

San-Er prickles when Galipei trips on the front stoop of a building, then stomps his boot hard into the entryway to gather his bearings. He's almost there. The Hollow Temple is on Loyan Back Street. It can be accessed only through a rear door in this low-rise because the temple is enclosed on all four sides by other buildings, tucked away like the cities' secret.

August has dyed his hair back to its original color. August won't go up to his study, as though he's forgotten about its existence. And when it comes to the kingdom, August may be putting through the reforms he lined up on his desk, but he does it with such a heavy hand that one would think he's stamping things into action without reading a thing or listening to any of his advisors.

The grumbles have already started about August being more vain than his adoptive father, more concerned about palace drama than the people's well-being, and there is no world in which that would be true, much less one where August would let that show to the public.

There have been too many missteps within such a short period of time. Too many items on the agenda that August has forgotten about, and at the end of the day, August is too *smart* to screw up like this.

Galipei's surroundings grow muffled the moment he leaves the sixth-floor marketplace and passes through a small door at the end. The stairwell echoes with dripping water. Something is squeaking on the second-floor landing while he descends. When he passes by, a family of rats burst out of the corner and chase each other down to the ground level ahead of him.

Galipei grimaces. At last, he steps out from the building. If anyone is going to make a fuss about his presence, it will be now. No other way to come in and out, unless he were to tear a hole through the mesh grille above the temple.

It's quiet. The grille creaks with the wind, bogged down by years of trash falling from the surrounding windows. He waits, observing a few Crescent Society members in conversation around the perimeter of the building. The Hollow Temple is the nearest place of worship to the palace. They come few and far between in the twin cities—it is not that San-Er has entirely abandoned its old gods, but the few devoted perform their piety in private. Kitchen shrines and small incense sticks stuck into hallway pots. Dried flowers taped to front doors and joss paper burned on the rooftops.

Truthfully, though, the temples do not serve those believers. The temples are the last remnants of San-Er's early years, continuing into the present only because the Crescent Societies have taken over the facade of religiosity for their operations.

Galipei steps into the Hollow Temple, nudging the heavy door aside. The vermillion paint chips off and sticks to the pads of his fingers. All sense of warmth drains from him as he walks down the pews, his breath appearing in clouds with each huff. He proceeds forward. Kneels before the statues erected at the front.

He recognizes none of them—by his parents' generation, the schools stopped teaching their names—but their watchful eyes are all-surrounding. The pantheon wants to fill the space of worship that Galipei has carved out inside himself. They're aware of what has changed. They know his ears are open to their whispers, seeking a new answer in the emptiness left behind.

When August asked for Otta to die, he seemed worried that she would wake up. Galipei can't comprehend it. Otta has woken indeed, fine, but *no one* has woken from the yaisu sickness before. In what world should he have assumed it was a possibility? Why *did* August consider it possible?

Galipei hears the approach of footsteps. These looming deities have shaken him. Their ten-foot, larger-than-life sneers; their frozen arms pulled back, ready to plunge their swords into an enemy.

Have I disappointed him? he asks the gods.

"Outsiders aren't welcome at the Hollow Temple."

A part of him wonders if he deserves to be shut out, if he's been lacking on the fronts where August needs strength. Another part is certain that something lurks beneath the surface here, some surprise attack gearing up unwatched. Otta has woken. August is acting different. Two impossible matters tend to be related, do they not?

"I'm not here for trouble," Galipei says slowly. "I only wanted to pray."

"Sure. That's why you sent a message ahead asking to speak to the eldest occupant of the temple."

Galipei shifts on his knees. He turns slightly, running a courtesy glance over the temple elder standing to his side. The elder has a slight hunch in his back, his white beard running cleanly down his chin. He has dark eyes: near-black, Galipei thinks at first, but then the old man faces him, and he discerns that it is a shade of deep green, swallowed up by the red temple lights.

"It's rather empty in here," Galipei remarks, gesturing around them.

"Numbers are down," the elder replies evenly. "Palace arrests. Palace executions. You know how it is."

"Ah."

August hasn't had time to deal with the Crescent Society members arrested after Leida was hauled in. Those stacks were left in his study, because Galipei wanted to discuss them.

"Might I ask, then," the elder says, "whether I may aid your prayer?"

"No need. I only sought a space. There aren't any shrines in the palace."

"Plenty of havoc in the palace these days." He must have heard about Otta Avia and her miraculous recovery. "It cannot be difficult to smuggle a shrine through those doors if you have become devout."

Galipei has considered this matter deeply. He has had no epiphanies, except that he does not know enough.

"There may be too much smuggled into the palace already." The old gods stare down at him. They are apathetic to the desperation in his voice when he asks, "When might cinnabar heal instead of kill?"

If the elder reports him for asking this question, the palace guard could easily put together the crime committed at Northeast Hospital. Fortunately for Galipei, the Crescent Societies have no speck of loyalty to the palace, no desire in the slightest to protect the kingdom without reward.

"It can't," the elder replies. "It is poisonous."

"Humor me," Galipei presses. "Your walls and doors are painted with cinnabar. The stories speak of it as the crystal for immortality. Why?"

The elder scoffs. He laces his hands behind his back, then turns to go. "Here I was, thinking this might be something worth my time. Those are legends, boy. There are gods and there are mortals; there exists little in between. Cinnabar has no function other than coloring some pretty lacquerware."

Galipei shoots to his feet. He moves with the aggression of someone looking for a fight, and the temple murmurs a complaint.

"No," he snaps. The elder halts in his path, between the pews on either side. "We can switch bodies at will, and the best explanation for it is *genetics*. Stories don't come out of nowhere."

"This kingdom hides more of its past than you could ever imagine." Though the elder remains facing the other direction, his voice is a low rumble through the entire space, each word enunciated without room for mistake. "There have been human soldiers who can change their features without jumping. Human aristocrats who've torn off their own limbs in sacrifice, hoping to match their qi to the crown. There was even once a human queen who sacrificed droves of her own people, hoping to achieve reincarnation."

The elder must take Galipei for some fool, spouting off folktales that province farmers have made up to scare their children out of trusting strangers. Galipei lifts his gaze. He meets the eyes of a figure painted onto the ceiling, one much smaller than the rest, an archaic Talinese character written on its forehead.

You weren't assigned to me until after Otta was gone, so I don't expect you to understand. Kill her.

"I ask if there has ever been a past where cinnabar was used to heal someone's qi."

The elder starts to walk again.

As you wish.

Galipei didn't go to his aunt for cinnabar without reason. He could have used anything. Otta Avia was comatose in a hospital room that had neither cameras nor medical personnel who cared enough to monitor the visitors coming in and out. It could have been a pillow over her face until she stopped breathing. Any one of the drugs that circulated through San-Er injected directly into her bloodstream to stop her heart. It didn't have to be a toxic powder. He got cinnabar only because August had asked him to. Only after August had summoned him to his study later that day to apologize—*he shouldn't order Galipei around, he knew they were closer than that, the pressure was getting to him.*

Cinnabar, August had declared, swiveling suddenly from the window overlooking the coliseum. *A peaceful yet slow method. The hospital won't notice. If someone investigates, they won't think to look for those signs.*

"You asked, actually, when cinnabar might heal instead of kill." The old man disappears from the main hall of the temple, but his words echo tenfold from the hallway. "There's a simple answer. When a god is involved, of course."

CHAPTER 11

"Your Majesty!"

Fuck.

The moment they exit Anton's old rooms, Seiqi calls out, still waiting at the end of the hallway. Anton considers his options, panic rapidly spreading from the twist in his stomach. If he isn't careful, Otta may expose him right now to make a game out of it. *She knows,* he spins in a cycle, *she knows, and it would only take one slipup—*

"Your Majesty," Seiqi says again, falling into step when he and Otta pass her. Otta doesn't look particularly bothered. Anton can hear his pulse beating in his ears, keeping in tune with his quick pace. "The gala starts soon. The council is asking for permission to allocate some Weisannas among the councilmembers for protection at the function."

"Yes, sure," Anton says. Whatever it takes to get her away from them.

Seiqi pauses. She's still walking at their side, her lips pursed. They proceed into the main hall of the east wing. This part of the palace isn't often used, and the provisions reflect that state. Statues of mythical flying horses decorate each atrium entrance, gray not by choice but by a thin layer of dust.

"If I may," Seiqi begins, "it would be wiser to call off the gala rather than disperse the guards. We don't know what Leida is planning. She could be waiting for the ideal time to slip out and run—or perhaps she wants to finish her plans and attack the palace."

"She doesn't exactly have the means, does she?" Otta asks. Though her voice is sugary sweet, there is no invitation for argument.

Seiqi winces. She clearly doesn't want to refute Otta. The guards are taught to obey instructions from their charges, and though Otta may not be a princess in the technical sense, she comes close enough by proximity. Close enough to order Seiqi into exile if anything upsets her. Anton urges silently, *Please, give it up. Go do your job and stop caring so much.* For her own sake, if not his sanity.

"There are still guards loyal to Leida," Seiqi says in a rush. "Not everyone thinks she was in the wrong. It will only take—"

In the same moment, Otta collapses midstep and Seiqi cuts off abruptly. Anton springs to catch Otta with a sharp inhale, grabbing her by the elbows. Her body softens, turning to deadweight.

"Shit," he hisses. "Otta? Otta, what's wrong?"

His first suspicion is that the yaisu sickness has caught up with her. It has allowed her a momentary awakening and come knocking again when she thought she was in the clear. He shakes her shoulders, pulls her closer to him. She doesn't respond. Her eyes stay closed, her face taking on a pallor.

Then, beside him, Seiqi says: "Oh, come on now. Don't be slow."

Anton whirls around. Seiqi—*Otta*—tilts her head toward the door beside them: a playroom, its curtains drawn and interior dark. Empty, since the palace children are being kept in their own quarters while the halls are in lockdown.

"Hurry up. I don't want surveillance to think anything's wrong," she says. Otta leaves Anton to lug her body through. She's already at the other side of the room when he enters. Shock has rendered him sluggish. This should be impossible. It should be, and yet she turns around in a Weisanna's body, and her eyes have changed accordingly. Midnight black with a flash of blue, just like August's.

"Otta," he says stupidly.

"You can set me down over there," she responds, pointing to a couch. "Remember this room? We came here all the time. One camera, only for the door."

Anton doesn't remember, to be honest. Seven years have passed for him, and that was since Otta fell ill. Never mind how many years it has been since they were last in this room, since they felt carefree enough to be sneaking around after hours when most people were sleeping. Those last few months in the palace were frantic with the longing to leave. Escape the twin cities, flee to the provinces, rob the vault cleanly enough to build their own house and garden.

He lays Otta's body gingerly onto the couch. She's had a strange gleam to her appearance from the moment she woke, and it's taken Anton until now to realize that it reminds him of King Kasa's television screens. The broadcasts where his complexion was smoothed over, made without flaw. There is no screen before Otta, but her skin glistens anyway. She resembles a doll kept in plastic wrapping for the shelf, unperturbed by the elements and the day's settling dust. Her time asleep has made her ill-fitting to reality, belonging to a different age.

"Anton," Otta prompts. "What's wrong?"

"You must be out of your mind," he says, the words bursting from him. "Jumping into a Weisanna is what got you into this mess to begin with."

"I didn't do it right back then," Otta says. She nudges the curtain, humming under her breath. Night is falling, so San-Er is growing brighter. A beam of golden yellow comes through the window, shining from the bulbs strung atop the coliseum. She doesn't behave like someone who is newly cured, someone who is a medical marvel despite the odds.

"You shouldn't be doing it at all." Anton stops. Backtracks. "In fact, you shouldn't be *able* to. Otta, what the *fuck*?"

"I thought you'd be more open-minded than this." Her eyes skirt up to the corner of the room, and he knows she's watching the camera. Otta beckons him, and Anton draws closer, out of the camera's view. It is only the sensible thing to do.

"Open-minded?" he echoes. "It's . . ." *Impossible. Unfathomable.* Just like his jump in the arena after the final battle. Just like him, surviving his own death and using the qi of that sacrificed vessel to invade August.

"What?" Otta asks. He's come near enough to be within her reach, and her hands land on his chest. They're calloused: the hands of a trained guard. One who must have lived her whole life believing she was among the chosen few of the kingdom who could never be invaded. The Weisannas are the only bloodline to be born as if they are doubled, though they in fact possess only one set of qi. Invasion should be an incomprehensible feat, just as it is to jump into someone doubled. How would Seiqi Weisanna react if she knew she could be jumped and used, like the regular people of Talin? How would the kingdom, hearing that this marker of difference has dissolved?

"You know," Anton says carefully, "I'm really starting to consider the warnings that you may be an imposter."

Otta snorts. "You already know I'm not."

"The Weisannas being insusceptible to invasion is a core facet in our ability to jump."

"And so is a flash of light, being within ten feet, and having a target before your eyes." Otta's hands glide up his chest to his neck. "I watched the footage from the Juedou. I saw what you did."

"I didn't mean to," Anton says. He can hear himself sounding defensive, though Otta speaks with an edge of amusement. She doesn't need to deliver an accusation outright. She has already gathered enough of the truth. "When did you figure it out?"

Her hand seizes his chin. Otta turns his head, putting his face against the electric light slinking through the curtain.

"I can tell the difference between shades, Anton."

"No one else can."

"I know yours very well. Let's say I'm particularly sensitive to the change." Though Otta doesn't let go of his chin, she changes her hold. Her fingers dance along his jaw with an indifferent air. He doesn't dare pull away, just as he's never dared to tell Otta he disagrees with her.

"And anyway," she goes on, "you asking about your family back there confirmed my suspicions. What was that about?"

The Dovetail. Under King Kasa, the council was prohibited by the crown from acknowledging its existence.

When Anton first invaded August's body, there were flashes of overlaid memories, thoughts that weren't entirely his. He's never experienced a brief merge like that, never jumped and felt a wave of fear that he might not come out on top. He shouldn't have been surprised that August's qi would put up a fight. Anton might have won out, but the wisps of August that leaked through were potent. He's certain he saw a dove pressed into a wax seal. He doesn't know if that's enough to go pointing fingers.

"Did you know that Kasa had my family killed?"

Otta freezes. For the first time since she woke, perhaps for the first time in her life, she looks genuinely concerned. Her lips part. Her eyes grow wide.

"Oh," she says. "Oh, I'm sorry, Anton."

"August sure isn't." The bitterness on his tongue is nauseating. "He knew."

"If we penalize August for the number of secrets he keeps and won't speak about, his punishment would be eternal."

Otta's lips purse. She is considering the matter, but something about her expression feels faraway. He's seen Otta jump in their younger years—sometimes that was how they snuck out of the palace—but he cannot wrap his mind around seeing her in a guard's body. A *Weisanna*. She gave herself the yaisu sickness on her first attempt, and now she's done it so easily on her second? What has changed?

"What's that look on your face?" Otta skates her hands down his arms, gently brushing the sleeves of his jacket. Before he can stop her, they're tucking inside the jacket, smoothing out the fabric of his shirt against his stomach, his torso.

"You know something too."

Otta's gaze snaps up. Ink black. These days, he should really start getting used to impossible acts: there's another in this palace who jumped a royal at eight years old and was never caught.

"I'm sorry?" Otta asks. She peers at him with the innocence of a convent disciple, and Anton can't help but get the impression he's being played. Through his exile, he spent his every effort keeping her alive. This is what he wanted. Otta awake should be a miracle upon miracles, but . . .

Her fingers graze his thighs. But this isn't what he expected. The Otta he kept alive was Otta asleep, a darling of a girl, a soft face who stayed unmoving, unprotesting no matter what he confessed at her bedside. Otta awake is something else entirely.

"Stop," he whispers.

"No one can see us," Otta says, her breath hot against his cheek.

For a thoughtless moment, he gives in. He misses her; he misses their time in the palace. Her fingers hook into his waistband; her lips graze his and make firm contact. Anton inhales the kiss, grasps her face, her hair, breathes the smell of something rich—something like praline, like plum candy.

Then she nudges closer, presses into him with unmistakable intent, and the wrongness of the situation is a slap to his face. Anton tears himself away, stumbling back two steps.

Otta watches him carefully. She laces her hands in front of her.

"Is something wrong?"

"I—" Anton gathers himself. Exhales. "*Yes*, something's wrong. Otta, it's been seven years. You've been under, but I . . . I've been alone this whole time. We can't just pick up where we left off."

"I didn't expect we would." Her scrutiny increases. The hairs on the back of Anton's neck lift. "But at the very least, I didn't think you'd abandon me either."

"I did *not* abandon you," Anton returns. "I'm the one who kept you alive."

"While cozying up to a princess."

Anton ventures a glance at the door. They may be out of camera view, but it doesn't mean they are unwatched. Forget it. He's not having this debate with her.

"Be reasonable." He takes another step away. "You grew up in the palace too, so I don't need to explain it to you. It's a little hard to keep up the act as August if I'm fucking my half sister, don't you think?"

She barely flinches. He had, at least partly, meant to hurt Otta with the crude defense, but her lip quirks.

"As you say, I am your sister. You are the throne. There is plenty of reason why I should be at your side."

When she sidles forward, Anton grabs her hand before she can put it back on his chest. He encircles her wrist, holding her at a distance, but he doesn't let go.

"You can't have it both ways, Otta," he says. "It sounds like you want me to stay as August for good."

"What did you have to gain living as Anton Makusa anyway?" Otta asks in return.

You. I had you, he thinks, stung by the question. He had Otta, and the entirety of San-Er stood in the way. The overspilling hospitals, the shortage of beds. The factories he never lasted long at, the paltry money he made with his useless noble hands.

"Not much," he says instead. "Exile. Picking rich businessmen's pockets."

"And look at the difference here," Otta says. "The kingdom at your beck and call."

Anton shakes his head, letting go of her wrist. "Don't try your tricks on me. You don't think I know your games by now?"

"I'm sure you're telling yourself you're only staying until you get revenge on August." Otta, intent on getting one more prod in, flicks his ear. Then she dances away, skipping to her body on the couch. "But I know your games too. You like it here. I'll help you, Anton. Just back me up and don't fight it. Understand?"

"What are you talking about—"

She collapses. On the couch, Otta opens her eyes again, having returned to her body, and she hops to her feet with a renewed energy. She hurries to shake Seiqi's shoulders.

"Are you okay?"

Ah.

Seiqi blearily returns to herself. She doesn't understand what happened. Of course, she wouldn't even consider that she was invaded, because she's a Weisanna.

"What on earth?" the guard mutters. "Did I—"

"You fainted," Otta says plainly. "Must be the air in the east wing. Let me help you." In brisk fashion, Otta tugs Seiqi to her feet.

"You were speaking about the gala," Anton reminds her, smoothing his expression over and following Otta's lead. "Shall we?"

Seiqi clears her throat. Shakes herself back into order. "Yes. Yes, some of the councilmembers would like to clear certain matters with you first."

Anton gestures for her to lead the way.

"I should change," Otta decides when Seiqi turns a questioning look on her. "I'd like to make a speech at the gala too." Before Anton can grant approval, she spins on her heel and prances for the door. She throws a wink over her shoulder. "See you there, *August.*"

CHAPTER 12

The first attendant that Calla runs into tells her the gala is starting soon, so the palace nobles will be gathering in the banquet hall.

"Ridiculous," Calla mutters to herself, pushing her sleeves up while she storms forward. As far as the rest of them are aware, Leida Miliu is loose in their corridors, and they have decided to go ahead with this frivolous display. They would probably keep holding galas if the seas swept in and flooded the cities, if a new round of influenza breezed in through the ornate doors and infected everyone within.

A patrolling guard startles at the sight of Calla turning the corner at high speed. When he calls out, asking if she requires assistance, Calla fires back a fast "It's fine!" without pausing. She has no time to waste. She needs to find Otta Avia, preferably before the gala starts and every aristocrat in this palace bears witness to Calla throttling her.

Main atrium. Calla's jaw makes a noise when she lifts her head and gauges the fastest route up the stairs to the banquet hall. Her teeth are clenched hard enough to hurt. In an attempt to look less frazzled, she scrapes her hair back while she climbs the stairs, tying everything high upon her scalp and out of her face.

A decade ago, she used to stomach every lofty remark Otta made within earshot of these rooms. They have renamed these long arches and tall atriums the Palace of Union, but the echoes of its origins remain. The velvet-green color schemes, the gold-threaded curtains. Alas, most of its undercoat weighs far too much now, and Calla finds the space even less tolerable than before. The corners sprout electric wires; the walls jam together as a palimpsest, so tightly crowded with costly decoration that each section overgrows into the next. There is no union, only half a capital refusing to give up the whole it has bitten off, stuffing itself far beyond capacity.

Calla rears to a stop, pausing for a brief moment to catch her breath at the threshold into the banquet hall. A guard steps forward. He says, "Your Highness, you're not dressed correctly."

"Oh, fuck off."

She's sighted her target. Before any guard can move to stop her, Calla surges forward and pierces the edge of the crowd. This banquet had been decorated for its last revelry merely weeks earlier, its space filled with excited palace nobles celebrating the conclusion of San-Er's games. Each corner was illuminated with an open bulb, leaving it only to chance that King Kasa didn't recognize his long-lost niece when she walked in with half her face obscured.

The lighting is dim tonight. In the Hollow Temple, there was a red bulb just like the ones dangling above Calla as she picks her way forward. It illuminated the Crescent Society members while they were marking themselves with blood, wearing vials of deep crimson like regalia. The light was the perfect shade to blend together the bodies of their victims, their hearts carved out and left to rot as vessels clumped in the middle of the room.

Calla makes it through half the crowd. They've brought in a large rug for the center of the hall. No amount of scrubbing could erase the stains after all that blood and gore soaked into the wooden panels, and no councilmember wanted to be the first to suggest a complete renovation of the floor where their previous monarch lost his head.

The last time Calla stood here, she was ready to die. To answer for every wrong she'd committed in the name of revenge, and the greatest wrong she had committed in that arena.

"*You.*"

Before Otta Avia can turn around, Calla yanks her by the elbow, forcibly dragging her out of a conversation.

"Ow!" Otta yelps, stumbling over her feet. Though she attempts to pull away, she's no match for Calla's physical strength. Calla, who towers over her by a head and then some. "Let go of me! What do you think you're doing?"

She hauls Otta through a side exit. The banquet hall chatter fades as the smooth door closes with a thud, camouflaging back into the floral wallpaper. This is a servants' passage, made for quick movement in and out to serve food. Calla releases Otta, if only to push her onto the carpet.

Otta lands with a disgruntled wince. Unlike Calla, who isn't *dressed correctly,* Otta very much is. She's changed out of her extravagant red getup from earlier. Her new dress is noiseless with movement, pale-pink silk wrapping a band around her chest before a darker sheer fabric flows to her knees in a triangle. *Aristocratic* isn't the right word anymore. She looks as delicate as a petal, and the thought practically grinds Calla's molars to dust.

"Can I *help* you?"

"I tolerated you all through our childhood, Otta," Calla says coldly. "But propriety isn't going to save you this time. Leida Miliu has named you as her source. She says she learned everything she knows about qi from *you.*"

Otta lets out a single laugh. Though she remains sprawled on the carpet, she props an elbow behind her, lounging with no hint of discomfort.

"Do you have any evidence? Or are you working off the baseless accusations of a woman imprisoned for treason?"

"Surveillance in this palace certainly goes back seven years." Calla's eyes lift. Even here, there's a camera blinking above them. "Do you want me to look? I'll have them find every bit of footage capturing the two of you together."

"You are so insufferable." In a smooth motion, Otta stands again. She dusts off her skirts, sniffing when she finds creases marring the silk. "If her claims are true, then it's not like I taught her on purpose. Go look through the footage—you won't find anything. She was the daughter of the captain of the guard. She must have been spying on me."

Calla can't believe what she's hearing. So Otta is *admitting* to it. Long before Leida started spreading impossible practices across San-Er, Otta Avia knew how to do it first. Some part of Calla still doubted it, despite her rampage to confront Otta.

Seriously? she can't help but think. The same Otta Avia who calls for servants to hold up a straw so she can have her hands free from the glass? The Otta Avia who gave herself the yaisu sickness from being stupid enough to attempt jumping into Weisannas?

"If you were a little nicer to me, I'd teach you." Otta bounces on the tips of her toes, just like she did to get closer to Anton's ear during the meeting. "Too bad."

Something in Calla snaps. Her hand plunges into her pocket. Barely enough time passes for her to process the gesture herself, never mind for Otta to realize what she's doing and get out of the way. Logic kicks in at the last millisecond. Just as the knife whips out of her palm, she jerks her wrist, redirecting it to draw a bit of blood rather than embedding somewhere more serious.

But that turns out to be for naught.

Her knife doesn't land.

Calla watches with absolute incomprehension as the blade pauses midair, hovering a second in front of Otta's face before falling to the floor with a lackluster clatter. A shudder moves through the passageway. A strange smell sears Calla's nose, like burning rubber.

"Oops!" Otta says brightly. "You're losing your touch, aren't you?"

What . . . the fuck.

The side door slams open. In that moment, Calla is so taken aback that her mind falters. August has entered the servants' passage, half bathed in shadow; the words are already forming on her tongue to demand he get his sister under control. Then he comes closer, and the sight of him gives her a physical jolt. His eyes catch the light; she remembers. August isn't here. This is Anton, training his gaze on Otta with a concern that Calla has certainly never seen.

"What's going on?" he asks evenly.

"Your *hair*," Calla exclaims, as though this is the most pressing matter at hand. The freshly dyed black makes August's face look shrewd again, in a manner that didn't photograph well when he was younger and new to the palace, in the way that other noble children didn't like the look of for a reason they couldn't explain.

"Otta?" Anton prompts. "Are you all right?"

At the other end of the hall, a cluster of servants have arrived with plates, but they come to a quick stop upon seeing the passageway already occupied. A few of them scramble to turn around and get out of sight. Others stand and wait, watching. Anton has noticed too, his attention flickering over, then back. Despite the easy demeanor of his words, his shoulders are stiff underneath his black jacket. He's also changed since Leida's interrogation. August has never worn these clothes, so it must be brand-new from the tailor.

"Would you like to tell him?" Otta asks. "Or shall I?"

"Rincun," Calla says. She pretends Anton isn't there, forging on with her interrogation. He's doing a mighty fine job doing the same to her, anyway. "Did you have anything to do with it?"

"Whatever could you mean?"

Calla's eyes narrow. A finger of cold has started to trail down her spine. "The massacre there," she says in a low voice. "Last week."

"Oh, silly me," Otta says, examining her nails. "Of course not. Why would I know anything about a massacre in *Rincun*? May I be excused to make a toast, Majesty?"

Anton doesn't immediately grant her permission. He tilts his head, catching the same tone in her voice. "Why did you say that? About Rincun."

Otta strides to the door. She brushes by Calla, their sleeves grazing against each other with all the friction of sandpaper. "I have something to announce. May I go?"

"No." Calla throws her arm out, blocking Otta's path. "You may not."

"Majesty?" An edge has entered her voice. This time, when Otta calls for Anton, it is nonnegotiable, and Calla understands why. Otta knows.

"Remember," Otta goes on, "I'm doing this for you."

This isn't the voice she would use with August. This is the expectation that Anton ought to be standing up for her, and when Anton's mouth simply opens and closes, he's taken too long. A flash of anger darkens her gaze.

"Enough." Otta smacks Calla's arm out of the way. The contact stings much more than Calla would have expected. Though she's quick to recover and shoves her arm out again, Otta is equally prompt. She catches Calla's wrist and bends it backward.

"Ow, *ow*," Calla says before she can stop herself. Where was this strength before, when Calla was dragging Otta across the hall?

"I can't work out exactly who you are," Otta hisses, "but it's only a matter of time. You've already burned your palace down. This one is mine."

Otta releases her grip, pushing away. While Calla is still wincing, grumbling profanities under her breath, she feels a faint, cool sensation on her wrist. There's a small blot of blood. Quickly, she lifts her sleeve and inspects her arm, searching for a cut, but no source appears. Otta left the mark there—it's almost the perfect shape of her finger.

Calla chases through the door at once and presses back into the rumble of the banquet hall.

"Galipei," she mutters out loud. "Where is Galipei?"

"I would like to make a toast!" Otta declares at the front, stepping onto a plush chair.

Calla scans the space, her heart kicking up a cacophony beneath her ribs. Otta is going to do something destructive. She can feel it, just as she can smell a bad monsoon before it comes down. The lights are turning brighter, each bulb showing the wire aglow inside and shining onto the crowd. There's Rehanou. Mugo. Venus Hailira, shifting uncomfortably. Finally, closer to the other side, she spots Galipei Weisanna, and he's already watching her. *Get her,* Calla mouths, pointing aggressively at Otta. *Stop her!*

Galipei moves in an instant. His silver eyes flash, and then he parts the crowd like string through gelatin, pushing cleverly at every loose pocket.

"Calla." Anton appears suddenly from behind, grabbing her arm. He's followed her out. "Leave her be."

She tears her arm out of his grip. "Don't touch me."

"I am delighted that we could join together tonight after so much strife," Otta bellows. She clasps her hands in front of her. "The annual gala was always my favorite event."

Above the heads of other attendees, Galipei meets Calla's gaze again, pausing near a cluster of councilmembers to maneuver around without jostling anyone. She sees him clearly mouth: *What the fuck is she talking about?*

I don't know, Calla mouths back.

"Before I fell ill," Otta goes on, "I found something monumental in King Kasa's vault. I kept it to myself out of fear, but with him gone, I think it is about time the kingdom and the council know the truth. I don't know how it has escaped notice for so long. Perhaps each royal advisor has run their eyes past this finding and chosen to keep quiet."

At this, several people nearby turn their attention to Calla. Curious. Wondering.

"Calla." Anton's voice, beside her.

"If she's about to tell the whole kingdom that they can jump without light and invade people at a moment's will, I'm going to kill her here and now," Calla hisses back. "It's going to tear the masses *apart*—"

"There is an object out in the borderlands, imbued with enough qi to annihilate a village with a mere wave of the hand," Otta says. To her left, Galipei has finally made his way to the front, but here he halts, equally perplexed as the rest of the room. Though Calla gestures him forward, asking him to shut Otta up, he isn't looking in her direction anymore.

"As a matter of protection, it was hidden at the site of the first battle when the war began with Sica. Once Talin won, we never went back for it." Otta pauses. The hall is silent. Confusion has settled thickly like a blanket over these aristocrats, keeping their movements confined and responses muted.

"The divine crown in San-Er is a fake. Talin's true crown remains in the borderlands, and each reign since the war has been a lie. We have not tested any ruler by its mandate since then."

Of everything Otta could have said, Calla did not expect this. A beat passes, utter disbelief reverberating through the crowd of nobles like a shock wave.

Then the banquet hall explodes with noise.

CHAPTER 13

"Did you know she was going to do this?"

Her question catches Anton off guard. The very situation catches Anton off guard, because he's dropped his usual flat imitation of August. His current expression belongs wholly to himself, and Calla knows this because she can catalogue it against the other times she's seen it. The last instance was the arena, when they pulled that bag off his face and he found himself surrounded by spectators, forced into the final battle.

At the front of the banquet hall, Galipei Weisanna marches forward and plucks Otta away, both hands on the sides of her arms to steer her firmly toward the exit.

"Of course I didn't," Anton hisses. "I would have had to *know* about the crown first."

Give it ten more seconds, and the demands coming at them from all directions are going to get out of control. Calla can pick out the bits and pieces from the nobles nearby, the councilmembers who are pushing toward Anton to get his ear first for their recommendations in light of this news. Even if it isn't true, even if the Palace of Union tries to deny the proclamation and write Otta Avia off as a madwoman, they will need proof to claim otherwise. And somehow, Calla doesn't think Otta is lying.

"Come with me," she says.

Anton's face changes. He snaps out of his stupor and smooths his features down, trying to decide how August would act here. "I need to respond to this."

The voices press in. *Heaven's mandate is only determined with the crown . . . This has been a scheme all along . . . We knew the crown was supposed to reject someone outside the bloodline . . . If those outside royal lineage are made fit to rule, then what is stopping the kingdom from swapping rulers over and over again—*

Calla doesn't have the patience to argue. She takes Anton's elbow and escorts him sharply toward the exit. By some miracle, he doesn't resist. Her focus locks into place, and she navigates through the obstacles before her as she would any strategic encounter in battle. They're out the door and past the guards. Down the hallway, left then right, into the first sitting room she finds.

Empty. Good. Calla slams the doors after them.

"Explain. From the beginning."

Anton drags his hands through his hair. There's no sign of August in this room anymore, the act vanishing the moment they came through.

"She said she was going to do something. I didn't think it would be *this*."

Calla watches Anton repeat the gesture. His black hair parts down the middle, falling in soft curls. This must be a nervous habit, yet it's somehow the first time she's seen him do it. She hasn't known him long, after all. Whatever love existed between them, it had a limited run before taking a tumble into damnation.

"Is this some ploy for your attention?" she taunts. "You haven't spent enough time with her, so she's forced your hand. She will inevitably lead the delegation out to fetch it, and your attendance will be mandatory."

Anton shoots her a glare, but he doesn't deny it. She's guessed correctly:

Otta Avia has already figured out that Anton is Anton—if Anton himself wasn't the one to tell her.

"Not that I have to explain myself to you, but I didn't imagine Otta possessed such information. Nor was I prepared for her to make a scene. There's nothing to be done about it. She's always been this way—we can only minimize impact."

Calla crosses her arms tightly around her chest. There's cold air coming in from the windows, and she doesn't want to resort to shivering. She bites on her thumbnail instead, clamping her teeth tight.

Anton is trying to make this sound simple, as though Otta's attitude is only a personality flaw, but Calla doesn't buy it. *I can't work out exactly who you are,* Otta said to her, *but it's only a matter of time.* Those aren't the words of another haughty aristocrat playing palace politics. That's the threat of someone who knows the truth, or at least has an inkling of it.

"Who is Otta Avia, Anton?" Calla asks lowly.

"The fuck kind of question is that?" Anton fires back. "She's August's sister. The second child to the Avias. Entirely ordinary, if it weren't for her aunt marrying into the Shenzhi family."

The council will be scrambling to verify Otta's claims. Calla can imagine the current pandemonium in the south wing: they will bring out the divine crown, perhaps test it on some prisoner who was already due for execution, and when the heavens don't strike them down—because surely the heavens would not allow a convict to possess their approval—they must determine that Otta has told the truth. In a kingdom that made the divine crown their very basis of monarchy, they cannot brush this matter aside, or else their monarch is as common as a factory worker plucked from the streets. Without the divine right to rule, the king has no legitimacy. Without the king's legitimacy, no councilmember has been rightfully appointed either, nor their hold over any province in Talin guaranteed.

"She's not ordinary." There's a ruckus coming down the corridor outside. "I watched her freeze a knife in midair."

Anton frowns, uncomprehending. "She caught it?"

"She *froze* it. With qi."

"That's imposs—"

"*Don't* say impossible," Calla interrupts. "*Impossible* is jumping without light. *Impossible* is qi swapping bodies at great distance. Yet somehow it keeps happening in this city, doesn't it?"

A funny look crosses Anton's expression. He must realize there's a jab in here for him too, a question that Calla has been wondering about since he survived the arena. Clearly, he doesn't consider it the time for those answers, because he refrains from a rebuttal. He turns and paces a few steps. His hand trails along the surface of a wooden table beside him, marking lines in the thin layer of dust. Three lines. Different from the ones the children drew, but the very reminder turns Calla cold nonetheless.

"Why are we in here arguing about this?" Anton asks slowly. "You spent the entire games working with August to put him on the throne. You were going to coronate him. If you could be blamed at any point, it would've been pertinent for him to mention to you that the crown was fake, don't you think?"

"You don't know if August knew," Calla returns.

"Calla. Be serious. What did August *not* know in this palace?"

New voices advance in the corridor outside. Calla strains to catch the commotion. It's a guard, giving orders to keep the nobles in the banquet hall. The Weisannas are going to try to stop the news from spreading. While Calla and Anton attempt to make sense of the situation, the kingdom is about to go to shit, because once the greater provinces find out, it's not only the palace that's going to want the divine crown in its possession. The crown, after all, promises to confirm a righteous ruler. There will be people wanting to put it on; there will be people wanting to find it and sell it on the black market, auction it off to the highest bidder. Then the crown might end up right back in San-Er, but in the hands of a councilmember launching a coup.

They're about to go up against every person who might want a chance at being Talin's ruler, every person who knows being accepted by the divine crown means a change in the centuries of Shenzhis and Tuoleimis ruling the kingdom.

"Where is this coming from?" Calla's anger gives way to frustration. There is no reason for them to be at odds. No extenuating circumstances, no rules set upon them. They could simply choose to stop being at each other's throats. "What is your problem with August?"

"You are more alike to me than you are to August," Anton replies. "Yet you insist on being his mouthpiece. You stormed the Palace of Heavens, Princess. Where did *that* Calla go?"

Calla flinches. "Don't."

"Oh, sorry. You're just some poor orphan from Rincun putting on a performance. Are you going to be giving that body back anytime soon?"

It was inevitable that he would take the argument there, yet Calla is shocked all the same. Her limbs lock; her lungs seize. The fear of being caught, of being dragged before the palace and executed, sweeps down her spine as muscle memory from her earlier years in this body. Anton may as well have swung a knife at her for the response he's triggered.

"Don't forget," Calla says icily. "You're not guaranteed to survive this. August might be too powerful. The longer you stay, the more likely it is that you could start to merge."

"Or maybe he'll disappear. Doesn't that sound terrific?"

"He was once your closest friend. Does that mean *nothing*—"

The door shudders. Calla's gaze whips over to it, but she must have locked it from the inside when she closed it. After another failed push on the other side, someone clears their throat in the hallway and calls:

"Your Majesty? Are you in here?"

Anton sighs. "And what about it?"

"We need a statement," the muffled voice continues.

"Seiqi, I am consulting with my advisor," Anton says. He pulls at his hair again, though it's more subdued this time.

"With all due respect, there are other royal advisors waiting for you in the war room, as well as the entire council. Could you perhaps continue the conversation there?"

Calla remains silent, watching Anton for his response.

"I'll have Seiqi escort me to surveillance to get a handle on the situation," he decides, heading toward the door. He's not waiting for Calla's permission.

"You don't have to do this."

She's dropped to a whisper. Seiqi Weisanna won't be able to hear her outside, but with the way Anton stops, he certainly does.

"I beg your pardon?"

"You could jump out. This is August's problem. The throne's problem. So why are you tending to it?"

Calla has always wondered why the crown would claim someone like Kasa, someone like her father. She suspected it called to a specific familial qi instead, that the palace had lied about what the object was supposed to do and drawn up its own mythos to support their royal family.

If the real crown is still out there, then it could truly function as it is said to. A Shenzhi or a Tuoleimi could be struck down. A peasant could become the next king. This goes beyond the scope of what game Anton is playing on the throne.

Seiqi is knocking on the door again. "Your Majesty? The news is going to spread through the cities very soon. We need to act before—"

"Are you afraid that I'll expose you, Highness?"

"I don't *care*," Calla hisses. "Expose me! Go on."

"—there are going to be riots, we will need to disperse guard units—"

Anton spins around. "Don't tempt me."

"I mean it." There's no doubt that Seiqi can hear some argument going on inside now, but they're keeping their volume so low that their words slur even to Calla's ears. "What do I care? The council is waiting for a chance to get rid of me anyway. Tell them—they may decide to investigate *you* while they're at it."

From the very beginning, their alliance was built on a terrible foundation: the outlaw and the exile. Two people on the precipice of falling off the very world, holding on to each other for balance. Now they are both planted too firmly, leagues of land and sea under their feet. She can't give Anton Makusa a simple shove anymore to get him out of sight; they can only continue this bizarre dance to see who can send the other teetering closer to the edge.

"I loved you," he spits, "and you chose to kill me."

"You wouldn't run with me," Calla returns in kind. "We could have left. You chose not to. What alternative would you have preferred? To kill *me* instead so you could live happily ever after with Otta Avia? I'm sure you wish I wasn't the one here right now."

"—open gaps at the wall," Seiqi continues, "and there are plenty of rural dwellers camped—"

Anton strides back. In two steps, he's before her, his jaw tight. A flush of red has started along his neck.

"How dare you."

"You are so *selfish*," Calla goes on, though she knows she's crossed the line. These are her darkest thoughts, the accusations that stem from their worst clashes. "All you wanted was your own little haven with Otta, and you couldn't give that up for me. I had the kingdom at stake. So *yes*, Anton, I chose to win."

Anton chokes out a laugh. The sound must be distinct enough to travel through the door, because on the other side, Seiqi Weisanna stops trying to summon his presence. She goes still, listening, and Calla shoots Anton a warning glance. He ignores her.

"This is rich," he hisses. "You replaced an ugly tyrant with a prettier one, Calla. One who will smile and shower pleasantries about your health, then release a brigade of soldiers to burn your village nonetheless."

"Shut up."

"Did you think King Kasa's only problem was being sadistic enough to let his civilians kill each other in his annual games? You don't think it might be the provinces he continued to starve for his wealth? The noble families he wiped out as soon as they disagreed with him? You didn't save the kingdom, Calla. Unless a new throne means Talin splintered back to its original form, your victory didn't change this kingdom *at all.*"

Calla staggers back. Her throat is closing. She doesn't register her legs moving, nor does she notice she's still trying to make distance until her neck is cold and flush with the wall. Her hands grope around to get her bearings. She buries her fingers into a tapestry, feeling the threads dig into skin.

"If you are so righteous," she gasps, "then why don't you do it? Pluck out the royal soldiers in each province. Stop taking their crops, stop collecting taxes. Let San-Er produce its own blood."

It's dangerous to say this. Someone like Anton might do it simply to prove a point. He will raze a trail wherever he flits and leave those remaining afterward to deal with the fallout.

"I don't want to," he replies easily. "Unlike someone"—*August*; he speaks of August, but he knows that Seiqi might hear him—"I can admit that I prefer it when everyone answers to me. I have everything at my disposal."

Calla releases the tapestry in her hands, forcing her posture straight with conviction. The fibers have carved markings into her fingers, drawing a map of mourning. Quietly, so quietly that she can barely hear herself, she says, "You don't have me, do you?"

Maybe there would have been a time when that meant something. Anton pauses, and he must know what she's saying. He must hear that she would still run with him now if he was willing; he must feel that her anger exists only in the space they've made before them.

"I should condemn you to execution." He turns away. "But I think it's better that you suffer the consequences of your actions. Open your eyes, Calla."

He yanks the door open. Seiqi Weisanna immediately scuttles back, trying to act like she wasn't struggling to make out what was happening in the room.

"Your Majesty," she greets. She peers over Anton. "Princess Calla, are you coming too?"

"Go ahead without me," Calla says.

Seiqi doesn't waste any time. She ushers Anton off, and then Calla is left alone in the sitting room, listening to activity rumble through the palace—through the walls, the floors, the ceilings.

She looks down at her wrist again. Otta's splotch of blood has dried, barely larger than a thumbnail.

Images of the Hollow Temple play again before her eyes. The bodies that the Crescent Societies had stolen, stacked, and sacrificed.

I want her heart, Pampi Magnes says in her mind's echo. *It is a very special one.*

The arena, then, flashes in vivid memory too. The body that Anton was wearing, bleeding out under the plunge of her knife. It was barely comprehensible in Calla's overwhelming grief. She shouldn't have needed to do it. She wouldn't be arguing with him now if they had left before the arena.

Calla scratches at the blood drop. It comes off easily, flaking to the carpet.

It's not fair, she wants to scream. *Why? Why* her*?*

How strange it is if their bodies have always had the ability to use qi like this.

How strange that ordinary civilians haven't stumbled onto it if that is the case. Instead, it's fucking Otta Avia who can freeze a knife in midair.

Resentment trickles down Calla's throat like a syrup. Once the council debates the severity of having a false crown, they are most certainly going to go looking for the real one. Calla needs her sword back. She needs answers.

Making up her mind, she zips up her jacket and storms into the hallway, in the direction of her rooms.

CHAPTER 14

Despite their best attempt to keep a clamp on the hysteria, news spreads in an instant.

Heavens knows how, given the palace is on lockdown. Yet the whispers travel beyond their doors, hit the streets before the clock can strike the new hour. San-Er has never been built for wide-scale chaos. The most it can handle is the king's games: a handful of players across the millions, uncaring of governance because all but one will be wiped out by the month's end anyhow. It used to be that anyone who disrupted the twin cities met a quick fate. The palace guards easily outnumbered the small outbursts. They would put a stop to the fuss, and San-Er would release a breath of relief that the clog in its arteries had been unblocked.

"Main thoroughfare is entirely gridlocked," Galipei reports into his field radio. "I've never seen anything like this before."

This time, it is a spontaneous eruption. Civilian after civilian, streaming out from their homes in the only display of discontent they are capable of. San-Er wants answers. They want a king chosen by the heavens. A king confirmed by the heavens. Without the crown's mandate, they haven't had a real kingdom since the war with Sica, and this is a terrifying prospect—as though the sky has fallen and the ground crumbles under every step. Without the crown's mandate, they may have tolerated a cruel monarchy for no reason other than someone's sly tricks centuries ago on Talin's first mass migration into the twin cities.

"We still have most of the guards waiting at the coliseum. Should we move some numbers?" one of his cousins responds on the radio.

"Stay where you are," Galipei says. "Let this run its course. Keeping the palace clear is most important."

From above, the crowd looks like a dark sea of heads. The last time there was movement of equal scale, a false alarm was screeching across San-Er, warning of flash floods that never came. That had been easy to fix. Easy enough to wave people back into their homes. Galipei was at the forefront of controlling the riots before the king's games too—the disgruntled residents asking for the cash prize to be equally distributed among those in need, asking for some solution to the hospital beds that were already full—and all the palace guard needed to do was herd them into a corner, then pluck them off the streets.

Galipei strains to hear the answer coming in on the receiver. Tonight, they can't exactly put everyone in a jail cell as King Kasa would've dictated. They would run out of jail cells.

"—hear it? They're—calling."

Galipei lowers the antenna and pulls the crackling field radio away from his ear. The people may have formed this protest on their own, but there is only one group in the twin cities with the organizational capability to take charge and make use of the circumstances. The Crescent Societies have been spreading word of their next goals: flock to the palace, keep resisting until the throne falls. Their battle call echoes down the thoroughfare, one wave after the other.

"*No throne without mandate. No throne without proof!*"

It's not that every resident in the twin cities has suddenly adopted Crescent Society anarchy. But give the masses a tangible reason to show their resentment, and they will take it. Give the Crescent Societies these numbers to use in chaos, and they will throw people at the palace like explosives to get in.

They have to disperse these protests before the Crescent Societies can take a firm hold.

"Crescent Society members are starting to jump. Suspected invasions on some guards. We need to get a handle on this *now*."

Galipei brings the radio close to his mouth. "Execute any Crescent Society jumpers immediately. No argument. We don't have cell space."

There's agreement and disagreement at instantaneous synchrony. Different units, different opinions. Times like these, he almost wishes Leida were still here. That they had one person making decisions.

"Some of them are still using what Leida taught—"

"We don't know if they've jumped without light—"

"Don't we need to clear executions with the council—"

Without a true crown, it is easy for unrest to reach a boiling point. The civilians whisper about their last cruel king and how he could have been allowed by their heavens to rule. If he wore the true crown, they say, Kasa would have lost the mandate while he governed so cruelly. August is the heir to a dynasty that should have been discarded. August should have been rejected at his coronation.

If there is one thing the Crescent Societies know how to do, it's seizing an opportunity in a power vacuum.

"August has ordered it," Galipei snaps, making the decision for him. He knows August, for better or for worse. "Get a move on and prepare palace proceedings to find the true crown. The last thing we need is some fucking farmer in Rincun putting it on and claiming the throne."

◇◇◇◇◇

The noise outside the palace is audible from the halls.

Calla slows by a window, peering through the night to catch a glimpse of the crowds. There's not much to be seen from this part of the south wing, though she can envision what the streets must look like. Impatience presses at her palms; she desires the grip of her sword. She nudges the glass, curious if the noise seems loud because it isn't closed properly, but the window doesn't budge.

"Highness."

The voice echoes from the far stairwell, sounding surprised to find Calla standing here, prodding a random south-wing window.

"I'm convinced everyone keeps calling me *Highness* to remind the council that they ought to get rid of me before I launch a coup for the throne."

Calla pushes at the corner of the glass. *Ah.* It's sealed down to the frame.

"Hmm. Well." Venus Hailira strides over with a preciousness in her steps, like she can't quite bear to set her feet all the way down. When she comes to a stop beside Calla, she's slightly breathless. She was definitely rushing around before Calla's presence caught her attention. "I would promise to not let that happen, but I think you and I both know I don't hold much sway."

"Not with that attitude."

Venus grimaces. "Are you coming to the second meeting?"

Second meeting?

Calla quirks a brow, turning away from the window and facing the councilmember. "I didn't know I was invited. What did I miss at the first meeting?"

"Otta Avia claims to know the location of the crown. First informal meeting was a vote on sending a delegation." The council must have been doing that while Calla and Anton were off arguing. "Second in an hour is to confirm who is attending. Miss Avia has personally requested your presence in the delegation."

Calla resists the urge to punch through the window and dive out. Maybe she'll survive the splat in the alleyway below. Maybe she'll fuse to the cement and won't have to look at Otta and her stupid tiny face ever again.

"May I ask why?"

"Uncertain. We all assumed you wanted to go." Venus hesitates. "To speak frankly, I don't think this is a good idea. San-Er is rioting, and we're the *capital,* packed with palace guards. By the time this news reaches Rincun, protest from the rural civilians won't be all the yamen has to worry about."

"You're afraid of mass entry into your province," Calla states. She has a headache emerging behind her ears.

Venus lowers her voice. "My soldiers can't handle that. They can barely handle the province as is. Anyone entering the borderlands must pass through Rincun, and there will be plenty of people entering to make a search for the crown. It will be havoc."

Calla resists a sigh. When it is *the divine crown* up for grabs, who can say how its seekers will go about the job? They might well kill everyone in their way for the infinitesimal chance of success, as though San-Er's annual games have expanded outside its wall and into the provinces.

"Look, Venus. Can I call you Venus?" If there is a delegation, it will likely set off at dawn. There is no time left for anything other than hurried plans. "Here's what you're going to do. Take your own delegation to Rincun immediately. Put out a proclamation to stay inside unless absolutely necessary. Dig into the Hailira pocketbooks and subsidize the food and rice your villages need. It won't stop what's unfolding, but it will prevent your soldiers from getting overwhelmed. It'll entice the people who live in Rincun to sit at home instead of venturing into the borderlands for the crown in a desperate bid to stay afloat."

Maybe Venus didn't expect Calla to offer an actual alternative. It takes her a beat to register Calla's words. Another long beat before she nods slowly, then more vigorously.

"All right," she says. "How—how long do I do that for?"

Calla shakes her head. She's got to go. She has business of her own to tend to.

"Don't make me draw up all your plans."

"But Highness"—as Calla tries to circle past her, Venus holds her arm out with more to say—"the entirety of Talin should enact this, if it is something councilmembers can manage. You should speak at the meeting."

There is such hope in Venus Hailira's voice. Calla tries to imagine how such an initiative would look. The farms settling into stillness. The village wells unattended.

"Be realistic, Venus. What will San-Er eat if Eigi is pushed into containment? You can do this because you are Rincun, and that is all. Get your delegation and go. You're out of time."

Before Venus can object, Calla pushes past her arm and hurries down the hallway again, resuming her quick pace. She makes only one detour: her sword, retrieved from the vault. She's lucky she hasn't done anything to draw the palace's suspicion quite yet, because the guards let her in and out without a problem. At some point, she's going to need to return the valuables she stole too, because it certainly doesn't look like she's leaving now.

She isn't leaving, but she *is* going to the borderlands with the palace delegation.

The very thought drives a nail through her skull. Calla may as well be banging her head repeatedly against the wall. *There's no reason to do this,* the sensible part of her says, the part that kept her tucked away for five years preparing a successful assassination, single-minded in her mission. Then blind annoyance overpowers everything else, and her ears are ringing with white noise, clearing for nothing except: *Anton, Anton, Anton. You know what,* fuck *you. I'll show you. You'll see.*

She glances over her shoulder. The corridors have cleared. Her sword hangs off her hip with a weight she's grown unaccustomed to. Significant time has passed since the games. Bearing the weapon again takes her back to her early days, trying to adjust to the way it brushes against the leather of her trousers.

Calla turns the handle to her rooms and slinks in, letting the door thud after her. Despite the measured manner of her movements, its echo is loud, foreboding, the toll of a funeral bell.

Leida looks up from the other end of the bedroom, still tied to the pipe.

"You'll be glad to hear that the cities are a mess, I'm sure," Calla says casually. "Riots all around the palace. Our divine crown is a fake and has no ability to determine the mandate of the heavens. Otta Avia declared that the true one is lost somewhere in the borderlands."

Leida reacts to her words woodenly. She doesn't appear surprised, and Calla thinks, *Of course*. If she was watching Otta long enough to learn about her control over qi, she must have also learned about the divine crown. She might even have known about it earlier, gleaning any information she could from August to eventually turn on him.

"I'm surprised it's taken this long for the kingdom to find out."

"Yes, well"—Calla breathes out, rubbing the corners of her eyes vigorously until her blurred vision clears—"as much as San-Er has left behind its belief in the old gods, it sure still believes in the cosmic determination of the heavens. Either that, or they've been waiting for a reason to riot after years of Kasa."

Leida doesn't respond. She's trained her gaze on a spot over Calla's shoulder, and she keeps it there.

"I passed a few guards on my way out of the vault," Calla continues. She knows what will trigger a response. "The palace has given the instruction to execute anyone found jumping in the cities at this time."

Leida meets her eyes in a snap. Only then does a line of shock finally crumple her brow.

"That's excessive."

Calla shrugs. "The palace has to make an example out of them somehow. They're already afraid of the Crescents' abilities, given recent circumstances. You caused this."

"I caused nothing." Offense crawls into Leida's voice. She prickles, evidently, at the accusation. "I only gave back knowledge that was rightfully theirs."

The more Calla tries to use logic on what is unfolding before them, the more her head hurts. She wouldn't put it past Kasa and his forefathers to lie to the kingdom. If an enemy came knocking on San-Er's door and obliterated the wall, King Kasa would have looked directly into a broadcast camera and insisted the brick formation remained standing. Still, to succeed in erasing decades of collective memory entirely is not only absurd, but wholly different from telling a lie that the people pretend to believe. For as long as *Calla* has been alive, it has been a given rule within Talin that jumping causes a flash of visible light and requires close proximity. If this hasn't always been the case, how long ago was the truth concealed?

"Leida," Calla says. "I already played in the games. I don't have time for more."

"I don't know what part of this seems like a game to you." Leida jostles about, exaggerating her confinement in the cord. "Either let me go or return me to the cells. It's not my fault that the king you put on the throne is showing his true colors."

She sounds like Anton. All Calla keeps hearing are accusations, yet no one seems to have a solution. What do they *want*? To burn the kingdom to ash and start over wearing threadbare clothes on flat plains? Calla has done her time going hungry in Rincun. She isn't going to volunteer to return to that way of life.

"What if he kills some Crescents and the provinces never starve again?" She doesn't know why she bothers trying to save face for August. "Can't exactly improve the kingdom if he's never given the peace to build."

Leida stays silent awhile. It's peculiar: there is no noise from the protests in here. The walls of her quarters have obstructed it entirely.

"You know," Leida says slowly, almost lethargically, "a fish in poisoned water won't be thankful to await a feeding every hour. It will want a new tank where it can swim uninhibited to find its own food."

"I don't really care for riddles."

"It's not a riddle. It's as plain as daylight."

Calla wanders over to the thick curtain. Brushes at the edge to peer outside, seeing little except shadows.

"What fine daylight we have today," she murmurs.

It is not a phrase that would be spoken in San-Er, with its claustrophobic alleys and looming, low buildings. That's why they chose it during the games, so Anton could identify himself no matter which body he was wearing.

"Look," Calla says firmly, tugging the curtain back before Leida can note her distraction. "Otta has summoned me for their delegation. You know what she is capable of. Tell me, and I'll let you go."

Leida narrows her eyes. "You don't mean that."

"Why wouldn't I?" Calla has already as much as admitted to Leida that she's an invader. "I don't need to keep you here. I don't actually give a shit if you want to bring down this palace."

At first, Leida stays quiet. Her eyes pointedly go to the bag that Calla abandoned near the door. Maybe Leida will call her bluff. When all's said and done, Calla is here prying for answers from an enemy of the throne instead of taking her stolen assets and leaving. An errant advisor is still an advisor: no matter her methods, she continues tending to the threats pressing on the monarchy.

She doesn't want to give a shit. Truly—she wishes she cared less. But the problem with destroying the palace is that Calla can't imagine what comes in the aftermath. Someone sneakier than Kasa, perhaps. Something that comes slithering out from Otta Avia's sleeve. Peace is not guaranteed. And if Calla lets that happen by turning the other way, maybe it'll come find her later anyhow in whichever province corner she hunkers down at.

It's why August was supposed to take over. It's why August was supposed to be their fair king, bringing in a new, just age.

"I want that backpack," Leida finally says.

Of course she does.

"Fine." Calla leans against the wall. "I'm listening."

Leida brings one ear to her shoulder, then does the same on the other side, stretching her neck. A few exaggerated motions later, she fidgets in her bindings, as though some godly intervention might come down from the heavens and save her from this bargain she's made if she holds out a little longer from speaking. Nothing comes.

"Leida, don't waste my time."

"I'm thinking about what you need to know," she retorts. Leida huffs, and, with each word practically dragging through her teeth, finally opens with, "Before the war, Talin's families used to have patron gods. You know this part?"

Calla puts her hands into her jacket pockets. "I could assume."

"They prayed to their patron god for protection and health. That part makes it into the history books sometimes. The part left out is that some of them went further than prayer. Some of them made sacrifices in exchange for heightened levels of qi. The only problem was, the gods were fickle. Merely sacrificing each time they wanted to be heard was unreliable. Sometimes killing a cow afforded new strength. Sometimes killing ten neighbors achieved nothing."

Calla, again, returns to Anton's dead body in her mind's eye. Her dagger, piercing his back and sinking to the hilt. All that blood spilling and spilling, dampening the arena ground.

"The old gods could choose when they wanted to listen if a mortal's sacrifice called for their attention among the pantheon," Leida goes on, "but each family possessed a sigil that called directly to their patron god. Patron gods were forced to listen if a sigil was marked after a sacrifice. It was the one foolproof method to unlock access to a god's ear."

"I need to stop you right there." Calla closes her eyes briefly, taking a deep inhale. "Do you think I'm stupid?"

"You *asked* to understand what Otta is doing."

Calla's eyes snap open. "The gods aren't *real*. Do you know how many people I have killed? How much qi I've released back into the ether, how much blood has run by my hand? Don't you think I would have noticed by now if *the gods* tuned in each time?"

"Highness, if you can't even fulfill the first component of believing in them, how would you ever make a sacrifice to them?"

With the way she speaks, Leida doesn't give the impression of lying. That doesn't have to mean it's true, though. Perhaps Leida really does believe this—perhaps the people of San-Er are more religious than Calla thought.

It must be explainable. Maybe it is not a god that allows access to new qi, but the mortal body, unlocking something when a sigil is drawn on. Before the kingdom spoke about jumping as a matter of genetics, the provinces threw around the word *magic* too. With further understanding, whether for jumping or for manipulating qi, there's always an explanation beyond gods and divination.

"The Crescent Societies," Calla says. She brings one hand out from her pocket and mimics two horizontal lines in the air. "They had this on their chests."

"One of the most basic sigils. Many families used to share it to call on one patron god. Probably the god of the sky."

Calla, slowly, looms closer.

"So which one have you been using?"

Subtly, she watches Leida's left arm twitch. The cord is still holding firm. If Leida were to make a sudden effort to free herself, it would make more sense for her to yank the right arm, since it is closer to the outside. It would have a far better chance at unraveling the binding.

"You asked to understand how Otta is capable of manipulating qi," Leida says. "I've told you."

"I'm sure you took the family sigil Otta was using. You must have been curious if you could use it too."

"No. I've never used it."

A lie, given the ease at which she jumps between bodies.

"There are sigils noted in the royal books," Leida goes on. "You can check for yourself. Before the war, families would use them as crests to represent their household when reporting to their yamen."

"But you said yourself"—Calla takes another step closer—"families also shared sigils that called to popular gods. That indicates common ones and rare ones. I want Otta's."

"Check the books," Leida says firmly. "I've told you what I know. The vault is going to be of more help to you than I am. She must have gotten it there. Keep your word and let me go."

"Fine, fine." Calla's eyes flit to the bag she left by the door. How tragic it is, to have escape waiting so closely, within reach. "If you leave now in the night, they might have unguarded window exits. Let me cut you loose."

Calla draws her sword. The silver flashes in the low light, the blade edge glinting.

With a muffled huff, Leida strains her wrists behind her, giving Calla maneuvering room. Calla draws closer, then crouches. Puts the point of her sword against the cord, sawing, sawing, sawing—

"I'm sorry, Leida."

"What—"

Calla shoves the sword through. It cuts between the side of Leida's ribs, into the heart, emerges from the other side. Before Leida can make a sound any stronger than a gasp, Calla pulls the sword out.

The long blade catches. Makes a wet, squelching noise. A mere few weeks of disuse is already affecting its function. Leida cries out; the initial trickle of blood transforms to an outright gush. Her hands remain bound. She cannot stanch the wound.

"This is what it comes to, then," Leida rasps.

"I'll use it well." Calla stares at the splatter of blood that has landed on the inside of her wrist. There is a twist in her throat, appalling and enormous, but she doesn't swallow it down. "I promise. I'll make this sacrifice worthwhile."

The long wheeze that Leida emits is a familiar one. "You claim to be an intruder, yet you are one of them nonetheless. You make your promises in vain."

Leida Miliu's eyes glaze over, turn into still-life crystals that might be harvested for portraits of death. Calla knows she will say nothing more afterward. Whichever guard she invaded has died in the process too. There will be no justice for this dual life taken.

Calla was willing to sacrifice Anton to get Kasa off the throne. She's willing to sacrifice whoever gets in her way if they won't yield to her now, including every other noble in this palace trying to wreak havoc on this kingdom. *Princess. King-Killer.*

It's about time she stops lying to herself.

She sets the sword down. Leida's blood has sunk into the carpet. The smell is pungent. The room sits quiet.

Calla takes Leida's left arm and pushes up her long sleeve.

"Goodness," she whispers beneath her breath.

In the Hollow Temple, the Crescent Society members marked themselves with blood. On Leida's arm, there's a sigil drawn not in blood, but glowing faintly in the appearance of liquid light, right underneath her skin. A left dot, a long and slanting curve with a dot above, then another dot to the right. It looks like it should be a word in Talinese. Calla doesn't recognize it. She does stare at it, committing it to memory until the body stops flowing with blood, until—before her very eyes—the sigil starts to turn faint, then disappears entirely.

"What the fuck?" she mutters. She gets to her feet, gathering her sword and sheathing it. In the bathroom, she washes the blood off her hands, scrubbing under the running tap until the crevices on her palms are clean. A heavy sensation clings to her when she leaves her rooms and enters the hallway, but she has a feeling that's not entirely her imagination. She keeps one of her fists clenched tightly.

None of the guards are particularly concerned by her presence in the hallways. Calla walks between the wings, to the palace cells, and then to the farthest door—the cells with maximum security. Though the Weisannas block her passage at first, she asks for them to find Galipei to confirm her permissions, and before Galipei has scarcely responded to the page they send, she slips between them and descends the stairs.

One yellow light glows from the walls. No windows. The ceiling hovers low enough that Calla's head brushes the top, forcing her to stay hunched. At the base, she finds a row of empty cells running down the left side.

They didn't bother locking Leida's body away securely. It is only a vessel, so it has been sat outside the cell they were keeping her in, preparing for the moment they found her and could force a return. Calla kneels at the vessel's side and pushes up its sleeve too. A chill skates up her arm.

The same sigil, marked with blood.

Calla unclenches her fist. Her palm is damp with water, and she presses it to the sigil, scrubbing it away.

"Calla!"

Galipei's voice bursts down the stairs a second before he does. Calla rises to greet him.

"What are you doing?" he demands. His eyes flicker between her and Leida's body.

"You're welcome," Calla says. She brushes past him. "The palace can come out of lockdown."

CHAPTER 15

Across Talin, throughout its twenty-eight provinces, there have been reports of spontaneous combustion at temples and shrines, all of which are burning without discernible cause.

Outside the wall, the kingdom still believes in the old gods. San-Er has lost its reverence for the mystical, but rural dwellers pass down the stories of their homes, their land, their ancestral encounters with minor gods who used to walk among mortals. Their shelves hold small labels—*plate retrieved with help from god of lost objects*; *guidebook drawn with aid from god of yellow flowers*; *bow gifted from god of pretty boys.*

If the old gods are to come down from the heavens, they will come to the provinces first. They will find their believers and exercise their influence. A shop shrine for the god of winter harvest burns red in Daol. A family shrine for the god of pottery bursts into flames and almost burns down half a village in Youlia before it is put out. The half-husk ruins of a temple erupt on a slow afternoon, and though they stand on Pashe's outer periphery, the smoke is visible from the yamen in the province center. No cleric has tended to that temple in decades. The councilmember for Pashe receives the reports and assures the province that it must have been an old lantern, its oil warmed by the sun and bursting.

The villagers nearby wonder about the god of the summer sun instead. Each time they are told there must be some explanation for these occurrences, the next occurrence grows more bizarre. Approved travelers from the capital have started bringing news about other feats of nature inside the wall, and the rumors spread fast. A noblewoman awakens from the yaisu sickness after seven years comatose. The captain of the royal guard is arrested only for trying to spread divinity. The princess has negotiated with the gods personally, because how else could she have stayed hidden in the cities for this long, save for protection from above?

I'll tell you what, some villagers say when the royal soldiers aren't in earshot, *maybe the gods had Calla Tuoleimi kill the king and queen of Er back then.*

Maybe they have been whispering into her ear from the very beginning.

Do you remember their names?

For the Tuoleimis? I haven't heard them spoken in so long.

It feels like the work of the gods. As if they are deciding who ought to remain and who ought to perish.

Then Otta Avia's declaration comes rippling into each village like a blazing gold arrow, and suddenly, it's an explanation, a reason why the gods have been striking again and again. The heavens never chose their king. Maybe it is time for the heavens to pick someone else. It all comes down to the crown, and whether it can be found. For the first time, the provinces have a hand in the kingdom's affairs, and maybe this is when it will change.

So the people begin to pray.

◇◇◇◇◇

Inside the wall, the remaining Crescent Society members are starting to merge temples.

They need the consolidation if their numbers are to operate functionally. There are structures to build and procedures to put in place. Their members have been striking across the board, afraid that they will be among the next killed or arrested.

Are we sure Otta Avia isn't one of ours? one Crescent asks. *The timing is almost too perfect.*

Murmurs down the table agree but confirm that this was certainly not a Crescent Society effort. This should be expected: at some point in the death of a kingdom, the nobility will begin fighting themselves.

We should coalesce an effort to intercept the crown, another says. *The common people will follow someone the heavens confirm. It is the easiest route to liberation.*

This meets dissent.

Unless you have some way of attaching yourself to the bottom of the palace carriages that leave tomorrow, we can't exactly get out of the capital.

The Crescent Societies, anyway, have always been the organization within the walls. They understand this. The unanimous decision settles quicker than usual. A tide has turned to push their agenda forward, and they won't miss the opportunity.

We must trust that the Dovetail will do their part. We keep our goals clear. Our job from the inside is to strike at the center.

◇◇◇◇◇

After they clear the body, Calla stands dumbly by the stain in the carpet.

Someone will come to clean it while she's away, they tell her. She should get some sleep. Especially if she agrees to accompany the delegation.

Slowly, she crouches and presses her finger into the stain. It hasn't dried yet. There's so much blood that when she pushes hard on the threads, it beads on the surface.

Left dot. Long and slanting curve. Dot above. Another dot to the right.

Calla lets her shirt collar snap back into place. The blood settles on her chest, drying where the sigil has been drawn.

As she crawls into her blankets for rest, she doesn't think she's imagining the rush of cold air that whispers down her spine.

◇◇◇◇◇

When dawn comes, there's already a crowd waiting at the wall.

After the riots and the many Crescent Society members dragged into the city's dark alleys, the civilians here now only wish to bear witness. They stand by curiously. Gape and peer at the horses brought out for transport, point and stare at the palace aristocrats who wait stone-faced.

The palace guards hold the civilians back, their weapons out in case they need to use force. No one pushes forward. A hush falls over the crowd, almost in disbelief that the palace has acted so quickly. They must really be worried about the crown. There must be a true possibility that King August could lose it.

The guards open the gate.

And the delegation enters the provinces.

CHAPTER 16

A long time ago, Anton Makusa used to make this exact journey with his family. San-Er was stifling, as was the palace, and if the occasion allowed it, his parents took them out to Kelitu for fresh air every few months. They would borrow a carriage from the palace, pile into the seats with his sister, Buira, giggling at being crammed against him. The carriage driver would ask if they were ready, clambering onto his seat with the horse reins, and his mother would shush them quickly before closing the door, signaling that they were all set to go. Only councilmembers could leave the capital whenever they pleased—they needed to govern their provinces, which did require being in the provinces on occasion—but that still required approval in advance, and all who went outside the wall were carefully logged. Resources for travel were scarce. After they reached Kelitu, the carriage driver would quickly return to San-Er in case he was needed by another councilmember, and he wouldn't return again until the date arrived when the Makusas planned to come back to the cities.

That was why it took them so long to rescue Anton after the attack. One full day, after he had cried himself out and resorted to sitting torpid in the carnage. He could only wait until the driver returned. Until the driver made a distress call and the call brought the palace guard in.

He cranes his neck up against the carriage window now. The carriage is shockingly well maintained—its gears oiled, seat linings soft. He doesn't remember the ride being this luxurious, but maybe someone on the council argued for an upgrade in the past few years, or maybe they only bring the best out for the king's use. Some miles back, the driver almost took them off-road before she got control of the horses again, and Anton barely felt it because the wheels moved through Eigi's minor flooding like it was nothing. The climate in Eigi is muggy, each step on the ground slapping wetly. One major road runs through Eigi before splitting in two for Pashe and for Leysa: the Apian Routes, shaped like a two-pronged instrument until the Jinzi River cuts off both ends. They'll be traveling through Leysa to get to the borderlands.

Back then, they went through Pashe to get to Kelitu, so he supposes the similarity to his family's route ends there. Maybe no one would think much of it if he asks to travel through Pashe on this journey too, just so he can see it again.

A knock comes on the window, jolting Anton for a moment. He peers through the foggy glass, and Calla takes shape, riding alongside the carriage on a horse.

His fists tighten in his lap.

"We're slowing," Calla says, muffled through the glass. "Rehanou is complaining."

Councilmember Rehanou shouldn't be on this delegation to begin with. But it was better to allow the councilmembers who insisted on coming than argue and delay the journey. There are four carriages rumbling after the one Anton occupies—five is the maximum number kept in surplus by the palace, and thank the heavens, because it limited the councilmembers who could claim that the delegation absolutely needed their assistance when passing through each of their provinces. There could be danger; there are most certainly other forces out here trying to fetch the crown too. It'll require defensive standby in each province. Smooth cooperation from the barracks and soldiers waiting to be summoned.

In truth, the councilmembers' presence implies a lack of faith that the soldiers out here will listen to instructions from their king. The chain of command is supposed to run from throne to council to general to soldier. Yet Talin is made up of mortals, and mortal loyalty is more oft sworn to the people they can see. In the provinces, the king might as well be as intangible as the old gods for how distant he is.

There's a reason Talin has so many provinces. No councilmember's power can grow too great this way. Less chance of leading a successful revolt against the throne.

"Stopping for the night?" Anton asks.

Through the glass, Calla nods. "Floods are bad up ahead," she says shortly. Then she trots forward on her horse, her nose in the air.

"Does she always do that?"

Otta's voice is a shock beside him. He isn't quick enough to disguise his reaction, and Otta pulls a face.

"Sorry," Anton says. Two Weisannas sit opposite them in the carriage. Though the elite guards may look like they're dozing off for their own rest, they're trained to be listening to every word. No room for speaking out of turn. "I'm not sure what you mean."

"Oh, I don't mean anything by it." Otta leans back with a sigh, lolling her head into the curtain on the other side. "It just seems tiring that you are running around keeping tabs on your leading royal advisor more so than said royal advisor is going about her job advising. She wasn't even going to come on this delegation until I requested her presence. Fancy that!"

Anton's eyes slide again to the Weisannas, and he bites his tongue. He hasn't had a moment alone with Otta since she played her hand at the banquet. He hasn't had the chance to ask plainly about what she's doing, why she's insisted on Calla Tuoleimi's obligation to be present for this retrieval mission. Surely she would prefer Calla stay out of it. Especially given the snide remarks she's been throwing whenever the opportunity arises.

But if Anton had to guess, he would say this: Otta doesn't go about anything half-heartedly. She's woken to him on the throne. She won't wait for a natural conclusion where Anton either decides to keep the role or jumps back into his birth body purely to beat the shit out of a conscious August. Anton may have the patience and wherewithal to wait for clarity in his circumstances before playing his hand. Otta will find power in her grasp and clutch tight immediately.

Remember, I'm doing this for you.

Why? Anton thinks, staring at Otta. She stares back, and maybe she can read his question in that gaze alone. *What comes after finding the crown?*

The carriage rolls over a cluster of hard rocks. A long creak sounds from the floor. The walls shift, then settle.

"I have to admit," Anton says aloud, "it would have been nice if you had told me about this in private first."

It's a risk to start this conversation in front of the Weisannas, but with this delegation now, Otta has more to lose by exposing him than by playing along.

"And why is that?" Otta returns easily. "I know you. You would have chosen the safe maneuver. You would have quietly sent a small force to the borderlands to fetch it and spent all your energy on making sure the news never got out."

"And what's wrong with that?"

"Really, August, perhaps I should be your advisor instead." The carriage is starting to slow. Otta shifts in her seat, crossing one leg over the other and letting the silk fabric of her green skirts flutter. "It is the *divine crown.* We must fetch it personally. Is there anyone in the palace that you trust enough to send for a task like this?"

Anton huffs. He gestures to the two Weisannas before them. "My guards are very trustworthy."

"Leida Miliu was a traitor."

The Weisannas can't help but frown. They resent the insinuation here, but it isn't in their place to speak. Otta smiles sweetly at them.

"Sooner or later," she goes on, "every secret comes to light. You would have preferred to risk the chance that the crown went missing along the way as long as the kingdom didn't find out. It doesn't work like that. The reward of this crown is far too great. You must act accordingly."

The carriage stops. Outside, one of the guards dismounts from her horse with an audible splash of her boots in the wet grass. They will check the perimeter before calling the all clear that lets the nobility disembark.

"You weren't worried that my council would turn against me?" Anton keeps his words tame for the listening guards, but Otta surely senses the warning underlying them. "It's not unimaginable that if they were feeling less generous, they could have voted to unseat me until the crown was brought back."

"Your Majesty," Otta says, sniffing. "You *are* still mandated to rule by the line of succession. They cannot simply decide you are not their king anymore."

"Ah, but they *can* decide to wait for a proper coronation. Treat me as they might handle an underaged heir apparent: appoint a regent from the council until the crown actually says I have divine right to rule."

Otta rolls her eyes. With the way that the two guards have perked up—a subtle shoulder tilted forward, an imperceptive shift of the knees—they would be nodding along if it were appropriate.

"All to say," Anton finishes, "we got lucky this time. You have my respect, Otta. But if you keep trying to decide what's best, I will have to rein you in. There's a reason you are only my sister, not my advisor."

Seven years have passed is the silent warning whispered between the words, under and over. *You must know we are not the same people anymore.*

"Your—"

The carriage door opens. "All clear. You're welcome to exit, Majesty."

Otta clamps her mouth shut. She flounces out first, not hiding her annoyance. When Anton follows after her, poking his head through the door, his gaze lands on a small cluster of midlevel buildings to their left. He pinpoints their current location immediately. They've barely passed the middle of Eigi. This used to be Eigi's capital, before King Kasa burned it down and built a security base instead. The yamen has since moved farther north, the villagers evacuated. When the reels reported the event and panned to those blackened buildings, the newscasters spent mere minutes on it before moving on to the total casualties of the games that day.

Slowly, Anton steps onto the grass. His shoe squelches into the earth. He's waved forward with Otta, the guards herding the delegation toward a large gray building in the distance, and Anton barely keeps his expression even.

He hasn't seen the provinces in so long. He doesn't remember the world outside the wall, not really. The memories exist as faint impressions in his mind, the same way he only retains flashes of what the palace felt like when his parents were still around. He remembers Kelitu through the longing in his chest when he breathes open air. He remembers Kelitu by its frequent echo of sound, miles and miles of wetlands waving in every direction. Though he can't envision what their vacation home looked like anymore, he hears Buira whooping while she runs alongside the tall fronds sprouting in a perimeter around their property. Kelitu is a seaside province. It smells of salt, screams with the caw of its cliff-climbing birds. Nothing like the pigeons of San-Er that he was used to, and when he hears Eigi's birds overhead and lifts his head to look, the fleeting images come rushing back, superimposed over the present like an exposed film reel.

"Cousin."

There's a tug on his elbow, then the slithering sensation of cold fabric when Calla loops her arm through his. To his left, Otta casts a glance over, frowning. Galipei keeps distance to their right, hovering in and out of his periphery.

"What is it, Calla?"

Calla doesn't answer immediately. When he looks to her, she's staring back at Otta, the displeasure in her eyes as bright as burning torchlight. He wouldn't put it past her to create conflict at the first opportunity. Calla brought along merely one attendant for staff. She showed up at the wall wanting to bring her *cat* too, before one of the Weisannas put down their foot and said it was a security hazard, to which Calla only rolled her eyes and pointedly asked a palace attendant to "take Mao Mao back and feed him some steak for the stress you're causing him."

"The flooding," Calla finally says. Her tone is curt. "A natural buildup wouldn't just clog a small part of the Apian Routes in the middle of Eigi. When we travel through the province, we're moving on a decline. The north is lower than the south."

Anton's brow furrows. Heavens. When did Calla Tuoleimi have time to be studying the provinces like this while she was training to kill a king? He certainly didn't pay enough attention during the academy to know this about Eigi.

"Floods don't always follow natural inclines," he says. "Maybe some farmers messed up the drainage. Or there's too much dirt blocking the roadside. Some rural dwellers bury their dead by the Apian Routes thinking it gets them closer to their gods."

"Sure." Calla turns over her shoulder. Her eyes narrow at Councilmember Mugo, who walks nearby with his cellular phone pressed to his ear. He's contacting his generals, gathering his soldiers stationed in the province. Eigi is his territory to govern, so he clamored to aid the delegation with security while they travel. "Or someone is trying to get us off route the moment we're out of the cities."

"Pray tell, why would they do that?" Anton asks. Despite himself, he sees Kelitu in his mind again. The attackers who barged in with knives. Their swift fury, cutting without hesitation until his parents were bleeding out on the hardwood floor. For so long, he had imagined this an inevitability, some tragedy that accompanied his family's stature, yet *all this time*—

Calla staggers in her step. At first, Anton thinks she must be responding to what he said, but it would be bizarre to show such dramatics to a mildly sarcastic question. The moment he grabs her arm, catching her before she can slip from the crook of his elbow, Calla crumples fully.

He feels a thrum from her hand.

Her eyes aren't merely bright from indignation. They're . . . *bright*. Emitting light.

"Your Highness," her attendant says sharply, breaking from the guard line and hurrying toward her.

"She's fine," Anton says quickly. He sniffs. It can't be a coincidence that the smell of burning rubber is pervading the air around them now too. "Let's get inside. It's probably the elements."

Otta steps in. "May I help—"

Anton tugs Calla away, avoiding Otta's reach. She can't see her like this. It'll open a fucking giant can of worms. "No need. I'll handle this."

Before Otta can argue, he hastens their pace, drawing ahead of the Weisannas and practically dragging Calla forward. She walks as though she's downed a gallon of wine. It would almost be impressive if she'd actually managed to smuggle that out, but unfortunately, that doesn't seem to be the case.

"Princess," Anton mutters under his breath. "What are you doing?"

"I'm not doing anything."

"Don't lie to me."

Councilmember Mugo hangs up his cellular phone to greet the soldiers stationed outside the gray building. Anton is already forging through the double doors, and Eigi's base takes shape like a backward mirage. What seemed like a cluster of buildings from farther away is nothing more than an illusion when looking up close; he mistook these thin towers for full-bodied interiors. The base unfurls in a gaunt, serpentine manner, letting its operations thread around and about the compact spaces as an endless maze, just like San-Er.

"Your Majesty," a soldier at the door says. "Lodgings are in the second wing—"

"I need a moment to speak with my advisor." Anton pulls ahead, taking Calla with him. In the foyer, the cold gray outer appearance transforms. His muddy shoes touch down on plush red; the wallpaper glistens a midnight blue. It is still daytime, but the foyer is dark, illuminated by candles glued to the window-sill and lanterns at the center mantel. In their haste, Calla stumbles again, barely keeping her feet straight before she recovers. It must be disconcerting to show weakness before others, because Calla's tone is wholly enraged when she hisses, "Your Majesty, you are yanking me around like a machine lever."

"Well, Highness, you ought to keep up if nothing is wrong."

Her hand thrums again. Stronger, this time. Anton pushes through a hall-way, where he finds a low ceiling and a string of lights taped to the wall. Why would they have such varying sources of lighting, and what is that *yellow*—

Anton's gaze flickers to his side. A glow emanates from Calla. The cutting, hard citrine of her eyes, faintly changing the hue of the hallway.

"Great heavens, Princess—"

Anton hauls her into the first room he finds. Someone's office, empty of life. The blinds are drawn tight, again creating the illusion of night with only a small electric bulb from the desk lamp. Though he makes the frantic effort to close the door behind him, it starts sliding on its own, clicking with a magnetic mechanism. Calla staggers away the moment he loosens his grip, preferring the table over his help.

"What the fuck did you do?"

"What the fuck did *I* do?" Calla echoes. "Why don't you ask your little lover whether she's poisoned me?"

Anton frowns. Whatever this affliction is, it's messing with her balance. Both her feet are planted firmly on the floor, yet her arm flails out, as though she needs the support to stop from falling over.

"Otta is capable of many feats," he says, "but she wouldn't resort to poison."

"Oh, *sure*."

With a sudden, barely suppressed noise, Calla yanks her arm back, then presses it hard against her sternum. The moment Anton inches forward to help, he reminds himself to get it together. His eyes pivot to the wall, and he unhooks a bronze plaque instead.

"Take a look at yourself."

He puts the bronze plaque in front of her. Calla flinches as soon as she glances at the surface. Rather than addressing why there is a yellow tinge to the room, she shoves the plaque away, letting it clatter to the floor.

"Don't."

"This is not a friendly request," Anton snaps. "This is a command: tell me what you did."

Calla's grip tightens. She isn't only clasping her chest—she's splayed her fingers and formed claws with her nails, as though the skin underneath is bothering her and she wants to tear through it to get at what's underneath. The burning smell thickens. A vibration has started within the room, and when Anton tilts his head, his ear doesn't pick it up as a sound so much as a feeling: movement that shakes the walls, the carpet, the ceiling slats until it's itching at the inside of his mouth. It's burrowing into bone. He would start plucking his teeth out one by one to make it stop.

Enough. Anton lunges forward. Before Calla can combat his approach, he hooks a foot around her ankle and takes her balance out. She yelps; he shoves her onto the desk.

"Hey!"

"I'm not *attacking*, god—"

When he squeezes her neck, he's exceedingly aware of each point of contact between them, each brush between his fingertips and her burning skin, between his palm and her throat. The feeling sears his nerve endings as though he's actually put his hand upon an open flame. The call to press closer into her is trancelike, near hypnotic. Calla jerks up in an attempt to get free, to push his hand off. She's unbalanced, and all she achieves is her nose nudging the side of his face. A whole-body shudder runs down his spine.

Anton, going exactly for what she's trying to protect, yanks at her shirt collar, revealing a glimpse of blood smeared on her skin. She bucks, forcing him away, but he's found what he was looking for.

"What have you done?" Anton demands. "Why are you messing around with Crescent Society experiments?"

"Not Crescent Society experiments," Calla manages, heaving. "Just qi."

"Stop it, then."

"I'm not *trying* to do this."

He grabs her face roughly with his other hand, keeping her still, flat on her back. "*Calla.*"

Calla makes a noise, her chest rising and falling. It isn't the whine of helplessness. It is a siren lure of hunger, and he wants nothing more than to bite down. Put his mouth on the vulnerable triangle of soft skin between her collarbones. There are so many ways to kill her right now, to turn the trap on her. A dozen objects on the table that he could use as a weapon: start with the ink pen and skewer it through her ribs, plunge through muscle and bone and split every important organ open until she's bleeding and repenting before him.

Her eyes are frantic, swiveling around.

Calla feels each groove of the hand on her jaw. Anton is wearing rings. Cold jade. Faintly, she takes inventory of what else is real around her body: the blue wallpaper, the stale air, the shriek of some alarm whining through the building. Then Anton says her name again, and she hears something else. He shakes her shoulders with a disgruntled "*Calla, come on*," and her ears spasm; her eyes go dark.

Sinoa, come on.

Calla blinks hard. "What did you say?"

"I said, you're trapping it in," Anton replies, and she realizes he wasn't the one to speak. At least not the last part she just heard. "The qi."

"Qi is *supposed* to be on the inside."

"Not if you're reacting like this! Let it out."

There's a second voice whispering in the room. Whispering in constant rhythm alongside Anton's words so that she can't pick apart what they're saying, save that they are getting closer and closer to her ear. She cranes her neck, searches through her blurring vision, and when Anton tightens his grip on her forcefully, she isn't in control of herself as her hand lifts to shove him away.

A pulse beats fiercely from her wrist. It collides with Anton's chest as if she has taken a wooden mallet to him, and the momentum pushes him hard enough that he skids across the carpet until his back collides with the far wall.

Calla heaves for breath. Anton swears, then stumbles a step, wincing and reaching for his shoulder. He doesn't look too badly injured.

The room settles. Calla rubs her eyes, and there's no more burning sensation. No glow. It has been building for the entire journey out—she simply couldn't have imagined that *this* would have been the result.

For the first time in fifteen years, she almost felt like she was about to jump.

"You did something," Anton states. He doesn't bother posing it as a question. "To cause this."

Calla's hand drifts down to her collar, her finger trailing the lining. In his bid to investigate—she must have been touching the sigil and drawn his attention, she realizes absently—Anton loosened the fabric. A clock ticks in the corner. The remains of heavy distress coat her tongue, but in the sharp taste there's vindication too, and she wants to lean over, wants to ask Anton to give it a taste so he realizes what she's achieved. He was close enough for it. He might have, if only she'd asked.

"Maybe."

"Calla, this isn't a joke."

"I'm not joking." She flexes her hand. She feels a new thrum skate down her arm, but it isn't intractable. It feels as though she's suddenly able to move a muscle she never knew she had. "Maybe I did do something. Maybe the gods willed it."

A muscle twitches at the side of Anton's face. "If you're trying to feign religiosity now—"

"I'm not." Calla pushes off the desk. "Go ask Otta if you want answers. It all started with her, anyway." She brushes by him and hits a latch on the wall that opens the office door. Noise floats in from the hallway.

Anton scoffs. "*What* is your problem with Otta?"

There's no need to reply. He should know. In fact, he should have questioned Otta the very moment she woke, because their current predicament begins with Otta Avia, and Calla is going to get to the bottom of it.

If not for the kingdom's sake, then for his. So he can see what Calla sees.

"As I was saying outside . . ." She walks off, letting her voice float back. "Summon the councilmembers to a meeting. I have concerns about our journey."

CHAPTER 17

Like other parts of the building, the makeshift meeting room is dark, the curtains drawn and the sloped ceiling crowded with shadows rather than light. Most factories in San-Er are built this way, especially the basement levels where produce is stored, and Calla wonders if they simply copied San-Er's existing construction plans out of laziness, rather than design a base that didn't need such a low roof.

She peers out the window. Night has fallen, slathering ink upon the wet ground. Eigi gives her the creeps, to be honest. It's too empty. Too quiet. It'll only get worse the farther they go into the provinces, because at least Eigi is close enough to San-Er that the terrain bears some resemblance to their streets. Central Talin will appear almost entirely unfamiliar.

Councilmember Mugo clears his throat at the table.

"Are we starting soon?" he asks.

Other than their esteemed king, Calla has allowed only councilmembers into the meeting room. No guards. No additions. No exceptions. That includes Otta Avia.

Slowly, Calla turns from the window and releases the curtain. The last councilmember they were waiting on—Councilmember Savin, who oversees landlocked Laho in the center of the kingdom—walks through the doors.

"Yes," Calla says. The low rumble of conversation starts to die down, at least across most of the table. Before her, Councilmember Rehanou and Councilmember Diseau are still in debate about one of Janton Province's sea exports.

Calla walks over to stand directly between them. The two men blink. Councilmember Diseau makes a noise, rears back in offense, but he can't quite tell her off for getting in the way when the room is entirely silent now, waiting on Calla's next words.

"Thank you very much," she enthuses. "I hope my meeting isn't interrupting your fun chat."

At the head of the table, Anton props his hands together, his lips thinning. He doesn't interject. If she were him, she would have long removed Rehanou as councilmember of Kelitu out of sheer pettiness. Then again, Calla can't quite speak to what she would do in Anton's position, because she also wouldn't be quietly pretending to be August. Either get out or rule *properly*.

Calla shakes out of her thoughts. Councilmember Rehanou has said something dismissive, but she didn't even register it. Her shoulder twitches. She tries to clamp it down, but then a muscle in her thigh tremors, and her leg jerks, hitting the edge of the table. It makes a small sound, and though no one else around the room seems to think much of it, Anton narrows his eyes.

"Let's begin here," Calla decides. She retrieves the photocopied papers she left on the windowsill and hands them to Rehanou to distribute. He takes one set of papers, lip curling, and passes the rest of the bundle down the line. "Leida Miliu claimed that her supernatural feats of qi stem from sigils. I need anyone in the room who was already aware of this to come clean now."

Silence. Calla doesn't know if she entirely buys that, but she figured it would take more for the councilmembers to admit to the knowledge. Members of the palace don't even believe that jumping should be allowed.

"Very well. I had my attendant, Joselie, do some research with me. We took some books out of the vault before the delegation. Hope you don't mind."

"You brought royal books into the provinces?" Mugo asks in disbelief.

"Yes, I'm a fucking idiot." Mugo doesn't seem to catch her sarcasm. "*No.* I photocopied everything."

Calla waits for the papers to make their way around the table. She took the time to staple them together and everything. Copies of ten pages. It wasn't easy getting everything printed in the dark. When Anton plucks up a set, he holds it only by the stapled corner, as though he's afraid that Calla has slathered poison over the text.

The last set of papers returns to Calla. She smooths it open down the middle. "We went through the few inventory books from before the war and scanned anything that could be described as *unfamiliar markings*. I want everyone to flip through the first five pages and tell me if there's anything you recognize."

The room fills with the sound of fluttering paper. A few seconds pass. Calla's eyes are already drifting to Councilmember Savin when she says:

"Oh. This one." Savin turns around her papers, which are folded to the third page. There, Calla photocopied a small etching she had found at the top of a village registry. A triangle with a line down the middle.

"I'm very glad you said that," Calla said, "because I would have been curious why you were lying if not. Turn to page eight, please."

After scouring the inventory books for sigils, Calla sent Joselie to find Matiyu Nuwa in the surveillance room, working the predawn shift. They needed a cross-reference. She figured there wouldn't be many instances of the palace logs using the word *sigil.* They didn't have the time to look through every suspicious occurrence logged within the kingdom to find when sigils might have popped up in their history. But if Leida was telling the truth and any marking before the war could be a sigil, then it was easy enough to type certain words into the palace system and see what came up once they had their suspicions. *Triangle. Line down the middle. Jumping.*

"Ayden Junmen, thirty years old," Calla reads aloud from the page. "Entered San-Er as a legal lottery entrant two years ago, his fourth time applying for the draw. He emigrated from Laho in the autumn, and by winter he had joined the Crescent Societies. Three weeks later, he was executed."

Half the councilmembers around the table lean in.

"I don't remember this coming before us," Rehanou says, almost sounding disappointed that he hadn't signed off on it.

"It would have been private," Anton interjects. It's the first thing he's said since the meeting began.

Correct, according to the Weisanna files that this account was pulled from. Public executions are ruled on by the council when the crimes are deemed serious, kingdom-wide affairs, like treason or mass murder. There hasn't been a public execution in years. Most daily crimes in San-Er are sorted with a callous sign-off by only the king, and then the Weisannas put those sentences into effect. Calla remembers her parents flipping through the stack of sign-offs within minutes before breakfast, back when the Palace of Heavens was still around.

"He was charged with the crime of excessive, illegal jumping, and apprehended when he attempted to pass as Daine Tumou, the head of the Evercent Hotel in Er. Some of you may also know Mr. Tumou as Number Seventy-Nine in the most recent games."

Anton visibly experiences a flash of recognition before smoothing down his expression. He and Calla almost lost their lives fighting Seventy-Nine's hired men in the games. They ended up fleeing instead of finishing the battle.

"Ayden Junmen occupied the body for a few days before getting caught, when one of Mr. Tumou's men finally got a good look at his eyes. Here's the kicker: among all the men giving statements, not a single one saw a flash of light, though there wasn't any moment Mr. Tumou was left in public without accompaniment. Ayden Junmen was extracted under torture, placed back into his birth body, and executed in the palace. He didn't give up any accomplices.

Under duress, he claimed he acted alone. When his body was processed, they found a marking on his chest drawn in blood, resembling 'a triangle with a line down the middle.'"

"This sounds like the Crescent Society experiments," Mugo says immediately. "Leida Miliu's work."

"Perhaps." Calla flips to the next page and continues reading from the quotes. "Ayden Junmen's record was clean when he was granted entry into San-Er, but upon further investigation from Councilmember Savin when asked how something like this happened, Laho's yamen found that he had two cousins with connections to the Dovetail."

Councilmember Savin sets her papers down. She's taken off her thin glasses and propped them atop her head, massaging the bridge of her nose

"Yes," she confirms tiredly. "That is true."

"Just to be very clear . . . ," the councilmember seated next to Anton cuts in. Deep-green eyes. A member of the Farua family, perhaps, but Calla doesn't remember which province they govern. "This is the same Dovetail group that is now committing attacks across the provinces?"

"Indeed," Calla says. "So what seems more likely, that Leida put in a random assignment through the Crescent Societies two years before she began her conspiracy against the throne, or that the Dovetail have known how to manipulate qi for a while now and taught this man two years ago?"

"Calla, speak plainly, would you?" Anton demands. He lifts his volume, an echo reverberating through the room. "I'm hearing story after story of context, but no reason as to why we are discussing this."

"In conclusion," Calla snaps, "I find it convenient that a rural group with remarkable capabilities is striking the provinces right when we hear the crown is false. The Dovetail are making their presence known to the kingdom after hiding for years, perhaps decades, and suddenly the Crescent Societies in San-Er are also yelling *No throne without mandate*? Something triggered that first attack in Rincun, and I will be the first to connect the dots aloud: Otta Avia is behind this."

Anton shoots to his feet. "That's enough."

"Will you deny it?" Calla returns just as quickly. "Will anyone in this room deny it?"

"I do ask," Savin interjects. "When would she have plotted this? In the few days since she's awoken from her seven-year coma? Or before she fell ill, when she was a mere teenager? There is no communication into the provinces from San-Er."

Calla scoffs. "As if a little lack of telephone wires is going to stop her."

"While I don't deny the aspects that line up," Councilmember Rehanou says, leaning back in his chair, "do you accuse her of making a play for the throne? What other reason is there to cause kingdom-wide chaos like this?"

Anton is shaking his head. Refusing to acknowledge what's in front of him. "This is ridiculous—"

"She's known the crown has been false for however long and bided her time until it was right to go after it," Calla says. "We are wasting time arguing about her motivation. She needs to be removed from this delegation—"

"This is *her* delegation, Princess Calla." Councilmember Mugo stands. "And forgive me, but it is starting to sound as though you bear a personal grudge. Of anyone in the room, you are the one who poses the biggest threat to the succession of the throne. Otta Avia has no blood claim. It would take a coup that eliminates every member of this council if she wants to wear the crown."

The room falls quiet. Calla, too, falters momentarily, scrambling to counter Mugo's point.

"I will increase security and ensure there's no intrusion from the Dovetail during our journey, given they are a real threat," Mugo continues before she can summon a retort. "But let us not invent further dangers where there are none, lest we think ourselves too self-important."

"Are you serious?" Calla demands.

Councilmember Mugo strides out of the meeting room, already pulling his cellular phone from his pocket. The rest of the councilmembers exchange glances. In the lull, Anton pushes his chair in and brushes dust off his sleeves.

"Meeting dismissed," he announces. "We will continue onward in the morning. Let's not waste time."

Without looking in Calla's direction, he exits the room too.

The councilmembers slowly follow suit. When Councilmember Farua walks past Calla, who remains rooted at the edge of the table, she offers a small nod.

The room clears.

"I can't believe this," Calla says aloud.

Her head twinges. She winces. Maybe she's losing it. Maybe this is a paranoia of her own making. The room rustles with sound, and then Calla hears a whisper.

Sinoa.

She swivels fast, but there's no one present but her.

That sigil she copied from Leida is doing this to her. There's no denying its effect: something peculiar is happening to her qi, something beyond unlocking the abilities that the Crescent Society experiments sought. She has been displaced anew. Out in the provinces, qi might behave differently from how it does in the cities—farmers might sense the seasons before they turn; villagers might move in tune with the crops and gauge the needs of the animals they keep. But they don't hear whispers that aren't there. They don't start phasing in and out of consciousness with their eyes wide open.

Calla allows herself a second of recovery, blinking frantically to get rid of the blots of yellow crowding into her vision. Before anyone can notice her delay, she hurries out of the room too, grumbling about the council's uselessness.

◇◇◇◇◇

There's an arcade at the security base.

Heavens knows how Anton stumbled onto it while walking around. The base comprises three buildings connected by multiple skywalks. Still, when he slipped out the window of his assigned room after failing to sleep, moving quietly to avoid notice from the guards in the adjacent lodgings, it seemed the base was easily made for ground movement too. The first door he opened ushered him into a laboratory of sleeping computers. He trawled deeper, picking up notepads and keyboards and a half-finished apple core that someone hadn't thrown out. Everywhere he went, a faint shroud of cigarette smoke hung in the air. He climbed the stairs to the second floor, where he found cabinet shelves and data drives. Third floor, where a faint beeping struck his ears, though he couldn't identify it quite yet while investigating the resting couches and teapots.

Now, on the fourth floor, he registers the sound as video monitors that have been left on through the night. Coins dropping and swords swinging, piped through the make-believe of a speaker. It's so jarring that he almost turns back on the stairwell and returns to his bed.

Then he spots her in the corner, sitting by the claw machines.

Anton approaches from behind. Drops silently into the velvet chair facing her, a low round table separating the space between them.

"Didn't like your bed either?" Calla asks.

Anton kicks a shoe up onto the edge of the table. "I'm only sleepwalking right now. Don't mind me."

She doesn't react. Despite the hour, she's wearing a dress that seems to have been torn in half to go with her leather trousers. Red bundles of fabric resembling flowers bloom at her shoulders, and her long sleeves run past her wrists in a wide bell shape, falling backward when she props her arm up to lean on her fist. Though there's a length of fabric covering her collar—and the sigil she's drawn onto herself—the rest of her neckline is absent in a thin triangular cutout, taunting past her heart and ending just above her navel.

Maybe it's the forsaken hour, but Anton has an urge to lick that exposed swath of skin.

He gestures forward. "I haven't seen you in much palace clothing."

"This old thing?" Calla shifts in her chair. "I repurposed a few pieces before we left. I was starting to get the impression no one would take me seriously as an advisor if I kept dressing like a street urchin."

Anton quirks a brow. "I'm not sure if *that* is why you're having trouble being taken seriously."

"As Mugo helpfully pointed out earlier, I am aware that being both the spare to the throne and a patricidal maniac is also not good for my reputation."

Anton almost laughs. But he gets ahold of himself before anything shows, because that is a slippery slope toward forgetting who she is, and who they are, and why they're here. For a moment, Anton and Calla merely stare at each other to the sound of the arcade. A machine nearby beeps incessantly, cawing "*Winner! Winner! Winner!*" without care for the fact that no one stands before it.

"What are you doing here?" Calla finally asks. "Why are you . . . being pleasant to me?"

He's not. Or he supposes he's eased off trying to provoke a reaction out of her, and in contrast, he almost seems kind. It's hard for him to pinpoint how he's coming across. This whole time, how he *feels* about her hasn't changed. It has never changed, whether from before he entered that arena or after that performance of a coronation. His impulse is still to reach forward, touch her mouth, cradle her hair. At every up-and-down flicker of her eyes, he begs for attention, craves that relish when her expression changes in reaction to something unexpected he's done.

There's only a stronger ache that has forced him to alter his behavior. Self-preservation, knowing that he will splay his arms open and allow her to kill him yet again if he forgets how she unstitched him with the blade of betrayal.

He won't come back from death a second time. Calla Tuoleimi has ruined him, so he'll have to ruin everything in return.

"I have something to discuss with you."

"What have we been doing these past few days *except* discussing things?"

Calla replies. Still, she doesn't sound unyielding. She strains her arm up, reaching for a folded game board on the shelf beside her. "Do you want to play?"

When she flips the board open, the surface shows a grid, ten by ten, each square numbered from one to a hundred. Its border is decorated with colorful depictions of the old gods, one midmotion while transforming into a cloud of dust, another sitting on a pillow and resembling a green-faced dog.

"'Chutes and ladders'?" Anton asks, recognizing the game. "What are we, twelve?"

The briefest smile crosses Calla's lips. "I always liked this game back in the Palace of Heavens." She unlatches the accompanying box and peers at its contents for a moment before offering it to Anton. "You remember how it works?"

"Of course." Three tokens and two dice wait inside the box. He takes one of the tokens. "It's hardly complicated. Land on a ladder and follow it up to the higher number. Land on a chute and follow it down to the lower number."

"Did you know that some of the boards look different depending on which city makes it?" Calla reaches for a token too, then takes out the dice. "Er usually prints theirs with an equal number of chutes and ladders. San is known to generate boards with more chutes."

Anton lifts a brow.

"We'll play the old way," Calla continues. "Ten rolls for each player." She throws the dice. They both land on a three, so she moves her token along the first row and stops at the sixth square. The next one would have offered a ladder directly up to number thirty-four.

Anton holds his hand out for the dice. Where their skin makes contact upon Calla's pass, his fingers whisper with recognition.

He rolls a seven. Slides right up the ladder. "It's about Otta—"

"Naturally." Calla takes the dice. Though her tone remains level, that single word is acidic.

"What is that supposed to mean?"

Calla moves her token again. "It means exactly what I said. *Naturally*. It's always Otta with you."

"May I finish? I was going to say you can't be so blatant about your suspicions. She'll recalibrate until it's harder to catch her."

Calla's gaze snaps to him. She didn't expect this. "So you believe me?"

"Obviously not that she plotted the Dovetail attacks," Anton hurries to correct. That's absurd. Although he hates to give Mugo any satisfaction in being right, it's true that Otta has had no time to put anything into effect since she woke up. If there *is* some coalition effort attacking royal soldiers across the kingdom, it was planned in advance.

"Then what?" Calla demands. She's paused with her next turn, clearly irritated.

"I don't know," Anton says honestly. "That's what I want to find out. Do you remember that day August summoned you to the wall? When he wanted a word with me first?"

Calla takes her turn, eyeing the board as she moves her token.

"Yes," she says. "The day Leida was caught red-handed."

"He asked about Otta. It seemed bizarre to me. Seven years go by, and he was suddenly thinking of her. Not only that, but he was inquiring what she last said to me. As if he feared whether she might have revealed something."

Anton takes a chute down. Calla's next roll has her on a ladder up.

"The crown, I gather."

"Maybe. Or maybe there were other secrets too. I think Otta knows far more than she's willing to give up at present."

One machine nearby abruptly jangles with chiming bells. Perhaps marking the hour, some distorted grandfather clock. Another ladder later, Anton has reached the middle of the board.

"You aren't worried that biding your time will endanger you?"

"I am more worried that scaring her will change her course and prolong the result further. I need to know what she's trying to do. There must be a grand motive up her sleeve with all these gambits. Releasing this information. Asking you along on this delegation."

In silent response, Calla rolls. Up. Down. Again. Her pointer finger is slow while she pushes her token around. They play a few rounds without speaking.

"Of course," she finally mutters, "because it is so terrible for me to be here."

"It's unnecessary, certainly."

Anton eyes the movement of her token. She's overtaken him, at seventy-five.

"Have you considered," she says, "that maybe I am here for you?"

"Sure," he replies. "Finding your opportunity to force me out of August."

Calla practically stabs her token down. "Protecting you. I acknowledge my wrongdoing in the Juedou, but outside of those coliseum walls, I was fighting *beside* you for most of the games. I am still that same person."

If he can help it, Anton tries not to think about that final battle. The moment he relives the bag being torn off his head to begin the Juedou, he remembers August's role in getting him there, and then he can concentrate only on August's silence over the years, saying nothing of his family. The moment he goes back to the image of the coliseum at night, crowds cheering on all sides, he can only hear Calla saying, *I love you. I love you, so this is a favor to you*, and enough fury boils in his blood to burn him inside out.

Anton, here, says nothing to preserve the temporary peace they've found. He rolls the dice. Pushes his token to eighty-nine. And despite being a gasp away from reaching the last row, it is this exact number that has a chute taking him all the way back to square one.

"Oh, that is so vile," he mutters beneath his breath, following the chute down. Anton sighs, gesturing for Calla to take her next turn. "Go on, then. Victory is yours."

"Can't."

Another machine screeches from a distant corner. "Excuse me?"

Calla shrugs. "I'm out of rolls. Game over."

Surely she is joking. Anton doesn't know any kid who still plays by the ten-rolls rule.

"Just like that?" he asks. "You'll accept loss while you're so close?"

"They're the rules, Anton. I can't change the rules." She pauses, scoffing. "I suppose I could do this." With one finger, Calla flips over the whole game board. Their tokens go flying across the table. "Now we both win."

He shakes his head. Any earlier humor dancing crookedly to fit between them has since disappeared.

"Don't push her, Calla," he says, returning them to the matter at hand. "For the good of the kingdom. You can do *that* for me, can't you?"

Calla puts the tokens back into the box. Then the dice. Her lips have thinned, and Anton reads the expression for irritation. That, at least, is what he expects before Calla looks up and meets him with misery in her yellow stare, and suddenly he wonders if he can read her at all.

"You have so quickly forgotten," she says quietly, "that I would have razed the twin cities for you. There was *one* irreconcilable matter in what you could ask of me, and you pressed on it too hard."

Winning in the arena. King Kasa dead.

Anton hesitates. "Princess—"

She's already stood up. Her sleeves flutter on either side of her. After spending so long in the games together, he has half a mind to warn her that she should detach those before they tangle her up in a fight.

"Yet now," Calla says, "now the irreconcilable matters between us grow and grow. But I'm in no mood to yell about that tonight, so fine. You can keep Otta compliant. Learn the secrets you need. But don't forget that you are *not* the one who's supposed to be acting for the good of the kingdom."

"And you are?"

Calla freezes in her step. "I beg your pardon?"

"You seem to like playing executioner," Anton continues, refusing to heed the warning in her voice. It's easier to speak to her like this, when she's turned away from him. She becomes a shadow of a woman, made up of hungry wisps and the smell of smoke, something impossible to grasp and therefore something he was only meant to lose. "Getting rid of the people you've deemed worthwhile sacrifices, so on and so forth."

He could be talking about himself. Or Leida Miliu, who used to be his friend, who used to insist she didn't mind dying on the job, until her mother did. What a terrible way to go instead—without the glory of a fight but the quick plunge of a profane princess's blade. Perhaps he should be grateful that, at least, Calla offered him the fight.

Without another word, Calla leaves the arcade, her sleeves sweeping after her like twin streams of blood. In her absence, Anton can only shake his head, listening to the hum and the clank that surrounds him. "*Winner! Winner! Winner!*" that persistent machine hawks, and Anton finally gets to his feet with a heavy breath. Maybe it is a reminder directed at him. San-Er didn't make him their victor, but he won the king's games nonetheless.

Winner! Winner! Winner!

"I sure don't think so," he says, dragging a hand through his hair. The truth is, his fight with Calla never ended with the Juedou. If they've been exchanging blows since then, San-Er's victor is still pending.

Calla has long disappeared from the stairwell. He waits a moment, paranoid that she is there, hiding, having decided to take him by surprise and shut him up.

Nothing.

Anton makes the slow amble back to his room.

CHAPTER 18

While a slow rain creeps into the southern provinces that next morning, San-Er receives less than a drizzle, which trickles down the cramped building exteriors at such slow speed that the rivulets have practically dissipated by the time they reach ground level.

Yilas doesn't like it when it rains. Before she scrimped together enough money to get corrective surgery on her eyes, the world was always blurry. Perhaps she could have worn her glasses more often, but the cities were too damp, and if she clamped on a mask during the colder, plague-ridden months, her glasses would fog up constantly. It felt easier to walk around squinting, her brow furrowed in a permanent frown. Other attendants working the palace thought she was so rude. She never smiled at familiar faces when they passed each other in the hallways. Chami had once offered a solution by suggesting that Yilas smile at everyone she passed, and Yilas decided she preferred it if they thought her unbearable.

Her world is usually crystal clear these days. When it rains, though, it brings back some of those old feelings, that weight in her chest. The water on the windows smudges the lights into amorphous blots. Mist congeals the neon signs, forms a muggy veil over the city.

"Good morning." Chami descends from the apartment above the diner, walks over, and drops a kiss on Yilas's bare shoulder. They've got a few minutes before opening. "You're up early."

"Couldn't sleep," Yilas says. She cups her mug of tea closer to her chest. Sadly, it has gone cold since she made it. "I hope I didn't wake you."

Chami shakes her head, and a lock of her hair drops into her pink eyes. Instinctively, Yilas reaches to tug the lock, which makes Chami smile. She's always reminded Yilas of the godlings in their storybooks, the deities that haven't grown power-hungry enough to claim a title of their own but still flit about the world prettier than anything a mortal mind can comprehend.

"You can always wake me." Chami leans forward, her eyes closing again for a momentary rest when her cheek meets Yilas's arm. Yilas is still dressed in her pajamas, the worn fabric fraying at the left shoulder strap. Chami must notice the detail too, because she loops her finger through it and tugs once.

"Didn't I buy you new pajamas last month?"

"These are perfectly fine, I'll have you know."

"Yes, but"—Chami shifts, only to bite on Yilas's shoulder, taking a solid chomp—"you can also buy new clothes for the sake of it. The city isn't going to strike you down for that."

The logical part of Yilas knows that. The frightened part still lives in that palace, counting forward the months that her savings could last if she finally ditched the job. She could have it worse, she knows. She could have been born outside the wall. She could have been born without two parents who spent every day of her childhood making sure she had food. Still, working in the palace opened her eyes to how *some* of them were allowed to live, and perhaps she didn't have it that bad, but it would only take a small hole opening in her beat-up safety net to land her there.

"I'll wear the new ones tonight," Yilas promises.

"Great," Chami says. "I can't wait to take them off."

"*You—*"

A loud thud on the diner's doors cuts off the rest of her teasing reproach. Immediately, she and Chami prepare for the worst, lunging for a spatula and a fork, respectively. When the doors thud again, Yilas hears "*It's me! It's meeeeee!*" and she rolls her eyes, setting the spatula down.

Chami blinks. "Is that Matiyu?"

"It sure is," Yilas mutters. She goes to unlatch the glass door, then hurries her little brother into the diner. His face is entirely obscured under a mask and a low hat, but she'd know his voice anywhere, however muffled. "What are you doing here?"

"I can't stay at the palace anymore." With a huff, Matiyu starts yanking off his layers. He slaps the mask covering down onto the table. Chami winces and uses the fork still in her hand to scoop it up for the trash can.

"What happened?" Yilas asks. "It's hardly dawn."

"People are *dying*! There are bodies showing up everywhere!"

"I heard that was Calla," Chami calls from the kitchen, where she's depositing Matiyu's mask.

Matiyu plucks his wool hat off. "She only went after Leida Miliu. Calla's not even in San-Er anymore—the delegation set off yesterday. They took lots of Weisannas with them too. Terrible idea, because the palace is clearly vulnerable and under attack."

A small *meowr!* chirps from under his jacket.

Yilas blinks hard. "Did you kidnap Mao Mao from the palace?"

"*Kidnap?*" Matiyu yelps. He opens his jacket. Pliant as ever, Calla's cat slowly pokes his face out from the crook of Matiyu's arm, not the slightest bit stressed. "I *rescued* him. I was hoping you still had contact with Calla and could get a message to her."

"About Mao Mao?"

"No!" Matiyu exclaims. He lets Mao Mao emerge from his jacket, leaping to the floor. The cat sniffs a sticky puddle by the booth. "The murders, Yilas! In the palace!"

He pulls a disk out of his pocket. Chami waves Mao Mao over in the kitchen doorway, cooing about feeding him raw meat, and he patters to her on his fluffy paws. Matiyu tilts his head in that direction too, shaking the disk in his hand vigorously.

"I suppose you'd like to use the computer." Yilas stands where she is. Maybe if she doesn't offer, she'll never have to see whatever it is on that disk, and Matiyu's problems will simply dissolve into thin air.

"I didn't smuggle surveillance footage out of the palace for fun and games, that's for sure."

Barely suppressing a sigh, Yilas nods and waves him to the back room, where their computer is. She has a feeling she's not going to like this.

"You couldn't tell your superiors about this?"

"Well, Yilas"—Matiyu puts the disk into the system unit slot—"my superior is a Weisanna who oversees the section of the south wing that I help keep watch over. When I clocked in this morning and ran a glimpse over my cameras . . ."

He navigates to a folder that pops up on the desktop. It takes some loading, but the file is local, so there's no buffering when the computer system pulls it open on a video player. Matiyu thins his lips. He starts the footage.

The first notable observation is the dead guard lying in the middle of the room. His neck has turned at an unnatural angle. A vase has shattered beside him, fallen off a dining table. Yilas doesn't recognize the room itself, but the Palace of Union was built similarly to the Palace of Heavens. The table is particularly long, so it is likely one of the main dining rooms that the nobles use to take meals. In an hour or so, the cooks will be bringing food into the room, and then this body will be discovered.

"Heavens," Yilas breathes. "Matiyu, you *have* to report this to your superior."

"Has it not occurred to you yet what the problem is?" Matiyu stabs a finger at the screen. "That *is* my superior!"

Oh. Oh, dear. "Okay," Yilas says slowly. "Who is your superior's superior?"

Matiyu shakes his head. "When the Weisannas rearranged security within the twin cities, the palace was affected too. They had to rid any chance there would be another treasonous captain of the guard, so most of the Weisannas stand equal now. They all report to the king."

"Find an equal, then. Someone who knows what to do."

"I'm *scared*," Matiyu hisses. "It's only rumors, but I've been catching bits and pieces from the Weisannas these last few days about attacks around the palace. They're never going to tell us the truth if there's something wrong."

Yilas laces her fingers in front of her. She stares at the image on the screen. It's still playing, though nothing is happening. Matiyu has pasted over a few minutes. Perhaps by now the body has already been discovered.

"What do you want me to do?" Yilas asks. "Get the message to Calla, have her running back to protect the palace? She carries a cellular phone, but I don't know if I'd reach her from inside San-Er."

Chami pokes her head into the back room then. She's frowning, concerned by the conversation. "Also, Calla said her traveling phone was for *extreme* emergencies."

"This *is* an extreme emergency," Matiyu insists. "Look." He clicks on a second file he dragged onto the disk. The video player pulls open the infirmary. Yilas doesn't know what she's looking at. With the way Chami draws closer and scrunches her nose, she can't tell either.

"At the back," Matiyu prompts, "six beds have pulled the sheets over their occupants. Dead bodies."

"To be fair," Chami says, "two of the bodies are likely Leida Miliu."

"Meowr," Mao Mao agrees from her feet.

"When there are more people around and it's safer, I'm going to go back into the palace and obtain footage that traces how they all died," Matiyu says. "Because I'm willing to bet they're guards, and something is happening to wipe them out."

The screen is starting to hurt Yilas's eyes. She shifts back. Extends her hands for Mao Mao and picks up the cat after he hurries over to her.

"I don't understand—you want to warn Calla about guards dying in the palace?"

"It doesn't really make sense, anyhow," Chami adds. "The palace may have loosened its entry since August took power, but employees and approved visitors still need to input their identity number at the turnstiles. Every entrance remains watched. If guards are dying, then someone authorized to enter the palace is doing it."

Matiyu goes quiet, thinking. Her brother doesn't often follow beats of logic: he prefers to hit a conclusion first and *then* go back to connect the pieces. It's great when it comes to solving problems at school and finishing his tests fast. Not so great when he's claiming there's a conspiracy unfolding at the heart of their capital.

"Look, I don't know how it's happening," Matiyu decides, hitting eject for the disk. "But *someone* needs to know that there might be a coup coming. What else could this be leading toward? What happens when there are no guards left?"

Anyone who wants to enter the palace can march right in.

"Exactly," Matiyu says to Yilas's expression, though she has spoken nothing aloud. "Get word to Calla as quickly as you can. I'll go get the rest of the footage, but I'm sleeping here from now on."

CHAPTER 19

For two days on the road, they encounter only peace and quiet through Talin's provinces.

Calla keeps her ears perked for chatter from the locals. She expects to hear gossip about travel surges beginning. Underground efforts to gather their best adventurers together and head for the borderlands. But the rural dwellers are much better at keeping mum than she expected, because Calla barely hears a peep. The silence can't be because the provinces have absolutely no interest in intercepting the crown. Perhaps the Dovetail's influence is widespread out here, and the people are doing their part not to ruin their plans.

Calla wipes sweat off her temple. Their surroundings have started to change from the flat fields of Eigi to the copses of trees farther north. They must be somewhere in the dead center of Leysa now, clattering through a dense forest along the Apian Routes. Though Calla rides near the third carriage and hovers safely at the middle of the delegation, she's not paying as much attention as she should. They're going so slowly—it'll likely be another week before they get to the borderlands, and that's already generous. In a week under her command, she would have reached Rincun by now. She *did*, in fact, last time she checked.

Her left ear thrums. Calla winces, her shoulder lifting to press against her eardrum. In these two days, her qi has mostly behaved too. She doesn't know what triggers the outbursts, but there may be more to come given she hasn't washed the sigil off her chest. She can feel its presence starkly. Not because she's a little dirty—though she is. The sensation is more akin to a light pulsation, just beneath the skin.

"Highness, a little to the left, please."

Calla grimaces, pulling her horse into alignment at the guard's prompt. Underfoot, the gravel has turned rough and sharp. It's been quite some time since the route was built—before the war, most definitely—yet the stones haven't worn down. She throws a look over her shoulder, catching the guard's eye.

"Pan, is it?"

Pan nods. He seems pleased that Calla remembers his name.

She gestures to the carriage beside her. "Not to toss blame, but this keeps gravitating closer and closer to me. What's going on? Where did we hire these drivers?"

The third carriage driver frowns atop his horse, clearly offended, but he doesn't say anything.

"It's not his fault, Highness," Pan replies. "There are probably eight people piled in there. The carriage is overloaded."

That doesn't seem right. Most of the guards are riding in accompaniment, so it is only councilmembers and staff within the carriages. With only eight councilmembers and roughly double the amount of attendants to aid their travel, surely there would be better distribution than that.

As Calla counts the vehicles, Pan must notice where her thoughts are going.

"Oh, the last carriage is empty," he tacks on. "King August's orders."

That last carriage would most certainly not be left empty for a journey like this. What did Anton bring with him?

"You're leaning again."

"Sorry, sorry," Calla grumbles, steering her horse to walk straight.

They ride onward. Overhead, the spindly ends of the tree branches wave in tune to their procession of hooves and wheels. Leysa's trees will stay green all year round. Just as San-Er hardly gets too cold—only wet and sweaty—Leysa is always slightly humid, bringing little change between seasons.

Calla remembers the first time she saw the forests. That earliest carriage ride from Rincun into San-Er, she forced herself to clamp down on her awe, craning her neck up and up and up to follow the claws stretching for the clouds.

Rincun doesn't grow many trees.

Midday turns to afternoon. The skies thicken with quiet gusts of an easterly wind. Along the Apian Routes, there are pockets where the two sides of trees will crowd so closely they block out the daylight, and other pockets where the trees only grow short and straight, letting in plenty of the skies.

Calla feels the disturbance in the forest before she sees anything.

A chill skates along her shoulders. She's irritated for a moment, suspecting that her qi is acting up again. She gives her left ear a harsh tug. The sting eases the prickle. Then the chill comes again, and her chest pulses hard.

She has no idea what incites her to do what she does next. Instinct tells her to put her index finger on the sharp edge of the saddle and press hard until she draws blood. When the trees rustle again, she hears it ten times as loudly. When the gravel path tremors underfoot, Calla pulls her horse to a sudden stop, listening.

There's a turn coming ahead. The forest will rise in elevation, and Leysa's fork of the Apian Routes pivots left on an acute angle to reach Talin's main river.

"Your Highness," Pan calls behind her. "Why have you—"

Calla leaps off her horse. "Get ahold of him," she shouts, gesturing to the reins she abandoned. "Halt! Everybody else, halt, right *now*!"

Her command echoes through the forest with explosive force. She sprints along the line of guards and carriages, hurrying for the front of the delegation line where the Weisannas leading the movement turn to look at her, concerned. Galipei is among them, directing his horse around quickly. By then Calla has already hurtled past him, skidding to a stop.

"Give me a crossbow."

The instruction doesn't leave room for argument. Though Galipei looks hesitant, he reaches into the weapons bag hanging off his horse and throws a crossbow at her, then the accompanying bolts. Calla catches the bow with one hand, secures the bag of bolts with the other. Before she's scarcely steadied her grip, she's loading the crossbow, aiming forward, and breathing out.

"Princess!"

Anton's voice. August's voice. She's left a smear of blood on the crossbow. Though she registers movement behind her—carriage doors opening and councilmembers wanting to see what is happening—she doesn't waste effort asking them to return. She puts every iota of focus she has on watching . . . watching . . .

Calla fires. Just as she pulls the trigger, she adjusts her aim, pointing higher than she needs.

The delegation, together, watches the bolt soar through the air. It fires straight while the road starts to bend; it hurtles into the trees right as a breeze blows in from the east, but because Calla has adjusted for the interruption, it pierces perfectly into the camouflaged man perched on a tree branch.

He cries out. Falls to the ground. So, too, does the veil he was holding in place, and when the large swath of camouflage drops, it reveals the people waiting in the forest, clutching swords.

Calla shoots forward without waiting for the guards, drawing her own sword from her belt. She trusts herself more than she trusts anyone here, and given that she ruined this surprise attack, there's only a brief moment when their opponents will be in disarray before they organize into a new formation. The Weisannas are yelling for the palace guards to take position. For the councilmembers to get back inside. Calla catches "*Your Majesty, you* cannot *be out here.*"

It must twist Anton up to have to feign incompetence. The Palace of Earth did not train August Shenzhi in the same way the Palace of Heavens trained Calla, so August shouldn't know his way around a sword. Maybe that's why

Kasa was the one who survived longer, the one smart enough to shut himself away after the mess the other palace made.

Calla slashes hard, charging into the offense. With barely any time to swing momentum into her arm, Calla cuts down one man. Ducks a woman's attack, parries for two clangs before she sees an opening, and plunges her sword through the woman's ribs. There couldn't have been more than twenty hiding in the trees. A small number have rushed out onto the road, while others pivoted and used the trees to go around, but it'll be harder to attack the delegation with the palace guards at the ready. If Calla hadn't caught the veil, then they might have broken in from the sides. Now all they have is brute force, but the numbers are on the palace's side.

Calla hauls her sword out of the woman. Blood arcs from the motion, falls like a sheet of rain onto her shoes. Though the woman coughs out a viscous spatter too, darkening her deep-green garb, she speaks nothing before she falls. No threat, no battle cry. Nothing to indicate what they're attacking for or where they came from.

Nothing to indicate whether this is the Dovetail, as Calla has been waiting for. But why *here*?

"Shit," Calla mutters.

A collision of metal draws her attention into the trees. The guards have joined the fray. Calla moves rapidly, plunging through the gaps of the forest and wincing against the sharp lower branches scratching her face. Beyond the scream of battle and the in-out panting of her breath, it's the unfamiliar thicket underfoot that rustles loudest. Her maneuvers do not change from the way she navigates San-Er, despite how substantially different the environments are. The cities swap bark for steel, dig up earth and let buildings put down roots instead, but Talin is a kingdom made up of labyrinths all the same. Here, Calla slams herself through a narrow space between trees, and just as she emerges into a small clearing, she barges in on a fighter getting the upper hand over a Weisanna. The guard hits the ground, fight finished. His opponent has enough momentum that he swings at Calla in the same exhale.

"Who are you?" Calla demands. "Who sent you?"

The man raises his sword. He doesn't spit curses or launch into a rallying cry. He plunges downward; when Calla dodges, he's quick to slash left to right, moving with untrained technique but fiercely strong conviction.

In another life, maybe Calla would have joined this group. The girl she was, rather—the one who's been lost, a name vanished into the wind. If she'd survived Rincun, she might have wanted more, might have traveled the kingdom to thank the gods for keeping her alive, plotting an attack on the capital to set the scene for Talin's liberation.

But in this life, Calla Tuoleimi is sick of messes in her way when she's trying to clean up a bigger one. For the grander survival of each small village dotting the kingdom, she will throw sacrifices onto the pyre. She was willing to kill eighty-seven civilians in the cities. She looked Leida Miliu in the eye before gutting her. Twenty nameless fighters in the forest is nothing. The heavens will understand their mission being cut short.

Calla ducks. She feels the sword meet her hair, taking off a lock that didn't move as fast as the rest of her. The metals thuds against a thin trunk; her dark hairs flutter into the twigs and sodden leaves. Before the man can tug his weapon from the bark, Calla returns the blow.

She hears metal scrape flesh. The man throws out an elbow, interrupting Calla's sword, but it's too late. An inch is a mile on an artery. Skin splits open; blood spurts in an instant. Before Calla can step back, slick liquid gets in her eyes, trickles down her throat as thickly as sludge. Though she swipes at her face and pulls away fast to break the close proximity, it takes a terrifying few seconds to clear her sight, to swallow down the pungent taste.

Palace training never covered this about battle. They taught her patterns of attack, pointed out technical calculations and logical flaws, but she learned desperation on her own. After the Palace of Heavens fell, the council deliberated for months before confirming it was Calla Tuoleimi who committed the massacre. *An intruder, surely,* half of the nobility argued. The princess on the surveillance footage fought with reckless abandon, and they didn't remember teaching that. They didn't remember giving her anger.

She knows this is what makes her good. She also knows this is what the palace tries to beat out of its generals, because desperation is fast, but it's also blinding.

A whisper, at her side. Calla brings her sword up, but someone else has blocked the attack for her. There are two new fighters on scene—when the second rears around to swing, Calla goes low, opting for a brute-force stab to push him off-balance.

"Calla, give me room."

Irritation prickles in her chest. Instead of making room, she changes her attack. Her opponent is still fighting despite his critical wound. She swerves to his other side and pushes him right in Anton's way, just as Anton incapacitates the first. He has a split second to flash a look of disbelief her way. Then he cuts down the second man too.

"What was *that*?" Anton demands. His voice booms through the trees. While their immediate surroundings have cleared, the sound of conflict rings loud at the tree line.

"What are you doing?" Calla fires back. She swivels around. Continues scanning the forest for movement. "You're going to get caught."

Anton Makusa has found himself a sword, likely filched from one of the Weisannas. It's a bizarre sight: August's level expression paired with the splatter of Anton's battle lust. Anyone looking upon him in this moment would know that he is an invader.

"I came here to help *you*." Anton swings his sword. "The Palace of Earth taught the basics, Princess."

That is how Anton Makusa learned to fight. But August Shenzhi did not go through the same teachings. August Shenzhi is a golden vase of the palace, protected by Galipei instead of his own glistening skin.

"You—" Calla's attention swivels to the right. There's a phantom click a few paces away. A hunched figure behind a bush, pointing something silver directly at them.

She shoves in front of Anton and throws her hand out. In that moment Calla isn't thinking of a command. She barely knows what she's trying to do, but she remembers her fight during the flash flood alarms, the way the brute of a man hadn't touched her, yet struck her hard enough to send her flying. She remembers the Hollow Temple and Pampi Magnes moving the world around her by mere gesture.

The air heaves. Just as a projectile flies from the attacker's weapon, it shoots backward instead, a flame engulfing the trees.

Heat flares hot and fast. When the smoke clears, Calla's throat closes tight, matching the vacuum in her chest.

"What the fuck?" Anton breathes. "That was gunpowder. It could have killed you."

A whisper hums at the base of her skull, splits to snake down the two sides of her arms, jolts at the rough surface of her elbows. It wants to wake up. It wants to wreak its full power.

"Get back."

Anton stares at her, unmoving. He can sense it. The air warps around her, refracting and shivering as it does above an open flame. Heavens, the pain, the *pain*—

"Calla," he says.

Calla gasps for breath, propping her palm against a tree for balance. Their surroundings suction with the impression of the atmosphere disappearing, and though it returns near instantly, the branches shudder to recover. Anton isn't as fortunate to experience a mere shudder. Without anything to root him in place, he skids back and collides with a thin tree trunk. He stills for a moment. The air clears.

And Anton lunges forward, swinging his sword at her.

"Hey!" Calla bellows. She barely manages to deflect the hit. "What are you—*fuck*—"

"Do that again."

"Stop it," she hisses, blocking his next strike. The reverberation travels to her very bones.

Anton gears up to swing again. When he wipes a splatter of blood off his cheek, it smears, running a dark line from the corner of his eye to his mouth. "Fight me off."

Fuck. Calla swings messily to counter his sword. She has never wanted any of this. She would have rather buried herself in the rocks of the sea than choose their current predicament. But it's impossible to start backtracking when she's already a thousand miles deep into dirty work. Just as it is impossible for her and Anton to stop antagonizing one another when they have each other's blood and guts spread in buckets between them. She keeps fighting him, but she's only here to keep him safe. She possesses such hatred for the crown and the way its fingers stretch from the electric wires in San-Er to the plain soil in Rincun, so why is she *here* when he doesn't even want her?

"You're out of your"—she narrowly avoids an overarm slash—"*mind.*"

"Let me see, Calla. Show me how you're doing this."

Her chest racks with new pain. A physical tearing sensation, like scissors slicing through the stem of her lungs. Her fingers spasm. Fine. *Fine.*

Calla drops her sword. "Okay."

"Okay?" Anton echoes in threat. They make a picture of stark contrast when he lifts his sword steadily. Raises it high, over his head, creating what should be a perfect arc down. "Pick up. Your weapon."

She went wrong long before she started on this crusade, from the first moment she decided to blame someone for Rincun, from that decision to enter the palace and take revenge into her own hands one day. If she wanted proper revenge, she should have prayed to the gods and asked for Talin to be incinerated off the map.

Anton lunges for the swing.

There's nothing more to do. He is angry. He is looking for an excuse to strike. And so Calla braces with her arm over her head. All she can think to use in her last line of defense is a carnal, mortal body.

A heavy *thud* strikes the ground.

Seconds pass. The fight continues in the distance. The opinionated hiss of the wind and the curious thorny branches are their only spectators.

Slowly, Calla peels her eyes open. Lowers her arm.

"It seems unfair, doesn't it?"

She doesn't look like she's been cut. As far as she can tell, each part of her remains intact, each beat of her rapid heart pulsing when it needs to.

"What does?" she asks. Her voice comes in a rasp.

"You killed me. You killed me, and yet I can't seem to strike you without feeling the wound as my own." He takes a step toward her. Without a doubt, Anton Makusa has stopped fighting, because as furious as his expression is, there are tears in his eyes. "Tell me this is some part of your work. Tell me you communed with the old gods and did this to me. What strength have you acquired that I lack?"

Calla shakes her head. The pain eases from her chest. The horrible thrumming fades from her ears.

"Is that what you think?" she returns. "The arena was the worst crime I have ever committed. I would have answered for it with my life. I still can."

She almost misses it: a flash of movement, incoming from the tree line. Deep green that blends with the forest instead of city-alley black, which means it is an attacker instead of reinforcements, heading right for them.

Two thoughts flash in her mind.

One, Anton won't turn around in time. Two, if she doesn't stop the attacker, it ends here—the palace collapses, and Talin . . .

But before her very eyes, the man *freezes*. His limbs lock, and Calla blinks in sheer incomprehension as he starts to fall, knees unmoving when anybody else's instinct would be to lunge forward and catch himself.

A blade flies from the left. It lands in his throat, as smooth as shearing through dough, and embeds to the hilt. The man collapses. As soon as Calla's gaze swivels wide in search of the culprit, she makes direct eye contact with Otta

Avia, who is standing between two stout trees, one hand holding back her long sleeve and the other still in the air from making the throw. Otta offers a smile.

Anton turns around, following Calla's line of sight. The battle has reached its last dregs, guards fanning deep into the trees and examining the premises. By the time Anton spots Otta too, the palace guards arrive in the vicinity, asking Otta to please return to the carriage. Galipei emerges among them, performing a fast inventory.

Calla charges forward.

"*You*," she snarls, pointing at Otta. She gets a few strides in before Galipei blocks her path. Calla tries to circle around. In response, Galipei grabs her properly, making a valiant effort to rein her back.

"Calla, this is unnecessary—"

"You did this." Calla has no proof. She's aware that she makes her accusation without proof, but she would much prefer to gather evidence after she's gotten her hands around Otta's slim white neck—

"I *saved* August," Otta calls from the trees. "*You* were about to let him die."

"I saw him coming. I had it handled!" Calla returns.

"Enough! Enough!" Galipei bellows. "Your Majesty, are you all right?"

One of the Weisannas picks up the sword Anton was using, shaking it free from the thistle. Another retrieves Calla's, then turns a questioning look her way. The forest is unnaturally quiet while they wait for his answer.

"I'm all right," Anton says plainly. Any tortured expression of his has disappeared. There's no sign of Anton Makusa.

The others in the clearing may not see it, but Galipei stiffens. He is still holding Calla steady; she senses the muscles in his arms prepare in defense, almost as though he didn't hear what he wanted to.

Galipei is suspicious. Of course he is. It was only going to be a matter of time until Galipei caught on that something was off, but what about *that* answer prompted the realization?

"You fought," the Weisanna holding Anton's sword says.

Anton's gaze flickers to Calla. "Princess Calla did most of the work. I hope I offered help."

"That's what *we're* here for, Majesty." Galipei, succeeding in redirecting the confrontation, releases Calla. He gestures rapidly at the other guards, and they go to lead Otta away, plucking her from the scene before Calla can lunge again.

Galipei doesn't glance at Calla when he takes her sword from one of the other Weisannas. He doesn't meet her eyes when he passes it back to her.

"In the future," he says, still speaking to his king, "there is no need for you to get involved."

Calla takes the sword.

"Understood," Anton says.

"All right. Let's return."

Galipei prompts Anton away from the clearing, returning to the delegation. Wind blows through the branches, and Calla feels a cool drop of liquid move along her arm. It's only when she looks that she sees the tear on her jacket and the first prickle of pain begins to smart on her upper arm. She grimaces, grabbing the cuff of her sleeve, and finds blood pooling inside her sleeve, dripping to her wrist. Someone cut her. She didn't even notice the sting.

Calla stands where she is. At this point, almost everyone has trudged out of the trees. A guard makes another summons, calling for her to move along.

Everything moved so fast. The attacker, running in. Otta from a distance, throwing that knife. Otta from a distance, using her qi to stop the man in his steps and render him entirely immobile.

Calla's teeth are gritted so hard that her jaw hurts.

"*Bitch*," she manages under her breath.

CHAPTER 20

The story goes like this.

There was a queen, many years ago, who didn't accept death for her final fate. Time has lost track of whether she was a Tuoleimi or a Shenzhi—the two family lines have been interchangeable for a while now, long enough that no one remembers what color eyes the Shenzhis might have started with before being swallowed up by Tuoleimi yellow. The Dovetail tell this story to the children they're teaching to jump when the gene kicks in. *Don't envision the limits,* they say. *The moment you expect a ceiling, your head will bump against it.*

Each time Bibi overheard the Dovetail embellish certain details for atmosphere, she had to hold in her laugh. The provinces don't have any grasp of the palace or what it is like. There are some details they make up that are entirely preposterous—toilets made of gold or crystal-studded windows. Machines that wait on royalty hand and foot or all-knowing sentience by the guards who patrol the hallways. Details aside, though, the larger story does the trick. The children stop believing what the kingdom says about mortal limitations.

Once, a queen knew that death was coming for her. Depending on who tells the story, it was either an early ground invasion from Sica or an internal coup from those she trusted most. The enemy was creeping closer, and she was out of time. She had always had the favor of the gods. Her qi was powerful—enough to fight at the front line when there was conflict between the unconquered provinces, enough to lead her soldiers herself and crush them to dust if they stepped out of line.

She prayed to the gods for the most defiant feat she could imagine. Forget jumping without a flash of light. Forget sending out a blast of qi as a mode of attack.

The queen wanted to be reincarnated after her death.

Bibi pauses at the end of the palace corridor, stopping to check her bangs in the reflective surface of a flower vase. Two attendants pass in the other direction without offering her a second glance. She proceeds onward.

This part of the story is what makes it believable. The Dovetail have always frowned upon violence as a method of sacrifice. They'll go as far as to say that if the sacrifice is unwilling, the gods refuse to listen. But Bibi knows. Death, no matter how it is dealt, is enough to catch a god's attention. Their ego comes first, and they'll smell blood the moment it splatters. When the queen conjured the prayer for reincarnation, she asked an entire village of her civilians to sacrifice themselves. Her life—it mattered to preserve it, she argued. There was no entitlement in the request. She had the privilege of being their queen, so she also had the burden of seeking their last route to victory. She would isolate the spirit of her qi and ask the gods not to let this be the last time she could fight for them. If they loved her, they would do this.

They did.

Hundreds of villagers laid themselves to rest, quietly going into the night. Their graves were dug, their gravestones carved by their own hands. When the queen's enemies came for her, she didn't resist. *Our victory is slated for the future,* she promised. *I will return, and your sacrifice will be worthwhile.*

A life is short. Legacy is forever.

The story doesn't really have an ending in any version that the Dovetail tell. Some conspire that she never came back; others swear they have heard accounts that she was reborn a generation later and wreaked havoc on her enemies. A few, even, have speculated that Princess Calla Tuoleimi is the reborn queen—though the terms of her sacrifice were that she would maintain her qi and the memory of her past life, so that doesn't hold water, short of being a rather interesting conspiracy. Surely Calla Tuoleimi has never heard this story before. When the wall was built, it didn't only keep out the province migrants. City civilians were banned from telling such frivolous stories about the gods.

Bibi reaches the surveillance room. How advanced the technology in the cities seems again, after she has spent so long in the provinces. Bright color created by pixels and movement mimicked in captured light. Wondrous.

"I will return," she whispers in echo.

"Excuse me. Did you need something?"

The summons draws her attention away from the large display screen, and she remembers where she is and what she's doing. There's a food tray in her hands. She has come to distribute bowls of rice for the palace employees working in surveillance, and Bibi hurries to get back on task.

"So very sorry," she says brightly. "I'm new."

"Are you?" The employee at the cubicle takes the bowl offered to him. "I thought I saw you last week too."

"That's still new. At least give me a year before expecting me to know my way around."

The employee quirks a brow, then turns back to work. Humming under her breath, Bibi finishes distributing to one row of cubicles, then circles around to the other side. The air conditioner in the corner of the room chugs heartily, struggling to keep up with the humidity building outside. She eyes the machines blinking against the wall, counting how many access ports each face has. The funny thing about the Palace of Union is that it possesses far more capabilities than it ever uses. King Kasa liked the ability to see well if he needed to, and he rarely needed to.

Bibi plugs a memory stick into an access port when she passes by. She continues distributing rice.

"... don't think this is evidence? This screams *suspicious*!"

"It's a guard forgoing his identity number, Matiyu. No one is going to take that as evidence."

Bibi slows, drawing nearer to the cubicle that sits second to the end. A palace employee is leaning close to his screen. A woman hovers over his shoulder, her lips pursed. They both have the same jade-green eyes. Siblings.

"Why didn't he type it in, then?"

"He clearly *knows* the guard keeping watch. It's laziness, not a murderer in the palace halls."

Oh, dear. Bibi shuffles just a bit closer and carefully sets down a bowl of rice in the cubicle next to the siblings. Her eyes swivel. She can't be too obvious, lest they realize she's spying.

"Yilas, I swear—"

The woman—Yilas—pushes away from the cubicle. "I have to get back to the diner. I'll keep trying the signal to Calla's phone, but I think we should leave out this stuff about a fake guard. She's going to think you're making it up."

"What!"

The seated employee spins too fast. Just as Bibi is leaning over to set the rice down, his elbow knocks into her, and the bowl goes flying. It isn't as bad as it could be. Yilas lunges forward to catch the bowl before it smashes to the ground. Half the rice stays inside.

"Oh no!" Bibi cries.

"You're fine, don't worry." The siblings are quick to grab a tissue and scoop up the discarded rice. Bibi extends her tray, and the brother—Matiyu—places the tissues on it.

"My fault," he says. "Thank you." To Yilas, he adds, "I'll search further. Maybe I can find more before tonight."

Yilas nods. While Bibi moves on, dropping the tissues into the trash can in the corner, she keeps track of which direction the woman is going. She counts a few seconds. Then, she circles back to the memory stick, plucks it out, and exits the surveillance room with her tray beneath her arm. She's supposed to find a new body now, make a quick exit out. She slips the memory stick into her pocket.

Around the next corner, she catches up with Yilas.

"Hello."

Though Yilas turns to look, her stride doesn't slow. Her bangs are dyed purple, nudging into the green of her eyes at every small movement of her head.

"Can I help you?"

"I didn't mean to eavesdrop, but I heard a bit of that conversation back there," Bibi says, keeping up with Yilas's pace. "When you said *Calla*, I don't suppose you were talking about Her Highness Princess Calla, were you?"

Yilas furrows her brow. "That's none of your business."

"Come on," Bibi whines. "Do you know if she's single? I only want to ask if she would go for a drink with me."

"She—*what?*"

The look that overtakes Yilas's face is full of such absurd disbelief that she forgets to be suspicious. Bibi is in.

"I suppose it's fine if not." Bibi sighs. "Maybe you would like to go for a drink instead?"

"For a—*no!*" Yilas splutters. "I have a girlfriend."

"Oh. A shame."

Yilas glances over her shoulder, as though she's checking whether anyone can overhear their conversation. The corridors around surveillance tend not to be busy. Nobles don't like how loud the wires are. They'll steer clear unless there's something they need.

"Who are you?" Yilas asks. She's recovered her hard expression, but it's too late. She's already confirmed to Bibi that she is in contact with the princess. "Your eyes. They're familiar."

Bibi shrugs. "Black eyes aren't uncommon."

"Don't tell me you're related to the king," Yilas continues pressing. Perhaps she aims to redirect the conversation. Scrub over what she admitted and hope that Bibi didn't take note. "I didn't think His Majesty had any more relatives."

"No. I'm not related to August Shenzhi."

Bibi slides a note out of her sleeve and passes it to Yilas. The moment Yilas takes it, hesitantly, Bibi stops walking and pivots. She's needed in the east wing. New body. New mission.

"For you. Consider it, would you?"

CHAPTER 21

After the attack, Otta is unusually quiet through the remaining carriage ride.

Anton doesn't notice at first, and in all honesty, he's busy enough trying to decipher what the fuck just happened. The delegation rides frantically through Leysa Province, aiming for Lankil Province across the long Jinzi Bridge before nightfall. Their original plan for the evening was to turn west and cross between provinces, where they could find lodging at the house that Councilmember Diseau owns in Janton Province. Given the possibility there were more attackers in the vicinity, though, it felt worthwhile to travel north quickly rather than stay in the area.

They're almost to the Jinzi River. Anton risks a glance through the window. He catches flashes of movement, but they're going at a pace fast enough to render riders and horses blurry with the burgeoning night. The sky is awash with deep orange—the horizon's setting sun slowly suppressed by the burgeoning dark.

He should have swung the sword.

Calla had been at his mercy. Her weapon was down. She'd practically begged to answer for her crime, palms open.

But if he wanted to, he could have put in the command days ago. The moment he found himself in that throne room, gasping while his qi settled into August's body, he could have ordered that Calla stay locked up and ready her execution. He didn't. Of course he didn't.

It's not that he wants her dead, not really. He wants her on his side.

Anton's eyes flicker across the carriage seats and land on Otta. Their vehicle lurches, the terrain changing from rough dirt to even stone. The bridge across the Jinzi River has stood for longer than their kingdom keeps records, built in the earliest years the moment there was travel between the north and the south. When the wheels lurch again and run onto smooth ground, they've finally found themselves in Lankil Province. The upper half of Talin, which the Palace of Heavens used to govern.

"You're staring."

Anton, slowly, reaches over. He loops his finger into Otta's sleeve and lifts it slightly to show her the small blot of blood there.

"You really shouldn't have entered the fight."

"This again." Otta rolls her eyes. "Relax, Majesty, I wasn't intruding on anyone's commands or anything of the like. You needed the help."

"I didn't. I don't *need* anything."

In fact, his bitterest innermost voice says, *you're supposed to need* me.

The carriage slows. Before it's pulled to a stop entirely, Anton gets to his feet and flings open the door, drawing protest from the two guards inside. The air is cool on his face. His neck has flushed underneath his jacket collar, sweat sticking to the nice fabrics.

Upon sighting him, the nearest Weisanna outside hops off his horse. The second carriage is immediately a frenzy when the door opens and the occupants bring out the injured. Most of the guards who fought against the attack will be fine. Scrapes and flesh wounds that need cleaning and wrapping.

"Talk to me," Anton says to the Weisanna.

"We have six casualties."

They counted five guards dead at the scene of the attack, but a sixth was bleeding out. Though the provinces are often short of resources, where there is a yamen, there must also be a healer. They'd hoped that he might hold out until they reached the yamen in the center of the province.

He didn't make it, then.

Anton tilts his head to the trees. "We'll dig graves. Bring them this way. Get them out of sight from the attendants; I don't want anyone fainting and hitting their head."

The Weisanna nods and disperses the instructions. The shield of night should give them an advantage when making camp out in the open. Though the delegation debated whether it was safe to find a random clearing off the main road after they crossed into Lankil, the numbers were on their side, and it was unlikely any rural group would best them in outright confrontation. The palace had brought almost double the number of guards as they had charges who needed protecting. Eight councilmembers, eighteen staff. Fifty guards, down to forty-four, ten of whom are standing in for the usual royal guard to accompany the king at all times. It ought to be perfectly fine. The only other option within traveling distance was an abandoned city that used to function as Lankil's capital, and the likelihood of getting crushed by prewar infrastructure while sleeping there overnight was far higher than getting attacked by a province group in the open.

Anton starts to trudge toward the trees. He feels Otta slinking up beside him before he hears her; the goose bumps at the back of his neck raise in warning before she actually curls her hand upon his shoulder.

"I'll say a few words," she says, "to lay them to rest."

"That really isn't necessary."

"Of course it is."

He had seven years to lay her to rest. If he had done so earlier, perhaps he wouldn't remain beholden to her now. Perhaps he would have found some other purpose in exile and never met Calla in the games either.

The guards begin to dig graves in the soft soil around the trees. To ensure their safety overnight, the Weisannas are surveying the perimeter, and Anton can see their movement through the thicket too. The councilmembers, meanwhile, remain in conversation at the roadside—something peculiar must be visible along the horizon, because they're whispering about how much they miss San-Er and how much they hate seeing this space go to waste. It's good that Lankil's councilmember didn't attend the delegation, or else they would be furious hearing these suggestions that are clearly economically infeasible.

"That should be fine," Anton says when the graves are deep enough.

The guards go to fetch the bodies. Otta turns absently to watch them push back through the trees. She hums a tune under her breath until they've disappeared. Then, she says:

"You should sacrifice them."

"I'm sorry?"

She tilts her head to the graves. "You managed it in the arena. You must know the power it can offer you."

Anton raises his fingers to his temples. He presses hard, applying the pressure to think, but it's also to get Otta out of his view, to use his hands to shield her away until he can resist the urge to snap at her.

"I'm not going to do that."

"It's lucky that the attacking group wasn't using their qi. If they strike again, you should know how to combat them. Once you have the crown, it'll give you inhuman strength. I can teach you more then."

"Otta." Anton faces her firmly, putting his hands behind his back. "This isn't . . . I don't think we're after the same goal here."

Otta's looking at her sleeve. She tucks it in once, then again to hide the stain. "How do you mean?"

The guards haven't returned yet with the bodies. The trees are whistling in accompaniment to Otta's jaunty tune from before, their flowering branches waving with the wind.

"I was hardly aware you knew this much about qi," he says, "and suddenly you're promoting yourself to my teacher. That's not going to work for me."

"You have no choice," Otta replies easily. "August is too strong. If you don't make the active effort to combat him, he'll overpower you with time."

"He'll *over*—" Anton cuts himself off, refusing to parrot her in his bewilderment. "Enough. If what you say is true, the crown will give me unlimited power. I require no additional teachings."

Now Otta is frowning. Her eyes swivel fast—the guards are returning. She has less than a few seconds to get her retort in before they are overheard.

"Why are you being stubborn about this? You didn't used to be this way."

"Yes, I used to listen to every word out of your mouth," Anton returns. When he thinks back to his last memory with Otta, she still looks the same. Yet when he looks into a mirror, he has changed countless times over. "Then you left me. I went into exile because of you, and you don't think that takes a toll? I can't be with you as we were, Otta. I won't ever be again."

Six dead bodies from the first half of the journey. The provinces are dangerous. People used to the comfort of the capital could never make it out here alone.

Otta stares him down. He expected a volatile argument, but there's barely any reaction save for a small frown turning down the corners of her pink lips.

The guards come back and settle the dead into their graves.

"Fine," she says. "I planned otherwise, anyway."

Before Anton can ask what on earth she is talking about, Otta pivots and flutters out from the trees. He lets her go.

◇◇◇◇◇

Lankil's former capital looms in the distance.

Calla bites on her thumbnail, suppressing a sigh. She wants a cigarette. She should have bought a pack before they left San-Er, because heavens knows where she can find any out here. Certainly not in what used to qualify as cities in the provinces.

Wind blows into her eyes, harshly enough for her to tear up. The moon clears behind a cloud. Silver glitters along the horizon.

There remain ten or so abandoned cities in provincial Talin: prewar settlements that were evacuated when or shortly after Sica invaded. This city in Lankil doesn't appear to have collapsed entirely, but it cannot have withstood the test of time either. Before the war, there was at least one city in each province, if not multiple in the provinces that were wealthiest. When Sica invaded, civilians either fled to San-Er, the last stronghold, or moved to the rural villages, where lifestyles were simpler. The luxuries of a city were too expensive to maintain—they couldn't keep the water pipes or electricity grids going. After the war, there simply weren't enough people left in the cities to rebuild.

Late-night documentaries in San-Er will sometimes run footage of abandoned cities that travelers took decades ago. Calla has watched a few in her sleepless hours, squinting at the screen with Mao Mao in her lap. They always seemed so uncanny. San-Er might have looked like this too, once. Buildings that rose proud with natural materials: browns and reds and yellows absorbing blue skies and rays of sunshine. Trees planted by the sidewalks. Grand arches and paved roads, a bird's-eye view that made sense when overlooking the city. While these places were left to languish, San-Er took all of their burdens. San-Er was forced to grow new limbs that festered between old ones, replaced warm wooden beams with harsh, unyielding steel. It braced its favored ground for people, for people, for an unending influx of people, and it has become ruination in the process.

Calla bites harder on her nail, staring intently at the shape of the city from afar. It does little to soothe her tension. She has so much volatile energy that she would chew off her own hand if she could, but that probably wouldn't grow back in the same way her nails will.

Who were they? Why launch an attack in the forest, of all places?

If Calla hadn't caught the telltale whiff of their presence, she doubts that they would have succeeded in killing a king—if that was even their goal—but they would have taken out a lot more of the delegation than six guards. Situating themselves on the curve of the road meant they were waiting for the delegation to pass by. It would have been difficult for the numbers at the front to see anything if the back had been attacked. The group was trying to incite chaos, rather than snatch the grand prize. Everyone knows royalty travels at the front.

They could have chosen somewhere with wider ground. Why hide in the trees, disguised with a camouflage veil?

"I can help you with that."

Calla doesn't turn her head, recognizing the voice. She swivels only her eyes to find Otta Avia holding a roll of bandages, standing much closer to her side than she would like. *Ugh.* She wishes she had accepted Joselie's earlier offer to dress her wounds.

"I'm ever grateful for the offer," Calla says, tugging her sleeve over the blood on her arm. "But I can find a healer in the next village."

"You'll bleed out before we reach the next village. I heard the Weisannas saying it will take another day of travel."

Much as Calla could keep refusing, Otta Avia must have some motive for approaching her. Better to hear this now than await a lingering viper. Silently, Calla pulls her sleeve up, offering the wound.

"How can I thank you?" she asks wryly.

"You'll find a way." Otta reaches into the small fabric bag she has hanging from her shoulder. It wasn't there earlier, at the scene of the attack. She pulls out a bottle of antiseptic.

A few moments of silence pass. Otta pours the liquid. Calla stoically bears the sting.

"So," Otta chirps, "I don't suppose you know why we were attacked?"

"I'm still not convinced you didn't have something to do with it, Otta."

Calla doesn't bother mincing her accusations, but she has to admit that said accusations are losing steam. It takes more energy trying to be nasty and pushing blame Otta's way than it does applying a neutral logic to the situation: Calla doesn't quite understand what Otta would have to gain when she's the one directing the delegation through the borderlands, and she's the one who claims she overheard enough information from King Kasa to find the crown.

"I don't know why," Calla says, answering properly when Otta doesn't return the dig. "All the bodies were collected, but there's nothing of note. Our best guess is an anti-monarchy guerrilla group. Nothing confirms it was the Dovetail."

"Of course." Otta unravels a length of the bandage. "Pockets of rebels have always existed. The king making a visit out into the provinces is sure to attract them."

"Did they seem like rebels to you?"

"They were definitive threats to our monarch. So it stuns me that you would let one come close on purpose."

Calla shifts. Her sword clatters, brushing against both her leather trousers and the fabric of the coat she's tied around her waist. Her head hums with noise.

"That wasn't what happened," she counters.

"Really?" Otta, with her clean robes and clean hands, keeps her tone as sweet as honey while she places one end of the bandage over the wound. "It certainly seemed so. Forgive me if I misjudged you."

Otta couldn't have caught much of the scene before the man was rushing at Anton, or else Calla would have spotted her presence through the trees. How much did she see? How much did she hear?

"You seemed perfectly capable of incapacitating the attacker, anyway."

"I shouldn't have had to."

"No," Calla agrees. She holds back a wince as Otta wraps the bandage over itself, tightening its hold upon her arm. "Because there was never danger to begin with. You've never seen your monarch fight. You've been gone so long that you have no idea how things have changed. He would have handled it fine."

"And what if he had been injured?" Otta returns. She looks up. Her eyes are pools of black, identical to the shadows darkening with the hour. "It's an age-old advisor tactic, I understand. He becomes bedridden, in need of rest. You prevent anyone else from coming near him so he has only your ear for guidance."

"You're paranoid."

Otta smiles. While her hands still, a small breeze blows her hair out of her face, letting the wisps fall into a perfect frame. "Aren't you?"

There's a commotion where the delegation is making camp, and they both turn to see the guards shooing off a councilmember who is trying to open the final carriage. By the king's orders, it is to be left alone. Even discounting the busyness occupying the rest of the delegation, Calla and Otta are far from anyone's hearing range. Still, Calla drops her volume when she says:

"You should stop trying to wage war against me, Otta. We don't have to be enemies. We are hardly even competitors."

"Oh, I know." Otta ties a bow on the bandage. "*Competitors* would be a terribly inaccurate word. You aren't even close to holding equal footing with me."

Is she fucking serious?

Calla yanks her arm back. Enough. She is wasting time arguing with Otta, as though they are schoolchildren sniping over the best toy on the playground. Otta lets her stride away, feigning innocence over why Calla would have reacted so suddenly.

"I am only doing you a favor by warning you," Otta calls after her. "You cannot keep what isn't yours."

Calla grits her teeth. A new headache is starting. Before Otta can piss her off further, she skirts around the carriages, making for the bags to help with unloading.

"Hello, Highness," Joselie greets, already building a tent. "You're looking a little pale."

"I'm fine," Calla says. She gestures for the rest of the pole. "Let me help."

There's brutal annoyance stirring in her chest, but beneath it, there's also clarity: the first indicator that maybe Calla has misunderstood what prowls before her. Here is where Otta has misstepped; here is the injured limb that she has put weight on during battle, exposing her weaker parts without knowing. If this were about Anton, she wouldn't speak about him so demeaningly. He is not a puppet on strings that Otta and Calla can take turns tugging. He is a player forceful enough to hold a throne—and Otta in her fancy sleeves and beautiful gowns must know that is not merely something to *keep*.

Calla looks up at the burgeoning stars. If she squints, she can imagine how the province dwellers see a pantheon in their shapes. She can imagine why they might believe in gods who live in the heavens, looking over mortal lives and injecting unnatural force into their qi when they commit sacrifices in their patron's name.

"Your Highness, you're turning the pole the wrong way."

Calla stops. She clears her throat. "You know what? Hand me the hammer and nails instead."

◇◇◇◇◇

Almost an hour after they've entered Lankil, Galipei announces that the perimeter has been thoroughly examined and they should settle into camp for the night. Anton hears it through his thin tent fabric while he's in the middle of inspecting a map he requested from one of the guards, shining an electric flashlight.

He's warned the guards that he will be resting. They are not to let anyone in. Not Calla, not Otta. It doesn't matter if they say the entire kingdom is burning down; it can wait for tomorrow when they're on the move again.

When the zip opens, he shouldn't be surprised that it is Galipei who has managed to enter. Anton cannot exactly lock the doors on a tent, as he can in his palace quarters to avoid Galipei.

"I had quite specific instructions for the guards out there," Anton says dryly.

"From experience, the guards know that instructions don't apply to me," Galipei replies. "It's strange. They must be wondering why you have forgotten."

Anton doesn't like where this is going. He turns his map facedown.

"Maybe it's time you stop expecting that you'll receive special treatment, Galipei."

"Given that I am the head of your royal guard, usually that's called *around-the-clock security.*"

The electric flashlight in his hand wavers. Instead of turning it off, Anton aims it directly at Galipei—a warning, a line drawn in caution. The guard barely flinches. He shouldn't be able to see anything past the glaring beam, but he stares straight at Anton.

"Did you need something?" Anton asks.

"I'd like to know if there's anything you wish to tell me."

The tent shivers. Its center pole clanks against a loose screw at the top, keeping in tune with a high-pitched cry that sounds across the camp. While the southern provinces are effectively barren of wildlife, overhunted with the intent of selling meat into the twin cities, the northern provinces stir with animals of the land. Lankil isn't as woodsy as Leysa, which means there's more open space, more room for sound to travel on each gust of wind.

Anton doesn't know how to respond. He can only assume that Galipei's suspicion has come to a head, and he needs to deal with the problem before it grows unmanageable. Still, Anton must take too long trying to decipher the tone of this confrontation, because Galipei strides forward without waiting for permission.

His hand closes around the flashlight; he pushes it up to get the beam away, lighting the top of the tent.

Something is happening. Where Galipei's fingers overlap Anton's, he loses sensation. His arms weaken, as though he has pinched a nerve. His left ear goes out, then tunes back in with frantic buzzing.

It's *August*. He's fighting for control.

"I saw the letters in your study before we left for the delegation," Galipei says carefully. "So I want to know what exactly happened back there."

Even if Anton wants to lie in that moment, he can't. If he opens his mouth, someone else will speak.

Back there . . . back in the palace? Or back at the scene of the attack?

Anton grits his teeth around a section of his inner cheek and bites down hard. A metallic taste floods his mouth, blood dripping down his throat. The pain shoves him back into the situation—and feeling returns to his fingers. Though he tries to pry out of Galipei's grasp, Galipei takes that as a challenge and turns the beam on him.

"Enough!"

Anton tosses the flashlight to the side. Though it clatters to the tent floor and rolls hard enough to dislodge the battery, flicking the beam off, the light has already seared an imprint into his vision. He blinks rapidly to clear it.

"I don't know what has gotten into you," Anton says, trying to summon force into his voice. "But this is out of line."

He expects Galipei to argue. To press further until he breaks past why exactly Anton has no idea what he's talking about. Instead, Galipei turns on his heel and exits, whacking the tent flap out of the way.

Which is arguably much worse, because that means Anton has already lost the charade.

Shit.

He's in trouble.

◇◇◇◇◇

When nightfall comes, the voices begin.

. . . don't . . . it'll work . . . listen to me . . . Sinoa, no, no—

Calla squeezes her eyes shut, bracing her head in her hands. She keeps hearing that name. Again and again, whether the words draw nearer or flitter farther, she's hearing the same name. *Sinoa.*

Across the tent, Joselie is fast asleep. Calla pushed all the pillows at the old woman and took station in the corner, sitting with her arms propped on her knees. Joselie—thank goodness—didn't bother protesting and promptly went to sleep.

. . . lose . . . can't defeat me.

Calla gets to her feet. Enough. She isn't so much of an idiot to think she's conjuring a *name* out of nowhere, so it can't possibly be delirium without cause. Every spasm at the base of her head prompts a hiss of voices, and each time they get louder, she has the peculiar sense that they are memories she's forgotten about.

This wasn't her original name, though. No way. She would know if it was. She would recognize it. The more she tries to bear it, the more she's certain these voices aren't talking to *her.* Certainly not the little orphan girl she would have been when she possessed a different name.

Calla tries to stretch out her arm. The wound complains as soon as she moves and, registering the feeling of the bandage soaking through, she winces and goes to undo it. Underneath, the cut has mostly stopped bleeding. Changing her bandages once more should do the trick to soak up the rest of the goop.

Calla stops. She leans back, putting her arm in the lantern light beaming through the tent fabric from outside. It's too dark. She tosses the bandage onto the floor and leaves the tent, goose bumps rising on her arms immediately.

With better light, she eyes the smear of blood below her puckered wound.

She feels deranged at first. The voices continue whispering in her ear—she must be searching for a place to put blame. But this isn't conjured. The smear of blood makes one straight horizontal line, then a double loop upward. This isn't an inadvertent stain. This is another sigil.

A new burst of pain explodes behind her eyes, as if confirming the realization. Stumbling, Calla goes back into her tent and grabs her sword, leaving her attendant to sleep. She moves quick and low, keeping out of the eyeline of the guards. Calla reaches Otta's tent in seconds, opens the flap before lunging in.

The tent is empty.

Calla pauses, drawing to a stop and recalculating. She scans the neat pallet and finds nothing of interest. It's not like there is anywhere on the campsite that Otta could go. Any guard who spots her would politely ask her to return to her tent.

Sinoa . . . now . . . now . . .

She reverses back out through the tent flap. There must be rainfall nearby in the province. Mist hovers low to ground, painting the surroundings with a gray haze. The voices echo, again again again, and by some instinct, Calla turns and gazes into the distance, toward the abandoned city.

Now I've got you.

"What the fuck?" Calla says out loud. "Otta?"

Come on.

Calla waits a moment, trying to determine whether she's hallucinating this entire episode. In her periphery, there stands a guard humming, bored, while he peruses his surroundings. He hasn't noticed her yet. Though Calla remains where she is, a terrible twisting sensation funnels up her nose, presses at her eyes, illuminates the space around her. She almost gags when she blinks and finds yellow light pressing behind her eyes.

"Shit," she spits. She clamps her arms around her head. The night tilts; the world tilts. All her other cheap tricks aren't working this time—when she tries to throw her hands out to push the feeling away, nothing ejects. She is an animal sealed inside a glass cage, shaken by a giant's hand for amusement.

"Stop," Calla gasps. She scrabbles for her collar. Maybe if she scrubs the sigil off, this will all be over. Maybe if—

The light in her eyes flares to an intolerable point. The moment the nearest guard turns away, Calla breaks into a dead sprint, heading for the city.

CHAPTER 22

The city is gated. Although Calla can see between the gaps of its tall bars, dirt has clumped around the structure over the centuries, sticking to the hinges and rusting over the latches. It would be quicker to climb to the top using the dirt mounds as support rather than attempt to pull the latch open.

She's scrambled up the bars in seconds, then leaps onto the other side with a hard crunch on the gravel. The half-moon is sufficient to light her way. The city streets take shape before her, glowing faintly with the yellow brightness coming from her own eyes.

The whine in her ears prompts her to keep going. No time to linger. She needs to find Otta, and then she's going to bash her head in until Otta tells her how she can stop *her* head from doing this.

Sinoa . . . don't do . . . to me . . .

The voices are persistent. Calla swallows hard, pressing down on her sword while she runs so it doesn't make noise knocking against her leg. The streets here are far wider than San-Er's. While she moves fast, the buildings stand sentry on both sides. Some windows have been smashed in, others smeared with enough dirt to turn them opaque. There aren't electric signs anywhere in sight. Stone tiles pave the roads, leaving enough room to push wooden barrows. One has been parked outside a white door.

"Otta," Calla ventures, "I'm here. Come out."

Silence. She slows. The structural damage worsens the deeper she goes into the city. A shopfront marked with PHARMACY is half caved in. A door on its other side appears to be the entrance into a residential block, the paper billing at the front asking prospective tenants to call a short number. Calla tilts her head. So it hasn't been long enough that the paper has rotted. Yet it has been long enough that the phone towers have since gone down in the provinces. This city was emptied before the war, not after.

A howl travels through the night. Some mixture between animal and the cold sting of wind. Calla has to suppress the shiver dancing down her neck. The provinces are too large, too wide. San-Er guarantees every threat is forced into close proximity, but out beyond the wall, in the arena of the grand kingdom, someone could be waiting for an immeasurable amount of time before playing their hand.

Sinoa . . . I won't let you . . .

Calla's breath comes short. She can't hold on to one thought for long; the pain is all-encompassing. Maybe Otta is trying to kill her. Maybe this is how she deteriorates until she goes entirely insane and runs herself through with her sword.

"What do you *want?*"

Calla draws her sword and swings. She only cuts through air, the whistle of her blade joining the night chorus.

Fuck. *Fuck.*

Forward she goes. Her vision blurs. She stumbles down alleys and up hills. Barely keeps her balance on descending stone steps and finally hurls herself into a pillar for something to clutch to. This cannot continue, but Calla can't return to the campsite like this, nor can she admit to anyone that something is wrong.

They would investigate. They would figure out that she's doubled. That she has occupied someone else for the entire life she remembers—and there's no reason she deserves the power she has.

Her fingers come off the pillar covered in ash. When Calla looks ahead and focuses, she recognizes the shape of the building before her as a temple. Its columns smolder white under the moon. The overhanging, upcurved eaves glitter gold.

"Please," she manages aloud. If there are gods in this world, she's begging for relief.

Calla staggers toward the temple, her foot crossing where dirt turns to marble flooring. She feels qi pulse the air around her. The thrumming behind her eyes sears with the physical press of a knifepoint.

Long live Her Majesty, a scream calls in her head, suddenly as clear as day. It's a chorus of voices in unison, not from this temple but from across the city, echoing and echoing. *Long live Her Majesty ten thousand years. May our sacrifice give her new life. May she be reborn, and win the war once our enemies have perished.*

Calla falls to her knees. Her sword scrapes against marble, brushing away a thin film of ash. There's color beneath, an inlay built into the base before the steps begin. She barely has the conscious capacity to make the decision, and yet she finds herself swiping at the ash, scratching and brushing until the image is clear.

She doesn't understand.

This is her face, staring back at her from the very composition of the temple floor. It's an impossibility. Calla today may be an invader, but Princess Calla Tuoleimi was still born like any other child, eight years before a girl from Rincun jumped in.

Calla clears the ash below her face.

SINOA TUOLEIMI

QUEEN OF THE PALACE OF HEAVENS

This must be a hallucination. She can't rein in the pain anymore. Something is trying to tear her apart from the inside out. She's going to die if she doesn't stop it.

"Calla, stay right there."

The night floods with yellow. Her chest shudders. The new sigil on her arm feels entirely aflame, as though she might possess the raging sun in her bones.

"Galipei?"

He comes into view. His sword is drawn. "Hands up."

Long live Her Majesty. Long live Her Majesty ten thousand years. Long live Her Majesty ten thousand years. Long live Her Majesty ten thousand years. Long live Her Majesty ten thousand years—

"Shut up!" Calla gasps, clasping her ears. "*Please.*"

You'll never win this war. The blood will be on your hands. The land will be lost—

"Calla Tuoleimi," Galipei bellows, "you have three seconds to surrender yourself before I bring you in by force."

The south is lost. Yi has burned. You have nothing but—

"One."

Sinoa, I will never see you again.

"Two."

Long live Her Eternal Majesty.

"Thr—"

For the first time in fifteen years, Calla jumps.

CHAPTER 23

Venus Hailira reaches Rincun accompanied by four guards on horses. They don't take a carriage. They barely take any belongings.

"I'm declaring a voluntary confinement period," she declares at East Capital's yamen. The mayor there hurries to send news to the mayor at West Capital. The generals receive the order, but they're told not to disperse soldiers, which incites great confusion wondering how they are to preserve order for any type of confinement, but Venus puts her foot down. Soldiers are to stay in their barracks too. She wants Rincun to turn into a land of ghosts.

"You know," East Capital's mayor says while Venus writes, leaning over her shoulder, "we might get people moving to Youlia because of this. You can't interrupt their livelihoods."

The lamp on the desk flickers. Venus puts one sheet aside. That's the calculation for one week. Next, she'll do a month. Then six months. By a year, she suspects the math will show that she can't keep them in anymore.

"I'm not forcing them to do anything," she replies simply. "They will be rewarded for staying put."

"What if this invites people to refuse to work after confinement ends?"

Venus gives him a look. "Are *you* going to stop working?"

The mayor grimaces. He hems and haws for a few seconds, but otherwise says nothing more.

Maybe mass migration to Youlia would be for the best. Youlia doesn't touch the borderlands. Even on the easternmost course toward the borderlands, a traveler must cross miles of Rincun before reaching the mountains. The panhandle-shaped province that the Hailiras govern is the final frontier before the edge of Talin, no matter which path one takes.

Venus turns back to her calculations. The mayor wanders off to tend to his own business. The yamen falls into silence, interrupted every few seconds only by the scratch of Venus's ink pen nib on lined paper. When an exclamation outside wafts in through the open window, it echoes loudly through the office, and Venus frowns immediately, rising to see what has happened.

"I thought I instructed everyone in the yamen to stay inside," she says, poking her head through the window.

Two of the yamen workers are sitting on a bench installed along the yamen exterior, cigarettes in hand. They can't exactly go home, lest they abandon yamen administration. Still, that doesn't mean they need to be in the open, inviting trouble.

"Councilmember, look," the one on the left says. Her blue eyes are wide. She points out into the distance.

At first, Venus can't tell what they're looking at. The sky is black, hanging with a handful of stars. She searches the clouds for a few seconds before her gaze settles lower, onto the mountains.

The blip is there then gone. She wouldn't have known that was what she was watching for if the two yamen workers didn't jolt excitedly.

"There!" they say. "There it is again!"

Venus understands. That was the light of someone jumping. There are people in the borderlands.

She hisses through her teeth, leaning back from the window.

"Get inside, would you?"

CHAPTER 24

The world falls quiet.

Calla exhales. Inhales. The voices disappear. The pain fades. Slowly, her surroundings take shape around her: the temple dusted in gray, the moonlight beaming up the path, the marble steps . . .

Her body.

Calla doesn't dare breathe as she approaches. Her head is lolled, her hair splayed. She can't see her face. She has no indication whether she's just freed a centuries-old entity onto the world, if Sinoa Tuoleimi was reborn as Calla Tuoleimi and was on a path toward vengeance against her enemies before her plans were diverted by a rural orphan.

Her wrist is still warm when she touches it. The fabric of her shirt rustles, responding to the push she gives her shoulder to turn herself around.

Calla goes cold. Her eyes are wide open.

Wide and *yellow* instead of an empty vessel's white.

With the bewilderment of a child, Calla merely freezes, thinking if she doesn't move she will not be attacked. But the body before her is unresponsive. Unblinking, even when a gust of wind howls through the night and sends ash flying about. Calla reaches forward and, as though this body is a corpse, she closes its eyes. An empty vessel wouldn't be damaging its eyes by keeping them open, so it doesn't matter. But an empty vessel isn't supposed to have the appearance of an eye color at all, because that signals the presence of a person's qi, and unless the real princess is still lurking in there, *why* would—

Calla rushes to lift the sword that was in Galipei's hand. She puts the blade close to her face, enough to catch a reflection in the moonlight.

She hears a delirious laugh, and it takes her a second to realize she's the one making that noise. She laughs and laughs with Galipei's reflection mimicking each move, then as quickly as the sound came, she settles into abrupt sobriety. In the silence, her eyes blinking silver, she finally has to reckon with the question that emerges, the question she's never thought too hard about lest it push something strange out into the open.

She's always known something peculiar happened to put her on this course: either she was born with Tuoleimi yellow as her natural eye color, or she didn't bring her own eyes with her when she invaded royalty. Either she was born with the most unlikely coincidence, or she was born with the fathomless ability to jump without the *one* indication that has marked invasion for as long as their kingdom has kept records.

First she jumps into royalty. Not merely a child but, if any of these voices are to be believed, someone with a qi much older, someone a hundred times more powerful. Now she's jumped into a Weisanna without really trying, which is an exercise that hovers at the cardinal baseline of impossibility.

"Who the fuck *am* I?" she whispers.

Her body doesn't answer. Doesn't move. If the princess were hiding in there and pretending to be immobilized, she would still need to breathe, would she not? It can't be an act. Her collar has fallen slightly astray; there is still a sigil marking her chest. Acting off a suspicion, Calla goes to push the shirt collar on Galipei's body and glances down cautiously.

A sigil made of light. It's the same as Leida, when she jumped between bodies and marked up the one she moved to. Calla scrubs a finger against the light sigil, and nothing budges.

She shoots to her feet, perturbed. Maybe she shouldn't have drawn something irremovable on herself before understanding what it was. There is a language to these sigils, and she doesn't have the first idea what this one does.

"Okay," she says aloud. "I'm okay."

Something catches her eye upon the temple's outer wall. She didn't notice it earlier, too distracted and delirious from the pain, but with her head clear, the flapping motion in her periphery is persistent. Calla turns properly to find a dagger buried to the hilt, fastening a folded piece of paper to the clay wall.

She's almost hesitant to leave her body unguarded, but she trudges over to the temple wall, keeping herself within view. Otta left this for her; there's no doubt about it. The dagger looks newer than anything in this city, shiny and metallic where everything else is covered in a layer of grit. As soon as Calla plucks it out—the blade emerging from the clay with a hard yank—the paper drops to the floor. Skeptical that this can be anything good, Calla's holding her breath when she picks it up and unfolds it.

COME ALONE.

The words show first. Below the instruction is a map, one black *X* marked beyond the border of Rincun, deep in the mountains. There's no debate regarding the purpose of the map. Otta has given her the location of the divine crown, and Calla cannot fathom *why*.

Calla glances over to the marble steps. Her body—if she can even lay claim and say it is hers—remains splayed. Though Otta came through this city to leave the map, she must be long gone. The city is eerily quiet, echoing Calla's breaths back at her.

She shoves the map into her body's jacket pocket, keeping it safe. Then, with a grunt, she picks herself up and drapes her collapsed vessel over her shoulder.

Galipei's strong. She shouldn't be surprised. Still, she doesn't remember how it feels to move in a body that's not hers, and it takes her considerable effort not to flail her new limbs, to adjust her center of gravity while walking back through the city's main road and avoid tripping when she's stepping over the mound of dirt at the city gate. Galipei must have forced it open when he followed her in. She didn't even hear him.

Her plan forms as she approaches the campsite, shifting her collapsed body off her shoulder and into a more appropriate hold. The few guards on night duty spot her coming toward them. They call out in alarm when they see the body in her arms, making the conclusion that they must be under attack again.

"It's all right," she calls, and Galipei's voice almost breaks under her use, pitched too high. She clears her throat, sinks into his natural timbre. "Where's Otta Avia?"

Two of the nearest guards exchange glances.

"Otta Avia?" one echoes. "Is she not in her tent?"

"No," she answers. "Go wake His Majesty."

"I'm awake."

Anton emerges from his tent at a speed that indicates he was already listening from inside. He's squinting for a moment—*that's right,* a gut feeling in Galipei supplies: August's vision isn't the best at night, and Calla takes aim. She shifts the body in her arms. Waits for the first sign of realization when the face turns toward the moonlight.

Maybe it'll be glee. Maybe annoyance, that someone got to her before he could.

Instead, she watches a visible wave of horror take over Anton's expression. He surges forward in a run, and it's the most he's ever broken character because August Shenzhi does not *run.*

"Is she—"

Anton doesn't finish his question. His hands come down on her body's neck, feeling for a pulse. *I would have answered for it with my life,* she said to him, the last thing she said before all of this. *I still can.*

Look where they have come to.

Calla doesn't rush to make reassurances. With Galipei's height, she looms over him while the clouds blow over the moon; the night darkens to utter shadow, and maybe Anton loves her after all, if he's breathing like this, ragged and desperate.

"I found her in the city," she says. "I heard her calling for Otta when I was nearing the scene."

Anton's head snaps up. "*What?*"

"I think Otta performed some ritual to gain power, and now she's gone after the crown herself."

With such a wild claim, Calla expected chaos to erupt. It's not entirely a lie: if Otta has gone missing, there's only one reason.

You've already burned your palace down. This one is mine. Otta spoke those words herself. Why leave a map and then disappear? Otta wants to get there first.

Calla is met with stunned quiet. Several councilmembers have been roused by the commotion and have clambered out of their tents, yet there's no uproar. They're in unknown territory—wondering how Calla was attacked, how long Otta has been plotting rebellion, whether they're in far more danger than they imagined. Through the gathering crowd, Joselie pushes forward, looking over Calla—the body—with mechanical inspection.

"Galipei, what are you saying?" Anton asks. He's blinking fast.

"We have to go after—"

"Is she still *alive*?"

The rest of Calla's answer dies on her tongue. It is in the dark that Anton appears most like himself. That the purple tinge in his irises comes to life when he meets her gaze, gives him away to those who know how to look.

"She's still alive," she says, pivoting quickly. "Check her eyes."

The moment she's given the instruction, Anton's hands move from her neck to her eyelids and push up lightly. Electric yellow, not replaced or dulled. Alive, undoubtedly, and stuck in there.

"Give her to me."

Calla falters.

"I will help," Joselie adds. They must think Galipei wants to be rid of this burden as soon as possible.

Recovering, Calla eases her body into Anton's arms. She's surprised that he receives the handover with care, that he tucks her head against his shoulder and adjusts for the sword hanging from her hip when he turns and walks. She hardly recognizes her own body when it's made into something fragile. With her height, she's never been small, yet somehow she's rendered into the flat imitation of a person the moment her qi is removed.

Calla watches them take her body to the last carriage. Anton delivers some instruction, and Joselie helps him move her in by pushing around some of the items before he places her body down. From afar, Calla catches a brief glimpse of three stacked boxes before Joselie closes the carriage door again.

Anton, what on earth did you bring in that carriage?

"Galipei, what are we to do?"

The voice comes at her shoulder. She turns to find a close cousin of Galipei's: Balen, or Bayen, or—

"We get to the borderlands as quickly as possible," she answers. The map sits safely in her body's pocket. "Even if we don't know the exact location without Otta, we travel as far as we can until we spread out to hunt her down. This isn't only about getting the crown to keep peace in San-Er anymore. It's about stopping her possible coup."

"And finding out what the fuck she did to Calla," Anton adds, returning to join the gathering crowd and rolling his sleeves up. When the guards blink at him, he claps his hands. "What are we waiting for? Break camp. Come on!"

Calla lets him issue the instructions. Lets him order around the guards and the other councilmembers, hurrying their mission. Quietly, she falls into line, joining their effort to gather up the campsite.

It would seem this has worked greatly in her favor.

CHAPTER 25

Yilas tossed the odd note in the office trash can the moment she returned from the palace. She didn't think anything about it, writing it off as nonsense. It requires a certain brand of peculiar to work in an environment like the Palace of Union, so she wasn't going to take it personally. She merely happened to be the person in view that day for the woman with black eyes to exercise her eccentricities on. Out of sight, out of mind.

"Baby, what is this?"

Until Chami walks into the apartment later that night with the note between her fingers.

"Don't tell me you plucked that out from the trash," Yilas groans, setting down her book. "I threw my orange peels in there afterward."

Yilas has put on new pajamas, as promised. The air conditioner blows gently from the window corner, its cold blast mostly absorbed by the overgrown indoor plants that line the floor before drifting into the rest of the bedroom. Though the diner closed an hour ago, Chami was on cleanup, pulling the blinds and locking the doors while Yilas came up first to rest.

"It looked strange, so I reached my hand into the trash." Chami raises a brow. Yilas's darling girlfriend, who laces her shoes in the correct order, has been wearing a fake piercing in her left eyebrow lately. She wants to branch out into new styles but needs to "try it out" before she "commits to a lifelong scar."

"You want to explain yourself to me?"

Chami turns the note around. Though it is clearly orange stained from Yilas's flippant peeling, the typewritten message in the middle remains clear and legible:

We need you.
441-819

"Well, first of all, it's not what it looks like."

Chami snorts. "Yes, I figured as much. Did you get it in the palace?"

"It was just someone who overheard my conversation with Matiyu."

A thump from downstairs sounds on cue, then an "*Ow!*" and a meow. Matiyu is sleeping downstairs on an air mattress in the office. He doesn't want to return to his designated lodging in the palace, for fear of his life. Yilas still isn't convinced that there is some conspiracy in the palace taking out the guards. People are murdered in San-Er all the time. The timing is suspect, but it could easily be a regular crime. Maybe some guards pissed off another employee, and now, while most of the Weisannas are away with the delegation, they're taking the opportunity to strike.

"They gave you a calling card because . . ." Chami trails off, appearing confused. "They heard your conversation?"

Yilas peers down the stairs, checking on the sound. "Are you all right?"

"Yes!" her brother exclaims. "The cat whacked a plate. I saved it!"

They better not break anything down there. Yilas sighs, then turns back and reaches to take the card out of Chami's hand. "I don't know what it is. I don't particularly care to find out."

Just before her fingers can make contact, Chami cranes her arm behind her, keeping the card away.

Yilas throws her arms into the air. She might as well be a fucking mind reader with how she's predicted this conversation. The Crescent Societies know that San-Er will not accept them easily—they are still a fringe group, after all, with a reputation for extremism and kidnapping civilians. The Crescent Societies desire change, and perhaps there genuinely are members among them that have sensible ideas, but they have operated as a black-market operation for far too long. Even if they are entirely successful in wiping out the palace, they will still have the people's disdain. For decades, Talin has been taught to accept the will of their heavens, to honor the aristocrats elevated by their bloodlines and let the nobles rule over the masses. For years, San-Er has warned their children to come home after dark because Crescents are lurking in the alleys. None of that goes away easily.

"You're going to have to give me more information than that," Chami counters. "I doubt a takeover is imminent."

"It is. We will seize the Palace of Union by force."

"How so?"

"Is this an interrogation? These aren't necessary details. The only critical component is that Calla's approval soothes the people. I'm sure she wants to work something out with us in exchange for a ruling title."

Chami examines her nails, leaning into the wall. She looks entirely unbothered, her tone no-nonsense. "If I'm taking something to Calla, I'm going to need details. Do you know how many people want an audience with her? How do I know you're not wasting her time with a plan doomed to fail?"

"I can't give you our exact time or method. I will tell you that we have the complete blueprints to the Palace of Union and a dependable route in—"

"And how do you have complete blueprints to the Palace of Union?" Chami interrupts. "That's not information maintained on any data server. Hidden entrances, servant passageways, and panic rooms are never told in full to attendants, staff members, or employees of the surveillance room. Without a full picture of lockdown plans, it is highly unlikely any palace offensive will be successful."

Yilas is so in love right now.

"So unless—I don't know—a *councilmember* has somehow sworn loyalty to the Crescent Societies and given up their inside knowledge, I doubt you have complete blueprints," Chami continues. "Nice try, though."

The silence draws long on the other end. Yilas has to assume that Bibi has been caught out, and this is the end of whatever scheme the Crescent Societies wanted to play tricks with.

"We do have a reliable source," Bibi finally says.

She speaks with hesitation, again. Yilas sidles nearer to the phone. There's no reason to carry this out any longer. It's not going to be successful. It will be another failed Crescent Society coup, and Calla has much more important things on her plate.

Yilas's finger is already hovering on the hook switch to hang up. Then:

"Before she was killed, Julia Makusa drew them up for us."

CHAPTER 26

By the first rays of morning, they're almost at the other end of long, curvy Lankil Province. They'll pass into Laho shortly, which shouldn't take more than another day to cross. Laho Province is shaped like two rectangles pressed together—a common feature among most of the provinces deeper inland, where they neatly sectioned the land apart for ease of governance. Provinces that formed around natural rivers and mountains must draw their lines accordingly, but Talin's north is smooth land and flat desert terrain, fit for straight borders. It causes spats between councilmembers sometimes when their generals slack off and don't patrol all the way to the edge of the province, assuming the neighboring soldiers will pick up the extra work.

Calla rides in the second carriage, digging through Galipei's bag. She's not a fan of sitting upright in his body. The carriage is past capacity, and she's jammed in tight with the other Weisannas working the councilmembers' protection detail. With his height, his head brushes the top of the carriage every time there's a pebble on the road and the wheels jostle, which is starting to cause static with his hair. Her hair. Whatever.

Calla pulls out a digital watch and turns it around in inspection. The numbers aren't moving, permanently stuck at 05:27. She doesn't know why Galipei is carrying around a broken watch. Maybe he stopped it on purpose at some point or another to track their journey. After Laho, there's Actia Province, known for being half sand. Some of it spills into Rincun to its north too, but Rincun's elements are harsher with the borderlands on its other side. Rather than sand, it is stone; rather than dunes, it sees cold steppes.

Three more provinces, Calla tells herself.

Her hand clunks against a cellular device at the bottom of the bag. It is small, like the one she keeps on herself too, tucked with her body stored in the last carriage, so she doubts it'll work in the provinces. Still, out of sheer curiosity, Calla plucks the phone out and pulls the cellular antenna to see if it will connect. Galipei's stupid thick arms make it so that she has to squirm against the guards on either side of her, and across the seats, Councilmember Mugo gives her a funny look. Calla ignores him.

No signal.

At that moment, there is another chirping sound in the carriage, though.

"Hello?" Mugo answers, practically yelling into his phone. His is larger, the size of his head. Made to pick up signal in the provinces and transmit all the way from San-Er. "Speak up. The cell towers are miles away."

Every passenger in the carriage turns to follow his conversation. It can hardly be helped when he's speaking at such volume.

"What?" He pauses. Before their very eyes, Mugo loses blood in his face, turning washboard pale. "Why would—*goodness*. I can inform His Majesty."

"What is it?" Calla asks the moment Mugo hangs up. They don't exactly have time to stop for Mugo to deliver a message.

"Councilmember Naurilus is dead. Murdered."

Murmurs travel through the carriage. Mugo tries to lower the antenna on his phone, and it makes a sharp noise, almost snapping sideways instead.

"Has the palace caught the perpetrator?" Savin asks, leaning over from the end, where she's seated.

Mugo shakes his head. "It happened a few minutes ago. They thought to call me first so I could speak to the king."

Calla wishes she had kept Otta's map on her so she could look more closely at it now. Though Otta used it to mark a location in the borderlands, the existing paper still shows the entirety of Talin. San-Er at the bottom, sticking out of the southeast. The provinces spreading past the wall: Eigi, encompassing most of that land border, giving way to Cirea on its immediate right. Cirea, which Councilmember Naurilus governed.

Calla reaches around the other guards and yanks the window curtain aside. Though there are occasional copses of trees, they're otherwise surrounded by green fields. It isn't a safe place to stop.

"We're almost in Laho," she says, pointing to the flat land outside. "You may deliver this news to His Majesty when we make camp for the night. We cannot idle here."

Mugo puffs up his chest. "Unchecked disruption in Cirea could severely impact the kingdom within one afternoon. His Majesty should appoint a temporary substitute immediately."

It isn't Mugo's civic responsibility to report a crime. This is a quick power grab when the opportunity presents itself. He already has Eigi. Adding Cirea would practically give him a small kingdom.

"We're about to enter the Dovetail's home base," Calla warns. "Stay put. No temporary substitute is going to change anything about Cirea in this current moment."

But Mugo is already standing. The councilmembers seated along his row cluck, annoyed to be jostled. "It would assuage the people."

"What? Knowing that one useless councilmember has been replaced by another?"

Mugo's eyes sharpen. Calla stifles a sigh, realizing she's giving far too much attitude for Galipei Weisanna's usual level.

"Look," she suggests, trying to smooth over the waves she just made. "You joined this delegation for a very important matter. We *must* get to the crown before Otta Avia claims it. Are you going to put that at risk to handle affairs in the capital? If Otta decimates the kingdom, your very role may dissolve, and then what?"

"Do not engage in fearmongering over how the council conducts its affairs." Mugo pushes through the carriage. "Please excuse me." The other council-members call complaints, asking him to sit back down, to calm down, but Mugo reaches for the door handle, meaning to throw it open and force the driver to a stop.

"Stop, *stop*." Calla rises too. "At least wait until we're sure we haven't entered Laho yet—"

Before Calla has finished her sentence, the carriage screeches to a halt, the driver outside giving a shout of alarm. She swivels, alarmed, looking out the window and spotting movement in the distance.

"What was *that*?" one of the Weisannas demands.

Mugo opens the door.

"Hey!"

Calla dives after him, pulling the councilmember back before he can step properly into the open. The moment she's exposed, though, something lands in her shoulder and pierces through muscle. The sight of a metal arrow jutting from her guard uniform is more shocking than the burst of pain in her shoulder. A weapon like that must cost an arm and a leg.

Another arrow whistles through the air and strikes the side of the carriage.

"Shit," Calla spits. "Get *in*! We're under attack."

◇◇◇◇◇

Civilians of San-Er, the television in the barbershop runs on a loop, *this is a hostile takeover.*

Councilmember Aliha rolls his eyes. He's almost home, walking from the palace to his second home in Er for a midmorning meal, and in that time he's passed three other screens with similar crowds gathered before them.

Look around. Is this the life that the old gods wanted for us when they forged Talin? We were born to jump, and yet the throne commands you stay on the ground.

The Crescent Societies have hacked into the palace broadcast system and connected to every channel across San-Er. It's ridiculous. If people really believed their religious nonsense, their groups wouldn't have been pushed to the shadows of the cities, left to practice only in the last remaining temples. Yet San-Er loves novelty, and whenever something comes along to disrupt their daily monotony, the people will give it their every bit of attention, regardless of what it is.

Aliha mutters and grumbles, pushing past the barbershop crowd. No one inside is working anymore, too fascinated with the broadcast. He's spent this whole morning looking at export numbers from Dacia to make sure their factories can get the produce they need to sell rice, to sort seeds, to distribute accordingly on the year's quotas, and what is San-Er doing in gratitude? Being useless and waiting on handouts from the council, of course. He's tired of the grumbling from Dacia that they can't meet the numbers, and he's tired of the grumbling from inside the cities that it's not enough. It's not his fault the farmers are lazy. His father's grandfather was the one who was handed Dacia Province the year the nobility were in tatters after the war with Sica. In a better world, the Alihas would have been given a more impactful province—he made a grab for Kelitu when the Makusas fucked up, but of course Kasa went with the Rehanous.

With a heft of his briefcase, Aliha ducks under a clothesline. Dirty water drips from a sock and onto his shoulder. He yanks the sock off the line and throws it onto the muddy ground, annoyed. This part of San is horrible. Full of miscreants and delinquents who will leave the windows wide open while they blast their televisions and lie on their beds the whole day. The ground-floor apartments he passes are all occupied at this hour, screen after screen after screen.

No council, no governance. The gods direct to the throne, direct to the people.

A bucket of water splashes into the alley behind him. Aliha whirls around, his curses prepared, but there's no one on the balcony to shake his fist at, as he expected. It fell on its own and is slowly rolling to a stop by a trash bag.

"Strange," he mutters. He'd better hurry out of here, before his daughter thinks he isn't going to join her for a bowl of noodles. She's been delicate since she was attacked unprovoked during the king's games, and she doesn't go outside anymore in fear of the danger.

The moment Aliha turns to proceed down the alley, though, he spots a man who's slunk in from the other end, tossing an orange in his hands.

"Councilmember," the man greets. "Do you remember me?"

Aliha frowns. If this is an attempted robbery, it won't be long before the surveillance cameras register the impending crime and send palace guards. Besides, he isn't carrying much cash, so it will be a lost cause.

"I'm afraid not," Aliha replies. "If you'll excuse me—"

The man's arm shoots out, blocking his way before he can move past. Underneath his sleeve, there's a crescent moon tattooed on his wrist.

A flutter of alarm shivers down Aliha's back. He doesn't want to risk it: he turns on his heel and moves in the other direction, but there's a blur of movement, and suddenly someone is leaping down from the balcony he thought empty before, blocking his path yet again. A woman this time, the two edges of a crescent moon peeking over the cut of her shirt collar.

"Get out of my way," he demands. "Who do you think you are—"

Something pierces his side. He doesn't register the feeling at first, only that it is cold, and foreign. Then the pain begins.

"Fuck you for putting me in jail," the woman whispers viciously. She pulls the knife out. Then shoves it in again, two inches to the left. "It was your daughter's fault for getting in my way. I'm not surprised she couldn't run fast when she was weighed down by five thousand fucking shopping bags on each arm. *Scum.*"

The knife tears out. Aliha touches the wound, holds the pouring red. If he could just get somewhere, if he could wait until the guards come . . .

He cries out, dropping to his knees. He's turned his back on the man at the other end of the alley, and something has been pushed right through his back, exiting through his chest. His vision swims. Gray shadows. Gray puddles. Only his red blood offers some sort of color on the wet floor when he spasms and falls to his side, his head smashing hard into the half-ripped remnants of a trash bag.

"They should have sent me after you earlier," the woman mutters. She wipes down her knife handle. "You belong with the trash. Have fun rotting in it."

Councilmember Aliha hears her throw the knife beside him, the clatter of metal as loud as a screeching factory reset. Then a gurgle of blood oozes from his mouth, filling his lungs, and he hears nothing more.

CHAPTER 27

Anton comes to with his head pounding.

His left eye is shielded with a veil of red. A scratch through his brow, he assumes, if blood is streaming directly into his vision. It doesn't seem like he's been out for long. He knocked his head hard when the carriage took a tumble. They've landed in a ditch.

He shifts, trying to find his footing with the carriage on its side. The two guards are entirely out, heads lolled back. Alive, but they're useless to him if they're this slow to recover.

Anton wipes his forehead, trying to stanch the blood. He stands, then shoves his elbow hard against the window above him. It takes three strikes before the glass shatters, crumbling inside the carriage in large shards.

What happened out there? How did their driver not see a giant *ditch*?

When Anton hauls himself through the window, his arm hits a net. He freezes. This is worse than he initially assumed. On the other side of the net, albeit muffled, he hears the clang of swords. He tries to yank at the covering, move it aside so that he can extricate himself, but it's too wide. Its very purpose is to keep him in.

Shit. How many carriages hit the ditch? Did they all crash, or did the rest have time to slow by the time they saw the first driving off course?

Anton rummages in his pockets for a knife, then slashes at the net wherever he can make contact. It doesn't cut. He tries between the lines, saws furiously at the interwoven knots, but nothing gives.

"Hey!" Anton starts shouting. "Someone—"

"*Shush! Shush!*"

A thump echoes from the carriage exterior, sounding like boots landing in the ditch. Seconds later, Galipei Weisanna appears on the other side of the net. His silver eyes scan their surroundings quickly, searching for an opening.

"Stay quiet. I assume they're coming for you. We'll make an escape before they get through the guards."

Galipei has sounded strange since last night. It still hasn't gone away. Maybe he's plotting something too. Maybe he's responsible for this.

"What's going on out there?" Anton demands. The ground shudders. Was that an *explosive*?

"We've entered Laho. I'm willing to bet anything we're being attacked by the Dovetail." Galipei's voice grows muffled while he slinks around the carriage, trying to find the end of the net. "Can you . . . other side?"

Although Anton doesn't hear most of Galipei's question, he can take a guess at what his guard asked. He pulls away from the orange light of the higher window and shifts to the lower one. It's almost pressed to the ground in the overturned carriage. He kicks it free too, letting the broken shards fall outward, then pokes his head through the hollowed window frame.

Galipei is crouching outside.

"Squeeze through."

"In the *mud*?" Anton grumbles.

Galipei rolls his eyes. Then . . . he blows a puff of air up, as if he's trying to get hair off his forehead.

There's no hair covering his forehead and falling into his eyes. Someone else, though, certainly does that often, but how could—

"Let's *go*. We don't have time to waste, and this is the only section the net doesn't cover. I can't lift it otherwise. They have some magnetic shit on the edges."

Gritting his teeth, Anton lowers himself out of the carriage window, squeezing into the small burrow. Someone screams, no more than ten paces away, and Galipei sucks in his breath, glancing over his shoulder. At the last few inches, he doesn't wait for Anton to finish crawling, and merely reaches in to yank him out and to his feet.

Shrapnel strikes the ground right beside the ditch. Dirt sprays in, and Anton flinches, uncomprehending. He's only seen this sort of weaponry in the textbooks, in Talin's battles with Sica. After the war was won, the palace removed everything from distribution, destroyed it en masse. Weapons remain outlawed in the capital to this day. They don't need them anymore, after all. No use risking them being wielded against the throne once their foreign enemy was vanquished.

"They've got good arrows too," Galipei supplies, seeing Anton's expression. He points to his shoulder; now that Anton's not looking through a net, he sees Galipei's enormous red stain, which is steadily growing. "I think I've still got the arrowhead in there somewhere."

"You should probably get that out."

"No kidding." Galipei waits a moment for the dirt to settle, then goes to peer over the edge. Anton is close behind him, although he has to strain to get his head—August's shorter head—over the edge of the ditch for visibility.

"Who is doing this?" Anton asks lowly. "Same group as the one in Leysa?"

"They're wearing the same clothes, so my guess is yes. They've outnumbered us this time. I only got a quick glance before ducking out of sight, but they're jumping, which means the Weisannas either need to fight back in kind, or we're going to be eliminated."

"Jumping?" Anton echoes. "They can't possibly be strong enough to invade palace guards."

"San-Er's bloodlines aren't inherently stronger than the provinces—they're palace *guards*, not palace aristocrats," Galipei mutters in reply. "It seems to be working plenty well, anyway. They're jumping in, killing us, then jumping out. We don't have enough Weisannas to put up a good defense by mere insusceptibility. Once the guards are overwhelmed, they'll go for the carriages and attack the councilmembers. I'm not sure the delegation will survive this."

Weisannas. The guards. Has Galipei always spoken like that?

"We'll take a horse and escape when the opportunity comes," he goes on. "We don't need everyone present to go after the crown—if anything, they're only useless baggage."

Anton finally spots where the other carriages have stopped, past the frantic scene of battling guards. The carriages are still lined up in an orderly fashion with the horses, relatively undamaged. The last one sits exposed, no lock on the door, no way to stop any random rural dweller from opening it and seeing what lies inside.

"No," Anton says.

Galipei looks back at him, flabbergasted. "No?"

"No, not yet—"

Another round of shrapnel strikes the ground right beside the ditch. This time, it's not an accidental misfire; it's an intentional projectile, dispersing plumes of smoke into the ditch. Though Anton turns, thinking they must move now or else be spotted, it's already too late.

A man lands in the ditch. He's followed by ten others, each one of them clutching a blade.

"Hands up," he says.

They're surrounded.

◇◇◇◇◇

Calla strains against the bindings on her wrists, but she can't find any give in the rope. If she were in her own body, her arms would be more limber, enough so that she might be successful getting her hands in front of her. Then she could untie her ankles and run. Galipei, though, is muscular for appearance, his wide shoulders more a burden in this moment than any privilege.

"Will you stop squirming?" a voice hisses beside her.

Although Calla has been blindfolded, they set her and Anton apart from the councilmembers in a quick rush, so it could only be him telling her off. After they were pulled from the ditch, they were rapidly bound and set down. Calla doesn't understand why they're not being killed. She can hear one of the councilmembers near the carriages protesting: the blindfold is too tight, the binding is too tight, the ground is too hard. Whoever keeps yapping doesn't understand that these people could take a knife to their throat in a heartbeat.

So why don't they?

"I'm trying to get us out," Calla replies lowly. "Maybe if you tried squirming too, you could get your skinny arms out of those binds."

That shuts Anton up for a minute. Perhaps he's wondering whether he ought to be offended when, technically, she's insulting August's arms.

"We're about to die and you're thinking about my arms."

"I'll kill you myself if you say one more word."

Anton snorts. "Galipei Weisanna, when did you develop such an attitude?"

That jolts Calla back to her senses. She tries to push her face against her shoulder, but it doesn't move the blindfold.

"Look," she says. "I don't know what they want us around for, but they won't keep us alive long."

There's chatter among the attackers, somewhere in the vicinity. Laho boasts the sort of flat plains made of rock and grass. Sound travels without restriction. Though Calla can't pick out exactly what they're saying, she knows they're deep in debate.

"There's an easy way out of this," Anton says suddenly. "Your shoulder is still bleeding. Focus on drawing qi out of the wound, and you can jump blindfolded."

Her chest pulses. The sigil is still there. She can hear the horses by the carriages too—it *would* be a quick escape.

"Why don't you do it, Majesty?" she asks. "You're a skilled jumper, after all."

"I don't want to."

"Don't be difficult on purpose."

"Am I? Surely you understand the hesitation to lose a powerful body, Calla."

Calla freezes midmotion, her wrists straining against the ropes. So he's figured it out.

"Look," Calla says slowly. "I did what I needed—"

"Did Otta even attack you?"

"Yes!" Of course the first question he asks is about Otta's guilt. "She lured me off the campsite, practically bashed me over the head with qi, and then left a map to a location in the borderlands. I don't know what her goal is. But I know where she's going, even if it's a trap."

Anton makes a low sound. "Classic. I wouldn't expect anything less from her."

That response infuriates her even more than him asking whether Otta actually attacked. Calla tugs hard once more on the ropes, but there is clearly no chance of getting free. The argument among the attackers is starting to quiet. Though Calla isn't putting her full attention toward eavesdropping, it occurs to her then that it's nevertheless strange she isn't picking up *anything.*

They're not speaking Talinese at all.

The field goes quiet. Something shifts. When Calla hears a rapidly nearing stride cutting through the dried grass, she knows they're coming directly for her, and that's before the fist slams hard into the side of her face.

Oh, fuck—

Calla bites down on her yelp, swallowing the sound. Her head strikes the grass; her shoulder crunches when it smacks into the ground. Her hands are still bound behind her so she can't brace when she falls, nor can she brace against the next kick on her chest. She's never been more glad to be wearing Galipei in the midst of this. That impact would have stung so badly upon her own chest.

"Was this some reverse ambush all along, then? Terribly stupid to think you wouldn't answer for it."

The attacker is speaking to her. *Confronting* her.

"What the fuck are you talking about?" Calla growls back.

Maybe the confusion captures their curiosity. Suddenly, her blindfold is yanked off, and a man takes shape before her. He hauls her chin up. Checks the color of her eyes.

"Are you," the man says, "Galipei Weisanna?"

Morning beams over the horizon. Brilliant red streaks through the skies, and a flock of birds takes flight overhead. Doves, native to the central provinces despite the unlikely, harsh environment.

"I am," she says. "Who are you?"

It is the wrong thing to say. The man strikes his fist into her nose, and she's entirely upside-down for a moment before realizing that her head is simply tilting upon the grass, her vision spinning, spinning—

"The one you communicated with," he spits. "The one you made agreement with. Now, why did we bury our fighters in Leysa, huh? You thought it would be worthwhile to take out some of our numbers that way?"

"Shit," Calla mutters.

Why would Galipei make an agreement with the Dovetail?

The man yanks her back up by her hair. She strains to catch a glimpse of Anton at her side. He's listening closely. He must be putting it together as she is.

"For your sheer stupidity and failure—"

"You didn't do your part," Calla interrupts in a rush. Her bottom lip is starting to swell. If she pushes the right buttons, she'll get answers. "The attacking group was caught early. That wasn't the agreement."

He throws her down. There's blood dripping from her face, painting the grass.

"We put everything at risk. We took your information and promised safety for your king. That is *more* than the agreement."

"I didn't see it that way." She's scrambling to make sense of the timeline. The attack in Rincun, the attacks across the provinces. Leysa in the forest, now this ditch in Laho. "I acted accordingly thereafter."

The man shakes his head. When he turns away, gesturing for another member to bring him his sword, Calla finally spots a small dove tattooed at the back of his neck.

"Affairs were conducted far more smoothly when we were speaking to Prince August directly. We don't want you near divine matters."

Divine matters. Prince August.

Her inhale lodges in her throat.

Galipei made an agreement with the Dovetail because *August* was speaking to the Dovetail. *August* instructed the attacks on the provinces; *he* dictated the instructions before his coronation, before Anton invaded him. It seems, in fact, that Anton interrupted a carefully laid set of plans. Send the provinces into a frenzy, blame the councilmembers, take complete control over Talin.

God. *She* put him on this throne.

"Anton," Calla says suddenly. It's the end of the line. A part of her knows that she's exposing him on purpose. Let there be no other option. Push him into the corner that will force his hand. Say whatever it takes to lock their convict chains together. "I'm going. Come with me. I need you."

She doesn't wait for an answer. It isn't the same panic that culminated in Lankil's city, but the moment she peers inward, the sensation is waiting inside her—an abyss merely zipped away in her mind rather than sealed over. An exhale, an inhale. Blood trickles from her shoulder, leaks down her arm, into her palms.

Pain darts down her spine, flashes a burst of light inside her head. When Calla opens her eyes again, she's staring up at the ceiling of a carriage, her body tingling with circulating blood and regained feeling. The moment she moves, she feels the grime of her dirty clothes, which are still covered with the ash of Lankil's city.

It worked.

There's a sound to her left. Calla is slow to turn, groggy. The last thing she expects to see is the lid suddenly flying off a long crate, and then someone sitting up inside.

"What the *fuck*—"

"My god, I'm as stiff as a board. I can't believe they left me lying around like this in storage."

Calla remembers the photo Anton kept in his apartment, the one of his younger self at the Palace of Earth. Black eyes and tousled hair, a strong brow and perfectly symmetrical features.

"You brought your birth body along on this journey?" she exclaims. "Are you out of your mind? Have we been wasting an entire carriage for this?"

"I brought it along because chances were high that you would force me out of August before the journey was over, and I was right," he snaps back. "Are we going? August and Galipei are waking up."

Shit. Shit shit shit—

Calla pushes the carriage door open. Before she's even gathered her bearings and determined which direction she should turn, she's drawn her sword, at the ready. Her body knows to react with the slightest prompt, senses the world around them and adjusts accordingly. Her legs prepare to spring. Her fingers flex, securing a grip. She's so happy to be back. No other body in this world is right for her.

In the bright morning light, Calla swings her blade on the rope connecting the horse to the carriage. She shoves her sword back into its sheath, then climbs into the saddle, teetering one way before gaining her balance.

"Come on!" she hisses.

With a frantic squeeze of her legs, she maneuvers the horse the other way. Anton stumbles out of the carriage; she holds her arm for him to grab and hauls him onto the horse just as there are shouts from the field. She spares a glance over.

Galipei is staggering to his feet.

"We're going north," Anton instructs, hands on her shoulders to veer her toward the right.

Calla nods. Before the Dovetail can start shooting their arrows, she tugs the reins and bolts away at high speed.

◇◇◇◇◇

August Shenzhi returns to consciousness as if he has awakened from a dream.

On his first blink, he knows that something is outrageously awry. On the second, he registers the blindfold, then the bindings on his wrists.

"*Enough of this*," he hears beside him. "*Who left? Get them back.*"

The air smells strange. Like something has burned, cradled in the sun's touch for too long. A grunt echoes beside him, and he recognizes Galipei's presence in an instant. Are they tied up? Are they out in the provinces?

Faintly, his memories flutter by when he tries to reach for them, but all that has happened outside of his control fades away like smoke through a sieve. His body is sore, indicating frequent movement in the last few days. He recalls nothing except the persistent tug of resentment. Though his qi was suppressed, he can feel every bit of effort it made to tear itself back to the surface, starting with the burst of rage that mottles the inside of his throat at present.

With a practiced ease, August leans his face onto his knees and scrapes the blindfold off. The people who take shape before him are entirely unfamiliar, but that doesn't change the matter that he has been tied up, and they are looming over him with swords. August jumps and lands in the nearest man without any struggle. He unsheathes the sword hanging at his side and sticks it into his occupied body, then jumps before he feels the pain, flashing light so furiously that he hears cries when he lands again.

He's found someone with a knife. Someone else screams, begs, "Wait, no! Stop!" and the knife is in his neck.

He moves. Again. Again.

By the sixth jump it seems most of the people nearby have fled, leaving the range of ten feet, and August wipes his hands, grimacing at how much this one is sweating. It doesn't give him pause—he kills them, then jumps back to his own body at last.

The ground is hard and uncomfortable under him. He pats around his limbs before he dares to stand, checks his clothes, his bruises, looking for some sign to show what they're doing out here.

"Galipei?"

His guard is woozy on his feet. In the time it took August to attack their opponents, Galipei has only just gotten his bearings. Blood smears the space from his neck to his torso. Though his hands remain bound, he is not blindfolded. When he looks at August properly, his eyes dilate, then focus, his pupils a pinprick in the silver.

"It's you," Galipei rasps. "August, you're back."

"What the fuck," August rumbles, "is going on?"

CHAPTER 28

The crown has slept for well past a century, and it doesn't take kindly to being awakened.

The last time it was worn, Talin looked different. The ocean hemmed every corner of the land, its tides brushing against the northern mountains. The provinces were tribute states, fractured in varying shapes, answering to the gods rather than the soldiers that prowled their fields. It didn't make anything easier, but Talin hadn't seen a real war yet. One might imagine the skies were brighter and the air sweeter.

Then the war came, and the gods angered. There needed to be natural order in the mortal world. Qi is born, and must die. Humanity may be granted blessings, but it should never think it, too, can play god.

The crown was a gift from the heavens. When its wearer dared not accept her heaven-mandated abdication, a godling of balance came down to restore order. She was so taken aback by the grievances committed that she had no choice but to curse the crown from being touched, to beg the gods to stay away. Let Talin recover. This was her terrain: balance had been upset, and she would pluck herself out of the pantheon to guard the crown for however long it took. Until the war resumed.

Deep in the mountains, the crown feels a presence draw close.

And it begins again.

◇◇◇◇◇

The Weisannas put a temporary curfew over San-Er. All civilians need to be inside by nightfall for their own protection, because the Crescent Societies have taken to the streets.

Councilmember Aliha's death is announced on the nighttime newsreels, the surveillance footage playing in high definition. That part of the city has recently installed color cameras. When the splatter of red hits the alley wall, the pattern resembles a bird spreading its wings.

Councilmember Bethilia of Yingu Province is attacked at the open market. Three masked figures home in on her with knives, and seconds later, she's already beyond saving or attempting a jump while she bleeds out beside the meat for sale. Over twenty witnesses report that the attackers had crescent moon tattoos on their hands. The Weisannas announce the Crescent Societies as the perpetrators, but they don't have further specifics on the attackers' identities. With that many members belonging to the temples, they must arrest either all of them or none of them.

The councilmember of Meannin—to the left of Laho—survives being struck multiple times by a blunt object, but she hasn't yet woken in the hospital. The councilmember of Ediso—atop Kelitu on the other side of the Jinzi River—has his hand amputated when he reaches for his dinner at the coliseum market, but the Crescent with the knife is already running before his stump starts spurting with blood.

It's anarchy.

But the regular civilians of San-Er have certainly noticed that they're not the ones getting attacked.

Yilas and Chami slink out from the back door of the diner, and no one is abiding by curfew. Faint bass music pumps from one of the facilities in the building. Chami squeezes Yilas's hand twice, and Yilas returns the gesture, acknowledging that she also sees the three women lurking at the end of the alley. They pass by with no problem.

"We've done a lot of ridiculous things in our lifetime," Yilas mutters, "but this might win a prize of its own."

"Nothing ridiculous about it," Chami assures her. "It's a perfect way to get communication out and help your brother."

"By working with the perpetrators he's accusing?"

Chami sighs, but it's a sound made with fondness, not exasperation. She doesn't say more. They've debated this no less than eight times since the phone call last night. When Yilas tried to end the call with the woman—Bibi—by claiming they actually had no way to contact Calla Tuoleimi since her phone signal was too poor, very sorry, better luck with another avenue, Bibi cut in immediately. The Crescent Societies had the technology to improve the signal, so long as they had Calla's phone number. That was an easy obstacle. Bibi would supply the method, and all she asked in return was to tack on her own message after Yilas communicated with Calla.

"Why . . . would you allow that?" Yilas asked, confused. "Do you understand the conversation you overheard in the surveillance room? My brother is trying to report you. I'm about to tell Calla that there's a nuisance in the palace she needs to deal with—*you*—and then you want to hop in and say hello?"

"I trust that the princess can make an informed decision." Bibi didn't sound worried.

And neither did Chami, after they hung up.

"Who cares what the Crescent Societies want to say?" she asked. "Calla can let it go in one ear and out the other. She's not going to do anything she doesn't want to."

Maybe Yilas is too used to chasing after Matiyu while they were growing up. Hardworking Matiyu, who did his homework and believed his classmates when they said they only wanted to see his assignments for inspiration. Easily gullible

Matiyu, who willingly joined a cult after graduating from the academy because it was the quickest way to climb the ranks of the capital and make quick cash before he was fast-tracked into respectable work.

The Crescent Societies have always been the most likely contender to bring down the palace. But *most* likely still doesn't mean likely. If the Palace of Union really wanted, it would take a day to tear down every temple in the capital. They've let them stand because the Crescent Societies would need colossal support to win over San-Er—hungry San-Er, desperate San-Er. Between a reliable next meal and revolution, the people of the cities would choose keeping their shitty job.

"Stop worrying so much," Chami says now. "Once we've passed the message to Calla, it isn't our business anymore. Especially with Matiyu interviewing in the financial district. They can burn down the palace, for all we care."

"That wouldn't be great either," Yilas replies. "I kind of prefer having a functioning economy."

Chami snorts. They proceed through San, and though it is quieter than usual, there is no sense of danger. Stores maintain the facade of closing, but their shopfront gates are only pulled halfway, letting people duck in regardless. Yilas squints through one of their windows. The Two Chicken Restaurant is certainly open: its patrons are only eating in the dark so that no patrolling palace guard tells them off.

San's most prominent cybercafe is only a ten-minute walk from the Magnolia Diner, so it isn't long before Yilas and Chami approach its front entrance and press their faces close to the glass door. The lights are off. Bibi said to meet here, but she didn't say whether they were supposed to go in or hover outside.

"Hear anything?" Chami whispers.

Yilas shakes her head. "This would be the first place the Weisannas shut down, so I doubt they'll operate openly. Let's try the back."

The cafe, although self-sufficient, is still located in the ground floor of a mall, and the mall's main entrance is a creaky revolving door on Mouco Street.

As soon as they approach along Mouco Street, though, sidestepping someone's abandoned bicycle out front—did they purchase it in Er, then realize it was too hard to ride bikes through San?—Yilas figures the revolving door must be locked. Yilas shakes the pushbar roughly, as though that might loosen the structure, and Chami giggles.

"Something funny?"

"You are, my darling. I think there's a door stopper here." Chami kicks away a triangular block jammed under one part of the revolving door. When she leans over to nudge the pushbar again, the door starts to move. "There we are."

Of course.

Yilas and Chami enter the mall quickly and pass the ghostly, empty stores. It is a matter of trial and error before they find themselves at the back of the cybercafe, and even then, Yilas isn't sure if the place is actually open, given that they've wandered through what she thinks must be the back entryway into absolute pitch dark. Her footsteps echo. Chami's grip on her hand tightens.

"The wait is about an hour, I'm afraid."

Yilas and Chami shriek at the same time, whirling around. The voice came from behind the counter. Suddenly illuminated by a square of blue light, an old man stands with a bottle of soda in his hands, a straw waving out the top. Though he is well dressed, his jacket hangs off him bizarrely, the padded shoulders at odds with his thin frame.

"Sulian, they're with me!"

That voice comes from behind the counter too, much lower to the floor. Yilas peers over and finds Bibi with her head sticking out of a square in the floor, waving happily. There's a basement level beneath the cafe.

"Don't I keep telling you to register your visitors' names in advance?" Sulian asks.

"Sorry." Bibi has already disappeared back down into the basement. "Please allow my visitors through. I'll tip nicely. Thank you!"

The old man looks tired. He turns to Yilas and Chami, then silently gestures for them to proceed.

"After you," Chami whispers.

"So I can get murdered first?" Yilas whispers back.

Still, she goes around the counter. Peers down the stairs into the blue basement, sniffing, before stepping onto the ladder carefully. It's a very small space—no more than three computers in use—echoing with the clatter of rapid typing. Yilas holds out a hand to help Chami behind her. When Chami steps onto the last rung, she loses her footing a little, her elbow knocking into a divider before she regains her balance. Yilas hurries to hold the divider still, then blinks, squinting through the gaps of its foldable hinges. She was mistaken: this isn't a small space at all; it's only a small space reserved for the computers. Behind the divider, rows and rows of bookshelves expand onward and onward, taking up most of the basement.

"Over here."

There are two teenagers present using the other computers, but they've got headsets glued to their ears. Yilas and Chami pick past them, shuffling tentatively to the computer that Bibi has occupied.

"We're going to use a VoIP program," Bibi says the moment they sit beside her, wasting no time for pleasantries. She clicks around on the screen, pulling open multiple windows.

"A voy-p?" Yilas tries to repeat.

"VoIP. Voice over Internet Protocol." She looks over. Gets blank stares. "Okay. Sorry. I can run a program that dials out into the provinces. Just input the number. It won't save it for me, if you're worried about that."

"Not like we would believe you, anyhow," Yilas mutters, covering her hand to type when Bibi nudges the keyboard in front of her. She's still not convinced that this isn't a trap. Give it a minute or two, and there will probably be Crescent Society members running in from behind those bookshelves to kidnap her again and carve out her heart.

"I asked around the temple about you earlier," Bibi says while Yilas finishes inputting the number. "They apologize about involving you with the experiments. Most of the members who were dabbling in that funny business are gone now. We're not all the same . . . Well, I suppose we mostly want the same things, but we have different ethics in how we go about it."

Yilas doesn't even bother dignifying that with a response.

She's more concerned with getting Calla's number right, but the moment she clicks the green CALL button, it displays a connectivity error. Bibi frowns at the screen.

"Weird," she says. "Even if it's not going to work, it should at least try calling first."

"Is the number right?" Chami asks, leaning closer to put her chin on Yilas's shoulder.

"It is," Yilas says. "I don't know why—" It occurs to her. "Hang on. I know."

She pulls open a browser and navigates to one of San-Er's online newspapers. On either side of her, Bibi and Chami silently watch as Yilas scrolls through the most recent articles and stops when she finds a write-up about the divine crown. She was reading this absently over lunch. The reporter has drawn a map for them, marked with arrows that indicate the royal delegation's route into the borderlands.

Chami points forward, understanding why Yilas is checking the delegation route.

"Try Laho's area code."

Yilas adds a two-digit province code at the start of Calla's traveling cellular number. Error.

"Lankil?" Chami suggests next, more uncertain. The delegation would be going too slowly if they're still in Lankil.

Error.

"May as well be generous about it," Yilas says, finally trying Actia Province's prefix.

The small window on the screen changes. Instead of a red box error, it turns into a green loading circle. Bibi sits up straight. Yilas and Chami hold very still.

It rings once. Twice.

"What the *fuck?*" are the first words emitted over the computer speakers, crackling with interference but otherwise audible. If Calla's voice wasn't immediately recognizable, her greeting sure is. "Who is this, and how are you getting through?"

"It's me," Yilas says in a rush. "Are you able to speak?"

"Erm, well . . . sure. Anton, take over the reins, would you?"

Yilas rears back. Chami blinks. Bibi, slowly, tilts her head.

"Anton?" she echoes. "Anton Makusa? Isn't he dead?"

"That's a long story I can't be getting into on the roads of Actia. This damn desert is no joke. What's happened? Is Chami okay?"

"I'm fine!" Chami chirps. "I'm here too!"

"Calla, the Crescent Societies are starting a coup in San-Er." There's no point beating around the bush. Yilas doesn't know where the microphone is located if they're calling from a computer, so she raises her voice. "They've been quietly killing guards and Weisannas in the last week, but it's escalated to a widespread broadcast calling for the deaths of the council. Most of the councilmembers who remain in the capital are being attacked."

The other side of the line hums. The pause goes on for long enough that Yilas wonders if the connection has dropped, though the green circle is still flashing on the screen.

"That is certainly a troublesome development." Interference over the line crackles and sputters. "But there's nothing I can do. Otta Avia went rogue, and we're racing her to the crown. San-Er will have to hold tight until the delegation returns."

Bibi gives Yilas a knowing look, as if to say: *See, she doesn't even care that much.*

Yilas grimaces. "One more thing. The Crescent Societies actually helped us make this call. I've got someone here for you."

"You've got *what?*"

"Hello, Highness," Bibi cuts in. "I'll keep this quick—I know you're a busy person. Upon your return to San-Er, you can count on our forces behind you. We only ask that you don't combat us. We have a lot in common."

"A lot in common—Yilas, is this a prank?"

"I assure you the temples have reached agreement," Bibi continues before Yilas can answer. "We've never wanted utter chaos. We only want the kingdom to live how the gods made us. With you on the throne as our symbol, it'll make for genuine and lasting change."

Calla must have pulled the phone away from her ear. There's faint muttering, the sort that doesn't sound very agreeable.

"The Crescent Societies are under new leadership," Yilas says weakly.

"Sure," Calla answers, her voice accompanied by a burst of static when she returns to the line, "whatever."

After all those years working with her, Yilas knows what one of Calla's brush-offs sounds like. She's strangely relieved, even though this is exactly what Chami predicted would happen. There had been a part of her afraid to hear interest when Bibi made her proposition. Yilas can't really explain why.

"Listen, Yilas, Chami, while I've got you," Calla says. Her words are growing more and more inaudible. If she's riding through Actia while speaking, she may be getting too far from the cell tower they've connected to. "Have you ever heard of a Sinoa Tuoleimi?"

Yilas and Chami exchange a look. Neither of them completed their schooling before dropping out to become palace attendants. Despite their unfinished education, though, they learned their history lessons early, like all children in

San-Er. One of the first units they are taught is that King Akilas Shenzhi in the Palace of Earth led the war effort against Sica. During the war, his brother King Potau Tuoleimi manned the Palace of Heavens—though he wasn't a real Tuoleimi, because the generation of Tuoleimis before him had no children and they moved over a Shenzhi instead.

"No clue," Chami answers. "Was she a ruler before the war?"

"Must be," Calla says, sounding thoughtful. "You've never heard the name? Maybe she was born a Shenzhi instead."

Name swapping among the royals has always been common practice, even after the kingdom consolidated their capital into San-Er. King Kasa's father, too, was a Shenzhi with two sons, while the other throne bore no children. King Kasa inherited San and the Palace of Earth, then Calla's father was reassigned into a Tuoleimi for Er and the Palace of Heavens. Shenzhi and Tuoleimi were the same blood. The name was a formality to echo the palace.

"I've never heard of a Sinoa, full stop," Yilas says. "What are you asking?"

". . . figured it was a long shot . . . bizarre history . . ."

Calla's connection is fading. Yilas leans forward, meaning to say something about Anton's mother and what the Crescent Societies know about her, but then the call drops, the green circle switching to a red line.

Bibi is up and moving immediately. She ejects a disk from the computer. Loops a pair of headphones around her neck.

"This was very productive," she declares. With a swipe of her hand across the keyboard, the screen clears and she has logged out of the system. "I have some affairs to get in order. You have my number if you need me for anything else."

Yilas and Chami let her go. Neither says anything in the affirmative; if they're lucky, they'll never have to be involved in this nonsense again.

"Oh!" Bibi says, spinning around before she ascends the ladder back into the main cybercafe. "It might be good to stay indoors for the next few days. Just a heads-up."

CHAPTER 29

August thought he heard the old gods once.

He would never have admitted to it. If he did, the palace would have deemed him insane long before he could climb its ranks. But he knows he wasn't mistaken, even if he can't entirely explain how it happened.

He was fourteen, and his father was dying. Annic Avia didn't offer August much as far as his lot in life went, but he taught August how to fold paper birds and took him to the city burial rooms every year, where he spent time going room to room with August, showing him which panels belonged to their ancestors. In San-Er, the respected dead are not buried; their ashes are placed into trays, and the trays slotted into the wall drawers, labeled with a two-inch panel for their name. August used to read each one with utmost care, looking closely at the color it had been engraved with. Very rarely did anything else represent a family in a city with this many people, and so their descendants printed the dead's names in the color of their eyes, for one small piece of unique remembrance in a sea of metal drawers.

The Avias are an old family, his father said on his deathbed. *Though we may not be special, we have history. That's something you must preserve. Take care of your mother and your sister.*

Later that year, Otta would get the yaisu sickness, and his mother would jump to her death by sneaking up to the top of the wall. Those two matters were not related. His mother was Annic's second wife and couldn't give less of a fuck about Otta, whose mother had passed in childbirth. Though he visited the two of them too, he mourned only his father regularly.

The new moon hid him slinking through the city when he went to pay his respects on the first day of every month, bringing fruit for gifts. He was nothing but a wraith, unknown by all and unknown most to himself. The kingdom owed him little, but he wanted more. August made sure his father got two drawers instead of one, purchasing both slots so the panel was larger than the rest. Still, each time he cleaned his father's grave, the black ink seemed terribly ordinary compared with the other names. Black eyes were supposed to be a mark of nobility, commonly found in the palace. To August, that spoke of insignificance. He could easily be replaced by the next lonely boy in the north wing. Written with the same pens, if he swapped his school essays with those on the desk next to him, no teacher would be able to tell the difference.

"I would like to know," he whispered aloud one night, polishing the drawers and helping the panels nearby with a coat of shine too, "whether there is more for me."

Hardly anyone knew who August was when Carneli Avia married King Kasa. Though the ceremony was extravagant, nobody cared about the scrawny eight-year-old nephew who entered nobility by proxy. In the years that passed, he charmed nobles and made sure he was well-liked among the most elite crowd. It wasn't enough. It didn't get him close enough to what he desired.

"I want to know what more there could be."

It was not a musing he expected to be answered. He was hardly awake at the late hour, so the echo that sounded could have been written off to his imagination. Only the flickering lights told him this wasn't an auditory hallucination, the shrines of every deity nearby pulsing red. He turned, and he heard *King, king, king* whispered directly from the heavens, and August made up his mind.

When he gave Aunt Carneli the cup of tea, it was supposed to damage her organs. Enough to rid the possibility of heirs, so that August could begin plotting one day. He didn't expect her to take ill.

He didn't expect her to die shortly thereafter.

Matters, however, worked out for him, as they tend to do. August likes to think the god of luck is particularly fond of him, and even if he can't imagine the old gods existing as entities that walk the earth like province dwellers believe, he does know their essence remains in the kingdom. A wind blows; a die is cast. Events fall into place, and August Shenzhi is king.

Too bad he's only lived a few hours of it thus far.

They ride into Actia Province after nightfall. It has gotten horrendously cold, and Galipei keeps glancing over from his horse, watching August urge forward faster and faster on his own. The guards have repeatedly asked August to please get into a carriage, but he refuses, preferring to ride. There's far more sitting room now, after the councilmembers were given the opportunity to return to San-Er. The ones who left will bring the announcement into the cities that Anton Makusa and Calla Tuoleimi are criminals conspiring against the throne, having plotted from the coronation onward.

Not every councilmember wanted to return, though. They've heard about the Crescent Society attacks. The unrest, building and building in San-Er.

"We must slow," Galipei calls. "We're approaching sand."

August nods his silent approval. As soon as they have reduced to a speed that allows it, Galipei nudges his horse closer. The other guards lag behind. They are free to speak.

"August, one moment," Galipei says. "Do you recall—"

"No," August interrupts. Unfairly, unrighteously, he cannot understand how Galipei didn't see he had been invaded for weeks . . . if not as his guard, then surely as someone who knows him, who should be his closest confidant.

From an early age, there was nothing August resented more than being overlooked. He spent too many nights alone as a child, sitting in the corner of the factory his father owned and wondering why he felt no more real than one of the rubber machines running in a row. A piece could break down, and it would not matter, because dozens more on the work floor would replace it in an instant. August couldn't bear an environment like that. He much preferred the palace afterward. He loved getting to speak with the nobility in the meeting rooms, his words rippling beyond the four walls and into written law.

August Shenzhi needs the kingdom to care about what he is doing. He needs the kingdom to know that he loves it deeply, tragically, profoundly. In return, their devotion will be real and lasting. For as long as they bear witness to the wonders he offers and think of him as their great burden bearer, he can grow larger than life. He can be their very representation of the heavens, taking mortal form.

The trouble with keeping Galipei around is that August tempts himself into believing he might have it both ways. That Galipei might truly see him, and he may receive total devotion anyway. It doesn't work like that. It shouldn't. Galipei was assigned to him. At the end of it all, none of it is real, and he ought to remember that.

"Don't take that tone with me," Galipei chides. "I knew something was wrong."

"And yet," August says, "we were all the way in *Laho Province* before something brought me back by chance."

"By chance? You underestimate me."

Anger tentatively releases its tight grip around August's spine. He hears a note in Galipei's tone. He knows what Galipei is implying.

"You saw the letter in the study."

The Dovetail appeared on August's radar when the palace guards raided the Crescent Societies after Leida's treason and found communication in and out of the capital. Though the Dovetail and the Crescent Societies are both revolutionary groups, they disagree on one major facet: the Crescent Societies want to abolish the monarchy and let the gods rule; the Dovetail only want to eliminate bureaucracy—get rid of the council, the generals, the soldiers—and let the gods channel through the monarch on the throne.

And August knew he had an opportunity to work with.

"I didn't find the letter until we were about to leave San-Er." Galipei pauses. "I got in contact on your behalf to resume communication."

August, maintaining his stride with his hands steady on the reins, casts a glance at Galipei and finds Galipei already watching him. His guard doesn't seem too upset that August didn't say anything about his plan. Eventually, he would have needed to—there's very little that Galipei doesn't see, and even less that August intentionally wants to keep from him. The pieces fell into place mere days before August was crowned. Between meddling in the games and making the necessary appearances in the palace to ease suspicion, he didn't even have time to take his meals. Galipei must know he would have been told the moment the coronation occurred.

If Anton Makusa hadn't behaved like the pest he is.

August tamps down that flare of rage as soon as it erupts. There will be time for that later.

"You did a fine job," he says. "The council won't survive this."

Actia's sand dunes blow fiercely with the wind. The harshness scratches at August's eyes, though he refuses to hunch down and protect his face.

"August."

Galipei's brow is furrowed when August looks over again. Whatever he is to say, he hesitates, and after a few seconds pass, August prompts:

"Go on."

His permission takes effect instantly. Galipei breaks his restraint.

"It didn't make sense at first, but I understand. You wanted Otta to wake. You knew that cinnabar would trigger it."

This was the one matter that August hoped Galipei wouldn't decipher. The rest he will tell when the time comes. The rest he has reason and endless defense for, no matter who needs to die. Yet it is saving his half sister that troubles him the most, because he doesn't believe in the gods, but it is impossible to explain why he figured there might be a chance this gamble would work unless the gods were real.

"It was a guess," August says evenly. "She was practically dead already. Either it killed her or it resurrected her."

The closer they crept to Kasa's execution, the more and more it weighed on August that his biggest threat thereafter was the council. He didn't have a true claim to the royal bloodline and the throne, as the gossiping aristocrats particularly liked to mention. It would take only one conniving councilmember to put the crown on someone else's head and insist that the heavens had claimed them too, thus starting a debate about who deserved to be the ruler. August already knew the crown wasn't real. He couldn't risk anyone using the loophole to claim the heavens' acceptance, yet he didn't have another way to distinguish himself either, save for the crown's will. He didn't have royal blood. Kasa's adoption was the only item that gave him any right to rule, and after Kasa was dead, what stopped the council from coming after that little fact the moment they were upset with him?

"August," Galipei says, and his voice is distant, faint. "Why did it work? What do you know?"

Many years ago, August and Leida Miliu had a scheme to leave San-Er and recover the true divine crown from a lost palace deep within the borderlands. It was rumored to have the power to raze cities and change sea tides, read minds and order armies. With it, they could launch a coup against King Kasa by force. Wage war against Talin from the north and work their way down until they liberated the capital.

The problem was that they needed Anton Makusa to join them, because the provinces were difficult to travel, and the borderlands even harder to navigate. If they wanted to survive, they needed to jump. Without Anton's skill set, their plan was the flimsy make-believe of children. Then Otta found out, and she didn't want him to go. Otta, in fact, was where Leida had learned about the crown, given how often Leida was spying, convinced that there was something *off* about that girl. His half sister had always been a bit peculiar. Though August warned Leida not to mind her, she continued downloading camera footage to keep an eye on Otta, until the day Otta noticed Leida lurking and snuck into Leida's bedroom to do her own snooping.

"I'll tell! I'll tell! I swear I will!" Otta had rushed to confront August in his quarters. No matter how much he tried to quiet her, she was incensed at what she had found: a half-written proposal, not yet finished but addressed to Anton. Leida had composed a letter to prevent anyone in the palace from overhearing a treasonous conversation, and still, a treasonous discovery had been made.

"What do you want, Otta?" August had spat. "An invitation too? This is bigger than your stupid fling—"

"You can't have him," Otta returned. "And you can't have *this*." She flapped the torn paper in her hand. "If Leida read that book closely, you'd see the crown is cursed. Do you think it is as easy as a mere retrieval? You need sacrifice. *Enormous* sacrifice—"

"I am willing," August interrupted. "I know what I'm trying to achieve. It's for the good of the kingdom."

Otta flung open the curtain beside her. The sunlight that streamed through his window that day was so harsh it hurt his eyes, rare for San-Er.

"Look at you, pretending to be good. You're worse for San than Kasa ever could be. You'll put us in cages and call us your loyal subjects."

There was no point arguing with Otta. August was aware of the ultimatum she was issuing him: take Anton away from her, and she would tattle. The next time he snuck into her rooms, hoping to steal the source that Leida had been reading from, he found the book in Otta's fireplace, burned to a charred remnant.

"I always wondered why someone as shrewd as my sister would be obtuse enough to believe jumping repeatedly into Weisannas would be a good idea," August says in the present. "She wasn't trying to escape that day—she was trying to perform a ritual, and it failed. Her qi got stuck, and that brought on the yaisu sickness. Cinnabar is a cleansing element of qi."

Galipei must know this explanation doesn't make sense. He watches the path ahead warily, his knuckles white on his horse's reins. He must know that there was more that pushed August's hands, but Galipei Weisanna does not ask further.

"Now she's awake," Galipei mutters, "and going after your crown."

"That's exactly why we woke her up." The desert is leveling out. They have entered Actia proper, and they must hurry. "She's going to lead us to it."

CHAPTER 30

They arrive in the capital of Actia Province after two days of nonstop riding, and Anton is close to passing out. He won't admit it if asked—and he's denied it each time Calla has asked throughout the ride—but it has started to show. When he gets off the horse, he holds still for a few moments, gathering his composure.

Calla eyes him suspiciously. Although her efforts are focused on tying the horse down outside the village stables, her face is pale too, not entirely a trick of the moonlight that rises slowly over the horizon. They need water. Food. Riding any farther without pause isn't sustainable.

The sand under their feet stirs. A southerly wind blows with the faint smell of ash, and Anton shudders at the same time that Calla does. They both feel it: every minute they spend inactive is time afforded for August to catch up.

"If anyone inquires," Calla says, "we're travelers heading for the borderlands after the rumors about the divine crown. I doubt we're the only ones taking refuge in Actia tonight."

Anton stretches his neck, then his arms side to side. There's a muscle strain at the left of his back, and he can't get it out no matter how much he throws his limbs around. "Otta's grand declaration was a week ago. Most travelers south of Actia would have passed through already."

"We're particularly slow travelers, along for the thrill rather than the appeal of acquiring treasure for the black market. No one's going to interrogate us too closely."

She decides it, and that is that. It's not like Anton has the energy to debate her anyway. By fortuity, they happen to be aligned now, but it's the days before the Juedou all over again. Anton is on the run to survive, still plotting a way to hit August while they proceed; Calla is clearly concerned about stopping Otta. They cannot press too hard on why they have decided to join together and continue onward as a unit, lest it give way and reveal what lies beneath.

Calla tilts her head toward the yamen, then gestures for him to turn his face down too when they begin to walk. It's late, so there are unlikely to be people working there, but a yamen always functions double as the gate into the village, and two palace soldiers are stationed on either side of the entrance. The soldiers let them pass without trouble, not bothering to call a greeting. Perhaps the warning hasn't been put out; perhaps August didn't spread the word that Princess Calla Tuoleimi and Anton Makusa were wanted, for fear it would incite trouble in the provinces.

The sand jostles with their steps before it fades to grass inside the yamen. Much as Anton tries to keep his gaze forward, his wandering eye automatically latches on to the doors on his left that lead deeper into the building. Someone's silhouette moves behind one of the papered panels. The mayor of Actia must be busy these days keeping a handle on affairs. He will be preparing for the royal delegation that is soon to pass through, assuming it wasn't entirely wiped out in Laho.

Somehow, Anton doubts that August will be that easy to kill—certainly not by a bunch of cult worshippers, even ones with tricks of qi at their disposal.

"Whoa."

Calla's soft exclamation comes the moment they step out the yamen's other side. The village unfolds before them, soft lantern light hanging from the shop sides and velvet shadows coating the space the orange glow doesn't touch. Stalls line the street, as do throngs of villagers flocking to the activity. Unless Actia is hiding a secret funnel of finances that Talin doesn't know about, this must be a special festival, its vendors hauling out food items and windup toys and incense sticks for sale. A kite cut to resemble a short, round man flies off one of the stalls, waving with the wind.

Somehow, they hadn't seen it from outside the yamen.

"A rendering of a god, I'd gather," Anton remarks, gesturing to the kite man.

Calla says nothing. Whatever she's thinking, she only strides forward, making an ambiguous noise. Anton's limbs are stone when he goes to follow. He makes an effort not to ram into people's shoulders in the crowd, but the street is narrow. At Calla's side, his birth body is considerably taller than her, tall enough to give the impression of looming. He has to resist the urge to fold his arms over his chest and slouch, the schoolboy urge to be flippant in the very manner he's walking. His birth body has never been comfortable for him—not by self-consciousness, but because it's too wholly his, and anything of his in full view of others is privy to being ruined. Anything an opponent can home in on is at risk of attack.

"Did you hear that?" Calla says under her breath. Her hand jerks to the side. When she pulls it back, she's stolen two sticks of roasted taro.

"What a delinquent," Anton says, but he takes one of the sticks.

"Listen."

They pause, as though there's something to inspect at the next stall selling joss paper, but Anton quickly determines which conversation Calla wants him to tune into.

"*—said he hasn't heard from him since then. I know there aren't exactly phone lines in there, but it doesn't bode well.*"

"*I wouldn't worry too much. They went in knowing it would require a search. It's not like he has a map.*"

"*Yes, but he wasn't going to throw his life away for it. He said if he couldn't find it in two days, he would come back. It's been a week.*"

They're speaking about the crown. With Actia located this close to the borderlands, there must be plenty of civilians who took the chance to trek into the mountains and take a look around.

Foolish of anyone to think they'd be able to stumble onto a centuries-old object in the borderlands in *two days.* Anton exchanges a judgmental glance with Calla. Nonetheless, goose bumps rise on his arms.

"Come on," Calla says.

As soon as she makes the command, though, Anton halts in his step, disrupting the flow of the festivalgoers. He isn't being difficult on purpose. He's just noticed that his breath is coming out opaque.

"Shit. What's going on?"

Calla stops short too, her eyes turning wide. The province goes cold—suddenly and without warning, as though an air-conditioning unit has been switched onto the maximum setting from the heavens. Some of the festivalgoers nearby shudder, mumbling in confusion. Actia isn't known for this sort of weather. The winters may be brisk in the desert, but not with such abrupt drops.

"In Rincun," Calla says, "it happened like this as well."

"The cold?"

Calla sucks in her cheeks, biting on them inside her mouth while she considers their surroundings. Her lips burn crimson red. Dehydration, most likely. Anton shouldn't fixate on the picture, but he does.

"The cold," she confirms. "And then we found an entire barracks of dead soldiers. Let's get inside."

They identify a tavern by the banner waving outside, and Calla ducks in first, her long hair swinging from the movement. Anton glances over his shoulder, checking their surroundings closely, before following her. At the bar, Calla is already speaking to the woman behind the counter, passing over cash.

"I didn't realize you were carrying any."

"Only enough to pay for room six upstairs," Calla mutters, propping her elbows against the bar. She taps her finger on the stone surface; Anton follows the direction of her subtle pointing and registers the man sitting at the end of the counter seats. He's the only lone figure present. The rest are families or groups, getting in a late meal. A thin set of uneven stairs goes to the lodgings upstairs. When one of the barkeeps ascends with a tray of food in his hands, the staircase groans like an instrument being played underfoot.

One possible threat, but quick exits in their favor.

"There you are, dearest." The first barkeep sets down two glasses of water in front of them. She pauses a moment, wiping the spilled drops, then says to Calla, "You look familiar."

"Thank you. I get that a lot."

The barkeep goes to clean another part of the tavern. Calla pushes the other glass nearer to Anton. He finishes the water in three gulps. Riding north through Laho meant the air was only getting drier and drier. Though he and Calla traded off on steering the horse forward, there wasn't any rest to be found in between.

"We need to talk about Otta."

"We'll find it before she does," Anton assures, but he should have known Calla couldn't be taken for a fool, because just as quickly, she replies:

"That's not what I'm talking about, and you know it." She summons the barkeep for more water. After the woman pours another glass and turns away, Calla reaches into her pocket, retrieves a piece of paper, and slaps it upon the stone counter.

Anton takes in the map slowly. *Come alone,* it says at the top, marked by a black *X* deep in the middle of the borderlands.

"This has nothing to do with my personal distaste for Otta Avia. Too many strange events have happened on this delegation, starting with why she took us out here claiming she wanted the crown for you, and why the Dovetail were targeting the delegation on August's behalf this entire time. They may be working together, Anton. If we're turning adversary against August, we have to prepare to counter Otta too."

Anton sighs. Of all times to have this conversation, it has to be now, when his head is pounding and his stomach is growling. Nonetheless, he's too worn to be sniping at Calla when she's the closest thing he has to an ally, so he'll entertain it.

"If you're asking whether I think they plotted together before she fell sick, I don't know," he says. "I couldn't tell you why Otta does anything she does, except that I turned down her offer to rule through me like some puppet king while we were in Lankil, and that's the last time I spoke to her."

Calla's expression turns thoughtful. She downs another glass of water. If she's trying to make sense of what sort of relationship Anton had with Otta, the truth is that he's never really understood it either. Otta always treated the world like it was play-pretend, like nothing she did had consequence and people's views toward her were record tapes she could rewind at will. Maybe she never actually wanted to run away with him: as much as she bemoaned the palace, she built her very sense of identity off how well she maneuvered it, and when the day came that they enacted their plan to raid the vault, perhaps there was some other ploy in progress he hadn't been privy to. Perhaps if they had been successful, Otta would have left him for dead and used the money she'd reaped.

"It must feel terrible," Calla states matter-of-factly. "You spent all this time keeping her alive as someone to hold on to, and you didn't actually know *who* you were holding on to. You didn't have a clue she could use qi that way. You were none the wiser that she alone possessed the location to some mythical object capable of uprooting the entire kingdom."

Anton sets his water glass down. "Room six, was it?"

He's walking toward the stairs before Calla can reply. He hears her tut, and seconds later, her footsteps are clattering after him.

"Did that make you *upset?*"

"I didn't say anything." The tavern trills alongside his climb. After one sharp turn and one almost-wrong pivot, Anton walks into the room labeled with a *6*. A small gas lamp in the corner burns to provide dim light. There's no lock. One of them is going to have to keep watch.

"You didn't have to say anything. You just stomped away like a petulant toddler."

Calla comes in after him and closes the door. Maybe he's going delirious, but he doubts he can find sleep despite his exhaustion. He wants to run the rest of the distance to the borderlands. Climb onto the top of the highest mountain and take a leap—see if that'll make Otta come back and claim to care about him, or if it'll prove that he was truly nothing more than a resting perch.

Seven years. He should have pulled her plug and sent himself into the incinerator alongside her corpse, saved them this trouble later on.

"It's not your fault."

Anton stops. His jacket is half-off, yanked in a fit of annoyance. "I beg your pardon?"

"This. Everything." Calla seems uncomfortable—which is certainly a first for Anton to witness. She scratches the inside of her wrist. "Some people spend their whole lives pretending to be someone they're not in pursuit of achieving a goal. It says everything about her machinations and nothing about you."

Anton can't help it: he laughs. "Thank you, Calla. Because I really needed you to try to make me feel better."

"You've always held her in such high esteem, so yes, I did figure you needed it."

Calla plunks herself down on the bed pallet capriciously. She doesn't look like she's going to shed any layers to prepare for rest, so Anton throws his jacket to the floor, then undoes the buttons on his shirt. Surely she won't mind.

"Oh, please." He throws the shirt to the floor too. He has no idea who put that on him, or when. Probably years ago, given how the hem is unraveling. "You killed me. You, of anyone, can't speak to what I need."

"Untrue." Calla unclasps her sword. Tosses it beside the pallet. "I killed you, but that doesn't mean I didn't care for you. I would have given up everything for the possibility of what we had—everything but one task. It's not my fault we were put in a position where I ended up having to choose."

It's hardly an apology. It's hardly even spoken with repentance. Yet when Anton stays quiet, considering her words, he resolves that it is perhaps his saving grace in this kingdom. Before him is the only person he knows won't lie to him.

Anton crouches. Calla tilts her head, staring back in a way that makes the hairs at the back of his neck lift. Her eyes flit, but it's too quick to track.

"And now?" he asks. "With the choice done?"

Cold seeps into the tavern. It isn't as severe as when they stood outside, but the chill has pried its fingers through the window, under the glass.

"I'm not sure what you mean."

He's acting without thinking. *Delirium*, *most certainly*, he insists. His hand reaches forward, takes Calla's chin, and tilts her face to the lamp in the corner. Her yellow eyes flare back at him, as though he's placed precious gold in direct sunlight.

"I'm warning you," Calla says dully. "I will not be your replacement merely because you cannot have your first love."

"Was that love?" Anton counters. "Is this?"

He thinks about the palace and its orderly sitting rooms, its silver candelabras. The twin cities, always tied to one another, the final battleground for a kingdom that barely won its war.

"If it wasn't, I wouldn't be here."

Anton's grip tightens. "You're here because there's a crown waiting at the end of it."

"I have no use for that crown."

"You were fighting to control it in the arena. After Kasa was dead, you got to decide who came next."

Calla closes her eyes. "No. *I* was willing to let go of everything after Kasa was dead," she says, and her volume fizzles to a whisper. "But you wouldn't leave Otta. You remained tethered. Then you had to go and jump into August, and look at what has unfolded since. What other reason do I *have*, Anton? I've followed you across the kingdom because I can't let you go a second time."

There's no venom in her words, yet each one lands with its own blistering wound. He swallows past a lump in his throat. The lamp flickers.

"Tell me, Calla," Anton says. "Tell me how I could have survived if I hadn't taken August in that moment."

Her palm lifts. She sets it gently atop his hand, weaving their fingers together. It worms a sensation through muscle, down his chest. It burrows into his heart, an infection taking hostage of his blood.

"Maybe," Calla murmurs, "neither of us should have survived."

He has no desire to rein himself in. Anton leans forward, and he's almost surprised when Calla doesn't push him away, when their lips make contact and she exhales into it, letting two seconds, three seconds, four pass before her hand pushes into his hair and she holds him closer.

His birth body has been awake since he jumped and burst out of that carriage, but it is only now it remembers being fully a part of the world. It is only now, when Calla's hand skates along his neck, down his chest, around his torso, leaving a trail of chills in its wake, that he knows what he has missed in these years occupying somebody else.

Anton pulls back a fraction. Calla lets him. She stares at him with those eyes, and he's no better than a believer hypnotized by the heavens.

"Is this a death warrant?" He curls a finger around a strand of her hair. It slithers like water, glides like silk. "Mutually signed, mutually enacted?"

"I'm glad you've realized." Calla's breath catches when his finger moves to her lower lip. She recovers, says, "You know what you're getting into. You know who I am."

"I know."

Her tongue takes him easily when he slides his finger into her mouth. A shiver seizes his spine, and though the room is getting colder, colder, he has never been warmer in any body. Every inch of his skin is ablaze.

He's tired of fighting her. No matter the warning signs that scream he is to be electrocuted if he grabs the live wire, he's willing to embrace his hubris in the belief that he will be different, that intent alone is enough to alter his course from every other mortal that has dared ask for too much. Anton breathes out, setting his forehead into the crook of Calla's neck, and he's safe in that moment, spitting at the feet of the gods. He pushes Calla onto her back and presses her arms over her head, and when she lets him, when she's compliant and amenable, he signs away any chance of emerging from this unmarked.

"Don't forget," Calla says, so softly that Anton strains to hear her. "We leave before dawn."

He almost laughs. "Are you trying to say you need rest?"

Calla frowns. Her hips shift, and Anton barely stops himself from wheezing aloud. One of her hands slinks free, traces down his stomach, along his waistband.

"Calla."

"Yes?" Her tone lilts. It's not a true call for response, not any request for further clarification. There's one demand: *Say it back.*

"Yes. You—"

Whatever he intended his next words to be, they are lost to an inhale when she tugs on his zipper.

"No lock on the door," she whispers into his ear. "If you're going to kill me, make it quiet and hide the body before the tavern calls the soldiers."

"I'll make it plenty quiet." His cock is so hard that it borders on the point of pain. Calla is doing it on purpose, her hand drawing out each second lowering the zip. He only bears it halfway before he releases her other arm to do it himself. "But I don't promise quick."

"A shame." She turns her gaze to the door, appearing to ignore him while he tugs her pants down and leaves them around her knees. "We're going to get caught, and I've hardly known you like this—"

He slides in. Their gasps merge, Calla's eyes snapping back to him, the guise of coyness flaring into hunger.

"Don't worry." She smells like flawless metal. Feels like a weapon made of flesh and blood under his hands, something that will call him to battle over and over until it has his life in sacrifice. "You'll know me plenty well by the end of this."

His mouth lands on everything it can, her mouth, her neck, her chest. There's something about the act that relieves him of these last few days in stillness, these last few days spent waiting for something to strike during their silent journey. She strengthens him as a preliminary battle drill would, marking out the offensive capabilities between them. He can feel Calla winding up when her legs fight to straighten beneath him, and Anton smooths his hands along her hair, holds her in place when she moans into his mouth and seizes up for a long while.

"There we are," he whispers.

She exhales. Arches against him, her fingers gripping into his arms on either side.

"Though you may think otherwise," she mumbles, "you are my anchor in this world. I'm sorry I tossed you adrift. I thought I was burying us instead."

The words do something odd to him. Anton breathes in, his face nudged against hers, and when he finishes, he can feel the whole world pulsating as a possibility between them, the kingdom and the wide seas beyond.

"You have me now," he says plainly.

CHAPTER 31

An hour before sunrise, when they are set to leave, Actia Province is still cold as shit.

"This is unnatural," Calla says between her chattering teeth. Her fingers are stiff without gloves. The moment her boots touch the ground, she shoves her hands into her pockets.

Anton lands with a grunt. Rather than risk being spotted, they're leaving their room through the second-floor window, and he's made the climb out from the tavern with slightly less grace.

"I don't suppose we have time to steal coats before we go."

Calla doubts the villagers in Actia will own coats that are sufficient, anyhow—and if they did, she's certainly not going to take them. It's not quite the same as swiping a roasted taro.

"We'll warm up en route," she says. The sky hovers before them in that black-muddled gray, both affronted by and resistant to the day that is to come. As far as Calla is aware, there has been no talk of an overnight massacre. No attacks have come of the sudden cold, not like in Rincun.

"What are you thinking about?"

Anton poses the question casually. In answer, she reaches out and smooths his tangle of hair. She doubts he needs to know this, lest his big head grow larger, but this body suits him most. The easy agility, the strong jaw. It gives him a look that closely resembles what is inside: simultaneously the steadfast soldier serving the kingdom and the rebelling noble it never should have armed. Anton Makusa in his birth body has acquired age well, much better than some vessels that are left stagnant for too long. He watches her while she inspects him, holds her gaze taking him in, and when her eyes lift to meet his face, he doesn't look away.

"What are *you* thinking about?" she returns. The question seemed like it was leading somewhere.

Anton breaks their staring contest to check over his shoulder, as though someone might be tailing them. It's entirely quiet. They're careful to keep their steps light while moving through the smaller streets of the village, avoiding the main thoroughfare. It is too easy to leave footprints in the mud and offer a traceable path for anyone searching.

"On that phone call, you asked your attendants about a Sinoa Tuoleimi."

Calla stiffens. "Have you heard the name?"

"It took me until now to remember why it was familiar, but yes. Otta owned a book that had her name on the front page. *Property of Sinoa Tuoleimi.* She destroyed it years ago. I watched her throw it into the fire after a fight with August."

This is bizarre. A whole Tuoleimi princess existed shortly before the war, and yet their history texts have no mention of her. How can the only records of her existence be one book that Otta Avia owned . . . and Calla's hallucinations?

"Strange," Calla says.

Anton casts her a look. They pause when they approach the inner side of Actia's yamen, waiting for movement, before nodding at each other and moving quickly through the center. It's empty. Dead silent.

"Think we were spotted?" Anton asks outside.

"Doesn't matter." Calla hauls herself onto their horse, taking on primary rider responsibilities for the first section of the journey. "We're going. Come on."

Anton pulls himself up behind her. The horse takes some adjusting, whinnying at the first appearance of the sand dunes, but Calla navigates onto a smoother path quickly. It's hard to see through the sand and in the dark. She's almost sure there's supposed to be a paved route here, cleared for travelers.

They ride without speaking. Anton must be deep in thought, because he does not remark on any of Calla's riding, even when she sends them over a particularly rough dune. Her constant motion keeps her sweating, fighting back the cold. Nonetheless, her nose loses feeling shortly into the journey. The temperature is plummeting further. It's coming from the mountains, funneling a cold that she can feel in her lungs each time she breathes in.

"Princess," Anton calls suddenly. "How far have we gone?"

Calla blinks, straining her ears to catch his question past the roaring wind. "We're entering northern Actia now. Why?"

"Look. There are people riding toward us."

At first, Calla thinks Anton must be mistaken, that their poor rest the previous night means he's seeing things in the horizon. She squints. The dunes have started to level out. In a few hours, as they approach the border between Actia and Rincun, it will become flat, dry land, made for crops to die.

Then, as they get closer, Calla realizes Anton is right. The distant shape is another delegation. Certainly not August's, nor any rural group.

"Flag them down," Calla commands. "Wave your arms."

Anton does as he is told without hesitating, rising slightly on the saddle and waving vigorously. Calla catches the moment the delegation must spot them, because the riders at the front of the group begin to slow. She counts only five people. Not wanting to risk any danger, Calla pulls to a complete stop while there's still distance between them and hops off with her sword clattering against her leg. Anton follows, nothing for a weapon but equally eager to move.

To the east, the sun has started to rise and bleed a murky violet semicircle. The delegation comes to a halt while they remain a field away too. Unlike Calla and Anton's sturdy approach, the moment the first rider alights from their horse, they stumble hard, taking two steps and faltering on the third.

"That's a councilmember," Anton says at once. "She voted against the delegation for the crown. What is she doing out here?"

As soon as Anton identifies the woman, Calla recognizes her as Venus Hailira too. Her clothes are torn. Days old for sure, dirt and blood smeared on the light fabric. The sun climbs higher. Ripples gold and yellow over the sand.

"She came to protect Rincun," Calla says, uncomprehending. "But what is she doing riding back south?"

Calla starts to move forward. The closer she gets, the clearer it is that Venus is seconds away from collapsing. Her lips are blue. Her skin is bloodless.

"Venus," she calls. "What are you doing out here? Are you okay?"

Venus keeps herself upright long enough for Calla to fully approach. The moment Calla grabs Venus by the arms to check for injuries, she keels over. Calla scrambles to prevent the councilmember from falling. When Calla lowers onto her knees, the ground might as well be made of ice for how it stings upon contact, even through her leather trousers.

"Venus," Calla says, panic sinking into her voice. "What happened? Who attacked?"

"Don't," Venus rasps. "Don't go in."

Calla doesn't understand. She glances over to Anton, who appears equally flabbergasted. His gaze lifts over the other members of the delegation, to the horizon where Rincun and its distant mountains reach for the sky. The sun has risen enough to show that the other riders are in similar condition. Near-frostbitten features, their clothes dirty.

"Don't . . . go?" Calla echoes. This must have something to do with the first attack in the barracks. This must have something to do with the borderlands and the object waiting in there, the grand prize that the kingdom is fighting for.

"Don't go into *Rincun*?" Anton adds, dragging his hands through his hair. "What happened?"

"Rincun has frozen over"—Venus shudders, the effort strained—"along with everyone inside."

◇◇◇◇◇

They return to Actia's yamen.

This time, Calla announces her arrival, asking for an audience with the mayor. The air has taken on a sunburned smell, even while the temperature plummets to freezing. Inside the yamen, the elements are substantially less severe. With the way the floors creak underfoot and the windows are faintly stained gray, Calla could fool herself into believing they sit in Eigi, or Dacia—somewhere close enough for her to grab her sword and quickly return through San-Er's wall if she wanted. The architectural plans for the provinces' yamen are all identical. She only needs to block out the scene outside.

But they're far, far from San-Er here. Yet they cannot move forward either.

"And you've received no communication from either yamen in Rincun?" Calla asks. She's clutching a cup of hot tea in her hands, but it does very little to warm her.

Mayor Policola, who is doing his best to appear genial, flounders with each new question Calla asks. He doesn't know how many travelers have passed through Actia to get to Rincun, therefore he cannot predict exactly how many civilians are trapped in Rincun at present. He doesn't know if Otta Avia came through. He doesn't have a clue why this is happening and why Rincun didn't issue an emergency call from either mayor in West or East Capital.

"If you don't mind me asking," the mayor says while Calla massages her forehead, at a loss for how they've found themselves in this situation, "how did Councilmember Hailira get out?"

"We had horses, and we fled," Venus calls from the other side of the room, overhearing the question. Before this, she'd only managed to nod yes or shake her head no to answer the healer. Her guards appear slightly worse for wear, slowly defrosting on the seats. "What are you trying to say?"

Policola scrambles to assure her he didn't mean anything by it. Meanwhile, Anton makes a thoughtful noise. He declined any tea. Instead, he's pacing the space around Calla, and she's letting him only because the movement is helping create heat in the room, no matter how little.

"It wasn't instantaneous," Anton says—a question, despite his tone.

"It . . . crawled," Venus answers. "As long as we kept moving, we could outrun it."

Anton pauses in his step. The room falls quiet. "So is everyone else in Rincun *dead*?"

Venus doesn't answer. She cannot: she does not know, and it shows plainly on her stricken expression. No one in this room has the faintest clue, half a day away from the border of Rincun.

"They can't be," Calla says. "Otta must be inside the province too. I'm willing to bet anything that she set this off."

"Even if she set this off, maybe she remains unaffected while the rest of Rincun falls dead." Anton starts pacing again. "It is an unnatural cold. That much is certain. It might not strike everybody the same."

It is possible that Otta is inside and perfectly unaffected. It is possible that she doesn't have anything to do with this and she's frozen like the rest of them. The problem is that they don't know enough to move forward, and soon, August will catch up with them and hold them captive out of spite.

As if he can read her mind, Anton trails his finger along her arm as he circles her again, maintaining contact while he's near. From the outside, it might appear a gesture between lovers, but Calla knows better. He is reminding himself she is nearby; she is assuring him that they stand united. There is no path out of this situation except through.

"Councilmember Hailira," Calla prompts suddenly. "Rincun has two cameras, yes?"

"Yes, at the two yamen."

Calla tilts her head to the computer in the room. There's only one camera in Actia, and two in Rincun at East and West Capital. The provinces aren't wired with the infrastructure for the type of electronics that San-Er runs. To make life easier for the councilmembers, the palace put in the bare basics for administration operations at each respective yamen and left it at that.

"Mayor Policola, would you turn that on, please?"

Though the mayor frowns, he walks over to start the machine. Calla gestures for Venus next, and when the councilmember looks to the healer for permission, he takes the blanket off her to confirm her examination is finished.

"Do you want me to log on?" Venus asks.

"If you don't mind," Calla replies.

Talin shares a network across its provinces. If Venus inputs her credentials, she can still access Rincun's server from here.

Venus leans over the keyboard, entering her details. "What am I pulling up?"

"Turn on the live footage from the West Capital yamen. I want to know what we can see."

Venus navigates slowly, her eyes flitting left to right in search of the right buttons. She doesn't appear too familiar with where each function is located, but she knows how to use a computer, and under her identity number, she has access to Rincun's administration, so she'll figure it out eventually. Calla's tea has gone cold. Anton has turned his back on the activity, opting to stare out the yamen window. Maybe he'll find a solution out there.

A soft knock on the door. One of the yamen workers brings papers to the mayor, murmuring softly under his breath. The conversation is largely inaudible, though Calla figures it can't be anything relevant to the situation.

The screen in front of Venus switches to a video player.

"Here we are."

Calla peers over the councilmember's shoulder. The rectangle of footage shows West Capital's yamen, two statues of lions placed on either side of the front entrance. The only indication that this is live footage and not a still image comes from the dusty, unpaved ground, where every gust of wind blows small pieces of dirt and grit off the surface.

"You said the cold *crawled.*" Calla ensures she's using Venus's exact wording. "What exactly did you see happen to the civilians left behind?"

There's something in the far distance, appearing in the corner of the camera by the barest smidgen. Try as Calla does to turn her own head this way and that, she can't get a better angle on what it is.

"They stopped moving," Venus says. "When the cold caught up, it froze them."

Calla thinks about the first descent of cold in Rincun. How it seized down from the heavens, and the qi was stolen from the barracks, and the cold faded. "The cold is some aftereffect of qi, though. It's not literal ice. That doesn't make sense."

"As I keep saying," Anton mutters by the window.

Calla leans closer to the screen. The slight movement in the distance is getting closer. She swears it is larger than the quarter of a pixel it was before. While Venus Hailira starts hypothesizing about other times they've seen strange feats of nature in Rincun—*I've been reading about it, you see, and it occurs more often than you'd think*—Calla taps the keys. The video rewinds. It confirms her suspicion, and she exits the screen.

The people in Rincun aren't frozen. They're moving really, really slowly. In fact, the person captured on the footage must be in the midst of trying to make it to the yamen as the closest place of shelter.

Out of the corner of her eye, Calla notices Anton turn, a brow raised. She's seen him in battle enough times to read his movements, the way his muscles stiffen. He's gauged a threat, and other than Venus Hailira, there's only the mayor in the room and the boy he's speaking to. Calla doesn't make a fuss by asking what he's noticed. Just as she would in battle, she syncs with his movements, switches her focal point of attention to tune out Venus and into the mayor's conversation instead.

In that initial second, she thinks she's hallucinating again. Since she jumped out of Galipei, she hasn't heard voices nor felt flashes of other people's memories. This, though, has nothing to do with her recent sigils and everything to do with her first jump. The girl she was.

"*—is the work of the gods. The city folk will make it worse.*"

"*Maybe they'll find the junndi and put a stop to it. I trust an official force more than I trust a criminal killer.*"

Actia almost entirely shares a dialect with Rincun. Calla understands their words.

"*Nevertheless, it is their business. None of them are our people. Remember what the throne did to Eigi.*"

"Mayor," Anton says loudly. "What are we talking about?"

He doesn't understand them. But he can discern that it's something suspicious. *Junndi,* Calla rolls over her tongue, squashing the two syllables against the back of her front teeth. What does that mean? She's never heard the word before. Her vocabulary is too stunted, capped at the year she left Rincun in a golden carriage.

"Low numbers for grain, sir," the mayor replies. In Talinese, he's bright and accommodating. No indication whatsoever that he was slamming them seconds ago as callous city folk, her as a criminal killer. "Lucin, why don't you close up around the yamen? It'll be an early day today."

The employee, Lucin, nods. He steps out through the door, and Calla pushes away from the computer desk too.

"I have to use the washroom," Calla says. "Please excuse me."

The mayor thinks little of her exit. Venus doesn't turn either. When Anton makes eye contact, Calla signals a simple up-down with her finger, then nods her head at the door and mouths, *Thanks!* She's not sure whether he understands what she's trying to say, but Calla has already stepped out, running her palm against the door hinge.

She slashes her hand hard against the metal. A jagged cut blooms to life, beads of blood pressing through the broken skin. Calla squeezes her palm tightly while she follows after the boy.

She jumps, the movement so smooth that Lucin raises his foot in one step and she's the one to put it down. A soft thump sounds behind her, but she doesn't turn her head back, wanting the benefit of the doubt if anyone is to ask why Princess Calla Tuoleimi suddenly fainted. She pushes through to a different set of rooms. The chatter doesn't stop when she enters. It is as ordinary as anything for her to walk toward the one desk that is unoccupied—Lucin's, surely—and scan through the contents, looking for some reason why he was whispering to Mayor Policola about city folk making matters worse.

"Hey," Calla calls aloud, directing the question at anyone in the vicinity, "anyone have any new thoughts about the junndi?"

"Are you on about that again?" someone across the tables replies. Interesting tone. "Better be quiet. They'll think we know more than we actually do."

What does that mean*?* Calla thinks frantically. She starts to rummage through the papers on the desk. She should get back in a few minutes, or else the mayor will wonder where she's gotten to, and she doesn't want to leave Councilmember Hailira to make the decisions . . .

Calla lifts one sheet of paper.

KEEP THEM THERE.

◇◇◇◇◇

Anton follows shortly after Calla, giving the excuse of wanting water, and stops dead in his tracks when he sees her body collapsed outside the door. *Ah*. So that's what her signal meant.

"My goodness," he mutters under his breath, scooping her up in a quick maneuver and throwing her body over his shoulder. He supposes he'll find the kitchen, then shove her somewhere out of sight until she gets back. If anyone can sniff out where he's gone, it'll be Calla Tuoleimi.

Anton stays in the shadows of the yamen, moving fast on his feet. The effort is wasted: there isn't anyone around anyway. He nudges into the kitchen and closes the folding door after himself. Calla's body is eerily still in his arms, and though he understands that she's been doing something funny with her qi, he's still unnerved when her eyes fall open a fraction, revealing her yellow irises perfectly intact inside.

"Stay here, Princess," he mutters, opening a large cupboard and setting her inside. Her body folds, malleable wherever he sets her head. To think he was actually afraid seeing her tucked into Galipei's arms, brought back unconscious from Lankil's city. That's the last time he'll ever be stupid enough to think Calla could go down so easily.

Anton fetches himself a glass of water and wanders back to the yamen's main office. Just as he's stepping through the door, the mayor rushes past him, looking harried. Seconds later, Venus Hailira follows too, calling after him in concern.

"We need your numbers," she's saying. "Actia's councilmember may not be here, but I can get in touch. It's to your benefit—"

"Councilmember, please, I have emergency warnings to put in place at the borders—"

"Mayor—"

Their voices fade. Anton takes a sip of water. Resumes his position by the window to watch the scene outside.

Seconds later, the door opens again. Calla has returned to her own body.

"We've got to go," she says. "*Now*, Anton."

CHAPTER 32

Actia's yamen takes shape ahead of the delegation. Despite the midday sun, the cold temperature has misted around the building and the surrounding walls, rendering the image hazy with white. As Galipei signals for the delegation to stop, August passes his reins to another of his guards. He recognizes one of the horses tied outside the yamen already. A palace creature. The one Calla took when they fled Lankil.

They must be here.

Mayor Policola hurries out from the yamen. A woman follows close on his heels—Councilmember Venus Hailira, though it takes August a moment to recall her name. She inherited the title from her father. He wouldn't have thought she'd last this long.

"Where is Calla?" August asks, in no mood to make pleasantries.

Mayor Policola grimaces. Hailira, meanwhile, does a quick double take, as though she's surprised to hear the question.

"I said to hold her until I arrive, so I better not hear that she's gone," August continues, his voice sharp.

"Your Majesty, by the time we received your message, she had already departed. We didn't realize it was Anton Makusa who accompanied her. We assumed him a mere travel companion."

Hmm. Fine. If they have shortly departed, they couldn't have gone far. In any case, it won't be long until August has them captured, because this is Anton Makusa they're talking about, and Anton is going to want the crown for himself. They have Anton and Calla's destination with certainty.

"Very well," August says. The mayor visibly relaxes. He was prepared for punishment. "Summon your generals. We're proceeding forward."

The mountains are already visible from here. Though Rincun is large, the borderlands are taller, casting their entire province neighbor in their shadows.

"Your Majesty, if I may," Venus cuts in. "It's a lost cause trying to enter Rincun. The province has frozen over. We've tried sending people through the border."

"Do they remain alive?"

Venus hesitates. "Yes, I suppose, but they move about an inch per minute. Once they cross, we cannot fetch them back."

The borderlands are sapping qi. If it extends all through Rincun, it isn't a one-off occurrence. It's something near-mythical.

"Otta has reached the crown," August says lowly. He's only speaking to Galipei, but Venus Hailira tilts her head curiously, trying to follow along.

"I will tell the councilmembers their journey ends here," Galipei declares. "The movement forward is no longer a delegation."

"You're not hearing me," Venus exclaims. She sweeps her arm out, in the direction of Rincun. "There is no forward. The cold will freeze you in place."

Galipei is already walking into the yamen. "Fetch your generals, Mayor."

"What?" Venus mutters, but she's lost her fight. Her expression is wholly confused, and when she catches August's eye, he offers no further explanation. Only a shrug, and then August begins toward the yamen too.

"It's not the cold we should be worried about, Councilmember," he calls back. "It's when it stops."

◇◇◇◇◇

"You're quiet."

Calla bites her thumbnail while she walks, peering over her shoulder to eye the village fading to a dot. With knowledge of August's impending arrival, there was no time to fetch the horse outside the yamen, no time to do anything except steal two cloaks from the main office and flee on foot.

They've made enough distance now to slow down. She turns back around to face the mountains ahead.

But they're also coming to the end of the line.

"Princess," Anton prompts again. "Are you ignoring me on purpose?"

She is. It's cold enough to freeze her brain from activity. She's trying to *think*, but she can only bump up against the conclusion that it is impossible to get any closer to the mountains, so how the fuck are they supposed to find—

"Princess. Sunshine. Sweet pea. Green beans. Red tea—"

"Are you quite entertained?" Calla finally answers. Her breath puffs out in thick, opaque clouds. "Enough. You're only naming items. I'm listening."

"I hadn't even started getting specific yet."

Maybe they could go *around*, push off the western seaboard of Rincun and ride a boat out into the waters to get to the borderlands, but that would take days. They don't have days.

"What's wrong with a little *dearest of my heart*?"

"*Tyrant of my heart* is far more fitting."

Calla's eyes snap over to him in a glare. He speaks in jest, and yet a poisonous part of her still rears up, spitting acid whenever it is provoked. "Don't demote me. That role wasn't exactly occupied well in the past."

Anton sighs. He can't counter the allegation, now that Otta Avia is somewhere deep in those mountains doing who knows what. His lips thin, and then he says:

"I still don't understand it, Calla. Why did she ask you to come, and come alone at that?"

A more careless Calla would have assumed it to be a matter of politics. A spurned woman, trying to prove a point. The Calla who watched Otta throw a knife directly into a man's neck, though—she isn't going to say the same. Otta Avia is far smarter than any of them were prepared for.

"I don't know," Calla says. "If something seems meaningless, rarely are we looking at it correctly."

Anton stops abruptly in his step. The wind howls, and his loose hair falls into his eyes.

"Did you see that?"

Calla looks toward the mountains. They are still. Gray giants, sleeping in the distance. "See what?"

"A beam of light." Anton points ahead, to the left. "It arced from there"—his finger moves slightly across the range, directing her gaze straight ahead next—"to there."

Calla scrambles to pull the map from her pocket. She smooths out its creases, holds it flat. "Anton, that's the crown."

"What?"

"I'm serious. The landing spot matches the location on the map."

Anton doesn't seem convinced. He tries to swallow, and his throat moves with a stuttering motion. The more they walk, Calla feels it too. The cold twists and warps her insides in a way she hasn't experienced since she was eight years old. It isn't quite right to call it pain. The sensation exists somewhere parallel to it: her organs at odds with her body, struggling to pull free.

"It seems a bit convenient for it to be shooting a light into the sky, don't you think?"

"*You* said it was arcing in," Calla replies, shoving the map back into her jacket. "It's not shooting light, it's taking it. Anton, it's qi. The site is absorbing it across the province. Sacrifice."

Anton closes his eyes. She doesn't understand what he's doing, nor does she think it's a very good idea when she hears something in the distance and sights movement coming toward them from the village.

End of the line. But if they keep going any farther, they will freeze.

"Calla," Anton says suddenly, "teach me what you drew on yourself."

It takes Calla a second to comprehend his demand. By then, Anton is already acting, unsheathing only a fraction of her sword and slashing his palm across the blade. Blood gathers on his fingers, and he offers it to her.

Anton Makusa was the one who stumbled onto the first of this practice on his own, who turned a dead body into his chance for survival. Who sacrificed so tremendously that he needed no guiding sigil.

"Here." Calla takes Anton's hand, his blood running onto hers. She's already marked—the sigil hasn't faded—and she pulls down his collar to trace the same sigil onto him. A rush of cold spirits down her spine. The world comes into sharp focus.

"Were you watching the order?" she asks, her voice low.

"No," Anton answers, and his eyes drop to her mouth. "You'll have to teach me again. I'll see you by the light."

And then he falls, collapsing as deadweight onto the cold ground.

"Hey!" Calla bellows. "You—"

August's delegation looms closer, riding at full speed. She can't waste time shouting at air, though she would have expected Anton to *wait* for her. With a huff, Calla turns in the direction of the mountains and closes her eyes, feeling for qi too.

She jumps.

◇◇◇◇◇

The first landing immediately feels bizarre. She's alive, conscious. But she can't blink. The world doesn't move around her—it is a hollow make-believe of shapes and colors, barely stitching together in her understanding of which way lies north and which is south.

Slowly, slowly, slowly, she turns her face. She cannot move her limbs, but she can feel the direction of the wind. It blows in from the western seaboard.

As far as she can stretch her own qi, she searches for the next body.

◇◇◇◇◇

Calla slams in with the sort of momentum that should cause her to stumble, but the body doesn't budge.

She's on the streets of Rincun again. The field looks familiar. There's a muddy puddle by her feet, and though it takes some time, Calla tilts her head enough to look at herself in the crystallizing reflection.

When she first saw the princess here, she looked so beautiful. Gems in every part of her headpiece. Her sleeves trailing pink, her dress glimmering with gold. The tears are dripping down Calla's face without any way to stop them. Her body cannot move outside these tedious speeds, but her tears fall and fall and fall without cessation.

She had wanted it so much. She wants so much . . . the world, the seas beyond.

Calla must go. If she gives in, she will remain here forever, just like the girl she left at the bottom of a puddle. She shutters her eyes closed, waiting for them to block the sights of Rincun out entirely.

◇◇◇◇◇

Her skin is frozen. She's dying. Her waist is buried in white snow, her palms split open on black rock.

Go, she urges herself. *Keep going.* If this mountain path continues north, there ought to be someone else—

◇◇◇◇◇

Her head is pressed to ice. There's blood in her mouth. This time, she has gotten entirely lost. Perhaps mere minutes pass, perhaps entire hours. She searches and searches with her slow-flickering eyes, but she sees only the white snow of the mountains.

The body has fallen. That's why. Inch by inch, Calla manages to get her head tilted up, staring into the sky.

Please, please . . .

A flash of light comes from the left. *There.*

◇◇◇◇◇

Her hand cradles into her chest. Her hand is so small. She's found herself among a group. They're turning in the wrong direction. They're fleeing. Calla keeps moving.

◇◇◇◇◇

This body is entirely numb. Approaching death. She feels how close she's getting to the site of the crown. That flash of light is nearer each time. The twisting sensation in her throat is unbearable.

◇◇◇◇◇

A knife in her stomach, her lungs awfully full—

◇◇◇◇◇

There are so many people in the borderlands.

◇◇◇◇◇

"About time you made it."

Calla's eyes fly open. She registers that in an instant: she can move. Whatever the limits were on the freeze, they've broken past it.

"Anton?" she whispers. The plain gray sky unfurls above her, pressing close enough to the earth that she might believe she could stretch her hand up and touch its folds.

"You can kiss me if you're unsure," his voice replies. Doubtlessly, although he possesses a higher pitch, it is Anton Makusa and not an imposter.

Calla turns. She barely stifles her gasp.

"I know," Anton says. "And we thought the Hollow Temple was bad."

Bodies upon bodies upon bodies. Anton has taken one that lies farther down the row from her—feminine, with hair falling in soft waves around his pinched, cold face. Calla counts ten bodies between them. On Anton's other side, the line of bodies continues as far as her eye can see, curving upward to make a semicircle of endless sleeping faces.

Calla looks down at herself quickly, finds gloved hands and a padded jacket. She feels hair curling around the nape of her neck, tucked behind her ears.

She exhales, a puff of visible breath dancing into view. Her eyes flit up, searching the mountain incline alongside the mounds of white. There's an entrance jutting out midway, gaping an open mouth into a structure built into the mountain. At first, the structure isn't visible, blending in with the snow and mountain face. Then Calla picks herself up and slowly trudges a few steps higher along the incline, craning her neck to look from a different angle. Its smooth exterior and round turrets wrap around the entire mountaintop, poking farther into the clouds. This is a palace.

"Junndi," Calla whispers under her breath. That's what it means.

Across the top of the palace entrance lies a plaque written in archaic Talinese. Though Calla can faintly sound out the characters, she can't understand what it says. Except for a name that has remained the same in today's Talinese.

TUOLEIMI

"These are all vessels," Anton reports, startling Calla's attention back to him. He's prying at the body next to him, opening its eyes. Blank. Better to be vessels, because there is no suffering.

It is quiet on the mountain. She doesn't want to be present at the site when that next flare of light comes. Heavens knows what that might do to them.

"Leave them be," she says, dusting her hands off. She gestures to the palace entrance. "We're needed up there."

CHAPTER 33

After all that frantic movement on horseback and all that frenzied jumping to cross an infamously impenetrable mountain range, Calla isn't accustomed to the silence that greets them in the palace atrium. Sound caves inward here, a quiet created by deliberate muffle rather than true tranquility.

"It's dark," Anton comments, stopping a few paces in. The light outside doesn't strike the windows at the right angle to illuminate the interior.

"Your eyes will adjust," Calla replies.

Though they are moving fine, it is still deathly cold. The climate in the borderlands isn't gentle, and Calla folds her arms tightly to preserve warmth, peering into the reflection of a vase at the entrance. There are no flowers inside, understandably. Her borrowed face blinks back at her, a long nose and teal eyes. Meanwhile, Anton's jump brought his black eyes over with him. Her lack of moving color isn't an effect of the sigil. Calla is just weird.

"Maybe Otta isn't here." Anton sniffs, craning his head to peer down the vestibule. There's a stale smell, or a rotting one. Nothing about the low ceilings and cement floors is particularly remarkable. The design is entirely different from the palaces in San-Er: no resemblance to the velvet-green wallpapers or the intricate banisters decorated with creatures of legend. Only beiges and whites, letting the site blend with the mountains.

"I'm sure the hundred sacrificed bodies are out in the snow just for fun," Calla replies.

"We don't know how long they've been there as vessels. It could be from before Otta."

Calla doubts it. She doesn't say it aloud, though, opting to save her breath.

When Calla walks to the end of the vestibule—carefully, in case she triggers some sort of trap—she finds herself in a wide hall with the ceiling almost brushing her head, as if it were some underground exhibit instead of the entrance into a grand palace. What *is* this place? The original Palace of Heavens was destroyed in the war, but it was located somewhere near the Jinzi River anyway.

Beyond the hall, an entranceway leads to a spiral staircase. She tilts her head at Anton, a signal to hurry it up.

"Wait," he calls. He's remained at the front of the hall, staring up at the decorative mural covering the shorter wall. "Look at this."

"Anton, we don't have time—"

"We do. What does this look like to you?"

For fuck's sake. Calla strides over, squinting up into the dark. Her eyes adjust on painted panels and dim colors, flowing from right to left. The borders bleed and intersect, drawing her attention across a coronation, then a battle, followed by a turret at the top of a mountain. It resembles the very palace they're standing within.

"It's like any historical mural," she says plainly. "Birth, war, death. All hail the throne, so on and so forth."

Anton doesn't take any offense at her tone. He presses a palm against the wall, almost reverent in his inspection.

"Princess," he whispers quietly. "You're everywhere."

There's a line of text at the bottom of the mural—archaic Talinese, again. Most of the script is gibberish to her eye. Most, except the names, because those do not change, even when the other words move on.

Tuoleimi, Tuoleimi, Tuoleimi, again and again.

"I don't understand any of this," Calla says. "It was the same on the plaque outside. Talin has never expanded into the borderlands. Even Rincun wasn't conquered until fifteen years ago, so how did they end up building something out here?"

"It's trying to tell you, isn't it?" Anton points to the first panel. "Birth. Three children."

The mural shows three swaddles, golden crowns floating above their heads. Calla always hated art history lessons. The art that remained after the war was terrible at saying what it meant, and the interpretations the tutors told her never made intuitive sense.

Anton points to the second panel. "Battle." He pauses. "Civil battle?"

The panel has the same colors on both sides. This mural actually doesn't seem so hard to decode. A river runs down the middle, parting the battle lines. Calla leans in closer.

"I think that might be the Jinzi River."

Anton frowns. "Surely not. What battle would that be depicting?"

The war with Sica is the only one that makes sense. The next panel shows a crowd of people witnessing an address by a royal on a balcony. It looks like . . . the Palace of Union, actually.

"That's the sigil."

Calla startles, blinking hard. She feels a peculiar flash of familiarity: some overlay on her vision, as though she's been here before, she's stood on the same floor, she's heard those same words. She hasn't. She knows that. Her entire body jolts regardless when it follows Anton's line of sight and finds a small, familiar shape hovering over the head of the royal giving the address. *Left dot. Long and slanting curve with a dot above. Another dot to the right.*

A chill sweeps into the hall. Calla strains her ears, listening hard through the howl of wind outside the palace. Without saying anything, she breaks from the mural and heads toward the spiral staircase, eyeing the structure. The metal groans when she yanks off her gloves and touches the handrail.

"Something isn't right."

Calla turns over her shoulder. Anton can't seem to help getting distracted by every item in the palace. He must know that she's preparing to tell him off the moment she opens her mouth, because he waves at her frantically.

"What?" Calla, sparing one more glance up the staircase, takes her hand off the rail and hurries to where Anton stands. "What is it?"

"Tell me this isn't the war with Sica."

He's found a map: a topographical map constructed to scale on a tall table. Each village is marked with a small white pin. Each mountain rises off the table surface with painstaking detail. The only peculiarity is how tiny the borderlands are. Most maps of the kingdom will depict the entire length of the borderlands, then extend the rendering to show a slice of Sica on the other side.

Here, the map ends curtly after the borderlands, as if the mountains drop right into the sea.

"This is definitely the war with Sica," Calla says plainly. She doesn't know why Anton would say otherwise. "Look at the arrows."

She's seen enough war plans during her time in the Palace of Heavens to know how to read them. Whoever was using this map last, they had arranged a configuration that shows one side advancing from the north and one side fleeing into the southeast. Certain sections have been marked with green. Others with red. Calla touches the plot of land where Ximili Province is, circling her finger along the green figurines there.

"Calla," Anton says. His enunciation is slow, gentle. As though he's trying to deliver bad news to her. "The colors. They're on the wrong side."

In truth, she knows what he's saying, but her mind refuses to make the conclusion. Ximili is marked in green. A victory. During their war with Sica, the first territory they lost in the initial invasion was Ximili. Then they would keep losing, and losing, and losing, until the tide of the war turned with their retreat into San-Er and brought hard-won victory.

This doesn't make any fucking sense. What could this be *except* the war with Sica? Yet if that were the case . . . this war plan is from Sica's side.

"I keep wondering about a Sinoa Tuoleimi," Calla says slowly.

Anton's eyes flit to the other side of the hall, to the mural and its archaic script. "Someone erased from Talin's history."

Calla touches her chest. On this body, the sigil has moved over as a faint marking of light. The real sigil is painted on the body collapsed at the border of Rincun, motionless with the rest of the province. Her stolen body. Her greatest heist.

Long live Her Majesty. Long live Her Majesty ten thousand years. Long live Her Majesty ten thousand years.

"She led the invasion."

The voices play in her mind. They have become a part of her memories, clinging like Lankil's ash stuck irremovably to her skin. *You'll never win this war. The blood will be on your hands. The land will be lost. The south is lost. Yi has burned.*

Anton's brows disappear into his hair. She knows he doesn't choose feminine bodies when he has the option, but he really ought to more often with how expressively he uses these features.

"For Sica?"

The pieces, at last, click into place. Calla pulls her eyes to the edge of the map, to the borderlands ending in the sea.

"Sica isn't real." She says the words, and the palace finally exhales in relief. One small statement, then the truth slots back into the world. "Sica is an invention to explain to later generations why the kingdom is war-torn. No foreign kingdom lies to the north of the borderlands. The crown was never hidden for safety. Talin fought a civil war, and when Sinoa Tuoleimi was vanquished, she fled here and died with her crown."

A loud *thunk* comes above them. Calla stiffens, waiting for something to follow, but the sound echoes and fades, turning the palace quiet again. Anton doesn't wait further: he runs for the staircase.

"Be careful, be careful!" Calla hisses after him.

They climb up the spiral staircase and enter a turret. It curves narrowly enough that Calla's shoulders start to scrape against the sides, centuries-old paint flaking off and dusting her jacket. A pulse beats in her ears. It accompanies her steps; it doesn't stop when they finally come to a halt at the top of the staircase, emerging into a cold room with glass for a sloped ceiling.

Calla tries to make sense of the scene. Before her eyes, a flare of light beams into the room. It enters the body sitting on the throne like an arrow wholly piercing into flesh, sharp tip and feathered stem alike absorbed.

The body is dead; that much is obvious. There must be some sort of qi at work, though, preserving her corpse in place instead of it turning to ash after so many years. Her skin sags broken and gray, reeking of rot. She's covered in a thick film of dust that smothers her eyelashes and the lines of her once-bright clothing. Nonetheless, Calla still recognizes the slope of her nose and the face she's seen for years in the mirror. However she did it, Sinoa Tuoleimi was reborn exactly as she appeared over a hundred years ago.

The only item on her body that isn't crumbling is her crown. A band of gold metal encircles her head, etched with decorative carvings—with mythical creatures and complex sigils—across the surface. The ridges at the top curve into sharp points, dotted with turquoise green gems. For all she doubted this crown, Calla can feel its power. It lodges in her throat, trembles through her lungs. Level a city, wage ten wars—she doesn't doubt that the previous wearer of the crown could do it.

And Otta sleeps at her feet.

"She's frozen too," Anton remarks.

A carpet runs the length of the room, ending at the throne seating the dead queen. He's right, to Calla's surprise. The rise and fall of Otta's chest is near-imperceptible, going so slowly as to appear absent. While Otta occupies one end of the carpet, Calla and Anton hover at the other. No makeshift weapons anywhere, unfortunately.

No matter.

Calla steps onto the carpet, and perhaps Anton reads her intent in the way she moves. His hand snakes out. Catches her elbow.

"She can't hurt you right now," he pleads. "It doesn't have to be like that."

Calla doesn't look back at him.

"You can't have us both, Anton." She tears her elbow out of his grasp. "Either kill me now to save her, or let me kill her."

It won't take much. A hard strike on the head—she won't feel anything. Calla nears, putting one foot in front of the other, and though she is walking toward Otta, she finds that she cannot look away from Sinoa Tuoleimi the moment her eyes flicker over. The crown ripples with power. If she listens closely, she can hear it humming, whispering promises of what it could achieve. It's not entirely selfish volition that has her pivoting, her fingers reaching for the crown. This is the one hard object in this room she could use as a weapon. If she's going to succeed . . .

Calla's fingers come down on the crown, and the room floods with light.

Qi heaves through the ceiling like the wind of a monsoon, sweeping through the glass and shattering each panel into dustlike fragments. Sinoa Tuoleimi bursts into ash, and when Calla is thrown back, thudding into the wall and staying pinned for seconds after, she knows there is enough qi swirling to kill them in an instant. It snarls and curls and grows fangs, but before the pure power can puncture through her throat and rip her apart, it dissipates, satisfied.

Calla gasps, scrambling for air the moment the room settles. The crown is warm in her hand. A droplet of blood trickles down her nose.

Sacrifice, she thinks absently, clambering upright. That explosion of qi didn't kill them because there were sacrifices made for it to consume, plucked from the vessels outside and funneled into the room. How did Otta know to do this? Where would any of these instructions have been kept, and if Calla didn't hear a peep as the fucking princess of the Palace of Heavens, then how *else* did Otta Avia stumble onto knowledge like this?

"You didn't follow instructions."

"Shit," Calla mutters. She missed her chance. While the throne is only occupied by ash now, Otta Avia slowly gets to her feet at the base of it, dusting off her hands. Her clothes remain pristine when she straightens up. Not a speck of dirt or any hint that she traversed the borderlands to get here.

"What is it?" Otta asks. "You thought I was going to lie there nicely while you decided how to bludgeon me?"

At the other end of the throne room, Anton has crumpled to the floor too. The blast pushed him back, near the edge of the spiral staircase.

"Don't be presumptuous," Calla returns. She's waiting for Anton to lift his head, but he doesn't stir. "Maybe I came to wake you so you could see the surprise I brought you."

Clearly, Otta doesn't find her very funny.

"You're a pest," Otta spits. "Nothing but a child wearing shoes that don't fit. You don't even know what you took."

Otta lunges. Calla spits a curse, then darts away, the crown still in her hand. It hums with every rough movement through the air.

"Tell me," Calla taunts. She holds the crown close. "I've heard plenty of conjecture."

"Not the crown."

Otta doesn't try to make another grab. Instead, she flings her arm hard, and an arc of light strikes Calla like a physical weapon, burning a mark on the arm she throws over her face in a panic. It takes the air out of her when she hits the floor again.

"You know what you took," Otta goes on. "Why else did I bother getting you here? Why else would I waste so much time? You didn't know what you were messing with, and now the rest of us have to suffer for it."

She flings her arm again. Calla avoids this attack, rolling, but she's getting too close to the wall. Shit, shit, *shit*—

Somehow, Otta knows that she is an imposter. That Calla is not Calla, but an invader from years and years previous, one who has been around long enough to snuff out the original princess.

"You'll inflate my ego," Calla says, trying not to sound breathless. "Don't tell me I'm the only one who could move this crown."

When Otta's expression flattens, Calla knows she's hit her mark. No one else could have picked it up. Queen Sinoa Tuoleimi was born again as Calla Tuoleimi, returned to the world for unfinished business, and then a desperate province child invaded her and absorbed all her might.

"Don't think so highly of yourself. Your use is done."

Otta lifts her foot, meaning to kick, and Calla takes her chance. She yanks hard on Otta's leg, sending her to the floor. Her offensive tactic clearly has a limited run, because Otta twists before she's fully fallen and lands on her knee rather than her full body. Calla hisses, jerking aside before Otta pivots and extends her leg in an attack. In the time it takes Calla to attempt scrambling upright, Otta throws a punch while on her knees, barely missing Calla's face when Calla dodges.

This is a shock.

Otta Avia fights like she was taught in the Palace of Heavens.

Calla shoves hard before Otta pulls back. Though Calla lands an attack, Otta is fast to recover, rising to her feet and staggering a few steps away. The Palace of Earth liked to teach defense. It's why August can't fight for shit—he will invade at a distance and spill blood in gallons, but he flinches before he hits.

Calla, going off a gut feeling she can't entirely put into words, stands and tries to jump.

Her eyes open and close in the same view of the world. She is blocked out. Otta Avia . . . is doubled.

Otta must feel the attempt. When she swings, Calla doesn't duck quickly enough. She's clipped in the shoulder; Otta swipes her feet out from underneath her. This all feels familiar; it's all an echo of *something*. Calla, cursing, grabs

Otta's arm and tries to incapacitate her, but she's made Otta angry in trying to invade her, and when Otta slams her head into hers, Calla flinches.

She can't give up the crown.

Calla twists around. In the corner of her eye, she finally sees Anton stirring. She doesn't give him any time to recover. She shouts, "Anton, catch!" and she throws the crown at him. In the same gesture, she lets her fury surge, and when her arm swings back around, she aims at Otta. Light unfurls from her hand in an arc, slamming Otta back.

It feels like firing energy out of her palms. As though she's turned herself into a weapon that uses gunpowder, exploding outward upon impact. But Otta is clearly better versed in this sort of maneuver. She wipes her face hard.

When she lifts her hand and clenches her fist in midair, Calla can't breathe.

"This could have been so easy," Otta says. She steps closer, her fist still extended. "You could have returned what you stole. We could have all gone about our merry way."

Calla pulls at her neck. Her nails are scratching lines down her throat, but she cannot get air.

"What I don't understand is how you did it." Otta is within reach. Black spots are clustering into Calla's vision. "Who *are* you? Do you yourself even know the answer? I gather not."

"Otta, stop."

When Otta turns toward Anton, her fist loosens the barest fraction, and Calla gets a gasp of air in. Anton has staggered to his feet by the staircase. One side of his temple is bruised red. His arm is bleeding from the shattered glass, smearing blood onto the crown he's got in his hand.

"Trying to come to her rescue?" Otta snaps.

"No," he replies, holding the crown up. "But I'm sure the heavens will when they strike."

Otta understands what he's doing a second before Calla does. Her fist releases its hold. Calla heaves and chokes to fill her lungs, the black spots in her vision darting away. By the time Otta throws her arm at Anton, meaning to attack him, it's already too late.

Anton puts the crown on his head, and the room floods with white light a second time.

◇◇◇◇◇

Calla can't have lost consciousness for more than a few minutes. When she comes to, her ears are picking up only a high-pitched whine.

It takes several more seconds for her vision to return, and then she sees Anton at her side, the crown sitting on the floor. She puts her hand on his neck. It's an unsteady pulse, but it is a pulse nonetheless.

She tries to lift up onto her elbow. Her muscles shriek, protesting with such calamity that Calla collapses back down. Her eyes flit sluggishly. There—Otta has been thrown near the throne. She stirs, raising a hand to her face.

Anton bought her enough time to even the battlefield. She has to end this.

Calla, carefully, eases herself to her knees, and remains steady. When she tries to reach for excess qi, for something to throw, she comes up empty. That flare from the crown did something: wiped everyone clean. There's no time to forge a new sigil.

She runs her palm along the glass shards on the floor and picks up a fragment with a particularly sharp point.

Anton's body jerks. He gasps for breath, his eyes flying open. He's trying to say something, but Calla focuses on getting to her feet. She can't hear anything. Her ears are taking a while to recover. Perhaps they've been blown out entirely, the eardrums ruptured by standing that close to the blast.

When Otta rises, she doesn't immediately shift into defense. She turns her back on Calla—even seeing what Calla holds, even knowing Calla's objective—and staggers to the window. It's not fear in her expression. It's steadfast resolve, as though this encounter has ended here and she's made up her mind about it.

The whine in Calla's left eardrum fades. The moment she picks up the first clatter of footsteps in the palace below, Calla knows what Anton was trying to say, why Otta is readying to flee. Calla's hearing returns like a jammed lock finally turning, and shouting floods the throne room, movement pouring from the stairs and surrounding her. They're quick to act. Before Calla can scarcely turn around, a blade flies through the air and embeds in her shoulder.

Weisannas. Calla searches through their faces desperately, trying to make sense of what is going on, and she understands. August's guards chased them through Rincun and the borderlands the very same way Calla and Anton traveled, then invaded the vessels outside the palace. Of course they did—the moment the guards caught up to their bodies collapsed by the border, they must have understood their tactic in an instant. One among the group marches forward, and she recognizes Galipei's gait.

"Wait," Calla says, her voice faint. "Wait—"

Galipei picks up the crown. He waves for his guards to surround Anton. Gestures for the others to get her, and though Calla tries to lunge away, three Weisannas converge upon her, holding her down. Despite their assorted, randomized bodies, their training moves with their silver eyes. They are too strong, and she is still too weak from the blast. She can do nothing except watch as Otta steps out from the window at the other side of the throne room. Before any of the guards can get to her, she drops silently into the snow below.

"No!" Calla rasps. She lurches her shoulder hard. It doesn't do anything. "Don't let her go! She's—"

"Bag over her head," Galipei instructs, coming in front of her. "Bind her tight, and for fuck's sake, knock her out."

CHAPTER 34

The councilmembers who departed from the delegation arrive in San-Er before His Majesty does. They were sent back when King August and his guards ventured forward to encounter what might evolve into a battle within the borderlands; he said that if it was no longer a delegation, then it wasn't safe for diplomatic representatives to be present. It was difficult to argue against this point—though some councilmembers, like Mugo, tried, claiming that the council needed to be present to verify whether the crown was true. August promised that was something to be done in the capital, and if they moved forward together, the council would only slow him down. He would bring back the crown. They needed to trust him.

So Venus Hailira returns with the rest of the council.

She did what she could for Rincun. It doesn't feel like enough. Through the journey, she ruminated on the sequence of events: her arrival declaring a province-wide lockdown, the few days when it seemed she'd achieved her task, the sudden freeze . . . and then everything thrown out the window. A cavity opens in her chest, blows dirt into her lungs. She takes a deep breath, and the week's events lodge in her throat, unable to be swallowed or digested. She ought to cough it out. She can't quite bear to.

When the delegation approaches the gates, Venus is jarred for a second. She forgot that they were expanding San-Er's wall. It is almost finished, and she recalls what King August announced, what was cleared when the council met to discuss the administrative work. If her perception is accurate, it would appear that the wall has gone much deeper into Eigi than initially planned. Mugo won't be happy about that. Neither will the rural dwellers who make a habit of camping outside the wall to wait for lottery selections, unless the new, expanded San-Er opens up spaces for them, and Venus doubts they'll let that many more in.

She peers out the carriage window. Taps her fingers on her knees, restless.

Instead, the dwellers outside the wall will be asked to relocate—*kindly pick up your tent, sir, before we do it for you*—and they will continue camping in hopes that maybe, maybe the next draw will be successful, ad infinitum until the palace guards do their rounds outside the wall to ensure order and find new dead bodies every week.

It's the way things are. Nothing to be done about it.

Venus holds her hands together primly. One of the migrants camped outside the wall pokes their head out from their tent and makes direct eye contact with Venus through the carriage window. The carriage starts to move.

"Maybe we should give them something," Venus finds herself saying aloud. "Food. Blankets."

In the seat opposite, Councilmember Farua leans forward, peering out the window too. She must be used to these sights while governing Daol Province. Venus, meanwhile, was raised in the cities, and had barely made a full trip outside the wall before she was handed Rincun's jurisdiction.

"That's a great idea," Farua adds. "King August will be glad to hear that."

The carriage passes through San's gate. Venus still can't quite get over the feeling that she's sitting on nails and wires, shifting in her seat without getting comfortable. She can't see the tents anymore, but she remembers her first trip to

Rincun and Princess Calla Tuoleimi rolling her eyes each time Venus said something about offering blankets.

Don't be such an aristocrat, Venus chided then.

That is what I am, after all, Calla said. *They don't like us. Let them have it rather than trying to feign generosity.*

The gates to San-Er close after them. Afternoon light suctions into gray dreariness, blocked by the tall, looming wall.

If you were truly generous, you would open the Hailira vault for them instead of giving bits and pieces.

Venus isn't sure why she's thinking about this now. The carriage stops, parking itself inside San-Er's wall, and Calla's words echo and echo and echo.

Say you won't. You're allowed.

A piercing scream tears through the air outside.

The sound doesn't register for a long moment. Venus sits there dumbfounded, unmoving even while the other councilmembers scramble up, scramble to the door, shove it open, run out. The ground trembles. Something that could be firecrackers bursts in the distance. The scream is coming from one of the other carriages.

Venus finally hauls herself to her feet. Her knees are weak. Farua is yelling at her to hurry and move, but when she finds that Venus isn't listening, she moves on, disappearing from view.

What is happening?

The carriage jolts. Just as Venus finally emerges, the vehicle tips over entirely and skids across the grass. Venus gasps, tripping over her ankles into the mud. There are miles of ground between the wall and the city now. The remnants of the construction remain: cinder blocks and long metal poles, stepladders and machines used to chop stone. When San-Er reorders its budget, it'll spread new buildings into this space. Maybe take off sections of existing levels elsewhere and move them wholesale.

On the other side of the carriage, the guards are fighting three men clothed in black. Venus picks herself off the ground and tries to hobble to safety. One carriage is still standing. Maybe if she hides in there, she'll be fine until palace reinforcements arrive. Most of the councilmembers have fled. The screaming has stopped. It doesn't seem like there is anyone harmed—

Venus clamps a hand over her mouth as soon as she opens the remaining carriage's door, stifling her gasp. Councilmember Rehanou has . . . exploded. As though there were some balloon of pressure in his chest that burst, flaying his skin and pushing his ribs outward, ribbons of flesh splattering the carriage walls. Though he isn't moving, his blood continues pumping, leaking through the protruding veins in every direction.

Venus inches closer. She shouldn't. She should run fast before vomit surges up her throat and sprays everywhere, yet something about this scene doesn't look right outside of its grotesque picture. Perhaps it is the angle at which she's gazing at Councilmember Rehanou. It could be a trick of the light causing something so incomprehensible.

She draws close enough to step on a chunk of something—maybe his stomach, maybe his guts—and she knows that she's not mistaken. Whatever caused this has carved a crescent shape into the gore of his chest.

Venus has to back away, her hand moving to press her nostrils down. This wasn't a weapon implanted in him, instructed to explode. This was a manipulation of qi.

The carriage shudders. Venus spins around, gasping. She's too slow; she's been cornered. There are new people on the scene, dressed the same as the men in combat with the guards across the grass. One woman in a ponytail, one man with a buzz cut.

"I know we only planned to handle one, but another can't hurt."

Venus throws her arms up, gesturing surrender. "No, please," she says. "There is no need. His Majesty is returning with the crown. He will prove himself."

"We're aware, Councilmember," the man says. He lifts his hand. Pain explodes behind Venus's eyes, like her brain is being squeezed, squeezed. Within seconds her head is going to look like Rehanou's exploded guts inside the carriage.

"Please, please, wait!" Venus gasps. "What do you want? Tell me what you want!"

"Enough—"

"If not the crown proving heaven's mandate, then what?" she yells. When she was sworn in, the palace taught her that distraction is the prime tactic to use against rural attacks. That, since the Makusas died in Kelitu, they have had to train their councilmembers to know to distract until the guards can arrive. Venus doubts that the guards will come to her rescue here in time. This isn't purely a distraction. She needs to understand what is happening. She needs to know—

"Freedom, Venus Hailira," the woman replies. "That cannot be hard to understand, can it?"

Her vision turns red.

"I'll help you!" Venus screams.

Suddenly, the squeezing sensation in her skull dissipates. She teeters, skids to her knees. Dizziness threatens her stomach. She fights against the vertigo.

"I beg your pardon," the man says lightly.

"Won't that be easier?" Venus gasps. She touches her eyes. There's blood leaking through her tear ducts, trailing down her cheeks. But she remains in one piece. Limbs intact. Guts preserved. "Let me live, and I will declare Rincun an independent province."

CHAPTER 35

In Actia, their ankle bindings are loosened. In Janton, after crossing the Jinzi River and returning to the south of the kingdom, the guards must feel content enough that there won't be any funny business for as long as their birth bodies are being held hostage, because they get their wrist bindings loosened too, the rope tight around only one wrist and looped to the seats of the carriage. It's not like Anton will be running anywhere. He can't jump Weisannas, and if he escapes into the provinces in this body, he's guaranteeing a slow death either by eventual starvation or by intense boredom.

The journey passes in a blindfolded blur. There are no more attacks—nary the slightest threat of danger from the kingdom outside, and Anton knows he's not the only one who finds that strange. He keeps feeling someone stomp on his toes every time the guards say something to mark their location. Calla, no doubt. Or maybe it's Galipei trying to throw him off, since he's riding in the same carriage to ensure there aren't any plans being exchanged. He's with them at every moment, even to use the bathroom.

Anton chatters meaninglessly every time a thought occurs to him, but Calla remains dead silent. No one in the carriage pays him any mind. He doesn't know what Calla is thinking. Whether she has something up her sleeve, because Anton sure as fuck has nothing.

"Here's what we're going to do," August declared when they were being loaded into the carriages in Rincun. "We're going to return to San-Er. You're going to take full responsibility for your misdeeds, and then you will await decision by the council. Don't even think about trying anything, because I'll burn both your birth bodies at the slightest provocation."

He didn't leave room for argument. August turned on his heel coldly, asking for the guards to hurry it up. The proclamation was comically performative anyway, meant for the benefit of the guards that surrounded them. What did it matter what the council's decision was? August was trying to get rid of the councilmembers, anyhow. Eventually, what was left of the council would descend into such shambles that King August could smoothly take over, becoming the one voice that the generals and soldiers answered to.

With every province they cross, Anton gets more and more restless. He likes to have a way out. In exile, survival meant constantly flitting off one burned bridge to another made of kindling. Even if it was a temporary path out, it was better than nothing.

Right now, he really has nothing. He doesn't have a shred of power. He has lost the body to play king. He has lost control over the masses, lost the right to click his fingers and be brought anything under the skies. Meanwhile, it takes one snap of August's temper, and Anton's head rolls.

It doesn't seem fair. August isn't even afraid of the dangers of keeping Anton alive; he makes no reference to wanting to kill him in punishment. August would, in fact, prefer to keep Anton alive to report to San-Er, to parade him around like some scampering rat caught eating in the back kitchen because he can reclaim the control that Anton took from him. Even if August has the inkling that Anton knows who was responsible for the attack in Kelitu, he doesn't *care*. He is August Shenzhi, with a kingdom operating under his thumb, and Anton is barely a Makusa anymore when there is no one else of his bloodline to make Makusa feel like anything more than a name.

A sudden, hard stomp comes on his toes, and Anton jolts. They are on day five of a journey that doesn't break for sleep. The drivers simply alternate with guards who take the reins when they grow too tired to go on. By nightfall, they will have reached San-Er.

Anton shifts his foot, tapping Calla back to ask what the matter is. He tries to imagine what life might look like if the council decides to pardon them and condemn him back to exile. With criminal status, Anton might pick up a small cult following amid the Crescent Societies, in the same way that many of them like to rewatch Calla's massacre footage every year as a holiday treat. Otherwise, the rest of his days will pass in relative insignificance.

It isn't as though the past seven years have had much significance either. Only an endless cycle of cobbling together money and making payments month after month to sustain a hospital bed. Otta needed him, though, and that's more than he can say at present. Without her, he's untethered.

Heavens knows that he'll never be tethered to her again. From what he overheard, August left guards behind to sweep the borderlands, but there hasn't been news on whether she's been found yet. Otta has disappeared.

Calla nudges his ankle, and Anton heightens his focus. Someone has answered a phone in the carriage. Though the words on the other end are inaudible, offering only a buzzy, low murmur outside the receiver, the carriage turns tense. Conversation on the opposite seats has died down. The other guards are waiting for the result of the call.

A button clicks.

It is the final plunge of an executioner's injection. The lock being turned in an eternal prison cell. Anton doesn't understand why Calla hasn't made a grab for Talin's throne. Princess Calla Tuoleimi, who—as far as Talin is aware—has as much claim to that crown as August does. Perhaps more. This Calla who sits bound with him claims to believe in what is good, but she didn't chase Otta into the borderlands out of concern for her civilians. She did it because Otta was making a power grab that she didn't care for, and she must realize someone who can fight a maneuver like that can also make one herself. She must realize that the two of them don't need to live by *August*—

The carriage stops.

"What's going on?" Anton demands, in perfect synchrony with Calla.

"There's some trouble in San-Er," Galipei replies, not sounding the least bit concerned. "We are making a stop in Eigi's security base overnight, until the disruption passes."

Anton scoffs. By *disruption*, he must mean people are once again marching on their streets, calling for an end to this rule.

"You don't want to get back quickly?" he goads. "I wonder if the threat has grown too big to contain."

Galipei is unfazed. Outside of August's body, nothing Anton says will prompt any reaction out of the guard, because Galipei Weisanna does not care about the opinions of anyone other than August Shenzhi.

"Stay put."

Movement flurries around them, guards streaming forth from the carriages and barking orders outside. Anton is sitting still—obediently, disgustingly—when a new set of steps climbs into the carriage. The door slams shut.

"If we're going to do this"—Calla's voice is a shock to hear, scratchy from uttering her first full sentence since they left Rincun—"can you at least take off our blindfolds?"

"Take them off yourselves," August returns. "They loosened one hand, didn't they?"

Anton doesn't wait for the next opportunity. He pulls the fabric from his eyes, blinking rapidly to adjust. This borrowed body has long hair, and it gets all over his face. While he's gathering himself and brushing everything back,

Calla is slow to remove her blindfold, easing it off as though she might be told halfway to stop.

Their eyes meet. Calla scrunches up the fabric and throws it to the floor. Without her yellow color, he doesn't know who else would believe that this is Calla, short of knowing her habits. Her bitten thumbnails and her chafed lower lip. Her instinct to stare awhile before answering a question, taking more time to read someone's expression than socially acceptable.

"I'm not happy, August," Calla says. She tugs her wrist, pulling taut the rope that connects her to the seats. "If you must act tough in front of your guards, fine. But I've been on your side from the beginning, and I should think that warrants more trust than being tied to a carriage."

"That trust dissipated the second you realized Anton Makusa was occupying my body and didn't kick him out," August returns. "Apologies if you feel that it isn't fair."

"She tried, don't worry," Anton interjects. "It's not her fault I wanted the throne."

August turns his glare on Anton now. "Where did you think this was going to end? That no one would notice? Impossible."

"Highly possible," Calla says. Unwittingly, she and Anton have become some sort of tag team, taking turns to counter August. "All he needed to do was kill Galipei. You should be thankful he showed mercy and avoided that route."

"I'm coming to regret being so merciful, actually." Anton can't help it. He lines up the shot and takes it: "Especially if you had anything to do with the death of my parents. Revenge was easily accessible. Take that into account for whatever trial you're about to give us."

He senses Calla grow still. This is the first she's hearing about this.

August, however, doesn't appear surprised to be confronted. He laces his hands in front of himself. His posture is overwhelmingly straight. Though his clothes are slightly ragged from the road, he has changed into a new jacket, a solid white that the cities would quickly dirty.

"I didn't," August says shortly. "But I did hear about it shortly thereafter, once Kasa's instruction went through. It was better you didn't know."

"Was it? Or were you afraid I'd revolt in the palace?"

To tell the truth, Anton has always been a little afraid of August, but he's aware the feeling goes both ways. Anton has witnessed August having no limit when it comes to climbing ranks in the palace. August has witnessed Anton exhibit the same behavior when it comes to the depths of his loneliness—his frantic jumping, his frivolous discarding of bodies. He moves fast to escape the fear that he could encounter a similar fate, because nothing in this world will scar him the way his parents' deaths scarred him, and he'll suffer eternity remembering what that day felt like.

"Don't be ridiculous," August says, but his black eyes flit away.

If, in Anton's youth, he had discovered that King Kasa ordered his parents to die, they wouldn't have needed to wait until Calla snapped and planned to kill him. Anton would have done it first, committed regicide from within the Palace of Earth, and then where would August be? Another forgotten noble, shoved around meaninglessly while the council battled to put someone onto the throne.

"There was nothing you could have done about it," August continues. He remains impassive, as he always is, as he always has been. "Your parents were working with the Crescent Societies to put themselves on the throne. It was high treason, and you should be thankful that they became victims of a rural attack rather than suffer your family name dragged through the mud if they were charged accurately."

Anton lunges, but the rope holds him back from reaching August. Calla stomps hard on his foot to tell him to ease off. He barely feels it, barely feels anything past the cold rage that slides liquid down his throat.

If it's the last thing he does, either Anton will kill August Avia, or he will accept death trying.

"Enough," August declares. He shifts toward the carriage door, easing himself out of the way lest Anton try again. It doesn't matter: the rope holds solid. "Out of respect for the both of you, I've come to share that we're not bringing you into San-Er. The climate is too volatile. You may testify on a broadcast we'll send into the capital, and you will stay at the security base to await trial."

This must be a joke. Testify on a *broadcast*? August isn't offering them a trial in the slightest. They are going to stay imprisoned at the security base until their bones turn to rot. They are going to give San-Er enough material to show that they have been defeated without being made into martyrs, and then Anton Makusa and Calla Tuoleimi are going to disappear.

"You need to be more specific," Calla says. A note of alarm threads through her words.

"What is there to specify? I am giving you the opportunity to speak your part. You can tell the whole truth, Calla. Tell them that we worked together to depose King Kasa. It doesn't matter to me."

August doesn't fear the council anymore. The council functions solely as a fail-safe to a king's achievement of total power, and he must believe that it is one push away from falling entirely if he is granting Calla permission to drag him down.

August opens the carriage door.

"One request," Calla says.

August stops. Turns back.

"If you want a broadcast, we need our bodies back." She leans into her seat. When she speaks, she's not looking directly at August, but she's not looking anywhere else in particular either. Her teal eyes are unfocused. Thinking. "Mine especially. San-Er will think you hired some actor otherwise. They will ask whether you take them for a fool, wanting them to believe that the first person who jumps without their qi changing the eyes is the princess in confession."

August is quiet for a moment. He considers her carefully.

"There's nothing to be afraid of, if that's what you're evaluating," Calla adds, matter-of-fact. "What is there left, August?" Her foot taps the side of Anton's ankle. "We can't fight you. We have no forces but ourselves. Who remains standing except you?" Another tap. This can't be an accident, but there is nothing that Calla would be prompting him to observe. It seems to be nothing except assurance. A reminder that she is here. A reminder that she knows he is there.

August rolls his eyes. "There is no need to flatter me, Calla."

"It is not flattery. I am stating the facts. You have plotted this long and this thoroughly to take Talin, and there is no remaining loophole. You will return to San-Er and tamp down the chaos with force. You will order your soldiers to take action in the provinces and wipe out any revolutionary groups that bear ill will to the throne. Nothing we do or say here changes a thing."

It's hard to tell whether August agrees with her. He makes a noise, then walks away, signaling for his guards to watch the carriage.

Anton fidgets, leaning forward to get a better look through the open door. The moment the thought of escaping crosses his mind, Calla shakes her head at him, a silent warning to stay put.

Five minutes later, Galipei appears with their birth bodies. They've so kindly made sure the bodies are already blindfolded and bound.

"All right," Galipei snaps. "Get back in."

CHAPTER 36

Calla eyes the metal chain they've secured around her ankle, the other end connected to an immovable loop in the corner of the room. If there is a god of fate, they must be laughing at her. To have thought herself smart for trapping Leida Miliu to an old radiator, only to suffer the same curse.

Midnight hangs heavy over Eigi's security base. An old clock tolled from somewhere in the building a few minutes ago, announcing the time. They are using the same lodgings as they were when the delegation first set out, only this time their numbers have vastly decreased. The councilmembers already took three of the carriages back to San-Er. Only Weisannas remain with August, watching the base closely for any signs of disruption.

Calla bites down on her thumbnail, pacing another round of the room. The chain, at least, is long enough for her to walk to the windows. She should feel nervous, fearful of what August has in store for her, but that's not what has her jittery.

August wants her to answer for betraying him. He wants her to repent for not raising the alarm during the coronation, but instead of a quick punishment where a sword strikes her neck, she will remain indefinitely at a security base removed from the kingdom. It won't be her small apartment in San, where she hunkered down to prepare for a grand task. It will merely be the rest of her life in perpetual waiting. That is far worse than spilling blood.

So she's not afraid of what August has in store for her, because it really can't be that bad. Knowing him, knowing his patience, Calla might as well get very comfortable with this chain on her ankle.

The nerve-racking part is that she knows how she gets out of this, but once she begins, she cannot take it back.

Calla leans her head against the cool window, trying to ease the pounding around her skull. The pain is no longer a consequence of experimenting with qi, at least. She's just tired, and cold, and likely dehydrated. In the corner of the room, the lamp is emitting a whine from the insulating cord to signal that something is broken inside the wires. Her brain is making that sound too. A flat screech as she scrambles to make sense of these ill-fitting pieces strewn across the past few days.

She keeps returning to her attempt to invade Otta during their fight. There is no science to qi. It is unpredictable, malleable, changeable just as the human spirit is. All the same, it can still be understood. It can be ordered by logic, such as: Calla invaded Galipei Weisanna, which should be impossible. Such as: Calla keeps jumping without moving her qi with her—properly, at least, or else her eyes wouldn't be changing color. Such as: from the very, very beginning, the fact that Calla jumped at such a young age already puts her in an outlandish tier, and no matter how hard she thinks, she cannot summon proper memories of her time in Rincun. She knows she was born there. She feels how the years passed in that village. Yet she has no warmth of a mother, no impression of a father. No home, no recollection of *anything* other than the sensation of wandering and wandering and wandering in hunger.

Calla can accept that there is more to her identity than she's been willing to acknowledge. But by that logic, there is no reason why Calla failed to invade Otta. Calla must be stronger. *Surely* she's stronger.

Calla bites too hard on her nail, a sting traveling down her thumb. Just as she's wincing, a soft knock comes on her door, and she freezes. Who would *knock*?

"Calla, it's me."

"Anton?" she hisses. "Come in. I can't reach the door."

The handle turns slowly, and Anton pokes his head in first. He is not bound by any ropes or chains. His collar is rumpled, loose with half his buttons undone. Most of his hair is pushed in opposite directions, crisscrossing at the back. He looks like he's been standing at the top of a mountain for hours, getting blown by furious winds.

"They didn't lock you down?"

Anton slips into the room and inspects the hallway for a long moment before closing the door behind him.

"They did. I got out."

Calla looks to her chain. She shakes her ankle. "Well, what am I doing wrong?"

"It's not your fault. They put all the guards with me. I jumped through each of them before I fetched the keys."

This journey through the provinces has been strange enough that such feats are sounding less and less bizarre. Still, Calla blinks, and says: "*What?*"

Anton shrugs. He tugs his sleeve up to show her the fabric bandaged around his lower arm, then the blood-smeared sigil drawn on his bicep. His birth body is pale from a lack of sun, his skin near-translucent at the inner flesh covered by clothing. Nevertheless, when he makes a fist, his arm flexes strong, the sigil glaring red and sharp.

"This works really well."

"I thought you didn't remember it when I showed you."

"My memory is better than expected."

Calla can't believe this. "And your sacrifice?"

"I used myself at first, but I didn't think a shallow cut would be enough for long. I left survivors."

On second thought, Calla doesn't want to ask further. She sighs, then points to her chain, and Anton retrieves the keys from his pocket.

"What is your plan with this?"

"I don't have one." The first key doesn't work. Anton tries another. "I only wanted to get myself free. Surely you can understand that."

An edge enters his tone. She holds herself very still, as though the grip of his hand over her ankle is a trap too.

"You're not free. There is no path out of this base."

Anton's hand tightens. He hasn't found the right key, but he's still attempting this one.

"There is no path *into San-Er* at present," he says. "There are plenty of paths out of this base. A wide terrain in fact, leading to any part of the provinces."

Calla jerks her ankle, rattling her chain loudly. Anton clearly doesn't expect the harsh motion, because he inhales sharply, leaning back to prevent being thrown off-balance. They both go still in the aftermath. Turn slightly, facing the door and preparing for intrusion, only it remains quiet outside. It is late, and August Shenzhi trusts himself too much. Lodgings at the base are located on different levels, and August has yet to understand that with this sigil, there don't seem to be limits to how they can use their qi. No one will discover the guards who watched over Anton. Not until morning comes and the group doesn't convene as expected.

"This is laughable," Calla says. "You didn't want to run when I offered to run. Then we hit the point of no return, and *now* the provinces are an option? There's no use even trying. We don't have connections. We don't have money. We would be more comfortable being imprisoned here."

"Fine." Anton tries a new key. This one finally slots in smoothly, and he turns the mechanism. "I don't like the sound of the provinces either. But that's not the best course of action here anyway. The best course of action is entering San-Er by force."

"And what force do we have?"

The cuff unlatches. Anton yanks the chain away. "You know very well, Calla."

"Stop," Calla says immediately.

"He can't be allowed to go on like this. He organized multiple attacks on the provinces for the sole purpose of weakening some of the council. He would throw his own guards into the fire for the chance that a councilmember catches an arrow and dies easily and quietly."

Rincun. Then Leysa. Calla hasn't forgotten.

"We are no better," she says. "We are murderers just the same—"

"When have we had the choice otherwise?" Anton returns.

"August could make the same argument." Their back-and-forth will only go in circles. She's been having this debate with herself since the moment she left Galipei's body, the moment she understood why the delegation was being attacked by the Dovetail across the provinces. "He acts for the sake of the kingdom. King Kasa gave him no choice; the council's restrictions forced him into a corner—"

"He is the *king*. He should order his councilmembers dead himself if he feels so strongly about it. Why murder hundreds of other innocents?"

Calla tilts her head. Anton hasn't risen, so he remains crouched before her, his breath heaving. He looks upon her like he has never seen her before, and maybe he hasn't. Maybe he's never truly known Calla Tuoleimi at her most cowardly: the child who wants to rest, who doesn't want to be told that her revenge isn't finished until she has cut down every nameless soldier that marched into Rincun. Where does it end, then? Has she doomed herself to unending hunger?

"He's fair," Calla says quietly.

"His fairness agreed that my parents needed to die. He would have sat on it forever just so he could remain Kasa's prized little heir. Calla, he *knew*."

The scorching burn in her chest is sudden, and unexpected. At least he knows who is to blame for taking his family from him. Calla almost wishes she could trace it to August too, adopt unshakable reason to widen her razor net. She's very good at holding personal grudges. Less so at being the judge of others and their grievances, others and the justice they should be granted, because Calla is neither a tolerable person nor an impartial judge.

Once she starts handing out penance, it will be hard to stop.

"I'm sorry," she whispers.

"Don't be. I don't need that from you."

"What do you need, then?" The question comes out in a rasp. "You want me to wage war on him, is that it?"

Anton shifts onto his knees, rising higher. Though he brings his palms to either side of her hips, he doesn't touch her. His hands hover in ritualistic prayer.

"You are the *only* person in this kingdom who can. San-Er will rally behind someone they believe was always in line for the throne. My mother and my father died attempting another way." His voice hitches. "You understand the cities just as well as I do: if they were caught, it is because they failed to garner support outside of revolutionary groups and Crescent Society temples. The rest of the kingdom still believes there might be good in their royals. The rest of the kingdom believes the heavens had a reason to select the ruling bloodlines. If August is to have an adversary who might actually succeed, it is you. You would be saving the kingdom from him."

Calla looks up. The lamplight wavers.

"I thought myself the kingdom's savior during the games too," she says. All those years spent training, tucked inside a ground-floor apartment swinging a blunt black-market sword. "Look at how that ended."

Anton's blood, running through the arena. The loudspeakers, luxuriating in his death.

"It doesn't have to be the same. It was still August who pitted us against each other."

"It was us, Anton," Calla says. Since the arena, she's lost track of how wholehearted her anger used to be. She wanted a righteous ending. The kings responsible for her hurt needed to die, and that had to be enough.

But she has no name, no history, no *anything* except the knowledge that one day she was lost on the streets of a far-flung province. Of course the blood of three royals is only an arbitrary payment.

"Calla—"

"I chose anger," she hisses. "And you chose Otta. There is no balance here."

"Is that all?" Anton demands. Now his hands come down and make contact. Though her stomach drops, she doesn't let it show on her face. "Needs change. I chose wrong. I am choosing again."

The words don't convince her. Calla grits her teeth and pushes a hand into his hair, grabbing the tufts roughly enough to pull his head back. A surge of satisfaction thrums down her spine. She likes seeing him wince. She likes that flash of pain darkening his eyes. She's seen Anton in so many different bodies, yet never has she seen his expressions reflecting exactly what he is thinking, as they do now.

"How do I know you're not lying?" she asks. "At this point, you would say anything if it meant avoiding the punishment that August has in store for us."

Anton Makusa knows who he is. Calla can't remember the first thing about herself.

"I wouldn't lie." He lets her pull his hair. He bares his throat for her, the surface smooth and unmarred in the lamplight. "I will swear myself to you here, if that's what it takes. From this moment onward, I am your follower. Your acolyte. Whatever it is you need, as my ruler or my deity."

The utterance sinks heavily into the room, like ingots in water. What a terrible promise. What a beautiful promise.

"You shouldn't offer that," Calla replies mildly. "I'll never be able to grant all your prayers."

"It doesn't need to be all of them. One is enough."

Anton moves to stand. As soon as he is shifting his balance, she pushes him hard, sending him back down. Either Anton is caught by surprise, or he lets her take her suppressed rage out on him. Either he freezes because he is ill-prepared when she crawls to the floor alongside him, or he wittingly stays put.

Calla can't decide what response she's trying to invoke from him. Her hands reach for his face, gentle despite herself. On each movement, her hair swings as curtains on either side of them. Anton gazes up at her. Hunger stirs plainly in his stare, but she cannot say whether it is for her or for power.

Maybe those are one and the same.

"Calla," he whispers. Slowly, ever slowly, his mouth presses to her neck. She sighs. "I know you can do it." The hollow of her collar. "Challenge August." Lower, into her neckline.

"Do you know what you call for?" she asks. His hands have found their way to the buttons of her shirt. One after the other, he commences her undoing. "It will be war."

"Maybe it's high time someone waged a war against the Shenzhis."

He tugs the zip at the front of her trousers. The leather fabric doesn't budge much, and Calla pulls back, drawing onto her knees. Anton tries to follow, but she keeps him down. Holds his gaze.

"The last civil war," she says, nudging the zips down the sides instead, nudging until the fabric dissolves into two pieces that she throws aside, "devastated this kingdom. Sinoa Tuoleimi ended up erased from history."

"And yet"—Anton catches her hands before she can press down on his torso—"she survived into a new time. You look identical. She was reborn."

Calla laughs once. "She was reborn, only to be replaced by a child in the provinces. Some great queen she was."

"Then don't you want to be better?" When Anton sits up, he has her arms trapped between them. He says her name again, again. "Don't you want to break every piece of the kingdom until it is nothing of the one that made you?"

Calla breathes out, and Anton finally kisses her. His skin is hot upon contact, near-feverish in temperature. His arms tighten to bring her closer, slot her exactly right, and their lips collide with a barely restrained frenzy. Her hands curl to grip his rumpled shirt, and Anton draws away for an exhale to pull it off, before he's right back where he was.

Every push and pull between them exists as a promise of mutual destruction. They're in no rush—not as they have been every previous time they've found themselves like this—yet there's always something thrumming under Calla's skin, something that tells her to grasp him with the panic of committing theft. Her nerves scream with sensation. Her entire counterfeit body, calling for some release.

"Please," Anton gasps, breathes into her mouth, her neck, her skin. It could be for the kingdom. It could be her. "Please, Calla."

She pulls at his waistband. Rather than breaking their proximity, she merely pushes everything in the way aside until she's sinking onto him, gasping into the crook of his shoulder.

"Promise me," she says. She moves, slowly. "Promise me you'll fight on my side. Don't give me a repeat of the arena."

"I promise," Anton says. He's barely holding himself back. The cords of muscle in his arms are strained, keeping himself still for her. "I will be your first soldier."

"My general."

His eyes look wholly black in the light. Anton can't keep still anymore. His hands lock on her hips.

"Your general," he confirms. "Rise for me, Princess."

Calla shifts with a soft exhale, her legs propped on either side of him, knees on the floor. The moment her arms slide around his shoulders, he's thrusting up, deeper and deeper. She moves with him until she can't, until her core entirely unravels, and then Anton breathes a self-satisfied laugh, pushing her onto her back so that he can continue, so that he can kiss her until she's barely able to string together two thoughts.

"Calla, Calla," he says, nudging his nose into her hair.

"Look at me," she commands. "Swear your devotion when you come."

Anton makes a ragged inhale. A strand of hair falls into his face; he's entirely uninhibited. Calla could reach through his rib cage, and in this moment, she knows he'd let her take whatever she wants.

"I swear it," Anton says. "You are my only place of worship. I swear it."

Lucky for him, she won't take a thing. If she reaches into his heart, she's only trying to leave herself there.

Anton stills with a shudder, and Calla gasps in, her every cell humming with life. For a moment, he stays unmoving, his forehead pressed into her neck, and Calla brushes his hair softly.

"Dearest Anton," she whispers, "I hope you keep your word."

"I am a man of my word," he returns, his voice alert even while the rest of him remains relaxed. "And if I break it, you may strike me down."

◇◇◇◇◇

Calla leaves Anton sleeping, slipping out from underneath his arm. If she asks him how to go about a plan, he will complicate it. Calla wants to proceed as straightforwardly as possible. She is no revolutionary. She is just the most furious orphan in the world.

Eigi has warmed in the days they've been away. The security base beckons in the smolder of an almost sunrise. When Calla exits the lodgings and approaches the main building, she sights two guards watching the door. She doesn't give them time to see her. She throws her hand out, her teeth gritted, and a beam of light slashes through the air. There is no need to knock them out for long. One doesn't even fall properly, but Calla only needs the opening to get past, shut the door, and pick up a standing lamp with a long pole to shove between the handles.

When August confiscated the crown, she knew he wouldn't keep it close to his person. Royal protocol says sacred people and sacred objects shouldn't stay together while there is the threat of danger, or else it splits the guards' attention.

"Your Highness," the guard exclaims when Calla slides open the next door inside. Cigarette smoke wafts around the space in plumes. He's been tearing through a pack.

"Very sorry for this," Calla says. She moves like a viper, arms grasped around his neck and held tight until the guard drops, unconscious.

The crown has been placed on a pillow in the middle of an office table. Calla wanders over. Picks it up.

She felt it in the borderlands too. An instant hum travels through her palm and along her arm, vibrating through her chest. With this, she needs no sigil. The screaming presence of qi is as blatant as a waving red flag, unfurling in her bones. Much more qi than a mortal body should be capable of. Enough qi to make her a god.

"Calla."

Calla turns over her shoulder and finds August at the door. The guards must have raised the alarm fast: he looks as though he was pulled from sleep. It's very unlike August. There's already the fact that Anton messed with his hair and dyed it black, taking him away from that golden appearance he's so carefully cultivated over the years.

"Yes?" Calla holds the crown up. Inspects it under the electric lights, letting its sharp edges glint bright.

She will be good. She promises she will serve the kingdom well, even if it means burning it down. This is how it's supposed to be, isn't it? This is how they all convince themselves they are deserving of total power.

"Put that down."

Agitation quivers through his voice. For the first time since she has known him, August might be panicking, recognizing what is spiraling into place. He made an assumption that the Calla before him is the same Calla who agreed to help him at the start of the games.

"No," Calla says, "I don't think I will."

She sets the crown on her head.

It is nothing but the heavy weight of metal on first contact, the hum of qi moving from her chest to her head. Then, to her shock, the crown begins to *melt*. She feels it turn liquid, feels the metal trailing down her forehead. She blinks rapidly, trying to keep it from entering her eyes, but she shouldn't have worried. The droplets stop right above her lashes. The crown solidifies back into gold the moment it finishes fusing with her hair, her skin.

August stares, bewildered, as though he might be misunderstanding, as though she might be playing in jest. He has forgotten so easily. From the moment he found her before the king's games, it has always been him who seeks her help. She does not answer to him.

"What are you doing?" August demands.

"I thought it was obvious." Calla lifts her arm, and the room pulses with her. "This is a coup. I am your king now."

CHAPTER 37

The Crescent Societies are privy to mutterings from every corner. There is havoc erupting outside the wall, in a security base where Eigi's capital used to stand. The qi is changing in San-Er, the twin cities overwhelmed by enormous volumes of it, more than they have seen in decades. The old gods are whispering. They have their hands on the underside of the kingdom, hefting for a great big turn.

Bibi gives a thumbs-up from the diner she's stationed herself inside. It has just opened, unlocking its doors with the sunrise, so she is their only patron. On the other side of the windows, Woya sets off the timer.

"You again."

The server puts down a pot of tea. Bibi, as she's reaching for the cup, lifts her eyes and sees the server's dyed purple bangs first. Yilas.

"What a coincidence," she says. "I knew we would run into each other again."

"We're one of the only diners open this early." Her same companion from the cybercafe comes to put tarts on the table too. Chami, who has jade dangling from her ears despite the oil stains on her apron. Her pink eyes are lined with electric-blue pencil. There's far more natural qi emanating from her than there is from Yilas. "It was bound to happen."

"I'm grateful for it."

Bibi takes a large bite, then checks her watch. This is her last meal under these circumstances, before San-Er returns to how it should be ruled. There are so many stories of the ones who came before her. The power-hungry, the desperate. Blinded by greed, damned to play god.

Bibi starts to get under the table. Yilas blinks, watching curiously.

"What are you doing?"

"I'd suggest you do the same."

When the watch hand strikes the top of the hour, San-Er tremors once, and the windows on the Magnolia Diner shatter, blown in by the blast.

◇◇◇◇◇

By the time Galipei arrives on scene, it's havoc.

He can't see anything. The lights have gone out across the whole building. There are other Weisannas already present in the hallways, shouting commands at one another with overlapping voices while they try to make sense of the situation, while they, too, rush to the room where they're keeping the divine crown.

"August?" he bellows. "August!"

Just as Galipei is approaching the room, a body flies out from inside, hitting the hallway. For a startling second, Galipei thinks he sees blond hair—he thinks he sees August, limp and broken. Then he blinks and his vision clears. It is not blond hair, only the tint of burgeoning daylight coming from the double doors he left open on his way in. Galipei recognizes the man on the floor as one of his second cousins, and he appears fine, twisting onto his shoulder with a groan.

An alarm is blaring throughout the security base. He doesn't know what the threat is or who is at risk. Even the yelling inside the office is indecipherable. Galipei warned August that the office wouldn't be a good room for the crown. He warned that for once they needed to defy protocol and keep it close by, because no number of guards would stop a truly hostile takeover, no number of windowless rooms would—

A loud *boom* rocks the office. At that point, Galipei merely shoves his way forward, losing all measure of patience. He ducks under a flailing arm and enters the room, where he finds the source of the noise to be a hole blown clean through the wall. It leaks in the morning's first orange wisps, illuminating Calla's outline when she strolls through the rubble and emerges into the daylight with the divine crown on her head.

"Calla."

Finally, now, Galipei sights August pressed to the wall on the far side. Perhaps there was some unnatural force keeping him there before, because when he pushes off now, he's furious.

"Calla, stop right there!"

"Tell me, August," she calls. Her voice amplifies across the base. Each word has the tremendous hollowness of shouting into a large cavern, ricocheting around and around and around. "Did you order the attack on Rincun?"

August pauses. The witnesses will not take that to mean anything particular, but Galipei knows, and Calla certainly knows too.

"No," August lies, recovering. "No, of course not. And besides, those were palace soldiers who died. Why would I do that?"

"There were *children* there, August," Calla seethes.

"My goodness, Princess Calla, I don't know what's gotten into you." August has perfected this voice he uses. The one that makes people doubt whether he was ever born a commoner, whether he might have been an actual progeny of Kasa Shenzhi, and everything the cities thought before was some mass hallucination. "I would never."

Galipei feels it building before the threat comes. His sixth sense for August is never wrong, solely purposed toward incoming danger. A tuning fork, emitting a protective measure at every glance. He bolts forward.

"They're just. *Children.*"

The air turns heavy, sour. Each of Galipei's steps strikes the ground hard.

"How dare your games touch them. How *dare* you bring them into it."

Galipei lunges into place the moment Calla turns back and flings an arc of light out of her hands. Before it can hit August, he takes the strike. It pierces through his stomach and ripples up his spine. In the place of blood, an electric current runs through his veins.

His world turns white. He sees a terrible bright light, as though a pantheon of gods might reach through the haze at any moment and haul him up.

Galipei's eyes roll into the back of his head.

Then, nothing.

◇◇◇◇◇

Two things occur to August in tandem.

First, Galipei is alive, but he needs a doctor immediately.

Second, Calla cannot be seen by San-Er with the crown on her head.

"Take him into the city now," August spits. "There's one carriage. *Go!*"

He sends three Weisannas off with Galipei, numbers that he should not be sparing during an attempted coup. August can't fathom this. Calla has no forces. No soldiers. Nothing that comes close to constituting an army.

But she has the crown, and August has only ten remaining guards.

Calla is almost out of sight, running for the far building. Makusa. He's still in there.

"Your Majesty," one Weisanna exclaims, "should we surround the building? She's going for Anton Makusa."

"No," August answers immediately. Fuck. *Fuck*. "Get to San-Er first. Guard the wall. We're keeping her *out*."

CHAPTER 38

Anton dreams of Calla surrounded by fire.

It's a restless sleep. One where he's right on the cusp of waking, fighting to surface while the dream holds him by the ankles. He reaches out his arm. His fingers brush the red-hot flames. The thick smoke floats up to form the clouds. There's the distant crash of the sea too, its waves rising higher against the rocks. If they don't move soon, the tide is going to take them. Ships loom on the horizon, pressing closer. It'll trap them with no route out.

Turn around, he wants to say. *Calla, turn—*

"Wake up."

Anton jolts out of sleep, his eyes flying open. His world is unbalanced. Some result of the dream, he's sure, but even as he rockets upright, reaching for Calla's elbow while she hovers over him, his sense of reality feels hazy.

"What's going on? Where did you go?"

"We're leaving."

Calla takes shape before him while he adjusts to the dark room. Her yellow eyes, her pink mouth. Her crown, bleeding metal down her forehead and clinging to her hair as though she had been born with it fixed onto her head.

"Shit, Calla. What gives?"

She offers a small smile. It is far from the appropriate time, but he's taken aback by the sight, that they are in the midst of what must be an active revolt on Calla's part and she affords this gesture at him. If there's anything about Calla Tuoleimi that he loves and despises in equal measure, it's that she's impossible to read.

"You wanted this."

"I didn't realize you'd act *this* soon."

"It was now or never. I couldn't let August tell lies to San-Er first." She turns over her shoulder, inspecting the open door. He thought it a remnant of his dreams, but there really is shouting coming from around the base. "I'm willing to bet he'll focus on keeping us out of the city and leave few guards behind. We might be able to get there before he situates himself fully."

Anton is barely blinking back the sleep in his eyes. Calla hauls him to his feet, and he shoves on his boots, pulls a jacket over his shoulders. An alarm screeches down the hallway as they hurry out, looking up and down to find empty corridors in both directions. They make it all the way outside the building. The sun floats directly above the horizon, an angry red ball that has been plucked from its hiding nook. A crossbow bolt flies directly toward them.

Before Anton can think to move, the bolt freezes on its own at the peak of its arc. It clatters to the ground. Calla watches it roll away.

"I wasn't aware you could do that," Anton remarks casually. The rapid clicks of other crossbows being loaded echo through the scene. Calla doesn't look concerned.

"It's the crown," she says. "Reach down."

Another guard takes aim closer. Calla bends down and kicks his legs out from underneath him, swinging her arm and yanking his sword off his belt without touching him. The sword skids through the dirt and comes to a stop by Anton's hand while he swoops to grab it. He unsheathes, then reverses his hold on the weapon. Before the guard recovers from kneeling to the ground, Anton rams the blunt pommel into his temple, and he goes down.

Then the remaining three guards rush in at the same time.

"You can't immobilize them?" Anton calls. He swings fast, but he can hardly combat in unison. A blade narrowly misses his ribs. Another fist catches him by the ear before he ducks and rolls.

"I don't know how. I can't concentrate on that many things at once—"

Calla emits a pulse of energy. It pushes the guards back a few paces, and she's on the move without hesitation, yanking hard at Anton's shoulder.

"Come on. That's only going to work once. Over there."

They run, heading for the pathway out of the security base. Calla's stolen a sword too, though it might as well be decoration compared with the metal on her head. She's got her eyes pinned on the group of guards lined up on their horses in ready defense, and Anton doesn't quite understand the plan until she says, "Go left. Break them apart."

"Oh, so I'm *bait*."

"Anton!"

He pivots fast, following instructions despite his back talk. While the guards expected the two of them in dual combat, he makes it appear that he's charging away from the line. One of the guards scrambles after him, steering the horse away from the cluster. Anton can't outrun him, so he veers until he's put enough distance from the other guards, and then he lets the guard catch up, acting as though he's growing winded. The guard leans down, reaches with his arm, wanting to make a grab.

Anton pitches into his path, ramming hard into the side of the horse.

The guard jostles. Before he's secured his balance, Anton grabs his foot and throws him clean off the horse. In an instant, Anton has latched on to the reins and gathered the momentum he needs to swing himself into the saddle.

He turns the horse around, searching the distance, and finds Calla in the midst of the other guards.

"Princess!"

The morning shines bright over Eigi, turning its plains into endless fields of gold. She looks up, and through the blood splattered down her face, she is the most glorious vision across Talin, second only to the sun.

Anton reaches his arm out as the horse dives into the gathering of guards. His hand grabs Calla's, their wrists meeting before he hauls her off the ground and into the saddle too.

"Go," Calla urges, her mouth near his ear, her arms curling around his shoulders. "Until we reach San-Er."

◇◇◇◇◇

San-Er's wall materializes out of nowhere, a mirage in the distance made of real stone and steel.

Calla gasps, holding tight when Anton pulls to a halt. With the guards in pursuit behind them, they've been going at a speed that could tear a rip through the ground. As soon as they see the forces around the wall, though, it's clear there isn't a visible way in, and Calla squeezes his shoulders once, signaling that they must stop.

August waits with his guards. Galipei is nowhere to be found, but the other silver-eyed Weisannas seem to be doing a fine job holding their stances in front of their king.

"Enough, Calla," August says. His voice is quiet. Calla glances to the side and finds regular palace guards lining the scene too, holding back the rural dwellers who camp outside the wall. With the ruckus, many of them have emerged, wanting to see what is going on. She knows they see what is on her head. Even outside the wall, removed from newsreels and slow-loading web articles, they have heard about the divine crown and the delegation that went out in search of it. The citizens of Talin know that their throne is contested.

Calla must emerge victorious in this encounter. If she doesn't, August will kill every person camping out here to erase the evidence of what passed through, to hide that Calla can wear the crown without being struck down by the heavens.

"I'd like you to step aside," she says.

The frantic pursuit has settled. The guards chasing from the security base warily form a semicircle, blocking her and Anton in.

"I can't do that. The two of you are a threat to San-Er."

Anton moves to get off the horse. Calla grips his hand quickly, stopping him. For as long as they're on equal height with the guards behind them, they can't be ambushed with a quick swing of the sword. Before the crown, August would have preferred to keep her alive to prevent the Crescent Societies from thinking of her as a martyr. Given current circumstances, she wouldn't put it past August to hack her head off here and now if it means getting the crown back.

"Are we a threat?" Anton calls in return. "Calla has been divinely chosen. If she is a threat, then the gods desire a threat, and you are nothing but a usurper. No royal blood. No heavenly approval."

August's expression grows tighter. There are more spectators gathering.

"Don't make this difficult."

Anton pushes them forward. The horse takes a step. Instantly, the Weisannas in front of August prepare to engage, and Calla reaches for the reins. She won't fight them at once. It is too risky, especially for Anton. One careless slip of a blade, and the mortal body crumples.

"You will take off the crown," August instructs. "You will return it to me."

"No," Calla says. "You have failed your kingdom, August."

August scoffs. He is, without charade, genuinely confounded that Calla would accuse him of wrongdoing. August Shenzhi has spent his whole life splitting apart what made Kasa terrible and what he will do differently. He thinks he knows what sets him apart from his adoptive father.

"Do you see me in lavish fabrics?" August asks. "Or holding feasts while the people starve?"

Calla almost feels pity toward him.

"You may not be a greedy king," she returns, "but you are still a hungry one."

When she and August were young, Calla's first real impression of him formed around that shattered vase. The servant broke it, King Kasa came in, and August accepted the blame. King Kasa's anger deflected; August wiped the blood off his arm like nothing. No one was punished that day. The servant lived blameless. How worthy August was, she used to think. Never mind that they could have brushed away the shards after the servant took responsibility for breaking it. Never mind that it was King Kasa at fault, not August in the right. She has given him so much credit for acting well, but he built a world where the sole choice was between him and Kasa, and of course she chose August.

"What is that supposed to mean?" August asks calmly.

It means that between two tyrants, Calla may as well become the third.

"The crown has chosen me. I am the rightful heir to the Palace of Heavens, and an inheritor of San-Er."

Anton pushes the horse forward another step suddenly, and half the Weisannas flinch. They are unsure if they should continue following instructions to attack.

"I invoke my claim to the kingdom of Talin," Calla bellows. "Every province shall swear their loyalty to me, and then I will free them from the throne. Surrender now. You have no other choice."

The spectators cry out. Exaltations. Hails.

Prayers.

"You cannot." August lifts his chin. "You will not."

"Cousin," she says. "You should know me better."

The crown pulses on her head. It tells her, *Go on.* In the Palace of Heavens, Calla could feel every spray of blood, could count each forced entry of metal cleaving into flesh. This time, it's so much easier. This time, she doesn't hold in the qi wanting to burst from her chest, and with nary a movement, she's slit the throats of the Weisannas in front of August, spurting carnage onto the ground.

There are screams from the spectators. Calla hears them as if the sounds are far in the distance. Most of the spectators, however, stay quiet. Most are watchful, waiting.

August stands surrounded by blood. He stares at his feet. Even with such posture, he looks every bit a royal, disgraced from a pedestal by force.

Please, she pleads silently.

Calla doesn't want to kill him, after all. Easy as it would be, she still sees him as her cousin, and she doesn't have any more of those ties left in the world. She has the blood of her family smeared up to her imposter elbows. It would be so tragic to add more.

Please.

Slowly, very slowly, August Shenzhi steps back. Surrenders.

They waste no time. Anton pushes the horse forward, taking them to the gate and through the thin open section. There is no safety until Calla occupies the palace and makes a proper bid for the throne, but the moment they enter San-Er, there is clearly something wrong. A plume of gray smoke rises from the distance. From the center of the city, where the Palace of Union stands.

"Be careful," Calla warns, letting Anton slide off the horse first.

Together they dive into the alleys, sprinting fast through the streets of San-Er. They have practice from the games, from the mornings they spent flitting through these shadows avoiding being seen and coordinating an attack on their next opponents.

"What the fuck is happening?" Calla asks. In the main thoroughfare, there are people running away from the palace, holding bleeding limbs and ash-smeared faces.

"Crescent Societies," Anton answers. "I would bet anything."

By the time they have made it to the Palace of Union, there isn't any further clarity to the situation. The turnstiles at the main entrance have been blown clean out of existence. Crescent Society members guard the front, holding swords for weapons. No palace guards to be seen.

"This doesn't make any sense," Calla whispers when they duck out of sight, taking a moment to hide behind a shop's front sign. "Even if they managed an attack, where are the guards?"

Anton grimaces. "We might not want to know the answer to that. How do we get in?"

Calla considers the matter of brute force. It would be straightforward enough to march right through, to push back anyone who comes toward her. Still, as she rises carefully, she recalls Yilas making contact, what she said about the Crescent Societies. If there is something expected of her here, she doesn't want to be making a greeting from the very front of the palace.

"I know a way in." Calla tilts her head left, around the coliseum and into the alleys. "Follow me."

The back alleys are quiet. Either the people have evacuated, or they are unmoving inside their apartments. Even the rats have stopped scampering around the trash bags. Nothing moves when Calla kicks aside some particularly bulky ones, clearing the space in front of the hidden door.

She doesn't know what Matiyu's identity number is, or any other number that should activate the panel to open the emergency passage, but the moment she touches the keypad, she finds it is unnecessary. The panel has been unplugged and hangs from the wall off a half-broken wire. Confused, Calla prods the door, and it opens on its own.

This passage was used for entry to attack the palace.

Calla steps in first, grimacing at the puddle her foot dips into. Anton is close behind; he attempts to close the door after him and finds the lock doesn't click anymore.

"Where are we going?"

"Throne room," Calla answers. Her original objective was greeting the cities from the throne room balcony. Seeing the state of the palace, she supposes their destination doesn't change. If there is any objective to an attack on the palace while its monarch has left, it is in the throne room.

They emerge from the passage. South wing. The throne room is close, but she doubts the palace will stay behaved through their entire route.

She's mistaken.

The first people they come across halt instantly. They stare, in the manner of a child caught with their hand in the candy jar rather than a threatening anarchist cult. Anton tries to ask what has happened, but Calla tugs him to keep moving. There are crescent moons tattooed on the inside of their elbows. As strange as the situation is, the Crescent Society members simply leave them be when Calla and Anton turn the corner. They proceed onward. Up the stairs and down the stairs. Through the smoky halls and around the shattered chandeliers.

It appears they may be in the clear to approach the atrium into the throne room, but another group awaits, lined up vigilantly. Calla braces. Her hand flies up, prepared to counter an attack.

But they do the opposite.

The Crescent Society members see her, and they drop to their knees.

"What the fuck," Anton says, "is going on?"

Silently, Calla continues onward, making sure Anton stays in her periphery. Her hands flex at her sides. They proceed through the line of Crescents, passing under the arch of the throne room entrance. Without any sound to her steps, Calla enters to find the throne room charred with the remnants of an explosion, vases shattered, and paintings dragged off the walls. The remaining councilmembers in San-Er have been gathered here. Ten people, Calla counts in her cursory inspection. She sights Mugo and Farua. No Venus Hailira. Perhaps Venus has already been killed.

No one in the room has noticed her entry yet. They're too busy watching a man pull Councilmember Farua from the circle and situate her in the middle of the room and onto her knees. He draws his sword. A crescent moon engraving decorates the blade.

"Stand down," Calla says.

At once, those surrounding the man whip their gazes over, locking onto Calla. The man, however, pays her no attention. He raises his sword high with both hands.

"I said"—Calla throws her arm out and flings the man and his sword alike into the wall, pressed tight without any chance of movement—"stand down."

He strains. He can't move. Only then does he look properly at Calla, and his brows fly up. The outer halves have been shaved off, the inner halves dyed white. It gives him a stronger appearance of shock when he states, "Calla Tuoleimi."

A morning breeze floats in from the open balcony. Its curtain drifts up and down, and ever casual, Anton strides over to push it aside so that the fabric isn't billowing at every moment. The room has utterly stilled. Then, just as the people outside did, the Crescent Society members fall to their knees, one by one by one. There is no opposition here.

And Calla can't help but wonder *why*.

"I want everyone to behave," she says. The instructions come as though someone else is delivering them. As though the original princess whispers in her ear, temporarily taking over with the right decisions. She knows that she is conscious, that she is the one present here, but it is easier to separate herself. Easier in the same way she detached herself when she was raising her sword to her parents.

Slowly, Calla releases the man from the wall. He staggers to regain his balance. The room quiets.

Then Councilmember Mugo lurches forward, breaking from the circle they have ordered him into.

"What is this?" he hisses. "Where is His Majesty?"

"Incapacitated," Calla answers.

Mugo thins his lips. His gaze flickers to the door. Behind him, the other councilmembers are shifting slowly, waiting to take his example, waiting to see if this is their moment to escape. Calla can't let him leave. The moment he raises his generals, they're going to march on San-Er. Eigi is too close to be risking that kind of funny business.

"You're excused from duty," Calla decides.

Though Mugo must have been eyeing his escape route, his attention snaps back to her in an instant. "I beg your pardon?"

"You heard me. You are excused. I don't think you're fit to continue working alongside me."

The other councilmembers have turned to stare at their feet. They're pretending that if they don't move, maybe Calla won't notice them and bring down judgment on them too.

"Enough." Mugo, seeing that none of the Crescent Society members are holding weapons to him anymore, brushes by. He heads for the door. For August, the reign that he believes will keep him around.

"You should stop now," Calla calls.

"You do not have claim to that crown." Mugo turns over his shoulder. "Nor authority in this palace—"

Calla only blinks. She doesn't use her hands for the gesture. She doesn't need to. A red line appears from Mugo's forehead down to his navel. A mere scratch, he must think. Mugo touches his neck with concern, feeling the sensation pierce him.

Then blood is pouring from the line at gushing speed. He topples over. When he falls, he splits where the wire thin cut is, his body collapsing onto the throne room floor like fruit half-peeled to access the innards.

The other councilmembers make an effort not to react. Someone stifles a sharp inhale. Their sounds blend, their faces blend. If no one stands out, Calla won't deal with them all at once.

"Princess Calla, we've been waiting for you."

The voice that booms through the room is familiar. Though it takes a beat, Calla searches fast through her memory and matches it to the woman who was speaking on the phone, the one who tagged along with Yilas's message. Calla turns and finds the woman lingering by the throne, the only one still standing while the rest kneel. Calla didn't notice her before in the shadows, where she was almost hiding from the light streaming through the balcony. She's dressed in black and leathers, as a city dweller who frequents casinos and nightclubs might. Calla can't get a good look at her eyes. The woman's hand drops from the back of the throne.

"Have you?" Calla asks. "I'm surprised. I didn't think the Crescent Societies had such goodwill toward me."

"Of course we do. We're logical people. We can help each other."

Around the throne room, the damage isn't deep. Charred walls and ruined floors, but nothing that can't be scrubbed away with some heavy-duty soap and fixed with carpet replacements. The gouges are shallow, made to frighten rather than incinerate.

The woman walks down the few steps from the throne, emerging from the shadows. Her hair has been pulled slick against her head and tied in a long braid. Her eyes are entirely black, lined charcoal dark.

Where Calla has no familiarity with her face, it's Anton who gasps. Anton who stares with such awe that one would think this was someone risen from the dead. He staggers forward a step.

"*Bibi.*"

Calla grabs his elbow at once, keeping him back instinctively.

"How do you know her name?" she demands.

Anton's mouth opens. Nothing comes out. He appeared fine charging into San-Er on the back of intense bloodshed, but it is here that he enters shock.

Bibi reaches the end of the steps. She comes closer and closer, until she goes to her knees too, the thud of each leg landing heavily on the deep green carpet.

"Because a long time ago, only he called me that," Bibi says, answering where Anton cannot. She inclines her head. "My full name is Buira Makusa. We have come to join your war, Your Majesty."

CHAPTER 39

Night sweeps over Eigi's security base.

Enough days have passed that Calla and her coup have settled in San-Er. With each new hour, August cools down. He could hardly think past his rage when she entered the city. Now, he finds any sort of indignant response to be a wasted effort. Calla can try, but she can't take the kingdom. No matter how thoroughly Calla wins the capital, it is impossible to claim Talin without claiming the provinces that provide its resources, so it doesn't matter, does it?

He hears the reports from those who leave San-Er. The wall has opened one section to allow people to freely exit. No one is getting forcibly expelled, but plenty of Weisannas and guards have left anyway, joining August's cause. Plenty of aristocrats have voluntarily packed up their things, fearing their time remaining in San-Er. Calla did not issue a warning. The hostility in the Palace of Union was enough of an unspoken one.

Under Calla Tuoleimi, this is not the same San-Er they've known with each new coronation. Crescent moons start appearing in shop windows. Weapons are distributed on the open market. These groups have always wanted anarchy. What more perfect way to begin that than the criminal princess finally coming back to end what she started?

August is starting to understand. How the pieces fell where they did. Who was moving which thread, whose hands were nudging where without him knowing.

Despite the Crescent attacks, some members of the council remain in San-Er, resolved to rule their jurisdiction. Ximili Province. Cirea Province. Gaiyu Province. Most of the councilmembers are dead, though, which means most armies in the provinces are also waiting, necks craned to see which way the wind blows, whether they ought to be listening to the queen who wears the crown or the king they coronated. It's hard to tell how any of it will play out. Never has Talin seen change like this. Not since the war.

And, allegedly, no one alive today remembers the war.

The door creaks open behind him.

"Your Majesty," a guard says. "You have a visitor."

August doesn't turn to thank the guard for bringing the news. Every unfamiliar face reporting in only reminds him of who he's missing. Though the Weisannas who left San-Er have replenished his numbers at the base, he feels more exposed than ever while Galipei remains in serious condition, refusing to wake.

If Galipei doesn't recover, August will personally take Calla's head as a war prize at the end of this.

The door shuts again. He hears the soft pad of footsteps, then Otta Avia approaches his side, staring at the map he's unfurled on the board. She showed up at the security base yesterday, not looking at all like she'd wandered in from the borderlands. When the guards brought her to him handcuffed, August took one look and asked for her to be released. He had some matters to discuss with her. She didn't need to be kept prisoner.

"It's not optimal, is it?" she remarks. She notes his markings on the map.

"Only because we're not fighting the same," August replies. "She has cheap tricks up her sleeve."

Otta makes a noise of disagreement. "I'm not sure if unfettered access to qi can be qualified as a cheap trick."

"It is," he says. "Take the crown away, and she is nothing. She follows instructions blindly passed down from other people, drawing sigils to reap its effects but failing to understand how any of it works."

"As if you understand any better."

August turns to Otta. He surveys her thoroughly, watches for the most minute change in her expression. When Otta says nothing more, he turns to check the door. She's closed it.

"Have you been my sister all along," he asks, "or did you come in later?"

The room darkens. Outside the base, the clouds weigh heavier and heavier, sure to bring another night he'll spend unsleeping. While August holds his scrutiny, Otta primly smiles. He hadn't doubted his conclusion, but it unnerves him that she doesn't bother denying it. How long has she been *expecting* him to know, and why has it taken until now?

"Would it change anything?" she returns. "You know me."

"I'm not sure I do. When did it happen?"

The seconds stretch long. He almost thinks she won't answer him.

Then: "Fifteen years ago. A stupid girl in Rincun took over my body without knowing what she was doing. The old gods favor her. They protected her. After all these years pondering this sequence of events, I gather she may be one of their own sent down to stop me, and she doesn't even realize it yet."

August has long suspected something strange under his nose, but with that, he finally comprehends the picture fully.

"I wasn't strong enough to win control over the body. My new mind was too young, so I yanked myself out before I could be entirely consumed," she goes on. "Found the next-best substitute."

"You escaped into Otta."

"I did."

The kingdom barely understands these recent developments with qi. Never mind this sort of magic. Never mind child royals and godlings playing jumping games without discretion.

"How long were you planning to pretend?" he asks. "Would you have schemed for the throne earlier if you hadn't fallen ill?"

"I wouldn't have schemed for anything," she returns. "I would have inherited the Palace of Heavens by birthright. Then it was taken from me, and I was forced to go another route. None of this is my fault. I am not the one who intruded."

August keeps quiet. It's not lost on him that when she lost the Palace of Heavens, her next route was to claim the Palace of Earth. Her eyes flicker to him, and she must realize that she needs to go about this in a far less threatening manner.

"None of it matters now. August, you don't want another enemy. Work with me. San-Er has always had two thrones. Nothing says we cannot reinstate that."

It's true enough. There are no what-ifs, no alternate pasts where his half sister swept the throne out from underneath him before he could receive it. The kingdom today knows him as its rightful ruler, and he ought to work with the one person who has power trembling right beneath her skin, waiting to be unleashed.

"Very well," August says. He takes a pen and draws a firm line through Talin. "And you think we can win this war?"

"Yes," Sinoa Tuoleimi answers without hesitation. "That crown was always mine. If there is anyone who knows how to get it back, it is me."

ACKNOWLEDGMENTS

In every battle, there are victors and losers. The yearslong siege that evolved into what history will term the BATTLE OF VILEST THINGS ended with one casualty: Chloe Gong's Sanity. However, the sacrifice was appreciated as *Vilest Things* gained the wealth it desired. There were many dedicated fighters in this mission to allow the book to emerge victorious:

Thank you to Laura Crockett, my spectacular agent, my greatest warrior. To Uwe Stender and everyone at Triada US literary agency. To Amara Hoshijo, dedicated frontline general, aka my wonderful editor. Also to Joe Monti and everyone at Saga Press: Savannah Breckenridge, Christine Calella, Caroline Tew, Jéla Lewter, Erika Genova, Lauren Gomez, Zoe Kaplan, Amanda Mulholland, Alexandre Su, Chloe Gray. To Will Staehle of Unusual Corporation for the stunning US cover art. And to Cassie Malmo at Malmo Public Relations, my publicist extraordinaire who I've been reunited with on the publishing battlefield.

Thank you to Molly Powell, dedicated frontline general across the pond, aka my superb UK editor. Also to everyone at Hodderscape: Sophie Judge, Callie Robertson, Kate Keehan, Matthew Everett, Natalie Chen, Lydia Blagden, Dominic Gribben. And to Corey Brickley for the glorious UK cover art. To the teams at Simon & Schuster Canada, especially superstars Cayley Pimentel and

Mackenzie Croft, and at Hachette Aotearoa New Zealand. Thank you too to every team in every country working on putting *Vilest Things* on shelves—I'm sending enormous air-kisses across the oceans.

Thank you to my readers, especially the ones who are now struggling to keep my books on just one shelf given the sheer volume of publications in these recent few years. Storytelling wouldn't be the same without your reception, your love, your passion, and it means the world to me that the Flesh & False Gods series has been allowed into your mindspace. Special thank you to Minju Kim, the supreme Chloe News Source who has been such a wonderful supporter from day one. And thank you to the booksellers, librarians, and advocates everywhere who have championed my books.

Finally, thank you to my family and my friends—especially the d.a.c.u., whom this book is dedicated to: Tino and Rocky and Tashie and Zoe. I love it when our brain cells rattle together in our enclosure. And, to Owen, resurrector of my sanity, the steadfast home I can go to after battle.